Praise for *New York Times* bestselling author Diana Palmer

"Palmer demonstrates, yet again,
why she's the queen of desperado quests
for justice and true love."
—*Publishers Weekly* on *Dangerous*

"The popular Palmer has penned another winning
novel, a perfect blend of romance and suspense."
—*Booklist* on *Lawman*

"Palmer knows how to make the sparks fly...
heartwarming."
—*Publishers Weekly* on *Renegade*

"Diana Palmer is a mesmerizing storyteller
who captures the essence of
what a romance should be."
—*Affaire de Coeur*

DIANA PALMER

A prolific author of more than one hundred books, Diana Palmer got her start as a newspaper reporter. A *New York Times* bestselling author and voted one of the top ten romance writers in America, she has a gift for telling the most sensual tales with charm and humor. Diana lives with her family in Cornelia, Georgia.

New York Times Bestselling Author

DIANA PALMER

True Blue

and

Carrera's Bride

HARLEQUIN® BESTSELLERS

Recycling programs
for this product may
not exist in your area.

ISBN-13: 978-0-373-60651-1

TRUE BLUE AND CARRERA'S BRIDE
Copyright © 2011 by Harlequin Books S.A.

The publisher acknowledges the copyright holder
of the individual works as follows:

TRUE BLUE
Copyright © 2011 by Diana Palmer

CARRERA'S BRIDE
Copyright © 2004 by Diana Palmer

Printed in U.S.A.

CONTENTS

TRUE BLUE

Chapter 1

"We could lose the case," San Antonio Detective Sergeant Rick Marquez muttered as he glared at one of the newest detectives on his squad.

"I'm really sorry," Gwendolyn Cassaway said, wincing. "I tripped. It was an accident."

He stared at her through narrowed dark eyes, his sensual lips compressed. "You tripped because you're nearsighted and you won't wear glasses." Personally, he didn't think the lack of them did anything for her, if vanity was the issue. She had a pleasant face, and an exquisite complexion, but she was no raving beauty. Her finest feature was her wealth of thick platinum-blond hair that she wore in a high bun on top of her head. She never wore it down.

"Glasses get in my way and I can't ever get them clean enough," she muttered. "That coating just causes smears unless you use the proper cleaning materials. And I can't ever find them," she said defensively.

He drew in a long, exasperated breath and perched on the edge of the desk in his office. In the posture, his .45 Colt ACP in its distinctive leather holster was displayed next to his badge on his belt. So were his powerful legs, and to their best advantage. He was tall and muscular, without it being obvious. He had a light olive complexion and thick long black hair that he wore in a ponytail. He was very attractive, but he couldn't ever seem to wind up with a serious girlfriend. Women found him useful as a sympathetic shoulder to cry on over their true loves. One woman refused to date him when she realized that he wore his pistol even off duty. He'd tried to explain that it was a necessary thing, but it hadn't given him any points with her. He went to the opera, which he loved, all alone. He went everywhere alone. He was almost thirty-one, and lonelier than ever. It made him irritable.

And here was Gwen making it all worse, messing up his crime scene, threatening the delicate chain of evidence that could lead to a conviction in a complex murder.

A college freshman, pretty and blonde, had been brutally assaulted and killed. They had no suspects and trace evidence was very sketchy already. Gwen had almost contaminated the scene by stepping too close to a blood smear.

He was not in a good mood. He was hungry. He was going to be late for lunch, because he had to chew her out. If he didn't, the lieutenant surely would, and Cal Hollister was even meaner than Marquez.

"You could also lose your job," Marquez pointed out. "You're new in the department."

She grimaced. "I know." She shrugged. "I guess I could go back to the Atlanta P.D. if I had to," she said with grim resignation. She looked at him with pale green eyes that were almost translucent. He'd never seen eyes that color.

"You just have to be more careful, Cassaway," he cautioned.

"Yes, sir. I'll do my best."

He tried not to look at the T-shirt she was wearing under a lightweight denim jacket with her jeans. It was unseasonably warm for November but a jacket felt good against the morning chill.

On her T-shirt was a picture of a little green alien, the sort sold in novelty shops, with a legend that read, Have You Seen My Spaceship? He averted his eyes and tried not to grin.

She tugged her jacket closer. "Sorry. But they don't have any regulations against T-shirts here, do they?"

"If the lieutenant sees that one, you'll find out," he said.

She sighed. "I'll try to conform. It's just that I come from a very weird family. My mother worked for the FBI. My father was, uh, in the military. My brother is…" She hesitated and swallowed. "My brother *was* in military intelligence."

He frowned. "Deceased?"

She nodded. She still couldn't talk about it. The pain was too fresh.

"Sorry," he said stiffly.

She shifted. "Larry died very bravely during a covert ops mission in the Middle East. But he was my only sibling. It's hard to talk about."

"I can understand that." He stood up, glancing at

the military watch he wore on his left wrist. "Time for lunch."

"Oh, I have other plans…" she began quickly.

He glared at her. "It was a remark, not an invitation. I don't date colleagues," he said very curtly.

She blushed all the way down to her throat. She swallowed and stood taller. "Sorry. I was… I meant…that is…"

He waved the excuses away. "We'll talk about this some more later. Meanwhile, please do something about your vision. You can't investigate a crime scene you can't see!"

She nodded. "Yes, sir. Absolutely."

He opened the door and let her go out first, noticing absently that her head only came up to his shoulder and that she smelled like spring roses, the pink ones that grew in his mother's garden down in Jacobsville. It was an elusive, very faint fragrance. He approved. Some women who worked in the office seemed to bathe in perfume and always had headaches and allergies and never seemed to think about the connection. Once, a fellow detective had had an almost-fatal asthma attack after a clerical worker stood near him wearing what smelled like an entire bottle of perfume.

Gwendolyn stopped suddenly and he plowed into her, his hands sweeping out to grasp her shoulders and steady her before she fell from his momentum.

"Oh, sorry!" she exclaimed, and felt a thrill of pleasure at the warm strength of the big hands holding her so gently.

He removed them at once. "What is it?"

She had to force her mind to work. Detective Sergeant Marquez was very sexy and she'd been drawn to him since her first sight of him several weeks before. "I meant to ask if you wanted me to check with Alice Fowler over at the crime lab about the digital camera we found in the murdered woman's apartment. By now, she might have something on the trace evidence."

"Good idea. You do that."

"I'll swing past there on my way back to the office after lunch," she promised, and beamed, because it was a big case and he was letting her contribute to solving it. "Thanks."

He nodded, his mind already on the wonderful beef Stroganoff he was going to order at the nearby café where he usually had lunch. He'd been looking forward to it all week. It was Friday and he could splurge.

Tomorrow was his day off. He was going to spend it helping his mother, Barbara, process and can a bushel of hothouse tomatoes she'd been given by an organic gardener with a greenhouse. She owned Barbara's Café in Jacobsville, and she liked to use her organic vegetables and herbs in the meals she prepared for her clients. They would add to the store of canned summer tomatoes that she'd already processed earlier in the year.

He owed her a lot. He'd been orphaned in junior high school and Barbara Ferguson, who'd just lost her husband in an accident, and suffered a miscarriage, had taken him in. His mother had once worked for Barbara at the café just briefly. Then his parents—well, his mother and stepfather—had died in a wreck, leaving a single, lonely child all on his own. Rick had been a terrible teen, always in trouble, bad-tempered and moody. He'd been afraid when he lost his mother. He had no other living relatives of whom he was aware, and no place to go. Barbara had stepped in and given him a home. He loved her no less than he'd loved his real mother, and he was quite protective of her. He never spoke of his step-father. He tried not to remember him at all.

Barbara wanted him to marry and settle down and have a family. She harped on it all the time. She even introduced him to single women. Nothing helped. He seemed to be an eternally on-sale item in the matrimonial market that everybody bypassed for the fancier merchandise. He laughed shortly to himself at the thought.

Gwen watched him leave and wondered why he'd laughed. She was embarrassed that she'd thought he was asking her to lunch. He didn't seem to have a girlfriend and everybody joked about his nonexistent love life. But he wasn't attracted to Gwen in that way. It didn't matter. No man had ever liked her, really. She was everybody's confidante, the good girl who could give advice about how to please other women with small gifts and entertainments. But she was never asked out for herself.

She knew she wasn't pretty. She was always passed over for the flashy women, the assertive women, the powerful women. The women who didn't think sex before marriage was a sin. She'd had a man double over laughing when she'd told him that, after he expected a night in bed in return for a nice meal and the theater. Then he'd become angry, having spent so much money on her with nothing to show for it. The experience had soured her.

"Don Quixote," she murmured to herself. "I'm Don Quixote."

"Wrong sex," Detective Sergeant Gail Rogers said as she paused beside the newcomer. Rogers was the mother of some very wealthy ranchers in Comanche Wells, but she kept her job and her own income. She was an amazing peace officer. Gwen admired her tremendously. "And what's that all about?" she asked.

Gwen sighed, glancing around to make sure they weren't being overheard. "I won't give out on dates," she whispered. "So men think I'm insane." She shrugged. "I'm Don Quixote, trying to restore morality and idealism to a decadent world."

Rogers didn't laugh. She smiled, very kindly. "He was noble, in his way. An idealist with a dream."

"He was nutty as a fruitcake." Gwen sighed.

"Yes, but he made everyone around him feel of worth, like the prostitute whom he idealized as a great lady for whom he quested," came the surprising reply. "He gave dreams to people who had given them up for harsh reality. He was adored by them."

Gwen laughed. "Yes, I suppose he wasn't so bad at that."

"People should have ideals, even if they get laughed at," Rogers added. "You stick to your guns. Every society has its outcasts." She leaned down. "Nobody who conformed to the rigid culture of any society ever made history."

Gwen brightened. "That's true." Then she added, "You've lived through a lot. You got shot," Gwen recalled hearing.

"I did. It was worthwhile, though. We broke a cold case wide-open and caught the murderer."

"I heard. That was some story."

Rogers smiled. "Indeed it was. Rick Marquez got blindsided and left for dead by the same scoundrels who shot me. But we both survived." She frowned. "What's wrong? Marquez giving you a hard time?"

"It's my own fault," Gwen confided. "I can't wear

contacts and I hate glasses. I tripped in a crime scene and came close to contaminating some evidence." She grimaced. "It's a murder case, too, that college freshman they found dead in her apartment last night. The defense will have a field day with that when the perp is caught and brought to trial. And it will be my fault. I just got chewed out for it. I should have, too," she said quickly, because she didn't want Rogers to think Marquez was being unfair.

Rogers's dark eyes searched hers. "You like your sergeant, don't you?"

"I respect him," Gwen said, and then flushed helplessly.

Rogers studied her warmly. "He's a nice man," she said. "He does have a temper and he does take too many chances. But you'll get used to his moods."

"I'm working on that." Gwen chuckled.

"How did you like Atlanta?" Rogers asked conversationally as they headed for the exit.

"Excuse me?" Gwen said absently.

"Atlanta P.D. Where you were working."

"Oh. Oh!" Gwen had to think quickly. "It was nice. I liked the department. But I wanted a change, and I've always wanted to see Texas."

"I see."

No, she didn't, Gwen thought, and thank goodness for that. Gwen was keeping secrets that she didn't dare divulge. She changed the subject as they walked together to the parking lot to their respective vehicles.

Lunch was a salad with dressing on the side, and half a grilled cheese sandwich. Dessert, and her drink, was a cappuccino. She loved the expensive coffee and could only afford it one day a week, on Fridays. She ate an inexpensive lunch so that she could have her coffee.

She sipped it with her eyes closed, smiling. It had an aroma that evoked Italy, a little sidewalk café in Rome with the ruins visible in the distance...

She opened her eyes at once and looked around, as if someone could see the thoughts in her head. She must be very careful not to mention that memory, or other similar ones, in regular conversation. She was a budding junior detective. She had to remember that. It wouldn't do to let anything slip at this crucial moment.

That thought led to thoughts of Detective Marquez and what would be a traumatic revelation for him when the time came for disclosure. Meanwhile, her orders were to observe him, keep her head down and try to discover how much he, or his adoptive mother, knew about his true background. She couldn't say anything. Not yet.

She finished her coffee, paid for her meal and walked out onto the chilly streets. So funny, she thought, the way the weather ran in cycles. It had been unseasonably cold throughout the South during the spring then came summer and blazing, unrelenting heat with drought and wildfires and cattle dying in droves. Now it was November and still unseasonably warm, but some weather experts said snow might come soon.

The weather was nuts. There had been epic drought throughout the whole southern tier of America, from Arizona to Florida, and there had been horrible wildfires in the southwestern states. Triple-digit temperatures had gone all summer in south Texas. There had been horrible flooding on the Mississippi River due to the large snowmelt, from last winter's unusually deep snows up north.

Now it was November and Gwen was actually sweating long before she reached her car, although it had been chilly this morning. She took off her jacket. At least the car had air-conditioning, and she was turning it on, even if it was technically almost winter. Idly, she wondered how people had lived in this heat before air-conditioning was invented. It couldn't have been an easy life, especially since most Texans of the early twentieth century had worked on the land. Imagine, having to herd and brand cattle in this sort of heat, much less plow and plant!

Gwen got into her car and drove by the crime lab to see if Alice had found anything on that digital camera. In fact, she had. There were a lot of photos of people who were probably friends—Gwen could use face recognition software to identify them, hopefully—and there was one odd-looking man standing a little distance behind a couple who was smiling into the camera against the background of the apartment complex where the victim had lived. That was interesting and suspicious. She'd have to check that man out. He didn't look as if he belonged in such a setting. It was a mid-range apartment complex, and the man was dingy and ill kempt and staring a little too intently. She drove back to her precinct.

Her mind was still on Marquez, on what she knew, and he didn't. She hoped he wasn't going to have too hard a time with his true history, when the truth came out.

Barbara glared at her son. "Can't you just peel the tomato, sweetie, without taking out most of it except the core?"

He grimaced. "Sorry," he said, wielding the paring

knife with more care as he went to work on what looked like a bushel of tomatoes, a gift from an organic gardener with a hothouse, that his mother was canning in her kitchen at home. Canning jars simmered in a huge tub of water, getting ready to be filled with fragrant tomato slices and then processed in the big pressure cooker. He glared at it.

"I hate those things," he muttered. "Even the safest ones are dangerous."

"Baloney," she said inelegantly. "Give me those."

She took the bowl of tomatoes and dunked them into a pot of boiling water. She left them there for a couple of minutes and fished them out in a colander. She put them in the sink in front of Rick. "There. Now they'll skin. I keep telling you this is a more efficient way than trying to cut the skins off. But you don't listen, my dear."

"I like skinning them," he said with a dark-eyed smile in her direction. "It's an outlet for my frustrations."

"Oh?" She didn't look at him, deliberately. "What sort of frustrations?"

"There's this new woman at work," he said grimly.

"Gwen." She nodded.

He dropped the knife, picked it back up and stared at her.

"You talk about her all the time."

"I do?" It was news to him. He didn't realize that.

She nodded as she skinned tomatoes. "She trips over things that she doesn't see, she messes up crime scenes, she spills coffee, she can't find her cell phone…" She glanced at him. He was still standing there, with the knife poised over a tomato. "Get busy, there, those tomatoes won't peel themselves."

He groaned.

"Just think how nice they'll taste in one of my beef stew recipes," she coaxed. "Go on, peel."

"Why can't we just get one of those things that sucks the air out of bags and freeze them instead?"

"What if we have a major power outage that lasts for days and days?" she returned.

He thought for a minute. "I'll go buy twenty bags of ice and several of those foam coolers."

She laughed. "Yes, but we can't tell how the power grid is going to cope if we have one of those massive CMEs like the Carrington Event in 1859."

He blinked. "Excuse me?"

"There was a massive coronal mass ejection in 1859 called the Carrington Event," she explained. "When it hit earth, all the electrics on the planet went crazy. Telegraph lines burned up and telegraph units caught fire." She glanced at him. "There wasn't much electricity back in those days—it was in its infancy. But imagine if such a thing happened today, with our dependence on electricity. Everything is connected to the grid these days, banks, communications corporations, pharmacies, government, military and the list goes on and on. Even our water and power are controlled by computers. Just imagine if we had no way to access our computers."

He whistled. "I was in the grocery store one day when the computers went offline. They couldn't process credit cards. Most people had to leave. I had enough cash for bread and milk. Then another time the computers in the pharmacy went down, when you had to have those antibiotics for the sinus infection last winter. I had to come home and get the checkbook and go back. People without credit cards had real problems."

"See?" She went back to her tomatoes.

"I suppose it would be a pretty bad thing. Is it going to happen, you think?"

"Someday, certainly. The sun has eleven year cycles, you know, with a solar minimum and a solar maximum. The next solar maximum, some scientists say, is in 2012. If we're going to get hit, that would have my vote for the timeline."

"Twenty-twelve," he groaned, rolling his eyes. "We had this guy come in the office and tell us we needed to put out a flyer."

"What about?"

"The fact that the world is ending in 2012 and we have to have tin-foil hats to protect us from electromagnetic pulses."

"Ah. EMPs," she said knowledgeably. "Actually, I think you'd have to be in a modified and greatly enlarged version of a Leiden jar to be fully protected. So would any computer equipment you wanted to save." She glanced at him. "They're developing weapons like that, you know," she added. "All it would take is one nicely placed EMP and our military computers would go down like tenpins."

He put down the knife. "Where do you learn all this stuff?" he asked, exasperated.

"On the internet." She pulled an iPod out of her pocket and showed it to him. "I have Wi-Fi in the house, you know. I just connect to all the appropriate websites." She checked her bookmarks. "I have one for space weather, three radars for terrestrial weather and about ten covert sites that tell you all the stuff the government won't tell you…"

"My mother, the conspiracy theorist," he moaned.

"You won't hear this stuff on the national news," she

said smartly. "The mainstream media is controlled by three major corporations. They decide what you'll get to hear. And mostly it's what entertainer got drunk, what television show is getting the ratings and what politician is patting himself on the back or running for reelection. In my day—" she warmed to her theme "—we had real news on television. It was local and we had real reporters out gathering it. Like the Jacobsville paper still does," she added.

"I know about the Jacobsville paper," he said with a sigh. "We hear that Cash Grier spends most of his time trying to protect the owner from getting assassinated. She knows all the drug distribution points and the drug lords by name, and she's printing them." He shook his head. "She's going to be another statistic one day. They've killed plenty of newspaper publishers and reporters over the border for less. She's rocking the boat."

"Somebody needs to rock it," Barbara muttered as she peeled another tomato skin off and tossed it into a green bag to be used for mulch in her garden. She never wasted any organic refuse. "People are dying so that another generation can become addicted to drugs."

"I can't argue that point," he said. "The problem is that nothing law enforcement is doing is making much of a dent in drug trafficking. If there's a market, there's going to be a supply. That's just the way things are."

"They say Hayes Carson actually talked to Minette Raynor about it."

That was real news. Minette owned the *Jacobsville Times*. She had two stepsiblings, Shane, who was twelve, and Julie, who was six. She'd loved her stepmother very much. Her stepmother and her father had died within weeks of each other, leaving a grieving Minette with two little children to raise, a newspaper to run and a ranch to manage. She had a manager to handle the ranch, and her great-aunt Sarah lived with her and took care of the kids after school so that Minette could keep working. Minette was twenty-five now and unmarried. She and Hayes Carson didn't get along. Hayes blamed her, God knew why, for his younger brother's drug-related death, even after Rachel Conley left a confession stating that she'd given Bobby Carson, Hayes's brother, the drugs that killed him.

Rick chuckled. "If there's ever a border war, Minette will stand in the street pointing a finger at Hayes so the invaders can get him first."

"I wonder," Barbara mused. "Sometimes I think where there's antagonism, there's also something deeper. I've seen people who hate each other end up married."

"Cash Grier and his Tippy," Rick mused.

"Yes, and Stuart York and Ivy Conley."

"Not to mention half a dozen others. Jacobsville is growing by leaps and bounds."

"So is Comanche Wells. We've got new people there, too." She was peeling faster. "Did you notice that Grange bought a ranch in Comanche Wells, next to the property that his boss owns?"

Rick pursed his sensual lips. "Which boss?"

She blinked at him. "What do you mean, which boss?"

"He works as ranch manager for Jason Pendleton. But he also works on the side for Eb Scott," he said. "You didn't hear this from me, but he was involved in the Pendleton kidnapping," he added. "He went to get Gracie Pendleton back when she was kidnapped by that exiled South American dictator, Emilio Machado."

"Machado."

"Yes." He peeled the tomato slowly. "He's a conundrum."

"What do you mean?"

"He started out, we learned, as a farm laborer down in Mexico, from the time he was about ten years old. He was involved in protests against foreign interests even as a teenager. But he got tired of scratching dirt for a living. He could play the guitar and sing, so he worked bars for a while and then through a contact, he got a job as an entertainer on a cruise ship. That got boring. He signed on with a bunch of mercs and became known internationally as a crusader against oppression. Afterward, he went to South America and hired on with another paramilitary group that was fighting to preserve the way of life of the native people in Barrera, a little nation in the Amazon bordering Peru. He helped the paramilitary unit free a tribe of natives from a foreign corporation that was trying to kill them to get the oil-rich land on which they were living. He developed a taste for defending the underdog, moved up in the ranks of the military until he became a general." He smiled. "It seems that he was a natural leader, because when the small country's president died four years ago, Machado was elected by acclamation." He glanced at her. "Do you realize how rare that is, even for a small nation?"

"If people loved him so much, how is it that he's in Mexico kidnapping people to get money to retake his country?"

"He wasn't ousted by the people, but by a vicious and bloodthirsty military subordinate who knew when and how to strike, while Machado was on a trip to a neighboring country to sign a trade agreement and offer an alliance against foreign corporate takeovers."

"I didn't know that."

"It's sort of privileged info, so you can't share it," he told her. "Anyway, the subordinate killed Machado's entire staff, and sent his secret police to shut down newspapers and television and radio stations. Overnight, influential people ended up in prison. Educators, politicians, writers—anyone who might threaten the new regime. There have been hundreds of murders, and now the subordinate, Pedro Mendez by name, is allying himself with drug lords in a neighboring country. It seems that cocaine grows quite nicely in Barrera and poor farmers are being 'encouraged' to grow it instead of food crops on their land. Mendez is also nationalizing every single business so that he has absolute control."

"No wonder the general is trying to retake his country," she said curtly. "I hope he makes it."

"So do I," Rick replied. "But I can't say that in public," he added. "He's wanted in this country for kidnapping. It's a capital offense. If he's caught and convicted he could wind up with a death penalty."

She winced. "I don't condone how he's getting the money," she replied. "But he's going to use it for a noble reason."

"Noble." He chuckled.

"That's not funny," she said shortly.

"I'm not laughing at the word. It's Gwen. She goes around mumbling that she's Don Quixote."

She laughed out loud. "What?"

He shook his head. "Rogers told me. It seems that our newest detective won't give out on dates and she groups herself with Don Quixote, who tried to restore honor and morality to a decadent world."

"My, my!" She pursed her lips and smiled secretively.

"I don't want to marry Gwen Cassaway," he said at once. "I just thought I'd mention that, because I can read minds, and I don't like what you're thinking."

"She's a nice girl."

"She's a woman."

"She's a nice girl. She has a very idealistic and romantic attitude for someone who lives in the city. And I ought to know. I have women from cities coming through here all the time, talking about unspeakable things right in public with the whole world listening." Her lips made a thin line. "Do you know, Grange was having lunch next to a table of them where they were discussing men's, well, intimate men parts," she amended, clearing her throat, "and Grange got up from his chair, told them what he thought of them for discussing a bedroom topic in public in front of decent people and he walked out."

"What did they do?"

"One of them laughed. One of the others cried. Another said he needed to start living in the real world instead of small town 'stupidville.'" She grinned. "Of course, she said it after he'd already left. While he was talking, they didn't say a word. But they left soon after. I was glad. I can't choose my clientele and I've only ever ordered one person to leave my restaurant since I've owned it," she added.

She dragged herself back to the present. "But the topic of conversation was getting to me, too. People need to talk about intimate things in private, not in a public place with their voices raised. We don't all think alike."

"Only in some ways," he pointed out, and hugged her impulsively. "You're a nice mother. I'm so lucky to have you for an adoptive parent."

She hugged him back. "You've enriched my life, my sweet." She sighed, closing her eyes in his warm embrace. "When I lost Bart, I wanted to die, too. And then your mother and stepfather died, and there you were, as alone as I was. We needed each other."

"We did." He moved away and smiled affectionately. "You took on a big burden with me. I was a bad boy."

She groaned and rolled her eyes. "Were you ever! Always in fights, in school and out. I spent half my life in the principal's office and once at a school board meeting where they were going to vote to throw you right out of school altogether and put you in alternative school." Her face hardened. "In their dreams!"

"Yes, you took a lawyer to the meeting and buffaloed them. First time it ever happened, I heard later."

"I was very mad."

"I felt really bad about that," he said. "But I put my nose to the grindstone after, and tried hard to make it up to you."

"Joined the police force, went to night school and got your associate degree, went to the San Antonio Police Department and worked your way up in the ranks to sergeant," she agreed, smiling. "Made me *so* proud!"

He hugged her again. "I owe it all to you."

"No. You owe it to your hard work. I may have helped, but you pulled yourself up."

He kissed her forehead. "Thank you. For everything."

"You're my son. I love you very much."

He cleared his throat. Emotions were difficult for him, especially considering his job. "Yeah. Me, too."

She grinned. The smile faded as she searched his large, dark eyes. "Do you ever wonder about your mother's past?"

His eyebrows shot up. "What a question!" He frowned. "What do you mean?"

"Do you know anything about her friends? About any male friends she had before she married your stepfather?"

He shrugged. "Not really. She didn't talk about her relationships. Well, I wasn't old enough for her to confide in me, either, you know. She never was one to talk about intimate things," he said quietly. "Not even about my real father. She said that he died, but she never talked about him. She was very young when I was born. She did say she'd done things she wanted forgiveness for, and she went to confession a lot." He studied her closely. "You must have had some reason for asking me that."

She put her lips tightly together. "Something I overheard. I wasn't supposed to be listening."

"Come on, tell me," he said when she hesitated.

"Cash Grier was having lunch with some fed. They were discussing Machado. The fed mentioned a woman named Dolores Ortíz who had some connection to General Machado when he lived in Mexico."

Chapter 2

"Dolores Ortíz?" he asked, the paring knife poised in midair. "That was my mother's maiden name."

"I know."

Rick frowned. "You mean my mother might have been romantically involved with Emilio Machado?"

"I got that impression," Barbara said, nodding. "But I wasn't close enough to hear the entire conversation. I just got bits and pieces of it."

He pursed his lips. "Well, my father died around the time I was born, so it's not impossible that she did meet Machado in Mexico. Although, it's a big country."

"You lived in the state of Sonora," she pointed out. "That's where Machado had his truck farm, they said."

He finished skinning the tomato and reached for another one. "Wouldn't that be a coincidence, if my mother actually knew him?"

"Yes, it would."

"Well, it was a long time ago," he said easily. "And she's dead, and I never knew him. So what good would it do for them to dig up an old romance now?"

"I have no idea. It bothered me, a little. I mean, you're my son."

"Yes, I am." He glanced at her. "I love it when people get all flustered and start babbling when you introduce me. You're blonde and fair and I'm dark and obviously Hispanic."

"You're gorgeous, my baby," she teased. "I just wish women would stop crying on your shoulder about other men and start trying to marry you."

He sighed. "Chance would be a fine thing. I carry a gun!" he said with mock horror.

She glowered at him. "All off-duty policemen carry guns."

"Yes, but I might shoot somebody accidentally, and it would get in the way if I tried to hug somebody."

"I gather that somebody female mentioned that?"

He sighed and nodded. "A public defender," he said. "She thought I was cute, but she doesn't date men who carry. It's a principle, she said. She hates guns."

"I hate guns, too, but I keep a shotgun in the closet in case I ever need to defend myself," Barbara pointed out.

"I'll defend you."

"You work in San Antonio," she said. "If you're not here, I have to defend myself. By the time Hayes Carson could get to my place, I'd be…well, not in any good condition if somebody tried to harm me."

That had happened once, Rick recalled with anger. A man he'd arrested, after he'd been released, had gone after Rick's adoptive mother for revenge. It was just chance that Hayes Carson had stopped by when he was off duty, in his unmarked truck, to ask her about catering an event. The ex-convict had piled out of his car and come right up on the porch with a drawn gun—in violation of parole—and banged on the door demanding that Barbara come outside. Hayes had come outside, disarmed him, cuffed him and taken him right to jail. The man was now serving another term in prison, for assault on a police officer, trespassing, attempted assault, possessing a firearm in violation of parole and resisting arrest. Barbara had testified at his trial. So had Hayes.

Rick shook his head. "I hate having you in danger because of my job."

"It was only the one time," she said, comforting him. "It could have been somebody who carried a grudge because their apple pie wasn't served with ice cream or something."

He smiled. "Dream on. You even make the ice cream you serve with it. Your pies are out of this world."

"Don't you have an in-house seminar coming up at work?" she asked.

He nodded.

"Why don't you take a couple of pies back with you?"

"That would be nice. Thank you."

"My pleasure." She pursed her lips. "Does Gwen like apple pie?"

He turned and stared at her. "Gwen is a colleague. I never, never date colleagues."

She sighed. "Okay."

He went back to work on the tomatoes. This could turn into a problem. His mother, well-meaning and loving, nevertheless was determined to get him married. That was one area in which he wanted to do his own

prospecting. And never in this lifetime did he want to
end up with someone like Gwen, who had two left feet
and the dress sense of a Neanderthal woman. He laughed
at the idea of her in bearskins carrying a spear. But he
didn't share the joke with his mother.

When he went to work the next day, it was qualifying
time on the firing range. Rick was a good shot, and he
kept excellent care of his service weapon. But the testing
was one of the things he really hated about police work.

His lieutenant, Cal Hollister, could outshoot any man
in the precinct. He scored a hundred percent regularly.
Rick could usually manage in the nineties but never a
perfect score. He always seemed to do the qualifying
when the lieutenant was doing his, and his ego suffered.

Today, Gwen Cassaway also showed up. Rick tried
not to groan out loud. Gwen would drop her pistol, accidentally kill the lieutenant and Rick would be prosecuted for manslaughter...

"Why are you groaning like that?" Hollister asked
curtly as he checked the clip for his .45 in preparation
for target shooting.

"Just a stray thought, sir, nothing important." His
eyes went involuntarily to Gwen, who was also load-
ing her own pistol.

On the firing range, shooters wore eye protection and
ear protection. They customarily loaded only six bullets
into the clip of the automatic, and this was done at the
time they got into position to fire. The pistol would be
held at low or medium ready position, after being carefully drawn from its snapped holster for firing, with
the safety on. The pistol, even unloaded, would never
be pointed in any direction except that of the target and

the trigger finger would never rest on the trigger. When in firing position, the safety would be released, and the shooter would fire at the target using either the Weaver, modified Weaver, or Isosceles shooting stance.

One of the most difficult parts of shooting, and one of the most important to master, was trigger pull. The pressure exerted on the trigger had to be perfect in order to place a shot correctly. There were graphs on the firing range that helped participants check the efficiency of their trigger pull and help to improve it. Rick's was improving. But his lieutenant consistently showed him up on the gun range, and it made him uncomfortable. He tried not to practice or qualify when the other man was around. Unfortunately, he always seemed to be on the range when Rick was.

Hollister followed Rick's gaze to Gwen. He knew, as Rick did, that she had some difficulty with coordination. He pursed his lips. His black eyes danced as he glanced covertly at Gwen. "It's okay, Marquez. We're insured," he said under his breath.

Rick cleared his throat and tried not to laugh.

Hollister moved onto the firing line. His thick blond hair gleamed like pale honey in the sunlight. He glanced at Gwen. "Ready, Detective?" he drawled, pulling the heavy ear protectors on over his hair.

Gwen gave him a nice smile. "Ready when you are, sir."

The Range Master moved into position, indicated that everything was ready and gave the signal to fire.

Hollister, confident and relaxed, chuckled, aimed at the target and proceeded to blow the living hell out of it.

Rick, watching Gwen worriedly, saw something incredible happen next. Gwen snapped into a modified

Weaver position, barely even aimed and threw six shots into the center of the target with pinpoint accuracy.

His mouth flew open.

She took the clip out of her automatic, checked the cylinder and waited for the Range Master to check her score.

"Cassaway," he said eventually, and hesitated. "One hundred percent."

Rick and the lieutenant stared at each other.

"Lieutenant Hollister," the officer continued, and was obviously trying not to smile, "ninety-nine percent."

"What the hell...!" Hollister burst out. "I hit dead center!"

"Missed one, sir, by a hair," the officer replied with a twinkle in his eyes. "Sorry."

Hollister let out a furious bad word. Gwen marched right up to him and glared at him from pale green eyes.

"Sir, I find that word offensive and I'd appreciate it if you would refrain from using it in my presence," she said curtly.

Hollister's high cheekbones actually flushed. Rick tensed, waiting for the explosion.

But Hollister didn't erupt. His black eyes smiled down at the rookie detective. "Point taken, Detective," he said, and his deep voice was even pleasant. "I apologize."

Gwen swallowed. She was almost shaking. "Thank you, sir."

She turned and walked off.

"Not bad shooting, by the way," he commented as he removed the clip from his own pistol.

She grinned. "Thanks." She glanced at Rick, who was still gaping, and almost made a smart remark. But she thought better of it in time.

Rick let out the breath he'd been holding. "She trips over her own feet," he remarked. "But that was some damned fine shooting."

"It was," the lieutenant agreed. He shook his head. "You can never figure people, can you, Marquez?"

"True, sir. Very true."

Later that day, Rick noted two dignified men in suits walking past his office. They glanced at him, spoke to one another and hesitated. One gestured down the hall quickly, and they kept walking.

He wondered what in the world was going on.

Rogers came into his office a few minutes later, frowning. "Odd thing."

"What?" he asked, his eyes on his computer screen where he was running a case through VICAP.

"Did you see those two suits?"

"Yes, they hesitated outside my office. Who are they, feds?"

"Yes. State Department."

He burst out laughing as he looked at her with large, dancing brown eyes. "They think I'm illegal and they're here to bust me?"

"Stop that," she muttered.

"Sorry. Couldn't resist it." He turned to her. "We have high level immigration cases all the time where the State Department gets involved."

"Yes, but mostly we deal with the enforcement branch of the Department of Immigration and Naturalization, with ICE. Or we deal with the DEA in drug cases, I know that. But these guys aren't from Austin. They're from D.C."

"The capitol?"

"That's right. They've been talking to the lieutenant all morning. They're taking him to lunch, too."

"What's going on? Any idea?"

She shook her head. "Only that gossip says they're on the Machado case."

"Yes. He's wanted for kidnapping." He didn't add what Barbara had told him, that his own birth mother might have once known Machado in the past.

"He's not in the country."

"And how would you know that?" Rick asked her with pursed lips. "Another psychic insight?" he added, because she had a really unusual sixth sense about cases.

"No. I ran into Cash Grier over at the courthouse. He was up here on a case."

"Our police chief from Jacobsville," he acknowledged.

"The very same. He mentioned that Jason Pendleton's foreman is on temporary leave because of Machado."

"Grange," Rick recalled, naming the foreman. "He went into Mexico to retrieve Gracie Pendleton when she was kidnapped by Machado's men for ransom."

"Yes. It seems the general took a liking to him, had him investigated and offered him a job."

Rick blinked. "Excuse me?"

"That's what I said when Grier told me." She laughed. "The general really does have style. He said somebody had to organize his mercs when he goes in to retake his country. Grange, being a former major in the army, seemed the logical choice."

"His country is Barrera," Rick mused. "Nice name, since it sits on the Amazon River bordering Colombia, Peru and Bolivia. Barrera is Spanish for barrier."

"I didn't know that, only having completed two years of college Spanish," she replied blithely.

He made a face at her.

"Anyway, it seems Grange likes the idea of being a crusader for democracy and freedom and human rights, so he took the job. He's in Mexico at the moment helping the general come up with a plan of attack."

"With Eb Scott offering candidates, I don't doubt," Rick added. "He's got the cream of the crop at his counterterrorism training center in Jacobsville, as far as mercs go."

"The general is gathering them from everywhere. He has a couple of former SAS from Great Britain, a one-eyed terror from South Africa named Rourke whose nickname is Deadeye…"

"I know him," Rick said.

"Me, too," Rogers replied. "He's a pill, isn't he? Rumored to be the natural son of K. C. Kantor, who was one of the more successful ex-mercs."

"Yes, Kantor became a billionaire after he gave up the lifestyle. He has a daughter who married Dr. Micah Steele in Jacobsville, and a godchild who married into the ranching Callister family up in Montana." His eyes narrowed. "Where is the general getting the money to finance his revolution?"

"Remember that he gave Gracie back without any payment. But then he nabbed Jason Pendleton for ransom, and Gracie paid it with the money from her trust fund?"

"Forgot about that," Rick said.

"It ran to six figures. So he's bankrolled. We hear he also charged what's left of the Fuentes cartel for protection while he was sharing space with them over the border."

"Charging drug lords rent in their own turf?" Rick asked.

"And getting it. The general has a pretty fearsome reputation," she added. She laughed. "He's also a incredibly handsome," she mused. "I've seen a photograph of him. They say he has a charming personality, reveres women and plays the guitar and sings like an angel."

"A man of many talents."

"Not the least of which is inspiring troops." Rogers sighed. "But it has to be unsettling for the State Department, especially since the Mexican government is up in arms about having Machado recruit mercs to invade a sovereign nation in South America while living in their country."

"Why are they protesting to us? We aren't helping him," Rick pointed out.

"He's on our border."

"If they want us to do something about Machado, they could do something about the militant drug cartels running over our borders with automatic weapons to protect their drug runners."

"Chance would be a fine thing."

"I guess so. None of that explains why the State Department is gumming up our office," he added. "This is San Antonio. The border is that way." He pointed out the window. "A long, long drive that way."

"I know. That's what puzzled me. So I pumped Grier for information."

"What did he tell you?"

"He didn't. Tell me anything," she added grimly. "So

I had my oldest son pump his best friend, Sheriff Hayes Carson, for information."

"Did you get anything from him?"

She bit her lower lip. "Bits and pieces." She gave him a worried look. She couldn't tell him what she found out. She'd been sworn to secrecy. "But nothing really concrete, I'm sorry to say."

"I suppose they'll tell us eventually."

"I suppose so."

"When is this huge invasion of Barrera going to take place? Any timeline on that?"

"None that presented itself." She sighed. "But it's going to be a gala occasion, from what we hear. The State Department would have good reason to be concerned. They can't back a revolution…"

"One of the letter agencies could help with that, of course, without public acknowledgment."

Letter agencies referred to government bureaus like the CIA, which Rick assumed would have been in the forefront of any assistance they could legally give to help install a democratic government friendly to the United States in South America.

"Kilraven used to belong to the CIA," Rick murmured. "Maybe I could ask him if he knows anything."

"I'd keep my nose out of it for the time being," Rogers cautioned, foreseeing trouble ahead if Rick tried to interfere at this stage of the game. "We'll know soon enough."

"I guess so." He glanced at her and asked, "Hear about what happened on the firing range this morning?"

Her eyes brightened. "Did I ever! The whole department's talking about it. Our rookie detective outshot the lieutenant."

"By a whole point." Rick grinned. "Imagine that. She

falls into potted plants and trips over crime evidence, but she can shoot like an Old West gunslinger." He shook his head. "I thought I'd pass out when she started firing that automatic. It was beautiful. She never even seemed to aim. Just snapped off the shots and hit in the center every single time."

"The lieutenant's a good loser, though," Rogers commented. "He bought a single pink rose and laid it on her desk after lunch."

Rick's eyes narrowed and his expression grew cold. "Did he, now?"

The lieutenant was a widower. Nobody knew how he lost his wife, he never spoke of her. He didn't even date, as far as anyone knew. And here he was giving flowers to Gwen, who was young and innocent and impressionable...

"I said, do you think that could be construed as sexual harassment?" Rogers repeated.

"He gave her a flower!"

"Well, yes, but he wouldn't have given a man a flower, would he?"

"I'd have given Kilraven a flower after he nabbed the perp who blindsided me in the alley and left me for dead," he said, tongue-in-cheek.

She sighed. She felt in her pocket for the unopened pack of cigarettes she kept there, pulled it out and looked at it with sad eyes. "I miss smoking. The kids made me quit."

"You're still carrying around cigarettes?" he exclaimed.

"Well, it's comforting. Having them in my pocket, I mean. I wouldn't actually smoke one, of course. Unless we have a nuclear attack, or something. Then it would be okay."

He burst out laughing. "You're incorrigible, Rogers."

"Only on Mondays," she said after a minute. She glanced at her watch. "I have to get back to work."

"Let me know if you find out anything else, okay?"

"Of course I will." She smiled.

She felt a twinge of guilt as she walked out of his office. She wished she could tell him the truth, or at least prepare him for what she knew was coming. He had a surprise in store. Probably not a very nice one.

"But I made corned beef and cabbage," Barbara groaned when Rick phoned her Friday afternoon to say he wasn't coming home that night.

"I know, it's my favorite, and I'm sorry," he said. "But we've got a stakeout. I have to go. It's my squad." He sighed. "Gwen's on it, and she'll probably knock over a trash can and we'll get burned."

"You have to think positively." She hesitated. "You could bring her home with you tomorrow. The corned beef will still be good and I'll cook more cabbage."

"She's a colleague," he repeated. "I don't date colleagues."

"Does your lieutenant date colleagues?" she asked with glee. "Because I heard he left her a single rose on her desk. What a lovely, romantic man!"

He gnashed his teeth and hoped the sound didn't carry. He was tired of hearing that story. It had gone the rounds at work all week.

"You could put a rose on her desk…"

"If I did, it would be attached to a pink slip!" he snapped.

She gasped, hesitated and turned off the phone. It was the first time he'd ever snapped at her.

Rick groaned and dialed her number back. It rang and rang. "Come on. Please?" he spoke into the busy signal. "I'm sorry. Come on, let me apologize…"

"Yes?" Barbara answered stiffly.

"I'm sorry. I didn't mean to snap at you. I really didn't. I'll come home for lunch tomorrow and eat corned beef and cabbage. I'll even eat crow. Raw." There was silence on the end of the line. "I'll bring a rose?"

She laughed. "Okay, you're forgiven."

"I'm really sorry. Things have been hectic at work. But that's no excuse for being rude to you."

"No, it's not. But I'm not mad."

"You're a nice mother."

She laughed. "You're a nice son. I love you. I'll see you at lunch tomorrow."

"Have a good night."

"You have a careful one," she said solemnly. "Even rude sons are hard to come by these days," she added.

"I'll change my ways. Honest. See you."

"See you."

He hung up and sighed heavily. He couldn't imagine why he'd been so short with his own mother. Perhaps he needed a vacation. He only took time off when he was threatened. He loved his job. Being sergeant of an eight-detective squad in the Homicide Unit, in the Murder/Attempted Murder detail, was heady and satisfying. He assigned lead detectives to cases, reviewed cases to make sure everything necessary was done and kept up with what seemed like tons of paperwork, as well as reporting to the lieutenant on caseloads. But maybe a little time off would improve his temper. He'd talk to the lieutenant about it next week, he resolved. For now, he had work to do.

Gwen had been assigned as lead detective on the college student's murder case downtown. It was an odd sort of case. The woman had been stabbed by person or persons unknown, in her own apartment, with all the doors locked and the windows shut. There were no signs of a struggle. She was a pretty young woman with no current boyfriend, no apparent enemies, who led a quiet life and didn't party.

Gwen wanted very much to solve the case. She'd told Rick that Alice Fowler had found prints on a digital camera that featured an out-of-place man in the background. Gwen was checking that out. She was really working hard on the mystery.

But in the meantime, she'd been pressed into service to help Rick with a stakeout of a man wanted for shooting a police officer in a traffic stop. The officer lived, but he'd be in rehab for months. They had intel that the shooter was hiding out in a low class apartment building downtown with some help from an associate. But they couldn't find him there. So Rick decided to stake out the place and try to catch him. The fact that it was a Friday night meant that the younger, single detectives were trying to find ways not to get involved. Even the night detectives had excuses, pending cases that they simply couldn't spare time away from. So Rick ended up with Gwen and one young and eager patrol officer, Ted Sims, from the Patrol South Division who'd volunteered, hoping to find favor with Rick and maybe get a chance at climbing the ladder, and working as a detective one day.

They were set up in a ratty apartment downtown, observing a suspect across the alley in another run-down apartment building. They had all the lights off, a telescope, a video camera, listening devices, warrants to allow the listening devices, and as much black coffee as three detectives could drink in an evening. Which was quite a lot.

"I wish we had a pizza." Officer Sims sighed.

Rick sighed, too. "So do I, but the smell would carry and the perp would know we were watching him."

"Maybe we could put the pizza outside his door and he'd go nuts smelling it and rush out to grab it and we could grab him," Sims mused.

"What do you have in that bottle besides water?" Gwen asked, with twinkling green eyes.

Sims made a face. "Just water, sadly. I could really use a cold beer."

"Shut up," Marquez groaned. "I'm dying for one."

"We could ask Detective Cassaway to investigate the beer rack at the local convenience store and confiscate a six-pack for the crime scene investigation unit," Sims joked. "Nobody would have to know. We could threaten the owner with health violations or something."

Gwen gave him a cold look. "We don't steal."

Marquez gave him an even more vicious look. "Ever."

He flushed. "Hey," he said, holding up both hands, "I was just kidding!"

"I'm not laughing," she returned, unblinking.

"Neither am I," Marquez seconded. His face was hard with suppressed anger. "I don't want to hear talk like that from a sworn police officer."

"Sorry," he said, swallowing hard. "Really. Bad joke. I didn't mean I'd actually do it."

Gwen shrugged. Sims was very young. "I'm missing that new science fiction show I got hooked on," she groaned. "It's making me twitchy."

"I watch that one, too," Rick replied. "It's not bad."

"You could record it," Sims suggested. "Don't you have a DVR?"

She shook her head. "I'm poor. I can't afford one."

Rick glared at her. "We work for one of the best-paying departments in the southwest," he rattled off. "We have a benefits package, expense accounts, access to excellent vehicles…"

"I have a monthly rent bill, a monthly insurance bill, a car payment, utilities payments and I have to buy bullets for my gun," she muttered. "Who can afford luxuries?" She glared at him. "I haven't had a new suit in six months. This one looks like moths have nested in it already."

Rick's eyebrows arched up. "Surely, you've got more than one suit, Cassaway."

"Two suits, twelve blouses, six pair of shoes and assorted…other things," she said. "Mix and match and I'm sick of all of it. I want haute couture!"

"Good luck with that," Rick remarked.

"Luck won't do it."

"Hey, is this the guy we're looking for?" Sims asked suddenly, looking through the telescope.

Chapter 3

Rick and Gwen joined him at the window. Rick snapped a photo of the man across the street, using the telephoto feature, plugged it into his small computer and, using a new face recognition software component, compared it to the man he'd photographed.

"Positive ID. That's him," Rick said. "Let's go get him."

They ran down the steps, deploying quickly to the designations planned earlier by Rick.

The man, yawning and oblivious, stepped out onto the sidewalk next to a bus stop sign.

"Now," Rick yelled.

Three people came running toward the stunned man, who started to run, but it was far too late. Rick tackled him and took him down. He cuffed his hands behind his back and chuckled as the man started cursing.

"I ain't done nothin'!" he wailed.

"Then you don't have a thing to worry about."

The man only groaned.

"That was a nice takedown," Gwen said as they cleared their equipment out of the rented apartment, after the man had been taken away by the patrol officer.

"Thanks. I try to keep in shape."

She didn't dare look at him. She was having a hard enough time not noticing how very attractive he was.

"You know," he mused, "that was some fine shooting down at HQ."

She beamed. "Thanks." She glanced up. "At least I do have one saving grace."

"Probably more than one, Cassaway."

She shouldered her purse. "Are we done for the night?"

"Yes. I'll input the report and you can sign it tomorrow. I snapped at my mother. I have to go home and try to make it up to her."

"She's very nice."

He turned, frowning. "How do you know?"

"I came through Jacobsville when I had to interview a witness in that last murder trial," she reminded him. "I had lunch at the café. It's the only one in town, except for the Chinese restaurant, and I like her apple pie." She added that last bit to make sure he knew she wasn't frequenting his mother's café just because she was his mother.

"Oh."

"Has she owned the restaurant a long time?"

He nodded. "She opened it a couple of years before

I was orphaned. My mother worked for her as a cook just briefly."

Gwen nodded, trying to be low-key. "Is your mother still alive? Your biological mother?" she asked while looking through her purse for her car keys.

"She and my stepfather died in a wreck when I was almost in my teens. Barbara had just lost her husband and had a miscarriage the month before it happened. She was grieving and so was I. Since I had no other family, and she knew me, she adopted me."

She flushed. "Oh. Sorry, I didn't mean to pry. I was just curious."

He shrugged. "Most everybody knows," he said easily. "I was born in Mexico, in Sonora, but my mother and stepfather came to this country when I was a toddler and lived in Jacobsville. My stepfather worked at one of the local ranches."

"What did he do?"

"Broke horses." The way he said it was cold and short, as if he didn't like being reminded of the man.

"I had an uncle who worked ranches in Wyoming," she confided. "He's dead now."

He studied her through narrowed eyes. "Wyoming. But you're from Atlanta?"

"Not originally."

He waited.

She cleared her throat. "My people are from Montana, originally."

"You're a long way from home."

"Yes, well, my parents moved to Maryland when I was small."

"I guess you miss the ocean."

She nodded. "A lot. It wasn't a long drive from our

house. But I go where they send me. I've worked a lot of places—" She stopped dead, and could have bitten her tongue.

His eyebrows were arching already. "The Atlanta P.D. moves you around the country?"

"I mean, I've worked a lot of places around Atlanta."

"Mmm-hmm."

"I didn't always work for Atlanta P.D.," she muttered, trying to backpedal. "I worked for a risk organization for a year or two, in the insurance business, and they sent me around the country on jobs."

"A risk organization? What sort of work did you do?"

"I was a sort of security consultant." It wasn't quite the truth, but it wasn't quite a lie, either. She glanced at her watch as a diversion. "Oh, goodness, I'll miss my television show!"

"God forbid," he said dryly. "Okay. We're done here."

"It didn't take as long as I expected," she commented on the way out. "Usually stakeouts last for hours if not days."

"Tell me about it," he said drolly. "Is your car close by?"

She turned at the foot of the steps. "It's across the street, thanks," she said, because she knew he was offering to walk her to it. He was a gentleman, in the nicest sort of way.

He nodded. "I'll see you Monday, then."

She smiled. "Yes, sir."

She turned and walked away. Her heart was pounding and she was cursing herself mentally. She'd almost blown the whole thing sky-high!

* * *

Barbara was her usual, smiling self, but her eyes were sad when Rick showed up at the door the night before he was due home.

"You said tomorrow?" she murmured.

He stepped into the house and hugged her, hard, rocking her in his arms. He heard a muffled sob. "I felt bad," he said at her ear. "I upset you."

"Hey," she murmured, drawing away to dab at her eyes, "that's what kids are supposed to do."

He smiled. "No, it's not."

"Want some coffee?"

"Yes!" he said at once, pulling off his suit coat and loosening his tie as he followed her to the kitchen. He swung the coat around one of the high-back kitchen chairs at the table and sat down. "I've been on stakeout, with convenience-store coffee." He made a face. "I think they keep it in the pot all day to make sure it doesn't pass for hot brown water."

She laughed as she made a fresh pot. "There's that profit margin to consider," she mused.

"I guess."

"Did you catch a crook?"

"We did, actually. That new face recognition software we use is awesome. Pegged the guy almost immediately."

"New technology." She shook her head. "Cameras everywhere, face recognition software, pat downs at the airport…" She turned and looked at him. "Isn't all that supposed to make us feel safer?"

"No, it's supposed to actually make you safer," he corrected. "It makes it harder for the bad guys to hide from the law."

"I guess so." She got out cups and saucers. "I made apple pie."

"You don't even need to ask. I had a hamburger earlier."

"You live on fast food."

"I work at a fast job," he replied. "No time for proper meals, now that I'm in a position of responsibility."

She turned and smiled at him. "I was so proud of you for that promotion. You studied hard."

"I might have studied less if I'd realized how much paperwork would be involved," he quipped. "I have eight detectives under me, and I'm responsible for all the major decisions that involve them. Plus I have to coordinate them with other services, work around court dates and emergency assignments... Life was a lot easier when I was just a plain detective."

"You love your job, though. That's a bonus."

"It is," he had to agree.

She cut the pie, topped it with a scoop of homemade ice cream and served it to him with his black coffee. She sat down across from him and watched him eat it with real enjoyment, her hands propping up her chin, elbows on the tablecloth.

"You love to cook," he responded.

She nodded. "It isn't an independent woman thing, I know," she said. "I should be designing buildings or running a corporation and yelling at subordinates."

"You should be doing what you want to do," he replied.

"In that case, I am."

"Good cooks are thin on the ground." He finished the pie and leaned back with his coffee cup in his hand, smiling. "Wonderful food!"

"Thanks."

He sipped coffee. "And the best coffee anywhere."

"Flattery will get you another slice of pie."

He chuckled. "No more tonight. I'm fine."

"Are you ever going to take a vacation?" she asked.

"Sure," he replied. "I've already arranged to have Christmas Eve off."

She glared at him. "A vacation is longer than one night long."

He frowned. "It is? Are you sure?"

"There's more to life than just work."

"I'll think about that, when I have time."

"Have you watched the news today?" she asked.

"No. Why?"

"They had a special report about violence on the border. It seems that the remaining Fuentes brother sent an armed party over the border to escort a drug shipment and there was a shootout with some border agents."

He grimaced. "An ongoing problem. Nobody knows how to solve it. Bottom line, if people want drugs, somebody's going to supply them. You stop the demand, you stop the supply."

"Good luck with that" She laughed hollowly. "Never going to happen."

"I totally agree."

"Anyway, they mentioned in passing that one of the captured drug runners said that General Emilio Machado was recruiting men for an armed invasion of his former country."

"The Mexican Government, we hear, is not pleased with that development and they're angry at our government because they think we aren't doing enough to stop it."

"Really?" she exclaimed. "What else do you know?"

"Not much, but you can't repeat anything I tell you," he added.

She grinned. "You know I'm as silent as a clam. Come on. Talk."

"Apparently, the State Department sent people into our office," he replied. "We know they talked to our lieutenant, but we don't know what about."

"State Department!"

"They do have their fingers on the pulse of foreign governments," Rick reminded her. "If anybody knows what's really going on, they do."

"I would have thought one of those other government agencies would have been more involved, especially if the general's trying to recruit Americans for a foreign military action," she pondered.

His eyebrows arched.

"Well, it seems logical, doesn't it?" she asked.

"Actually, it does," he agreed. "I know the FBI and the CIA have counterterrorism units that infiltrate groups like that."

"Yes, and some of them die doing it," Barbara recalled. She grimaced. "They say undercover officers in any organization face the highest risks."

"The military also has counterterrorism units," he replied. He sipped his cooling coffee. "That must be an interesting sort of job."

"Dangerous."

He smiled. "Of course. But patriotic in the extreme, especially when it comes to foreign operatives trying to undermine democratic interests."

"Doesn't the general's former country have great deposits of oil and natural gas?" she wondered aloud.

"So we hear. It's also in a very strategic location, and the general leans toward capitalism rather than socialism or communism. He's friendly toward the United States."

"A point in his favor. Gracie Pendleton says he sings like an angel," she added with a smile.

"I heard."

"Yes, we had that discussion earlier." She was also remembering another discussion over the phone and her face saddened.

He reached across the table and caught her hand in his. "I really am sorry, Mom," he said gently. "I don't know what came over me. I'm not usually like that."

"No, you're not." She hesitated. She wanted to remark that it wasn't until she asked about the lieutenant giving Gwen a rose that he'd gone ballistic. But in the interests of diplomacy, it was probably wiser to say nothing. She smiled. "How about I warm up that coffee?" she asked instead.

Gwen answered the phone absently, her mind still on the previews of next week's episode of her favorite science fiction show.

"Yes?" she murmured, the hated glasses perched on her nose so that she could actually see the screen of her television.

"Cassaway, anything to report?"

She sat up straighter. "Sir!"

"No need to get uptight. I'm just checking in. The wife and I are on our way to a party, but I wanted to make sure things are progressing well."

"They're going very slowly, sir," she said, curling up in her bare feet and jeans and long-sleeved T-shirt on her sofa. "I'm sorry, I haven't found a diplomatic way to get him talking about the subject and find out what he knows. He doesn't like me…."

"I find that hard to believe, Cassaway. You're a good kid."

She winced at the description.

He cleared his throat. "Sorry. Good woman. I try to be PC, you know, but I come from a different generation. Hard for us old-timers to work well in the new world."

She laughed. "You do fine, sir."

"I know this is a tough assignment," he replied. "But I still think you're the best person for the job. You have a way with people."

"Maybe another type of woman would have been a better choice," she began delicately, "maybe someone more open to flirting, and other things…"

"With Marquez? Are you kidding? The guy wrote the book on staunch outlooks! He'd be turned off immediately."

She relaxed a little. "He does seem to be like that."

"Tough, patriotic, a stickler for doing the right thing even when the brass disapproves, and he's got more guts than most men in his position ever develop. Even went right up in the face of a visiting politician to tell him he was putting his foot in his mouth by interfering with a homicide investigation and would regret it when the news media got hold of the story."

She laughed. "I read about that."

"Takes a moral man to be that fearless," her boss continued. "So yes, you're the right choice. You just have to win his confidence. But you're going to have to move a little faster. Things are heating up down in Mexico. We can't be caught lagging when the general makes his move, you know? We have to have intel, we have to be in position to take advantage of any opportunities that present themselves. The general likes us. We want him to continue liking us."

"But we can't help."

He sighed. "No. We can't help. Not obviously. We're in a precarious position these days, and we can't be seen to interfere. But behind the scenes, we can hope to influence people who are in a position to interfere. Marquez is the obvious person to liaison with Machado."

"It's going to be traumatic for him," Gwen said worriedly. "From the little intel I've been able to acquire, he has no idea about his connection to Machado. None at all."

"Pity," he replied. "That's going to make it harder." He put his hand over the receiver and spoke to someone. "Sorry, my wife's ready to leave. I have to go. Keep me in the loop, and watch your back," he added firmly. "We're trying to get the inside track. There are other people, other operatives, around who would love nothing better than to see us fall on our faces. Other countries would do anything to get a foothold in Barrera. I don't need to tell you who they are, or from what motives they work."

"No, sir, you don't," she agreed. "I'll do the best I can."

"You always do," he said, and there was faint affection in his tone. "Have a good evening. I'll be in touch."

"Yes, sir."

She hung up the cell phone and sat staring at it in her hand. She felt a chill. So much was riding on her ability to be diplomatic and quick and discreet. It wasn't her first difficult assignment; she was not a novice. But until now, she'd had no personal involvement. Her growing feelings for Rick Marquez were complicating things. She shouldn't care so much about how it would hurt him, but she did. If only there was a way, any way, that she could give him a heads-up before the fire hit the fan. Perhaps, she thought, she might be able to work something out if she spoke to Cash Grier. They shared a similar background in covert ops and he knew Marquez. It was worth a try.

So Friday morning, her day off, Gwen got in her small, used foreign car and drove down to Jacobsville, Texas.

Cash Grier met her at the door of his office, smiling, and led her inside, motioning to a chair as he closed the door behind him, locked it and pulled down the shade.

She pursed her lips with a grin. "Unusual precautions," she mused.

He smiled. "I'd put a pillow over the telephone if I thought there might be a wire near it. An ambassador's family habitually did that in Nazi Germany in the 1930s. Even did it in front of the head of the Gestapo once."

Her eyebrows arched as she sat down. "I missed that one."

"New book, about the rise of Hitler, and firsthand American views on the radical changes in society there in the 1930s," he said as he sat down and propped his big booted feet on his desk. "I love World War II history. I could paper my walls with books on the European Theatre and biographies of Patton and Rommel and Montgomery," he added, alluding to three famous World War II generals. "I like to read battle strategies."

"Isn't that a rather strange interest for a guy who worked alone for years, except with an occasional spotter?" she asked, tongue-in-cheek. It was pretty much an open secret that Grier had been a sniper in his younger days.

He chuckled. "Probably."

"I like history, too," she replied. "But I lean more toward political history."

"Which brings us to the question of why you're here," he replied and smiled.

She drew in a long breath and leaned forward. "I have a very unpleasant assignment. It involves Rick Marquez."

He nodded and his face sobered. "I know. I still have high-level contacts in your agency."

"He has no idea what's about to go down," she said. "I've argued with my boss until I'm blue in the face, but they won't let me give Marquez even a hint."

"I think his mother knows," he said. "She asked me about it. She overheard some visitors from D.C. talking about connections."

"Do you think she's told him anything?"

"She might know that his mother was romantically involved with Machado at some point. But she wouldn't know the rest. His mother was very close about her private life. Only one or two people even knew what happened." He grimaced. "The problem is that one of the people involved had a cousin who married a high-level agent in D.C., and he spilled his guts. That started this whole chain of events."

"Hard to keep a secret like that, especially one that would have been so obvious." She frowned. "Rick's stepfather must have known. From what little information I've been able to gather about his past, he and his stepfather didn't get along at all."

"The man beat him," Grier said harshly. "A real jewel of a human being. It's one reason Rick had so many problems as a kid. He was in trouble constantly right up until the wreck that killed his mother and stepfather. It was a tragedy that produced golden results. Barbara took him in, straightened him out and put him on a path that turned him into an exemplary citizen. Without her influence..." He spread his hands expressively.

Gwen stared at her scuffed black loafers. Idly, she noticed that they needed some polish. She dressed casually, but she liked to be as neat as possible. One day her real identity would come out, and she didn't want to give the agency a black eye by being slack in her grooming habits.

"You want me to tell him, don't you?" Grier asked.

She looked up. "You know him a lot better than I do. He's my boss, figuratively speaking. He doesn't like me very much, either."

"He might like you more if you'd wear your damned glasses and stop tripping over evidence in crime scenes," he said, pursing his lips. "Alice Mayfield Jones Fowler, who works in the Crime Scene Unit in San Antonio, was eloquent about the close call."

Gwen flushed. "Yes, I know." She pushed the hated glasses up on her nose, where they'd slipped. "I'm wearing my glasses now."

"I didn't mean to be critical," he said, noting her discomfort. "You're a long way from the homicide detective you started out to be," he added. "I know it's a pain, trying to relearn procedure on the fly."

"It really is," she said. "My credentials did stand up to a background check, thank goodness, but I feel like I'm walking on eggshells. I let slip that my job involved a lot of traveling and Marquez wondered why, since I was apparently working for Atlanta Homicide."

"Ouch," he said.

"I have to remember that I've never been out of the country. It's pretty hard, living two lives."

"I haven't forgotten that aspect of government work," he agreed. "It's why I never had much of a personal life, until Tippy came along."

Everybody local knew that Tippy had been a famous model, and then actress. She and Cash had a rocky trip to the altar, but they had a little girl almost two years old and it was rumored that they wanted another child.

"You got lucky," she said.

He shrugged. "I guess I did. I never could see myself settling down in a small town and becoming a family man. But now, it's second nature. Tris is growing by leaps and bounds. She has red hair, and green eyes, like her mama's."

Gwen noted the color photo on his desk, with himself and Tippy, with Tris and a boy who looked to be in his early teens. "Is that Tippy's brother?" she asked, indicating the photo.

"Rory," he agreed. "He's fourteen." He shook his head. "Time flies."

"It seems to." She leaned back again. "I miss my dad. He's been overseas for a long time, although he's coming back soon for a talk with some very high-level people in D.C. and rumors are flying. Rick Marquez has no idea what sort of background I come from."

"Another shock in store for him," he added. "You should tell him."

"I can't. That would lead to other questions." She sighed. "I'd love to meet my dad at the airport when he flies in. We've had a rough six months since my brother, Larry, died overseas. Dad still mourns my mother, and she's been gone for years. I miss her, too."

"I heard about your brother from a friend in the agency. I'm truly sorry." His dark eyes narrowed. "No other siblings?"

She shook her head.

"My mother's gone, too. But my dad's still alive, and I have three brothers," he replied with a smile. "My older brother, Garon, is SAC at the San Antonio FBI office."

"I've met him. He's very nice." She studied his face. He was a striking man, even with hair that was going silver at the temples. His dark eyes were piercing and steady. He looked intimidating sitting behind a desk. She could only imagine how intimidating he'd look on the job.

"What are you thinking so hard about?" he queried.

"That I never want to break the law in your town." She chuckled.

He grinned. "Thanks. I try to perfect a suitably intimidating demeanor on the job."

"It's quite good."

He sighed. "I'll talk to Marquez's mother and plant clues. I'll do it discreetly. Nobody will ever know that you mentioned it to me, I promise."

"Least of all my boss, who'd have me on security details for the rest of my professional life," she said with a laugh. "I don't doubt he'd have me transferred as liaison to a police department for real, where he'd make sure I was assigned to duty at school crossings."

"Hey, now, that's a nice job," he protested. "My patrolmen fight over that one." He said it tongue-in-cheek. "In fact, the last one enjoyed it so much that he transferred to the fire department. It seems that a first-grader kicked him in the leg, repeatedly."

Her fine eyebrows arched. "Why?"

"He told the kid to stay in the crosswalk. Seems the kid had a real attitude problem. The teachers couldn't deal with him, so they finally called us, after the kicking incident. I took the kid home, in the patrol car, and had a long talk with his mother."

"Oh, dear."

His face was grim. "She's a single parent, living alone, no family anywhere, and this kid is one step away from juvy," he added, referencing the juvenile justice system. "He's six years old," he said heavily, "and he already has a record for disobedience and detention at his school."

"They put little kids in detention in grammar school?" she exclaimed.

"Figure of speech. They call it time-out and he sits in the library. Last time he had to go there, he stood on one of the library tables and recited the Bill of Rights to the head librarian."

Her eyes widened in amusement. "Not only a troublemaker, but brilliant to boot."

He nodded. "Everybody's hoping his poor mother will marry a really tough hombre who can control him before he does something unforgivable and gets an arrest record."

She laughed. "The things I miss because I never married," she mused, shaking her head. "It's not an incentive to become a parent."

"On the other end of the spectrum, there's Tippy and me," he replied with a smile. "I love being a dad."

"It suits you," she said.

She got to her feet. "Well, I have to get back to San Antonio. If Sergeant Marquez asks, I had to talk to you about a case, okay?"

"In fact, we really do have a case that might connect," he said surprisingly. "Sit back down and I'll tell you about it."

Chapter 4

Sergeant Marquez came into the office two days later, looking grim. He motioned to Gwen, indicated a chair and closed the door.

She remembered her trip to Cash Grier's office, and wondered if Grier had had time to talk to her superior officer's mother and the information had trickled down.

"The cold case squad has a job for us," he said as he sat down, too.

"What sort of job?"

"They dug up an old murder. It was committed back in 2002 and a man went to prison on evidence largely given by one person. Now it seems the person who gave evidence has been arrested and convicted for a similar crime. They want to know if we can find a connection."

"Well, by chance, that was the case I just spoke to Chief Grier about down in Jacobsville," she told him, happy that she could make a legitimate connection to her impromptu trip out of town. "He has an officer who knew the prisoner's family and could place the man at a party during the murder."

"Did he give evidence?" he asked.

She shook her head. "He was never called to testify," she said. "Nobody knows why."

"Isn't that interesting."

"Very. So the cold case squad wants us to wear out some shoe leather on their behalf?"

He grimaced. "They have plenty of manpower, but they've got two people out sick, one just transferred to the white collar crime unit and their sergeant said they don't want to let this case get buried. Especially not when a similar crime was just committed here. Your case. The college woman who was murdered. It needs investigation, and they don't have enough people." He smiled. "Besides, there's the issue of not stepping on the toes of another unit's investigation."

"I can understand that."

"So, we'll see if we can make a connection, based on available evidence. I'm assigning you as lead detective on this case, as well as on the college freshman murder. Find a connection. Catch the perp. Make me proud."

She grinned at him. "Actually, that might be possible. I just got some new information from running a check on the photo of that odd man in the murder victim's camera. The one I mentioned to you?"

"Yes, I recall that."

She pulled up a file on her phone. "This is him. I used face recognition software to pick him out." She showed him the mug shot on her phone. "The perp. His name is Mickey Dunagan. He has a rap sheet. It's a long one.

He's been prosecuted in two aggravated assault cases, never convicted. Here's the clincher. He has a thing for young college girls. He was arrested for attempted assault a few months ago, on a girl who went to the same college as our victim. I have a detective from our unit en route to question her today, and we're interviewing people at the apartment complex about the man in the photograph. If his DNA is on file, and I'm betting it is since he's served time during his trials, and there's enough DNA from the crime scene to type and match..."

"Good work!" he said fervently.

She grinned. "Thanks, sir."

"I wish we could get ironclad evidence that he killed the victim." He grimaced. "Not that ironclad evidence ever got a conviction when some silver-tongued gung-ho public defender got the bit between his teeth."

"Impressive mixing of metaphors, sir," she murmured dryly.

He actually made a face at her. "Correct my grammar, get stakeout duty for the next two months."

"I would never do that!" she protested with wicked, twinkling eyes.

He smiled back. She was very pretty when she smiled. Her mouth was full and lush and sensuous...

He sat back in his chair and forced himself not to notice that. "Get busy."

"I'll get on it right now."

"Just out of curiosity, who was the officer who could place the convicted murderer at a party when the other murder was committed?"

"Officer Dan Travis," she said. "He's at the Jacobsville Police Department. I'm going to drive down and talk to him tomorrow." She checked the notes on her phone. "Dunagan was arrested for assault by a patrolman in South Division named Dave Harris. I'm going to talk to him afterward. He might remember something that would be helpful."

"Good. Keep me in the loop."

"I will." She got up and started for the door.

"Cassaway."

She turned at the door. "Sir?"

His dark eyes narrowed. He seemed deep in thought. He was. He had a strange sense that she knew something important that she was hiding from him. He read body language very well after his long years in law enforcement. He'd once tripped a bank robber up when he noticed the man's behavior and deliberately engaged him in conversation. During the conversation, he'd gotten close enough to see the gun the man was holding under his long coat. Rick had quickly subdued him, cuffed him, and taken him in for questioning. The impromptu encounter had solved a whole string of unsolved bank robberies for the cold case unit, and their sergeant, Dave Murphy, had taken Rick out to lunch in appreciation for the help.

"Sir?" Gwen prompted when he didn't reply.

He sat up straight. His eyes narrowed further as he stared at her. She was almost twitching. "What do you know," he said softly, "that you aren't telling me?"

Her face flushed. "No…nothing. I mean, there's… nothing," she faltered, and could have bitten her tongue for making things worse.

"You need to think about your priorities," he said curtly.

She drew in a long breath. "Believe me, I am."

He grimaced and waved his hand in her direction. "Get to work."

"Yes, sir."

She almost ran out of the office. She was flushed and unsettled. Lieutenant Hollister met her in the hall, and frowned.

"What's up?" he asked gently.

She bit her lip. "Nothing, sir," she said. She drew in a long breath. She wanted, so badly, to tell somebody what was going on.

Hollister's black eyes narrowed. "Come into my office for a minute."

He led her back the way she'd come, past a startled Marquez, who watched the couple go into the lieutenant's office with an expression that was hard to classify.

"Sit down," Hollister said. He went behind his desk and swung up his long, powerful legs, propping immaculate black boots on the desk. He crossed his arms and leaned back precariously in his chair. "Talk."

She shifted restlessly. "I know something about Sergeant Marquez that I'm not supposed to discuss with anybody."

He lifted a thick blond eyebrow. He even smiled. "I know what it is."

Her green eyes widened.

"The suits who came to see me earlier in the week were feds," he said. "I know who you really are, and what's going on." He sighed. "I want to tell Marquez, too, but my hands are tied."

"I went to see Cash Grier," she said. "He's out of the loop. He can't do anything directly, but he might be able to let something slip at Barbara's Café in Jacobsville.

That would at least prepare Sergeant Marquez for what's about to go down."

"Nothing can prepare a man for that sort of revelation, believe me." His eyes narrowed even more. "They want Marquez as a liaison, don't they?"

She nodded. "He'd be the best man for the job. But he's going to be very upset at first and he may refuse to do anything."

"That's a risk they're willing to take. They don't dare interfere directly, not in the current political climate," he added. "Frankly, I'd just go tell him."

"Would you?" she asked, and smiled.

He laughed deeply and then he shook his head. "Actually, no, I wouldn't. I'm too handsome to spend time in prison. There would be riots. I'd be so much in demand as somebody's significant other."

She laughed, too. She hadn't realized he had a sense of humor. Her face flushed. She looked very pretty.

He cocked his head. "You could just ask Marquez to the ballet and tell him yourself."

"My boss would have me hung in Hogan's Alley up at the FBI Academy with a placard around my neck as a warning to other loose-lipped agents," she told him.

He grinned. "I'd come cut you down, Cassaway. I get along well with the feds. But I'm not prejudiced. I also get along with mercenaries."

"There's a rumor that you used to be one," she fished.

His face closed up, although he was still smiling. "How about that?"

She didn't comment.

He swung his long legs off the desk and stood up. "Let me know how it goes," he said. He walked her to the door. "It's not a bad idea, about asking him to the ballet. He loves ballet. He usually goes alone. He can't get girlfriends."

"Why not?" she asked. She cleared her throat. "I mean, he's rather attractive."

"He wears a gun."

"So do you," she pointed out, indicating the holster. "In fact, we all wear them."

"True, but he likes women who don't," he replied. "And they don't like men who wear guns. He doesn't date colleagues, he says. But you might be able to change his mind."

"Fat chance." She sighed. "He doesn't like me."

"Go solve that murder for the cold case unit, and they'll lobby him for you," he teased.

"How do you know about that?" she asked, surprised.

"I'm the lieutenant," he pointed out. "I know everything," he added smugly.

She laughed. She was still laughing when she walked down the corridor.

Rick heard her from inside his office. He threw a scratch pad across the room and knocked the trash can across the floor with it. Then he grimaced, in case anybody heard and asked what was going on. He couldn't have told them. He didn't know himself why he was behaving so out of character.

The man Gwen was tracking in her semiofficial disguise was an unpleasant, slinky individual who had a rap sheet that read like a short story. She'd gone down to Jacobsville and interviewed Officer Dan Travis. He seemed a decent sort of person, and he could swear that the man who was arrested for the murder was at a holiday party with him, and had never even stepped outside.

He had told the assistant DA, but the attorney refused to entertain evidence he considered hearsay. Travis gave her the names of two other people she could contact, who would verify the information. She took notes and arranged for a deposition to be taken from him.

Her next stop was Patrol South Division, in San Antonio, to talk to the arresting officer who'd taken Dunagan in for the attempted assault on a college woman a few months ago, Dave Harris. He was working that day, but was working a wreck when she phoned him. So she arranged to meet him for lunch at a nearby fast food joint.

They sat together over hamburgers and fries and soft drinks, attracting attention with his uniform and her pistol and badge, conspicuously displayed.

"We're being watched," she said in a dramatic tone, indicating two young women at a nearby booth.

"Oh, that's just Joan and Shirley," he said. He looked toward the women, waved and grinned. One of them flushed and almost knocked over her drink. He was blond and blue-eyed, nicely built, and quite handsome. He was also single. "Joan's sweet on me," he added in a whisper. "They know I always eat here, so they come by for lunch. They work at the print shop downtown. Joan's a graphic artist. Very talented."

"Nice," she murmured, biting into the burger.

"Why are you doing a cold case?" he asked as he finished his salad and sipped black coffee.

"It ties in with a current one we're working on," she said, and related what Cash Grier had told her.

His dark eyebrows arched. "They never called a prime witness in the case?"

"Strange, isn't it?" she agreed. "That would be grounds for a mistrial, I'd think, but I'll need to talk to the city attorney's office first. The man who was convicted has been in prison for almost a year."

"Shame, if he's innocent," the patrolman replied.

"I know. Fortunately, such things don't happen often."

"What about the suspect in your current case?"

"A nasty bit of work," she replied. "I can place him at the scene of the crime, and if there's enough trace evidence to do a DNA profile, I think I can connect him with it. Her neighbors reported seeing him around her apartment the morning before the murder. If he's guilty, I don't want him to slip through the cracks on my watch, especially since Sergeant Marquez assigned me to the case as chief investigator."

"Really? How many other people are helping you with the case?"

"Let's see, right now, there's me and one other detective that I borrowed to help question witnesses."

He sighed. "Budget issues again?"

"Afraid so. I can manage. If I need help, the cold case unit will lend me somebody."

"Nice group, that cold case unit."

She smiled. "I think so, too."

"Now about the perp," he added, leaning forward. "This is how it went down."

He described the scene of the assault where he'd arrested Dunagan, the persons involved, the witnesses and his own part in the arrest. Gwen made notes on her phone and saved the file.

"That's a big help," she told him. "Thanks."

He smiled. "You're very welcome." He checked his watch. "I have to get back on patrol. Was there any other information you needed?"

"Nothing I can't find in the file. I appreciate the summary of the case, and your thoughts on it. That really helps."

"You're welcome. Any time."

"Shame about the latest victim," she added as they got up and headed to the trash bin with their trays. "She was very pretty. Her neighbors said she went out of her way to help people in need." She glanced at him. "We had one of your fellow officers on stakeout with us the other night. Sims."

He paused as he dumped the paper waste and placed the tray in its stack on the refuse container top. "He's not our usual sort of patrol officer."

"What do you mean?" she asked, frowning.

"I really can't say anything. It's just that he has an interesting background. There are people in high positions with influence," he added. He smiled. "But he's not my problem. I think you'll do well in the homicide unit. You've got a knack for sorting things out, and you're thorough. Good luck on the case."

"Thanks. Thanks a lot."

He smiled. "You're welcome."

She drove back to the office with her brain spinning. What she'd learned was very helpful. She might crack the case, which would certainly give her points with Rick Marquez. But there was still the problem of what she knew and couldn't tell him. She only hoped that Cash Grier would be able to break some ground with her sergeant.

Cash Grier had a thick ham sandwich with homemade fries and black coffee and then asked for a slice of Barbara's famous apple pie and homemade ice cream.

She served it with a grin. "Don't eat too much of this,"

she cautioned. "It's very fattening." She was teasing, because he was still as trim as men ten years his junior, and nicely muscled.

He pursed his lips and his black eyes twinkled. "As you can see, I'm running to fat."

She laughed. "That'll be the day."

He studied her quietly. "Can you sit down for a minute?"

She looked around. The lunchtime rush was over and there were only a couple of cowboys and an elderly couple in the café. "Sure." She sat down across from him. "What can I do for you?"

He sipped coffee. "I've been enlisted to get some information to your son without telling him anything."

She blinked. "That's a conundrum."

"Isn't it?" He put down the coffee cup and smiled. "You're a very intelligent woman. You must have some suspicions about his family history."

"Thanks for the compliment. And yes, I have a lot." She studied his hard face. "I overheard some feds who ate here talking about Dolores Ortíz and her connection to General Machado. Dolores worked for me just briefly. She was Rick's birth mother."

"Rick's stepfather was a piece of work," he said coldly. "I've heard plenty about him. He mistreated livestock and was fired for it on the Ballenger feedlot. Gossip is that he did the same to his stepson."

Her face tautened. "When I first adopted him, I lifted my hand to smooth back his hair—you know, that thing mothers do when they feel affectionate. He stiffened and cringed." Her eyes were sad. "That's when I first knew that there was a reason for his bad behavior. I've never hit him. But someone did."

"His stepfather," Grier asserted. "With assorted objects, including, once, a leather whip."

"So that's where he got those scars on his back," she faltered. "I asked, but he would never talk about it."

"It's a blow to a man's pride to have something like that done to him," he said coldly. "Jackson should have been sent to prison on a charge of child abuse."

"I do agree." She hesitated. "Rick's last name is Marquez. But Dolores said that was a name she had legally drawn up when Rick was seven. I never understood."

"She didn't dare put his real father's name on a birth certificate," he replied. "Even at the time, his dad was in trouble with the law in Mexico. She didn't want him to know about Rick. And, later, she had good reason to keep the secret. She married Craig Jackson to give Rick a settled home. She didn't know what sort of man he was until it was too late," he added coldly. "He knew who Rick's real father was and threatened to make it public if Dolores left him. So she stayed and Rick paid for her silence."

Barbara was feeling uncomfortable. "Would his real father happen to be an exiled South American dictator, by any chance?"

Grier nodded.

"Oh, boy."

"And nobody can tell him, because a certain federal agency is hoping to talk him into being a go-between for them, to help coax Machado into a comfortable trade agreement with our country when he gets back into power. Which he certainly will," he added quietly. "The thug who took over his government has human rights advocates bristling all over the world. He's tortured people, murdered dissenters, closed down public media outlets… In general, he's done everything possible to outrage anyone who believes in democracy. At the same time, he's pocketing money from sources of revenue and buying himself every rich man's perk that he can dream up. He's got several Rolls-Royce cars, assorted beautiful women, houses in most affluent European cities and his own private jet to take him to them. He doesn't govern so much as he flaunts his position. Workers are starving and farmers are being forced to grow drug crops to support his extravagant lifestyle." He shook his head. "I've seen dictators come and go, but that man needs a little lead in his diet."

She knew what he was alluding to. "Any plans going to take care of that?" she mused.

"Don't look at me," he warned. "I'm retired. I have a family to think about."

"Eb Scott might have a few people who would be interested in the work."

"Yes, he might, but the general isn't lacking for good help." He glanced up as one of Barbara's workers came, smiling, to refill his coffee cup. "Thanks."

She grinned. "You're welcome. Boss lady, you want some?"

Barbara shook her head. "Thanks, Bess, I'm already flying on a caffeine high."

"Okay."

"So who has to do the dirty work and tell Rick the truth?" Barbara asked.

Grier didn't speak. He just smiled at her.

"Oh, darn it, I won't do it!"

"There's nobody else. The feds have forbidden their agents to tip him off. His lieutenant knows, but he's been gagged, too."

"Then how in the world do they expect him to find out? Why won't they just tell him?"

"Because he might get mad at them for being the source of the revelation and refuse to cooperate. And there isn't anybody else they can find to do the job of contacting Machado."

"They could ask Grange," Barbara said stubbornly. "He's already working for the general, isn't he?"

"Grange doesn't know."

"Why me?" she groaned. "He'll be furious!"

"Yes, but you're his mother and he loves you," he replied. "If you tell him, he'll get over it. He might even be receptive to helping the feds. If they tell him, he'll hold a grudge and they'll never find anyone halfway suitable to do the job."

She was silent. She stared at the festive tablecloth worriedly.

"It will be all right," he assured her gently.

She looked up. "We've already had a disagreement recently."

"You have? Why?" he asked, surprised, because Rick's devotion to his adopted mother was quite well-known locally.

She grimaced. "His lieutenant gave the new detective, Gwen Cassaway, a rose, and I mentioned it in a teasing way. He went ballistic and I hung up on him. He won't admit it, but I think he's got a case on Gwen."

"Well!" he mused.

That was a new and interesting proposition. "Couldn't she tell him?" she asked hopefully.

"She's been cautioned not to."

She sighed. "Darn. Does everybody know?"

"Rick doesn't."

"I noticed."

"So you have to tell him. And soon."

"Or what?"

He leaned forward. "Or six government agencies will send operatives down here to disparage your apple pie and accuse you of subverting government policy by using organic products in your kitchen."

She burst out laughing. "Yes, I did hear that a SWAT team of federal agents raided a farm that was selling unpasteurized milk. Can you believe that? In our country, in this day and time, with all the real problems going on, we have to send armed operatives against people living in a natural harmony with the earth?"

"You're kidding!" he exclaimed.

"I wish I was," she replied. "I guess we're all going to be force-fed Genetically Modified Organisms from now on."

He burst out laughing. "You need to stop hanging out on those covert websites."

"I can't. I'd never know what was really going on in the world, like us having bases on the moon."

He rolled his eyes. "I have to get back to work." He stood up. "You'll tell him, then."

She stood up, too. "Do I have a choice?"

"You could move to Greenland and change your name."

She made a face at him. "That's no choice. Although I would love to visit Greenland. They have snow."

"So do we, occasionally."

"They have lots of snow. Enough to make many snowmen. South Texas isn't famous for that."

"The pie was great, by the way."

She smiled. "Thanks. I do my best."

"I'd have to leave town if you ever closed up," he told her. "I can't live in a town that doesn't have the best food in Texas."

"That will get you extra ice cream on your next slice of apple pie!" she promised him with a grin.

But she wasn't grinning when she went home. It disturbed her that she was going to have to tell her son something that would devastate him. He wasn't going to be pleased. Other than that, she didn't know what the outcome would be. But Grier was right about one thing; it was better that the information came from his mother rather than from some bureaucrat or federal agent who had no personal involvement with Rick and didn't care how the news affected him. It did make her feel good that so far, they hadn't blurted it out. By hesitating, they did show some compassion.

Rick went to his mother's home tired. It had been a long day of meetings and more meetings, with a workshop on gun safety occasioned by the accidental discharge of a pistol by one of the patrol officers. The bullet went into the asphalt but fortunately didn't ricochet and hit anything, or anyone. The officer was disciplined but the chain of command saw an opportunity to emphasize gun safety and they took it. The moral of the story was that even experienced officers could mishandle a gun.

Privately, Marquez wondered how Officer Sims ever got through the police academy, because he was the officer involved. The same guy who'd gone on stakeout with him and Cassaway. He didn't think a lot of the young man's ethics and he'd heard that Sims had an uncle high up in the chain of command who made sure he kept his job. It was disturbing.

"You look worn-out," Barbara said gently. "Come sit down and I'll put supper on the table."

"It's late," he commented, noting his watch.

"We can have supper at midnight," she teased. "Nobody's watching. I'll even pull down the shades if it makes you happy."

He laughed and hugged her. "You're a treasure, Mom. I'll never marry unless I can find a girl like you."

"That's sweet. Thanks."

She started heating up roast beef and buttered rolls, topping off his plate with homemade potato salad. She put the plate in front of him. "Thank goodness for microwave ovens." She laughed. "The cook's best friend."

"This is delicious." He closed his eyes, savoring every bite. "I had a sandwich for lunch and I only had time to eat half of it between meetings."

"I didn't even eat lunch," she said, dipping into her own roast beef.

"Why not?"

"I had a talk with Cash Grier and afterward I lost my appetite."

He stopped eating and stared at her with narrowed eyes. "What did he tell you?"

"Something everybody knows and nobody has the guts to tell you, my darling," she said, stiffening herself mentally. "I have some very unpleasant news."

He put down his fork. "You've got cancer." His face paled. "That's it, isn't it? You should have told me…!"

He got up and hugged her. "We'll get through it together. I'll never leave your side…"

She pulled back, flattered. "I'm fine," she said. "I don't have anything fatal. That isn't what I meant. It's about you. And your real father."

He blinked. "My real father died not long after I was born..."

She took a deep breath. "Rick, your real father is across the border in Mexico amassing a private army in preparation for invading a South American country."

He sat down, hard. His light olive complexion was suddenly very pale. All the gossip and secrecy suddenly made sense. The feds were all over his office, not because they were working on shared cases, but because of Rick.

"My father is General Emilio Machado," he said with sudden realization.

Chapter 5

"My father is a South American dictator," Rick repeated, almost in shock.

"I'm afraid so." Barbara pulled up a chair facing him and held his hand that was resting on the table. "They made me tell you. Nobody else wanted to. I'm so sorry."

"But my mother said my father was dead," he repeated blankly.

"She only wanted to protect you. Machado was in trouble with the Mexican authorities when he lived in the country because he was opposed to foreign interests trying to take over key industries where he lived. He organized protests even when he was in his teens. He was a natural leader. Later, Dolores didn't dare tell you because Machado was the head of a fairly well-known international paramilitary group and that would have made you a target for any extremist with a grudge. He was in the news a lot when you were a child."

"Does he know?" Rick persisted. "Does he know about me?"

Barbara bit her lower lip. "No. She never told him." She sighed. "After Cash told me who your father was, I remembered something that Dolores told me. She said your father was only fourteen when he fathered you. She was older, seventeen, and there was no chance that her family would have let her marry him. She wanted you very much. So she had you, and never even told her parents who the father was. She kept her secret. At least, until she married your stepfather. Cash said that your stepfather got the truth out of her and used it to keep her with him. She didn't dare protest or he'd have made your real identity known. A true charmer," she added sarcastically.

"My stepfather was a sadist," he said quietly. "I've never spoken of him to you. But he made my life hell, and my mother's as well. I got in trouble with the law on purpose. I thought maybe somebody would check out my home life and see the truth and help us. But nobody ever did. Not until you came along and offered my mother work."

"I tried to help," she agreed. "Dolores liked cooking for me, but your stepfather didn't like her having friends or any interest outside of him. He was insanely jealous."

"He also couldn't keep a job. Money was tight. You used to sneak me food," he recalled with a warm smile. "You even came to visit me in the detention center. My mother appreciated that. My stepfather wouldn't let her come."

"I knew that. I did what I could. I tried to get our police chief at the time to investigate, but he was the sort of man who didn't want to rock the boat." She laughed. "Can you imagine Cash Grier turning a blind eye to something like that?"

"He'd have had my stepfather pilloried in the square." Rick smiled, then sobered. "My father is a dictator," he repeated again. It was hard to believe. He'd spent his whole life certain that his biological father was long dead.

"A deposed dictator," Barbara corrected. "His country is going to the dogs under its new administration. People are dying. He wants to accomplish a military coup, but he needs all the help he can get. Which brings us to our present situation," she added. "A paramilitary group is going down to Barrera with him, including some of Eb Scott's guys, some Europeans, one African merc and with ex-army Major Winslow Grange, Jason Pendleton's foreman on his Comanche Wells ranch, to lead them."

"All that firepower and the government hasn't noticed?"

"It wouldn't do them a lot of good. Machado's in Mexico, just over the border," Barbara said. "They can't mount an invasion to stop him. But they can try to find a way to be friendly without overt aid."

"Ah. I see. I'm the goat."

She blinked. "Excuse me?"

"They're going to tether me out to attract the puma."

"Puma." She laughed. "Funny, but one of my customers said that's what the local population calls 'El General.' They say he's cunning and dangerous like a cat, but that he can purr when he wants to." Her face softened. "For a dictator, he's held in high esteem by most democracies. He's intelligent, kind, he reveres women and he isn't afraid to fight for justice."

"Does he wear a red cape?" Rick murmured.

She shook her head. "Sorry."

"Who's in on this?" he asked narrowly. "Does my lieutenant know?"

"Yes," she said. "And there's a covert operative somewhere in your organization," she added. "I got that tidbit from a patrol officer who has a friend on the force in San Antonio. A guy named Sims."

"Sims." His face closed up. "He's got connections. And he's a total ethical wipeout. I hate having a guy like that on the force. He got careless with a pistol and almost shot himself in the foot. He's the reason we just had a gun safety workshop."

"Learning gun safety is not a bad thing."

He sighed. "I know." He was trying to adjust to the shock of his parentage. "Why didn't my mother tell me?" he burst out.

"She was trying to protect you. I'm certain that she would have told you eventually," she added. "She just didn't have time before she died."

He grimaced. "What am I supposed to do now, walk over the border, find the general and say, hey, guess what, I'm your kid?"

"I don't really think that would be wise," she replied. "I'm not sure he'd believe it in the first place. Would you?"

"Now there's a question." He leaned back in the chair, his dark eyes focused on the tablecloth. "I suppose I could have a DNA profile done. There's a private company that can at least rule out paternity by blood type. If mine is compatible with the general's, it might help convince him... Wait a minute," he added coldly. "Why the hell should I care?"

"Because he's your father, Rick," she said gently. "Even though he doesn't know."

"And the government's only purpose in telling me is to help reunite us," he returned angrily.

"Well, no, they want someone to convince the general to make a trade agreement with us once he's back in power. They're certain that he will be, which is why they want you to make friends with him."

"I'm sure he'll be overjoyed to know he has a grown son who's a cop," he said coldly. "Especially since he's wanted by our government for kidnapping."

She leaned forward with her chin resting in her hands, propped by her elbows. "You could arrest him," she pointed out. "And then befriend him in jail. Like the mouse that took the thorn out of the lion's paw and became its friend."

He made a face at her. "I can't walk across the border and arrest anyone. I might have been born in Mexico, but I'm an American citizen. And I did it the hard way," he added firmly. "Legally."

She grimaced.

"Sorry," he said after a minute. "I know you sympathize with all the people hiding out here who couldn't afford to wait for permission. In some of their countries, they could be killed just for paying too much attention to the wrong people."

"It's very bad in some Central American states," she pointed out.

"It's very bad anywhere on our border."

"And getting worse."

He got up and poured himself another cup of coffee.

His big hand rested on the coffeemaker as he switched it off. "Who's the mole in my office?"

"I honestly don't know," she replied. "I only know that Sims told his friend, Cash Grier's patrolman, about it. He said it was someone from a federal agency, working undercover."

"I wonder how Sims knew."

"Maybe he's the mole," she teased.

"Unlikely. Most feds have too much respect for the law to abuse it. Sims actually suggested that we confiscate a six-pack of beer from a convenience store as evidence in some pretended case and threaten the clerk with jail if he told on us."

"Good grief! And he works for the police?" she exclaimed, horrified.

"Apparently," he replied. "I didn't like what he said, and I told him so. He seemed repentant, but I'm not sure he really was. Cocky kid. Real attitude problem."

"Doesn't that sound familiar?" she asked the room at large.

"I never suggested breaking the law after I went through the academy and swore under oath to uphold it," he replied.

"Are you sure you didn't overreact, my darling?" she asked gently.

"If I did, so did Cassaway. She was hotter under the collar than I was." He laughed shortly. "And then she beat the lieutenant on the firing range and he let out a bad word. She marched right up to him and said she was offended and he shouldn't talk that way around her." He glanced at her ruefully. "Hence, the rose."

"Oh. An apology." She looked disappointed. "Your lieutenant is very attractive," she mused. "And eligible.

I thought he might find Miss Cassaway interesting. Or something."

"Maybe he does," he said vaguely. "God knows why. She's good with a gun, I'll give her that, but she's a walking disaster in other ways. How she ever got a job with the police, I'll never know." He didn't like talking about Cassaway and the lieutenant. It got under his skin, for reasons he couldn't understand.

"She sounds very nice to me."

"Everybody sounds nice to you," he replied. He smiled at her. "You could find one good thing to say about the devil, Mom. You look for the best in people."

"You look for the worst," she pointed out.

He shrugged. "That's my job."

He was thoughtful, and morose. She felt even more guilty when she saw how disturbed he really was.

"I wish there had been some other way to handle this," she muttered angrily. "I hate being made the fall guy."

"Hey, I'm not mad at you," he said, and bent to kiss her hair. "I just…don't know what to do." He sighed.

"'When in doubt, don't,'" she quoted. She frowned. "Who said that?"

"Beats me, but it's probably good advice." He put down his cooling coffee and stretched, yawning. "I'm beat. Too many late nights finishing paperwork and going on stakeouts. I'm going to bed. I'll decide what to do in the morning. Maybe it will come to me in a dream or something," he added.

"Maybe it will. I'm just sorry I had to be the one to tell you."

"I'll get used to the idea," he assured her. "I just need a little time."

She nodded.

* * *

But time was in short supply. Two days later, a tall, elegant man with dark hair and eyes, wearing a visitor's tag but no indication of his identity, walked into Rick's office and closed the door.

"I need to talk to you," he said.

Rick stared at him. "Do I know you?" he asked after a minute, because the man seemed vaguely familiar.

"You should," he replied with a grin. "But it's been a while since we caught Fuentes and his boys in the drug sting in Jacobsville. I'm Rodrigo Ramirez. DEA."

"I knew you looked familiar!" Rick got up and shook the other man's hand. "Yes, it has been a while. You and your wife bought a house here last year."

He nodded. "I work out of San Antonio DEA now instead of Houston, and she works for the local prosecutor, Blake Kemp, in Jacobsville. With her high blood pressure, I'd rather she stayed at home, but she said she'd do it when I did it." He shrugged. "Neither of us was willing to try to change professions at this late date. So we deal with the occasional problem."

"Are you mixed up in the Barrera thing as well?" Rick asked curiously.

"In a way. I'm related, distantly, to a high official in Mexico," he said. "It gives me access to some privileged information." He hesitated. "I don't know how much they've told you."

Rick motioned Ramirez into a chair and sat down behind his desk. "I know that El General has a son who's a sergeant with San Antonio P.D.," he said sarcastically.

"So you know."

"My mother told me. They wanted me to know, but nobody had the guts to just say it," he bit off.

"Yes, well, that could have been a big problem. Depending on how you were told, and by whom. They were afraid of alienating you."

"I don't see what help I'm going to be," Rick said irritably. "I didn't know my biological father was still alive, much less who he was. The general, I'm told, has no clue that I even exist. I doubt he'd take my word for it."

"So do I. Sometimes government agencies are a little thin on common sense," he added. He crossed his elegant long legs. "I've been elected, you might say, to do the introductions, by my cousin."

"Your cousin...?"

"He's the president of Mexico."

"Well, damn!"

Ramirez smiled. "That's what I said when he told me to do it."

"Sorry."

"No problem. It seems we're both stuck with doing something that goes against the grain. I think the general is going to react very badly. I wish there was someone who could talk to him for us."

"Like my mother talked to me for the feds?" he mused.

"Exactly."

Rick frowned. "You know, Gracie Pendleton got along quite well with him. She refused to even think of pressing charges. She was asked, in case we could talk about extradition of Machado with the Mexican government. She said no."

"I heard. She's my sister-in-law, although she's not related to my wife. Don't even ask," he added, waving his hand. "It's far too complicated to explain."

"I won't. But I remember Glory very well," he reminded Ramirez. "Cash Grier and I taught her how to shoot a pistol without destroying cars in the parking lot," he added with a grin.

Ramirez laughed. "So you did." He sobered. "Gracie might be willing to speak to the general, if we could get word to him," Ramirez said.

"We had a guy in jail here who was one of the higher-ups in the Fuentes organization. He's going on probation tomorrow."

"An opportunity." Ramirez chuckled.

"Apparently, a timely one. I'll ask him if he'd have the general call Gracie. Now, how do you get Gracie to do that dirty work for you?"

"I'll have my wife bribe her with flowers and chocolate and Christmas decorations."

"Excuse me?" Rick asked.

"Gracie loves to decorate for Christmas. My wife has access to a catalog of rare antique decorations. Gracie can be bribed, if you know how," he added.

Rick smiled. "An assistant district attorney working a bribe. What if somebody tells her boss?"

"He'll laugh," Ramirez assured him. "It's for a just cause, after all."

Rick started down to the jail in time to waylay the departing felon. He spoke to the probation officer on the way and arranged the conversation.

The man was willing to take a message to the general, for a price. That put them on the hot seat, because neither man could be seen offering illegal payment to a felon.

Then Rick had a brainstorm. "Wait a second." He'd spotted the janitor emptying trash baskets nearby. He took the man to one side, handed him two fifties and told him what to do.

The janitor, confused but willing to help, walked over to the prisoner and handed him the money. It was from him, he added, since the prisoner had been pleasant to him during his occupation in the jail. He wanted to help him get started again on the outside.

The prisoner, smiling, understood immediately what was going on. He took the money graciously, with a bow, and proceeded to sing the janitor's praises for his act of generosity. So the message was sent.

Gwen Cassaway was sitting at Rick's desk when he went back to his office, in the chair reserved for visitors. He hated the way his heart jumped at the sight of her. He fought down that unwanted feeling.

"Do they have to issue us these chairs?" she complained when he came in, closing the door behind him. "Honestly, only hospital waiting rooms have chairs that are more uncomfortable."

"The idea is to make you want to leave," he assured her. "What's up?" he added absently as he removed his holstered pistol from his belt and slid it into a desk drawer, then locked the drawer before he sat down. "Something about the case I assigned you to?"

She hesitated. This was going to be difficult. "Something else. Something personal."

He stared at her coolly. "I don't discuss personal issues with colleagues. We have a staff psychologist if you need counseling."

She let out an exasperated sigh. "Honestly, do you have a steel rod glued to your spine?" she burst out. Then she realized what she'd said, clapped her hand over her mouth and looked horrified at the slip.

He didn't react. He just stared.

"I'm sorry!" she said, flustered. "I'm so sorry! I didn't mean to say that…!"

"Cassaway," he began.

"It's about the general," she blurted out.

His dark eyes narrowed. "Lately, everything is. Don't tell me. You're having an affair with him and you have to confess for the sake of your job."

She drew in a long breath. "Actually, the general *is* my job." She got up, opened her wallet and handed it to Rick.

He did an almost comical double take. He looked at her as if she'd grown leaves. "You're a fed?"

She nodded and grimaced. She took back the wallet after he'd looked at it again, just to make sure it didn't come from the toy department in some big store.

She put it back in her fanny pack. "Sorry I couldn't say something before, but they wouldn't let me," she said heavily as she sat down again, with her hands folded on her jeans.

"What the hell are you doing pretending to be a detective?" he asked with some exasperation.

"It was my boss's idea. I did start out with Atlanta P.D., but I've worked in counterterrorism for the agency for about four years now," she confessed. "I'm sorry," she repeated. "This wasn't my idea. They wanted me to find out how much you knew about your family history before they accidentally said or did something that would upset you."

He raised an eyebrow. "I've just been presented with a father who's an exiled South American dictator, whose existence I was unaware of. They didn't think that would upset me?"

"I asked Cash Grier to talk to your mother," she said. "You can't tell anybody. I was ordered not to talk to you about it. But they didn't say I couldn't ask somebody else to do it."

He was touched by her concern. Not that he liked her any better. "I wondered about your shooting skills," he said after a minute. "Not exactly something I expect in a run-of-the-mill detective."

She smiled. "I spend a lot of time on the gun range," she replied. "I've been champion of my unit for two years running."

"Our lieutenant was certainly surprised when he found himself outdone," he remarked.

"He's very nice."

He glared at her.

She wondered what he had against his superior officer, but she didn't comment. "I was told that a DEA officer is going to try to get someone to speak to General Machado about you."

"Yes. Gracie Pendleton will talk with him. Machado likes her."

"He kidnapped her!" she exclaimed. "And the man she's now married to!"

He nodded. "I know. He also saved her from being assaulted by one of Fuentes's men," he added.

"Oh. I didn't know that."

"She's fond of him, too," he replied. "Apparently, he makes friends even of his enemies. A couple of feds I know think he's one of the better insurgents," he added dryly.

"He did install democratic government in Barrera,"

she pointed out. "He instituted reforms that did away with unlawful detention and surveillance, he invited the foreign media in to oversee elections and he ousted half a dozen petty politicians who were robbing the poor and making themselves into feudal lords. From what we understand, one of those petty politicians helped Machado's second-in-command plan the coup that ousted him."

"While he was out of the country negotiating trade agreements," Rick agreed. "Stabbed in the back."

"Exactly. We'd love to have him back in power, but we can't actually do anything about it," she said quietly. "That's where you come in."

"The general doesn't even know me, let alone that I'm his biological son," he repeated. "Even if he did, I don't think he's going to jump up and invite me to baseball games."

"Soccer," she corrected. "He hates baseball."

His eyebrows lifted. "How do you know that?"

"I have a file on him," she said. "He likes strawberry ice cream, his favorite musical star is Marco Antonio Solís, he wears size 12 shoes and he plays classical guitar. Oh, he was an entertainer on a cruise ship in his youth."

"I did know about that. Not his shoe size," he added with twinkling dark eyes.

"He's never been romantically linked with any particular woman," she continued. "Although he was good friends with an American anthropologist who went to live in his country. She'd found an ancient site that was revolutionary and she was involved in a dig there. Apparently, there are some interesting ruins in Barrera."

"What happened to her?"

"Nobody knows. We couldn't even ascertain her name. What I was able to ferret out was only gossip."

He folded his hands on his desk. "So, you're a fed, I'm one detective short and you're supposed to be heading a murder investigation for me," he said curtly. "What do I do about that?"

"I've been working on it," she protested. "I'm making progress, too. As soon as we get the DNA profile back, I may be able to make an arrest in the college freshman's murder, and solve a cold case involving another dead coed. I have lots of information to go on, now, including eyewitness testimony that can place the suspect at the murdered woman's apartment just before she was killed."

He sat up. "Nice!"

"Thank you. I have an appointment to talk to her best friend, also, the one who took the photo that the suspect showed up in. She gave a statement to the crime scene detective that the victim had complained about visits from a man who made her uneasy."

"They'll let you continue to work on my case, even though you're a fed?"

"Until something happens in the general's case," she said. "I'm keeping up appearances."

"You slipped through the cracks," he translated.

She laughed. "Thanksgiving is just over the horizon and my boss gets a lot of business done in D.C. going from one party to another with his wife."

"I see."

"When is Mrs. Pendleton going to talk to the general, did the DEA agent say?"

He shook his head. "It's only a work in progress right now." He leaned back in his chair. "I thought my father was dead. My mother told me he was killed when I was just a baby. I didn't realize I had a father who never even knew I was on the way."

"He loves children," she pointed out.

"Yes, but I'm not a child."

"I noticed."

He glared at her.

She flushed and averted her eyes.

He felt guilty. "Sorry. I'm not dealing with this well."

"I can understand that," she replied. "I know it must be hard for you."

She had a nice voice, he thought. Soft and medium in pitch, and she colored it in pastels with emotion. He liked her voice. Her choice of T-shirts, however, left a lot to be desired. She had on one today that read Save a Turkey, Eat a Horse for Thanksgiving. He burst out laughing.

"Do you have an open line to a T-shirt manufac-turer?" he asked.

"What? Oh!" She glanced down at her shirt. "Well, sort of. There's this online place that lets you make your own T-shirts. I do a lot of business with them, design-ing my own."

Now he understood her quirky wardrobe.

"Drives my boss nuts," she added with a grin. "He thinks I'm not dignified enough on the job."

"I'm sure you have casual days, even in D.C."

"I don't work in D.C.," she said. "I get sent wher-ever I'm needed. I live out of a suitcase mostly." She smiled wanly. "It's not much of a life. I loved it when I was younger, but I'd really love to have someplace per-manent."

"You could get a job in a local office."

"I guess." She shrugged. "Meanwhile, I've got one

right here. I'm sorry I didn't tell you who I was at first," she added. "I would have liked to be honest."

He sensed that. He grimaced. "It's hard for me, too, trying to understand the past. My mother, my adopted mother," he said, just to clarify the point, "said that the general was only fourteen when he fathered me. I'll be thirty-one this year, in late December. That would make him—" he stopped and thought "—forty-five." His eyebrows arched. "That's not a great age for a dictator."

She laughed. "He was forty-one when he became president of Barrera," she said. "In those four years, he did a world of good for his country. His adopted country."

"Yes, well, he's wanted in this country for kidnapping," he reminded her.

"Good luck trying to get him extradited," she cautioned. "First the Mexican authorities would have to actually apprehend him, and he's got a huge complex in northern Sonora. One report is that he even has a howitzer."

"True story," he said, leaning back in his chair. "Pancho Villa, who fought in the Mexican Revolution, was a folk hero in Mexico at the turn of the twentieth century. John Reed, a Harvard graduate and journalist, actually lived with him for several months."

"And wrote articles about his adventures there. They made them into a book," she said, shocking him. "I had to buy it from a rare book shop. It's one of my treasures."

Chapter 6

"I've read that book," Rick said with a slow smile. "*Insurgent Mexico.* I couldn't afford to buy it, unfortunately, so I got it on loan from the library. It was published in 1914. A rare book, indeed."

She shifted uncomfortably. She hadn't meant to let that bit slip. She was still keeping secrets from him. She shouldn't have been able to afford the book on her government salary. Her father had given it to her last Christmas. That was another secret she was keeping, too; her father's identity.

"And would you know Pancho Villa's real name?" he asked suddenly.

She grinned. "He was born Doroteo Arango," she said. The smile faded a little. "He changed his name to Pancho Villa, according to one source, because he was hunted by the authorities for killing a man who raped his younger sister. It put him on a path of lawlessness, but he fought all his life for a Mexico that was free of foreign oppression and a government that worked for the poor."

He smiled with pure delight. "You read Mexican history," he mused, still surprised.

"Well, yes, but the best of it is in Spanish, so I studied very hard to learn to read it," she confessed. She flushed. "I like the colonial histories, written by priests in the sixteenth century who sailed with the *conquistadores*."

"Spanish colonial history," he said.

She smiled. "I also like to read about Juan Belmonte and Manolete."

His eyebrows arched. "Bullfighters?" he exclaimed.

"Well, yes," she said. "Not the modern ones. I don't know anything about those. I found this book on Juan Belmonte, his biography. I was so fascinated by it that I started reading about Joselito and the others who fought bulls in Spain at the beginning of the twentieth century. They were so brave. Nothing but a cape and courage, facing a bull that was twice their size, all muscle and with horns so sharp..." She cleared her throat. "It's not PC to talk about it, I know."

"Yes, we mustn't mention blood sports," he joked. "The old bullfighters were like soldiers who fought in the world wars—tough and courageous. I like World War II history, particularly the North African theater of war."

Her eyes opened wide behind the lenses of her glasses. "Rommel. Patton. Montgomery. Alexander..."

His lips fell open. "Yes."

She laughed with some embarrassment. "I'm a history major," she said. "I took my degree in it." She didn't add that she came by her interest in military history quite naturally, nor that her grandfather had known General George S. Patton, Jr., personally.

"Well!"

"You have an associate's degree in criminal justice and you're going to night school working on your B.A.," she blurted out.

He laughed. "What's my shoe size?"

"Eleven." She cleared her throat. "Sorry. I have a file on you, too."

He leaned forward, his large dark eyes narrow. "I'll have to compile one on you. Just to be fair."

She didn't want him to do that, but she just nodded. Maybe he couldn't dig up too much, even if he tried. She kept her private life very private.

She stood up. "I need to get back to work. I just wanted to be honest with you, about my job," she said. "I didn't want you to think I was being deliberately deceitful."

He stood up, too. "I never thought that."

He walked with her to the door. "Uh, is the lieutenant still bringing you roses?" he asked, and could have slapped himself for even asking the question.

"Oh, certainly not," she said primly. "That was just an apology, for using bad language in front of me."

"He's a widower," he said as they reached the door.

She paused and looked up at him. He was very close all of a sudden and she felt the heat from his body as her nostrils caught the faint, exotic scent of the cologne he used. He smelled very masculine and her heart went wild at the proximity. Her head barely topped his shoulder. He was tall and powerfully built, and she had an almost overwhelming hunger to lay her head on that shoulder and press close and bury her lips in that smooth, tanned throat.

She caught her breath and stepped back quickly. She looked up into his searching eyes and stood very still, like a cat in the sights of a hunter. She couldn't even think of anything to say.

Rick was feeling something similar. She smelled of wildflowers today. Her skin was almost translucent and he noticed that she wore little makeup. Her hair was caught up in a high ponytail, but he was certain that if she let it down, it would make a thick platinum curtain all the way to her waist. He wanted, badly, to loosen it and bury his mouth in it.

He stepped back, too. The feelings were uncomfortable. "Better get back to work," he said curtly. He was breathing heavily. His voice didn't sound natural.

"Yes. Uh, m-me, too," she stammered, and flushed, making her skin look even prettier.

He started to open the door for her. But he paused. "Someone told me that you like *The Firebird*."

She laughed nervously. "Yes. Very much."

"The orchestra is doing a tribute to Stravinsky Friday night." He moved one shoulder. He shouldn't do this. But he couldn't help himself. "I have two tickets. I was going to take Mom, but she's going to have to cater some cattlemen's meeting in Jacobsville and she can't go." He took a breath. "So I was wondering…"

"Yes." She cleared her throat. "I mean, if you were going to ask me…?" she blurted, embarrassed.

Her nervousness lessened his. He smiled at her in a way he never had, his chiseled mouth sensuous, his eyes very dark and soft. "Yes. I was going to ask you."

"Oh." She laughed, self-consciously.

He tipped her chin up with his bent forefinger and looked into her soft, pale green eyes. "Six o'clock? We'll have dinner first."

Her breath caught. Her heartbeat shook her T-shirt. "Yes," she whispered breathlessly.

His dark eyes were on her pretty bow of a mouth. It was slightly parted, showing her white teeth. He actually started bending toward it when his phone suddenly rang.

He jerked back, laughing deeply at his own helpless response to her. "Go to work," he said, but he grinned.

"Yes, sir." She started out the door. She looked back at him. "I live in the Oak Street apartments," she said. "Number 92."

He smiled back. "I'll remember."

She left, with obvious reluctance.

It took him a minute to realize that his phone was still ringing. He was going to date a colleague and the whole department would know. Well, what the hell, he muttered to himself. He was really tired of going to concerts and the ballet alone. She was a fed and she wouldn't be here long. Why shouldn't he have companionship?

Gwen got back to her own office and leaned back against the door with a long sigh. She was trembling from the encounter with Rick and so shocked at his invitation that she could barely get her breath back. He was going to date her. He wanted to take her out. She could barely believe it!

While she was savoring the invitation, her cell phone rang. She noted the number and opened it.

"Hi, Dad," she said, smiling. "How's it going?"

"Rough, or don't you watch the news, pudding?" he

asked with a laugh in his deep voice as he used his nickname for her.

"I do," she said. "I'm really sorry. Politicians should
let the military handle military matters."

"Come up to D.C. and tell the POTUS that," he murmured.

"Why can't you just say President of the United
States?" she teased.

"I'm in the military. We use abbreviations."

"I noticed."

"How's it going with you?"

"I'm working on a sensitive matter."

"I've been talking to your boss about it," he replied.
"And I told him that I don't like having you put on the
firing line like this."

She winced. She could imagine that encounter. Her
boss, while very nice, was also as bullheaded as her father. It would have been interesting to see how it ended.

"And he told you…?"

He sighed. "That I could mind my own damned business, basically," he explained. "We're a lot alike."

"I noticed."

"Anyway, I hope you're packing, and that the detective you're working with is, also."

"We both are, but the general isn't a bad man."

"He's wanted for kidnapping!"

"Yes, well, he's desperate for money, but he didn't
really hurt anybody."

"A man was killed in his camp," he returned curtly.

"Yes, the general shot him for trying to assault Gracie Pendleton," she replied. "He caught him in the act.
Gracie was bruised and shaken, but he got to her just
in time. The guy was one of the Fuentes organization."

There was a long silence. "I didn't hear that part."

"Not many people have."

He sighed. "Well, maybe he's not as bad a man as I thought he was."

"We want him on our side. He has a son that he didn't know about. We're trying to get an entrée into his camp, to make a contact with him. It isn't easy."

"I know about that, too." He paused. "How's your love life?" he teased.

She cleared her throat. "Actually, Sergeant Marquez just invited me to a symphony concert."

There was a longer pause. "He likes classical music?"

"Yes, and the ballet." Her eyes narrowed. "And no smart remarks, if you please."

"I like classical music."

"But you hate ballet," she pointed out. "And you think anybody who does is nuts."

"So I have a few interesting flaws," he conceded.

"He's also a military history buff," she added quickly. "World War II and North Africa."

"How ironic," he chuckled.

She smiled to herself. "Yes, isn't it?"

He drew in a long sigh. "You coming home for Christmas?"

"Of course," she agreed. She smiled sadly. "Especially this year."

"I'm glad." He bit off the words. "It hasn't been easy. Larry's wife calls me every other night, crying."

"Lindy will adjust," she said softly. "It's just going to take time. She and Larry were married for ten years and they didn't have children. That will make it harder for her. But she's strong. She'll manage."

"I hope so." There was a scraping sound, as if he was

getting up out of a chair. "His commanding officer got drunk and wrecked a bar up in Maryland, while he was on R&R," he said.

"Larry's death wasn't his fault," she replied tersely. "Any officer who goes into a covert situation knows the risks and has to be willing to take them."

"I told him that," her father replied. "Damn it, he cried…!" He cleared his throat, choking back the emotion. "I called up Brigadier Langston and told him to get that man some help before he becomes a statistic. He promised he would."

"General Langston was fond of Larry, too," she said quietly. "I remember him at the funeral…"

There was a pause. "Let's talk about something else."

"Okay. How do you feel about giving chickens the vote?"

He burst out laughing.

"Or we could decide where we're going to eat on Christmas Eve, because I'm not spending my days off in the kitchen," she said.

"Good thing. We'd starve or die of carbon monoxide poisoning," he replied.

"I can cook! I just don't like to."

"If you'd use timers, we'd have food that didn't turn black before we got to eat it," he said. "I can cook anything," he added smugly.

"I remember." She sighed. "Rick's mom is a great cook," she replied. "She owns a restaurant."

"She does? You should marry him. You'd never have to worry about cooking again." He chuckled.

She blushed. "It's just a date, Dad."

"Your first one in how many years…?"

"Stop that," she muttered. "I date."

"You went to the Laundromat with a guy who lived in your apartment building," he burst out. "That's not a date!"

"It was fun. We ate potato chips and discussed movies while our clothes got done," she replied.

He shook his head. "Pudding, you're hopeless."

"Thanks!"

"I give up. I have to go. I've got a meeting with the Joint Chiefs in ten minutes."

"More war talk?"

"More withdrawal talk," he said. "There's a rumor that the POTUS is going to offer me Hart's job."

"You're kidding!"

"That's what they're saying."

"Will you take it?" she asked, excited.

"Watch the news and we'll find out."

"That would be great!"

"I might be in a position to do something more useful," he said. "But, we'll see. I guess I'd do it, if they ask me."

"Good for you!"

"Say, do you ever see Grange?"

"Grange? You mean, the Pendletons' foreman?" she asked, disconcerted.

"Yes. Winslow Grange. He was in my last overseas command." He smiled. "Had a real pig of an officer, who sent him into harm's way understrength and with a battle plan that some kindergarten kid could have come up with. Grange tied him up, put him in the trunk of his own car and led the assault himself. He was invited to leave the army with an honorable discharge or be court-martialed. He left. But he came back to testify against his commanding officer, who was dishonorably discharged after a nasty trial."

"Good enough for him," she said curtly.

"I do agree. Anyway, Winslow is a friend of mine. I'd love to see him sometime. You might pass that along. We could always use someone like him in D.C. if he gets tired of horse poop."

She wondered if she should tell her father what his buddy Grange was rumored to be doing right now, but that was probably a secret she should keep. "If I see him, I'll tell him," she promised.

"Take care of yourself, okay? You're the only family I've got left." His deep voice was thick with emotion.

"Same here," she replied. "Love you, Dad."

"Mmm-hmm." He wasn't going to say it out loud. He never did. But he loved her, so she didn't make a smart remark.

"I'll call you in a few days, just to check in. Okay?"

"That's a deal." His hand went over the receiver. "Yes, I'm on my way," he told someone else. "Gotta go. See you, kid."

"Bye, Dad."

He hung up. She put the phone back in her pocket. It seemed to be a day for revelations.

She had a beautiful little couture black dress, with expensive black slingbacks and a frilly black shawl that she'd gotten in Madrid. She wore those for her date with Rick, and she let her hair down, brushing it until it was shiny, like a pale satin curtain down her back. She left her glasses off for once. If she wasn't driving, she didn't need them, and a symphony concert didn't really require perfect vision.

Rick wore a dinner jacket and a black tie. His own hair was still in its elegant ponytail, but tied with a neat black ribbon. He looked very sharp.

He stared at her with disconcerting interest when she opened the door, taking in the nice fit of her dress with its modest rounded neckline and lacy hem that hit just at mid-calf. Her pretty little feet were in strappy high heels that left just a hint of the space between her toes visible. It was oddly sexy.

"You look…very nice," he said, his eyes taking in her flushed, lovely complexion and her perfect mouth, just dabbed with pale lipstick.

"Thanks! So do you," she replied, laughing nervously.

He produced a box from behind his back and handed it to her. It was a beautiful cymbidium orchid, much like the ones she had back at her father's home that the housekeeper faithfully misted each day.

"It's lovely!" she exclaimed.

He raised one shoulder and smiled self-consciously. "They wanted to give me one you wore around the wrist, but I explained that we weren't going to a dance and I wanted one that pinned."

"I like this kind best." She took it out of the box and pinned it to the dress, smiling at the way it complemented the dark background. "Thanks."

"My pleasure. Shall we go?"

"Yes!"

She grabbed her evening bag, closed the door and locked it and let him help her into his pickup truck.

"I should have something more elegant to drive than this," he muttered as he climbed in beside her.

"But I love trucks!" she exclaimed. "My dad has one that he drives around our place when he's home."

He grinned. "Well, maybe I'll get a nice car one day."

"It doesn't matter what you go in, as long as it gets you to your destination," she pointed out. "I even like Humvees."

His eyebrows arched. "And where do you get to ride in those?"

She bit her tongue. "Uh…"

"I forgot. Your brother was in the military, you said," he interrupted. "Sorry. I didn't mean to bring back sad memories for you."

She drew in a long breath. "He died doing what he felt was important for his country," she replied. "He was very patriotic and spec ops was his life."

His eyebrows arched.

"He died in a classified operation," she added. "His commanding officer just went on a huge bender. He feels responsible. He ordered the incursion."

His eyes softened. "That's the sort of man I wouldn't mind serving under," he said quietly. "A man with a conscience, who cares about his men."

She smiled. "My dad's like that, too. I mean, he's a man with a conscience," she said quickly.

He didn't notice the slip. He reached out and touched her soft cheek. "I'm sorry for your loss," he said. "I don't have siblings. But I wish I did."

She managed a smile. "Larry was a wonderful brother and a terrific husband. His wife is taking it hard. They didn't have any kids."

"Tough."

She nodded. "It's going to be hard to get through Christmas," she said. "Larry was a nut about it. He came home to Lindy every year and he brought all sorts of foreign decorations with him. We've got plenty that he sent us…"

He moved closer. His big hands framed her face and lifted it. Her pale green eyes were swimming in tears. He bent, helpless, and softly kissed away the tears.

"Life is often painful," he whispered. "But there are compensations."

While he spoke, his chiseled lips were moving against her eyelids, her nose, her cheeks. Finally, as she held her breath in wild anticipation, his lips hovered just over her perfect bow of a mouth. She could feel his breath, taste its minty freshness, see the hard curve of his lips that filled her vision to the exclusion of anything else.

She hung there, at his mouth, her eyes half-closed, her skin tingling from the warm strength of his hands framing her face, waiting, waiting, waiting…!

He drew in an unsteady breath and bent closer, logic flying out the window as the wildflower scent of her made him weak. Her mouth was perfect. He wanted to feel its softness under his lips, taste her. He was sure that she was going to be delicious…

The sudden sound of a horn blowing raucously on the street behind them shocked them apart. He blinked, as if he was under the influence of alcohol. She didn't seem much calmer. She fumbled with her purse.

"I guess we should go," he said with a forced laugh. "We want to have enough time to eat before the concert."

"Y…yes," she agreed.

"Seat belt," he added, nodding toward it.

"Oh. Yes! I usually put it on at once," she added as she fumbled it into place.

He laughed, securing his own.

Her shy smile made him feel taller. Involuntarily,

his fingers linked with hers as he started the truck and pulled out into traffic. He wouldn't even let himself think about how he'd gone in headfirst with a colleague, against all his best instincts. He was too happy.

They ate at a nice restaurant in San Antonio, one with a flamenco theme and a live guitarist with a Spanish dancer in a beautiful red dress with puffy sleeves and the ruffled, long-trained dress that was familiar to followers of the dance style. The performance was short, but the applause went on for a long time. The duet was impressive.

"What a treat," she said enthusiastically. "They're so good!"

"Yes, they are." He grinned. "I love flamenco."

"So do I. I bought this old movie, *Around the World in 80 Days,* and it had a guy named Jose Greco and his flamenco dance troupe in it. That's when I fell in love with flamenco. He was so talented," she said.

"I've seen tapes of Jose Greco dancing," he replied. "He truly was phenomenal."

"My mother used to love Latin dances," she said dreamily, smiling. "She could do them all."

"Is she still alive?" he asked carefully.

She hesitated. She shook her head. "We lost her when I was in my final year of high school. Dad was overseas and couldn't even come back for the funeral, so Larry and I had to do everything. Dad never got over it. He was just starting to, when Larry died."

"Why couldn't your father come home?" he asked, curious.

She swallowed. "He was involved in a classified mission," she said. She held up a hand when he started to follow up with another question, smiling to lessen the sting. "Sorry, but he couldn't even tell me what he was doing. National security stuff."

His eyebrows arched. "Your dad's in the military?"

She hesitated. But it wouldn't hurt to agree. He was. But Rick would be thinking of a regular soldier, and her dad was far from regular. "Yes," she replied.

"I see."

"You don't, but I can't say any more," she told him.

"I guess not. Wouldn't want to tick off the brass by saying something out of turn, right?" he teased.

"Right." She had to fight a laugh. Her father was the brass; one of the highest ranking officers in the U.S. Army, in fact.

The waiter who took their order was back quickly with cups of hot coffee and the appetizers, buffalo wings and French fries with cheese and chili dip.

Rick tasted the wings and laughed as he put it quickly back down. "Hot!" he exclaimed.

"I'm glad I'm wearing black," she sighed. "If I had on a white dress, it would be red-and-white polka dotted when I finished eating. I wear most of my food."

His dark eyebrows arched and he grinned. "Me, too."

She laughed. "I'm glad it's not just me."

He tried again with the French fries. "These are really good. Here. Taste."

She let him place it at her lips. She bit off the end and sighed. "Delicious!"

"They have wonderful food, including a really special barbecue sauce for the wings. Want to know where they got it?" he asked mischievously.

"From your mother?" she guessed.

He shook his head. "It seems that FBI senior agent Jon Blackhawk came here to eat with his brother, Kilraven, one night. Jon tasted their barbecue sauce, made a face, got up, walked into the kitchen and proceeded to have words with the chef."

"You're kidding!"

"I'm not. It didn't come to blows, but only because Jon put on an apron and showed the chef how to make a proper barbecue sauce. When the chef tasted it, so the story goes, he asked which cordon bleu academy in Paris Mr. Blackhawk had attended. He got the shock of his life when Jon named it." He grinned. "You see, he actually went to Paris and took courses. His new wife is one lucky woman. She'll never have to go in the kitchen unless she really wants to."

"I heard about them," she replied. "That's one interesting family."

He munched a French fry thoughtfully. "I'd love to have kids," he said solemnly. "A big family to make up for what I never had." His expression was bitter. "Barbara is the best mother on the planet, but I wish I'd had brothers and sisters."

"You do at least still have a father living," she pointed out.

"A father who's going to get the shock of his life when he's introduced to his grown-up son," he said. "And I wonder if Ramirez has had any luck getting his sister-in-law to approach the general."

As if in answer to the question, his cell phone began vibrating. He checked the number, gave her a stunned glance and got to his feet. "I'll be right back. I have to take this."

She nodded. She liked his consideration for the other diners. He took the call outside on the street, so that he wouldn't disturb other people with his conversation.

He was back in less than five minutes. He sat back down. "Imagine that," he said on a hollow laugh. "Gracie talked to the general. He wants us to come to the border Monday morning for a little chat, as he put it."

Her eyebrows arched. "Progress," she said, approving.

He sighed. "Yes. Progress." He didn't add that he had misgivings and he was nervous as hell. He just finished eating.

Chapter 7

Rick was preoccupied through the rest of the meal.
Gwen didn't talk much, either. She knew he had to be
unsettled about the trip to the border, for a lot of reasons.

He held her hand on the way to the car, his strong
fingers tangling in hers.

"It will be all right," she blurted out.

They reached the passenger door and he paused, looking down at her. "Will it?"

"You're a good man," she said. "He'll be very proud
of you."

He was uncertain. "You think?"

She loved the smell of his body, the warm strength
of it near her. She loved everything about him. "Yes."

He smiled tenderly. She made him feel tall, powerful, important. Women had made him feel undervalued
for years, mostly by thinking of him as nothing more

than a friend. Gwen was different. She was a working girl, from his own middle-class strata. She was pretty, in her way, and smart. And she knew her way around a handgun, he thought amusedly. But she also stirred his senses in a new and exciting way.

"You're nice," he said suddenly.

She grimaced. "Rub it in."

"No. Nice, in a very positive way," he replied. His expression was somber. "I don't like sophisticated women. I like brains in a woman, and even athletic outlooks. But I do mind women who think of themselves as party favors. You get me?"

She smiled. "I feel the same way about men like that."

He smiled. "You and I, we don't belong in a modern setting."

"We'd look very nice in a Victorian village," she agreed. "Like Edward in the *Twilight* vampire series of books and movies. I love those. I guess I've seen the movies ten times each and read the books on my iPod every night."

"I don't watch vampire movies. I like werewolves."

"Oh, but there are werewolves in them, too. Nice werewolves."

"You're kidding."

She hesitated. "I've got all the DVDs. I was wondering…"

He moved a step closer, so that she was backed into the car door. "You were wondering?"

"Uh, yes, if you'd like to maybe watch the movies with me?" she asked him. "I could make a pizza. Or we could…order…one…?"

She was whispering now, and her voice was breaking because his mouth had moved closer with every whispered word until it was right against her soft lips.

"Gwen?"

"Hmm?"

"Shut up," he whispered against her lips, and his crushed down on them with warm, sensual, insistent hunger.

A muffled sob broke from her throat as she lifted her arms and pressed her body as close as she could get it to his tall, powerful form. He groaned, too, as the insane delight pulsed through him like fire.

He moved, shifting her, so that one long leg was between her skirt, and his mouth was suddenly invasive, starving.

"Detective!"

He heard a voice. It sounded close. And shocked. And angry. He lifted his head, still reeling from Gwen's soft mouth.

"Hmm?" he murmured, turning his head.

"Detective Sergeant Marquez," a deep, angry voice repeated.

"Sir!" He jumped back, almost saluted, and tried to look normal. He hoped his jacket was covering a blatant reminder of his body's interest in Gwen's.

"What the hell are you doing?" Lieutenant Hollister asked gruffly.

"It's okay, sir," Gwen faltered. "He was, uh, helping me get my earring unstuck from my dress."

He blinked and scowled. "What?"

"My earring, sir." She dangled it in her hand. "It caught on my dress. Detective Marquez was helping me get it loose. I guess it did look odd, the position we were in." She laughed with remarkable acting ability.

"Oh. I see." Hollister cleared his throat. He shoved his hands in his pockets. "I'm very sorry. It looked, well, I mean…" He cleared his throat again. He scowled. "I thought you didn't date colleagues," he shot at Marquez, who had by reciting multiplication tables made a remarkably quick recovery.

"I don't, sir," Marquez agreed. "We both like flamenco, and there's a dancer here…"

Hollister held up his hand and declared, "Say no more. That's why I came. Alone, sadly," he added with a speculative and rather sad look at Gwen.

"She's a great dancer," Gwen said. "And that guitarist!"

He nodded. "Her husband."

"Really!" Gwen exclaimed.

"Oh, yes. They've appeared all over Europe. I understand they're being considered for a bit part in a movie that's filming near here next year."

"That would be so lovely for them," Gwen enthused.

Rick checked his watch. "We'd better go. I've got an appointment early Monday morning. I thought I'd brush up on my Spanish over the weekend," he added dryly.

"Yes, I heard about that," Hollister said quietly. "It will go all right," he told Rick. "You'll see."

Rick was touched. "Thanks."

Hollister shrugged. "You're a credit to my department. Don't let him talk you into going to South America, okay?"

Rick smiled. "I'm not much good with rocket launchers."

"Me, neither," the lieutenant agreed. He glanced at Gwen and smiled. "Well, sorry about the mistake. Have a good evening."

"You, too, sir," Gwen said, and Rick nodded assent.

Hollister nodded back and walked, distracted, toward the restaurant.

Rick helped Gwen into the truck and burst out laughing. So did she.

"Did I ever tell you that I minored in theater in college?" she asked. "They said I had promise."

"You could make movies," he said flatly. He shook his head as he started the truck. "Quick thinking."

"Thanks." She flushed a little.

Neither of them mentioned that they'd been so far gone that anything could have happened, right there in the parking lot, if the lieutenant hadn't shown up. But it was true. Also true was the look the lieutenant had been giving them. He seemed to have more than the usual interest in Gwen. He wasn't really the sort of man to put a rose on a woman's desk unless he meant it. Rick was thinking that he had some major competition there, if he didn't watch his step. Hollister's tone hadn't been one of outraged decorum so much as jealous anger.

Rick left Gwen at her door. He was more cautious this time, but he did pull her close and kiss her good-night with barely restrained passion.

She held him, kissing him back, loving the warm, soft press of his mouth on hers.

"I'm out of practice," he murmured as he stepped back.

"Me, too," she said breathlessly, her eyes full of stars as they met his in the light from the security lamps.

"I guess we could practice with each other," he murmured dryly.

She flushed and laughed nervously. "I'd like that."

"Yes. So would I." He bent again, brushing his mouth lightly over hers and forcing himself not to go in head-first. "Are you coming along, in the morning?"

She nodded. "I have to."

He smiled. "Good. I could use the moral support."

She smiled back. "Thanks."

"Well. I'll see you at the office Monday."

"Yes."

He turned and took a step. He stopped. He turned. She was still standing there, her expression confused, waiting, still...

He walked back to her. "Unlock the door," he said quietly.

She fumbled the key into the lock and opened it. He closed it behind him, his arms enveloping her in the dark hallway, illuminated by a single small lamp in the living room. His mouth searched for hers, found it, claimed it, possessed it hungrily.

His arms were insistent, locking her against the length of his powerful body. She moaned, a sound almost like a sob of pleasure.

He was feeling something very similar.

"What the hell," he whispered into her lips as he bent and lifted her, still kissing her, and carried her to the long, soft sofa.

They slid down onto it together, his body covering hers, one long leg insinuating itself between her skirt, between her soft thighs. His lean hands went to the back of the dress, finding the hook and the zipper.

She didn't even have the presence of mind to protest. She was drowning in pleasure. She'd never felt anything remotely similar to the sensations that were washing over her like ripples of unbelievable delight.

He slid the dress off her arms, along with the tiny straps of the black slip she wore under it, exposing a small, black-lace bra that revealed more than it covered. She had pretty little breasts, firm and very soft.

His hand slid under the bra, savoring the warm softness of the flesh, exciting the hard little tip, making her shiver with new sensations.

She hadn't done this before. He knew it without being told. He smiled against her mouth. It was exciting, and new, to be the first man. He never had been. Not that there had even been that many women that he'd been almost intimate with. And, in recent years, nobody. Like Gwen, he'd never indulged in casual sex. He was as innocent, in his way, as she was. Well, he knew a little more than she did. When he touched his mouth to her breast, she lifted toward his lips with a shocked little gasp. He smiled as his mouth opened, taking the hard tip inside and pulling at it gently with his tongue.

Her nails bit into the muscles of his arms as he removed his jacket and tie and shirt, wanting so badly to be closer, closer...

She felt air on her skin and then the hard, warm press of hair and muscle as they locked together, both bare from the waist up.

His mouth was insistent now, hungry, demanding. She felt his hand sliding up her bare thigh and she knew that very soon they would reach a point from which there was no return.

"N...no," she whispered, pushing at his chest. "Rick? Rick!"

He heard her voice through a bloodred haze of desire that locked his muscles so tightly that he could barely move for the tension. She was saying something. What? It sounded like...no?

He lifted his head. He looked into wide, uneasy green eyes. He felt her body tensed, shivering.

"I'm sorry..." she began.

He blinked once, twice. He drew in a breath that sounded as ragged as he felt. "Good Lord," he exhaled.

She swallowed. They were very intimate. Neither of them had anything on above the waist. His hand was still on her thigh. He removed it quickly and lifted up just a little, his high cheekbones flushing when he got a sudden, stark, uninterrupted view of her pretty pink breasts with tight little dusky pink tips very urgently stating the desire of the owner for much more than looking.

Embarrassed, she drew her hands up over them as he levered himself away and sat up.

"I'm sorry," he said, averting his eyes while she fumbled her dress back on. "I didn't mean to..."

"Of c-course not," she stammered. "Neither did I. It's all right."

He laughed. His body felt as if it had been hit with a bat several times in strategic places and he ached from head to toe. "Sure it is."

"Oh, I'm sorry!" she groaned. She wasn't experienced, but she had friends who were, and she knew what was wrong with him. "Here, just a sec."

She went to the kitchen and came back with a cold beer from the fridge. "Detective Rogers comes over from time to time and she likes this brand of light beer," she explained. "I don't drink, but I think people need to sometimes. You need to, a little...?"

He gave her an exasperated sigh. "Gwen, I'm a police detective sergeant!"

"Yes, I know…"

"I can't take a drink and drive!"

She stared at him, looked at the beer. "Oh."

He burst out laughing. It broke the ice and slowly he began to feel normal again.

She looked around them. His jacket and shirt and tie, and her shoes and his holster and pistol were lying in a heap beside the sofa.

His gaze followed hers. He laughed again. "Well."

"Yes. Uh. Well." She looked at the can of beer, laughed, and set it down. Her glasses were where she'd tossed them on the end table but she didn't put them on. She didn't want to see his expression. She was already embarrassed.

He put his shirt and tie back on and slipped into his jacket before he replaced the holstered pistol on his belt. "At least you don't object to the gun," he mused.

She shrugged. "I usually have a concealed carry in my purse," she confessed.

His eyebrows arched. "No ankle holster?" he asked.

She made a face. "Weighs down my leg too much."

He nodded. He looked at her in a different way now. Possessively. Hungrily. He moved forward, but he only took her oval face in his hands and searched her eyes, very close up. He was somber.

"From now on," he said gently, "we say good-night at the door. Right?"

He was hinting at a relationship. "From now on?" she said hesitantly.

He nodded. He searched her eyes. "There aren't that many women running around loose who belong to the Victorian era, don't mind firearms and like to watch flamenco dancing."

She smiled with pure delight. "I was going to say the same about you—well, you're not a woman, of course."

"Of course."

He bent and kissed her very softly. He lifted his head and his large brown eyes narrowed. "If Hollister puts another rose on your desk, I'm going to deck him, and I don't care if he fires me."

Her face became radiant. "Really?"

"Really." His jaw tautened. "You're mine."

She flushed. She lowered her eyes to his strong neck, where a pulse beat very strongly. She nodded.

He hugged her close, rocked her in his arms. He drew in a long breath, finally, and let her go. He smiled ruefully. "After we get through talking with the general, Monday, I'm going to take you to meet my mother."

"You are?"

"You'll love her. She'll love you, too," he promised. He glanced at his watch and grimaced. "I have to get going. I'll pick you up here at 6:00 a.m. sharp, okay?"

"I could drive to the office…"

"I'll pick you up here."

She smiled. Her eyes were bright with pleasure. "Okay."

He chuckled. "Lock the door after me."

"I will. I really enjoyed the flamenco."

"So did I. I know another Latin dance club over on the west side of town. We'll go there next time. Do you like Mexican food?"

"Love it."

He smiled. "Theirs is pretty hot."

"No worries, I don't have any taste buds left. I eat jalapenos raw," she added with a grin.

"Whew! My kind of girl."

She grinned. "I noticed."

He laughed, kissed her hair and walked out the door. After he climbed back into the pickup truck, he paused and waited until she was safely in her apartment before he drove off.

She didn't sleep that night. Not a wink. She was too excited, exhilarated and hungrily, passionately really in love for the first time in her life.

Rick was somber and nervous Monday morning when he picked Gwen up for the drive to the border. It had turned cold again and she was wearing a sweater and thick jeans with a jacket and boots.

"Summer yesterday, winter today," she remarked, readjusting her seat belt.

"That's Texas," he said fondly.

"Is Ramirez going to meet us at the border station?"

"Yes," he said. "He and Gracie."

Her eyebrows arched. "Mrs. Pendleton is coming, too? Isn't that dangerous?"

"We're not going over the border," he reminded her. "Just up to it."

"Oh. Okay."

He glanced at her, warm memories of the night before still in his dark eyes. She was lovely, he thought. Pretty and smart and good with a gun.

She felt his eyes but she didn't meet them. She was nervous, too. She worried about how he might feel when he learned the truth about her own background. She was still keeping secrets. She hoped he wouldn't feel differently when he learned them.

But right now, the biggest secret of all was about to be revealed to a man who had no apparent family and seemed to be content with his situation. Gwen wondered how the general would feel when he was introduced to a son he didn't even know existed.

They pulled up to the small border station, which wasn't much more than an adobe building beside the road, next to a cross arm that was denoted as the Mexican-American border, with appropriate warning signs.

A tall, sandy-haired man came out to meet them. He introduced himself as the border patrol agent in charge, Don Billings, and indicated a Lincoln town car sitting just a little distance way. He motioned.

The car pulled up, stopped and Rodrigo Ramirez got out, going around to open the door for his sister-in-law, Gracie Pendleton. They came forward and introductions were made.

Gracie was blonde and pretty and very pregnant. She laughed. "The general is going to be surprised when he sees me," she said with a grin. "I didn't mention my interesting condition. Jason and I are just over the moon!"

"Is it a boy or a girl?" Gwen wanted to know.

"We didn't let them tell us," she said. "We want it to be a surprise, so I bought everything yellow instead of pink or blue."

Gwen laughed. "I'd like it to be a surprise, too, if I ever had a baby." Her eyes were dreamy. "I'd love to have a big family."

Rick was watching her and his heart was pounding. He'd like a big family, too. Her family. He cleared his throat. Memories of last night were causing him some difficulty in intimate places. He thought of sports until he calmed down a little.

"He should be here very soon," Ramirez said.

Even as he spoke, a pickup truck came along the dusty road from across the border, stopped and was waved through by the border agent.

The truck stopped. Two doors opened. Winslow Grange, wearing one of the very new high-tech camouflage patterned suits with an automatic pistol strapped to his hip, came forward. Right beside him was a tall, elegant-looking Hispanic man with thick, wavy black hair and large black eyes in a square face with chiseled lips and a big grin for Gracie.

"A baby?" he enthused. "How wonderful!"

She laughed, taking his outstretched hands. "Jason and I think so, too. How have you been?"

"Very busy," he said, indicating Grange. "We're planning a surprise party." He wiggled his eyebrows at the border agent. "I'm sorry that I can't say more."

"So am I." The border patrolman chuckled.

Gwen came forward, her eyes curious and welcoming at the same time. "You and I haven't met, but I think you've heard of me," she said gently. She held out her hand. "I'm Gwendolyn Cassaway. CIA."

He shook her hand warmly, and then raised it to his lips. He glanced at the man with her, a tall young man with long black hair in a ponytail and an oddly familiar face. "Your boyfriend?" he asked, lifting an eyebrow at the reaction the young man gave when he kissed Gwen's hand.

"Uh, well, uh, I mean…" She cleared her throat. "This is Detective Sergeant Ricardo Marquez, San Antonio Police Department."

General Emilio Machado looked at the younger man with narrowed, intent eyes. "Marquez."

"Yes."

Machado was curious. "You look familiar, somehow. Do I know you?"

He studied the general quietly. "No. But my birth mother was Dolores Ortíz. She was from Sonora. I look like her."

Machado stared at him intently. "She lived in Sonora, in a little village called Dolito. I knew her once," he said. "She married a man named Jackson," he added coldly.

"My stepfather," Rick said curtly.

"I have heard about your late stepfather. He was a brutal man."

Rick liked Machado already. "Yes. I have the scars to prove it," he added quietly.

Machado drew in a long breath. He looked around him. "This is a very unusual place to meet with federal agents, and I feel that I am being set up."

"Not at all," Gwen replied. "But we do have something to tell you. Something that might be upsetting."

Nobody spoke. There were somber, grim faces all around.

"You brought a firing squad?" Machado mused, looking from one to the other. "Or you lured me here to arrest me for kidnapping Gracie?"

"None of the above," Gwen said quietly. She took a deep breath. This was a very unpleasant chore she'd been given. "We were doing a routine background check on you for our files and we came across your relationship with Dolores Ortíz. She gave birth to a child out of wedlock down in Sonora. Thirty-one years ago."

Machado was doing quick math in his head. He looked at Rick pointedly, with slowly growing comprehension. The man had looked familiar. Was it possible…? He moved a step closer and cocked his head as he studied the somber-faced young man.

Then he laughed coldly. "Ah. Now I see. You know that I have spies in my country who are even now planting the seeds of revolution. You know that I have an army and that I am almost certain to retake the government of Barrera. So you are searching for ways to ingratiate yourself with me…excuse me, with my oil and natural gas reserves as well as my very strategic location in South America." He gave Rick a hard glance. "You produce a candidate for my son, and think that I will accept your word that he is who he says he is."

"I haven't said a damned thing," Rick snapped back icily.

Machado's eyebrows shot up. "You deny their conclusion?"

Rick glared at him. "You think I'm thrilled to be lined up as the illegitimate son of some exiled South American dictator?"

Machado just stared at him for a minute. Then he burst out laughing.

"Rick," Gwen groaned from beside him.

"I was perfectly content to think my real father was in a grave somewhere in Mexico," Rick continued. "And then she showed up with this story…" He pointed at Gwen.

She raised her hand. "Cash Grier told your mother," she reminded him quickly. "I had nothing to do with telling you."

"All right, my mother told me," he continued.

"Your mother is dead," Machado said, frowning.

"Barbara Ferguson, in Jacobsville, adopted me when

my mother and stepfather were killed in an auto accident," Rick continued. "She runs the café there."

Machado didn't speak. He'd never considered the possibility that Dolores would become pregnant. They'd been very close until her parents discovered them one night in an outbuilding and her father threatened to kill Machado if he ever saw him again. He'd gone to work for a big landowner soon afterward and moved to another village. He hadn't seen Dolores again.

Could she have been pregnant? They'd done nothing to prevent a child. But he'd only been fourteen. He couldn't have fathered a son at that age, surely? In fact, he'd never fathered another child in the years since, and he had been coaxed into trying, at least once. The attempt had ended in total failure. It had hurt his pride, hurt his ego, made him uncertain about his manhood. He had thought, since then, that he must be sterile.

But here was, if he could believe the statement, proof of his virility. Could this really be his son?

He moved forward a step. Yes, the man had his eyes. He had Dolores's perfect teeth, as well. He was tall and powerfully built, as Machado was. His hair was long and black and straight, without the natural waves that were in Machado's. But, then, Dolores had long black hair that was smooth as silk and thick and straight.

"You think I would take your word for something this important, even with Gracie's help?" he asked Rick.

"Hey, I didn't come here to convince you of anything," Rick said defensively. "She—" he indicated Gwen "—got him—" he nodded at Ramirez "—to call her—" he pointed toward Gracie "—to have you meet us here. I got pulled into it because some feds think you'll listen to me even if you won't listen to them."

He shrugged. "Of course, they haven't decided what to have me tell you just yet. I presume that's in the works and they'll let me know when they can agree on what day it is."

Machado listened to him, pursed his lips and laughed. "Sounds exactly like government policy to me. And I should know. I was head of a government once." His eyes narrowed and glittered. "And I will be, once again."

"I believe you," Gwen agreed.

"But for now," Machado continued, studying Rick. "What evidence exists that you really are my son? And it had better be good."

Chapter 8

"Don't look at me," Rick said quietly. "I didn't come here to prove anything."

Gwen moved forward, removing a paper from her purse. "We were sure that you wouldn't accept anyone's word, General," she said gently. "So we took the liberty of having a DNA profile made from Sergeant Marquez's last physical when blood was drawn." She gave Rick an apologetic glance. "Sorry."

Rick sighed. "Accepted."

The general read the papers, frowned, read some more and finally handed them back. "That's pretty convincing."

Gwen nodded.

He glanced at Rick, who was standing apart from the others, hard-faced, with his hands deep in the pockets of his slacks.

The general studied him from under thick black eye-lashes, with some consternation. His whole life had just been turned upside-down. He had a son. The man was a law enforcement officer. He was not bad-looking, seemed intelligent, too. Of course, there was that severe attitude problem...

"I don't like baseball," Rick said curtly when he noticed how the general was eyeing him.

Machado's thick eyebrows levered up. "You don't like baseball...?"

"In case you were thinking of father-son activities," Rick remarked drolly. "I don't like baseball. I like soccer."

Machado's dark eyes twinkled. "So do I."

"See?" Gwen said, grasping at straws, because this was becoming awkward. "Already, something in common..."

"Get down!"

While she was trying to understand the quick command from the general, Rick responded by tackling her. Rodrigo had Gracie in the limo, which had bulletproof glass, and Machado hit the ground with his pistol drawn at the same time Grange opened up with an army-issue repeating rifle.

"What the hell...!" Rick exclaimed as he leveled his own automatic, along with Gwen, at an unseen adversary, tracking his direction from the bullets hitting the dust a few yards away.

"Carver, IED, now!" Grange called into a walkie-talkie.

Seconds later, there was a huge explosion, a muffled cry, and a minute later, the sound of an engine starting and roaring, a dust cloud becoming visible as a person or persons unknown took off in the distance.

Grange grinned. "I always have a backup plan," he remarked.

"Good thing," Gwen exclaimed. "I didn't even consider an ambush!"

"Your father would have," Grange began.

She held up her hand and gave a curt shake of her head.

"You know her father?" Rick asked curiously.

"We were poker buddies, a few years back," Grange said. "Good man."

"Thanks," Gwen said, and she wasn't referring totally to the compliment. Grange would keep her secret; she saw it in his eyes.

Rick was brushing thick dust off his jacket and slacks. "Damn. They just came back from the dry cleaner."

"You should wear cotton. It cleans better," Machado suggested, indicating his own jeans and cotton shirt.

"Who was that, do you think?" Gwen asked somberly.

"Fuentes." Machado spat. "He and I have parted company. He amuses himself by sniping at me and my men."

"The drug lord? I thought his family was dead!" Gwen exclaimed.

"Most of it is. This is the last one of the Fuentes brothers, the stupid one, and he's clinging to power by his fingernails," the general told her. "He spies on me for a federal agency. Not yours," he told Gwen with a smile.

Ramirez left Gracie in the car and came back. "I don't think she should risk coming out here in the open," he said.

"I agree. She is all right?" Machado asked with some concern.

"Yes. Gracie really has guts," he replied. He frowned. "Which agency is Fuentes spying for?"

"Yours, I think, my friend," Machado told the DEA agent.

Ramirez let out a sigh. "We know there's a mole in our agency, someone very high level. We've never found out who it is."

"You should set Kilraven on him," Gwen mused dryly.

"I probably should," Ramirez agreed. "But we have our hands full right now with Mexican military coming over the border to protect drug shipments." He glanced toward the border patrol agent, who was talking to Gracie through a cracked window. "Our men on the border are in peril, always. We almost lost one some months ago, an agent named Kirk. He was very nearly killed. He left the agency and went back to his brothers on their Wyoming ranch. A great loss. He was good at his job, and he had contacts that we now lack."

"I can get you all the contacts you need," Machado promised. He glanced toward the distant hill where the sniper had been emplaced. "First I must deal with Fuentes."

"I didn't hear you say that," Gwen said firmly.

"Nor I," Ramirez echoed.

"Well, I did," Rick replied coldly. "And you're still wanted on kidnapping charges in my country, even though Mrs. Pendleton refuses to press them."

Machado's large eyes widened. "You would turn your own father in to the authorities?"

Rick's eyes narrowed. "The law is the law."

"You keep a book of statutes on your person?" the general asked.

Rick glared at him. "I've been a cop for a long time."

"Amazing. I have spent my life breaking most of the laws that exist, and here I find a son, a stranger, who goes by the book." His eyes narrowed. "I think perhaps they rigged the DNA evidence." He gave the detective a disparaging look. "I would never wear a suit like that, or grow my hair long. You look like a—what is the expression?—a hippie!"

Rick glared at him.

The general glared back.

"Uh, the sniper?" Ramirez reminded them. "He may have gone for reinforcements."

"True." Machado turned to Grange. "Perhaps you should order a sweep on the surrounding hills."

Grange smiled. "I already have."

"Good man. We will soon have a proper government in my country and you will be the commander of the forces in my country."

Ramirez choked. Gwen colored. Rick looked at them, trying to figure out why the hell they were so disturbed.

"We should go," Ramirez said, indicating the car. "I promised her husband that I would have her home very quickly. He might send a search party for us. Not a man to make an enemy of."

"Absolutely," Grange agreed.

"Thank you for making this meeting possible," Machado said, extending his hand to Ramirez.

Ramirez shook it, and then grinned. "It wasn't my idea. I'm related to the president of Mexico. He thought it would be a good idea."

Machado was impressed. "When I retake my country, perhaps you can speak to him for me about a trade agreement."

Ramirez admired the confidence in the other man's voice. "Yes, perhaps I can. Keep well."

"And you."

Gwen and Marquez waved them off before turning back to Machado.

"We should be going, too," Marquez said stiffly. "I have to get back to work."

Machado nodded. He studied his son with curious, strange eyes. "Perhaps, later, we can meet again."

"Perhaps," Rick replied.

"In a place where we do not have to fear an attack from my enemies," Machado said, shaking his head.

"I don't think we can get to Mars yet," Rick quipped.

Machado laughed. "Grange, we should go."

"Yes, sir."

Machado took Gwen's hand and kissed the back of it tenderly. "It has been a pleasure to meet you, *señorita,*" he said with pure velvet in his deep voice.

Rick stepped in, took Gwen's hand and pulled her back. He glared at Machado, which made Gwen almost giddy with delight.

Machado's dark eyes twinkled. "So it is like that, huh?"

"Like what?" Rick asked innocently. He dropped Gwen's hand and looked uncomfortable.

"Never mind. I will be in touch."

"Thank you for coming," Gwen told the general.

"It was truly a pleasure." He winked at her, gave Rick a droll look and climbed back into the truck with Grange. They disappeared over the border. Rick stood staring after the truck with mixed feelings. Then he turned, said goodbye to the border agent and walked back to his truck with Gwen.

* * *

Rick kept to himself for the next couple of days. Gwen didn't intrude. She knew that he was dealing with some emotional issues that he had to resolve in his own mind.

Meanwhile, she went on interviews with neighbors of the murdered college freshman, the case she'd been assigned to as lead detective.

"Did she have any close friends that you know of?" she asked the third neighbor, an elderly woman who seemed to have a whole roomful of cats. They were clean, brushed, well fed and there was no odor, so she must be taking excellent care of them.

"Oh, you've noticed the cats?" the woman asked her with a grin that made her seem years younger. "I'm babysitting."

Gwen blinked. "Excuse me?"

"Babysitting. I have four neighbors with cats, and we've had a problem with animals disappearing around here. So they leave their cats with me while they're at work, and I feed them. It's a nice little windfall for me, since I'm disabled, and the owners have emotional security since they don't have to worry about their furry 'families' going missing."

Gwen laughed. "Impressive."

"Thanks. I love animals. I wish I could afford to keep a cat, but I can't. This is the next best thing."

Gwen noted several pill bottles on the end table by the elderly lady's recliner.

"By the time I pay for all those out of my social security check," she told Gwen, "there's not much left over for bills and food."

Gwen winced. "That's not right."

The woman sighed. "The economy is terrible. I expect something awful will have to happen to finally set things right." She looked at Gwen over her glasses. "I don't expect to still be around then. But if aliens exist, and they want somebody to experiment on…" She raised her hand. "I'm ready to go. To some nice, green planet with lots of meadows and trees and no greedy humans destroying it all for a quick profit."

"You and I would get along," Gwen said with a smile.

The woman nodded. "Now, back to my neighbor. I do keep a watch on the apartment complex, mostly to try to protect myself. I can't fight off an intruder and I don't own a gun. So I make sure I know who belongs here and who doesn't." Her eyes narrowed. "There was a grimy young man with greasy hair who kept coming to see the college girl. She was trying to be nice, you could tell from her expression, but she never let him inside. Once, the last time he came, the police went to her apartment and stayed for several minutes."

Gwen's heart jumped. If there had been police presence, there would be a report, with details of the conversation. She jotted that down on her phone app, making virtual notes.

"That thing is neat," the elderly lady said. "One of my cat-owning friends has one. He can surf the net on it, buy groceries, books, all sorts of things. I never realized we had such things in the modern world. I suppose I live in the past."

Gwen made a mental note to make sure this nice lady got a phone and several phone cards for Christmas, from an anonymous source. It would revolutionize her life.

"Yes, they are quite nice," Gwen said. She smiled. "Thanks for talking to me. You've been a very big help."

"It was my pleasure. I know you young folks don't

have much free time, but if you're ever at a loose end, you can come and see me and I'll tell you about the FBI in the seventies."

Gwen stared at her.

"I was a federal agent," the woman told her. "One of the first women in the bureau."

"I would love to hear some stories about those days," Gwen told her. "And I'll make time."

The wrinkled face lit up. "Thank you!"

"No, thank you. I'm fond of pioneers," she replied.

She told Rick about the elderly woman.

"Yes, Evelyn Dorsey." He nodded, smiling. "She's something of a legend over at the FBI field office. Garon Grier goes to see her from time to time." He was the SAC, the special agent in charge, at the San Antonio Field Office now. "She shot it out with a gang of would-be kidnappers right over on the 410 Loop. Hit two of them before they shot her, almost fatally, and escaped. But she had a description of the car, right down to the license plate number, and she managed to get it out on the radio before she passed out. They nabbed the perps ten miles away. Back in those days, the radio was in the car, not on a belt. It was harder to be in law enforcement."

"I expect so. Ms. Dorsey was very helpful on our college freshman case, by the way. We did have a patrol unit respond to the freshman's call. I'm tracking down the officer who filed the report now."

"I hope we can catch the guy," he replied.

"The cold case unit wants him very badly. They think he's connected to the old case they're working on," she said. "One of those detectives was related to the victim in it."

"Sad."

"Yes." She moved closer to the desk. "You doing okay?"

He grimaced. "No," he said, with a faint smile.

"Why don't you come over and watch the *Twilight* movies with me tonight? We can order a pizza."

He cocked his head and the smile grew. "You know, that sounds like a very good idea."

She grinned. "Glad you think so. I like mushrooms and cheese and pepperoni."

His eyebrows lifted. "Have you been checking out my profile?"

"No. Why?"

"That's my favorite."

She beamed. "Another thing in common."

"We'll find more, I think."

"Yes."

Rick wasn't comfortable with so-called chick flicks, but he was drawn into the movie almost at once. He barely noticed when the pizza delivery girl showed up, and only lifted his hand for the plate and coffee cup without taking his eyes off the screen.

Gwen was delighted. It was her favorite film. She kicked off her shoes and curled up beside him on the sofa to watch it again, sipping coffee and munching pizza in a contented silence. It was amazing, she thought, how comfortable they were with each other, even at this early stage of their relationship.

He glanced at her while the vampire was showing off his skills to the heroine on the screen. "You're right. This is very good."

"So are the books. I love all of them."

"I guess I'll have to buy them. It isn't often you find so many likable people in a story chain."

She sipped coffee. "You know, I hadn't thought of it that way, but you're right. Even the vampires are likable."

"Odd, isn't it? Likable monsters."

"But they aren't really monsters. They're just misunderstood living-challenged people."

He burst out laughing.

"More pizza?" she asked.

"I think I could hold one more slice."

"Me, too." She jumped up and went to get it.

After they finished eating, she curled up against him through the heroine's introduction to her boyfriend's family, the baseball game in the rain, the arrival of the more dangerous vampires, the heroine's brush with death and, finally, her appearance at the prom in a cast with her boyfriend.

"That was a roller coaster ride," he remarked. "Are there more?"

"Two more. Want to watch the next one?"

He turned toward her, his dark eyes on her radiant face. He pursed his lips. "Yes, I would. But not right now." He pulled her across his lap. "I'm suffering from affection deprivation. Do you think you could assist me?"

"Could I!" she whispered as his mouth came down on hers.

Each kiss became harder, more urgent. As they grew accustomed to the feel and taste of each other, the pleasure grew and it became more difficult to pull back.

He actually groaned when he found himself lying over her with half their clothes out of the way, just like before. He buried his face in her warm, frantically pulsing throat.

"I'm dying," he ground out.

"Me, too," she whispered back, shivering.

He lifted his head. His eyes were tormented. "How do you feel about marriage?"

She blinked.

He realized that he, the most non-impulsive man on earth, was doing something totally out of character. But he was already crazy about Gwen and the lieutenant was lurking. Even Machado had been giving her long looks. He didn't want her to end up with some other man while he was waiting for the right moment to do something. And besides, he was traditional, so was she, and there was this incredible, almost unbelievable physical compatibility.

He sighed. "Look, we get along very well. We're incredibly suited physically. We have similar jobs, outlooks on life, philosophies, and we're on the same social level. Why don't we drive over the border and get married? Right now. Afterward," he added with a speaking glance, "we can do what we're both dying to do without lingering feelings of guilt."

Her lips parted. She should have challenged that social level comparison immediately, but her body was on fire and all she could think of was relief. She loved him. He was at least fond of her. They both wanted kids. It would work. She would make it work.

"Yes," she blurted out.

He forced himself to get up and he pulled out his cell phone, scrolled down a list of names and punched in a button. "Yes. Ramirez? Sorry to call so late. Can you get

me a direct line to the general? I need his help on a—"
he glanced at Gwen "—personal matter."

Ramirez sighed. "All right. But you owe me one."

"Yes, I do."

There was a pause, another pause. Rick motioned
Gwen for a pencil and paper. He wrote down a number. "Thanks!" he told Ramirez, and hung up. He dialed the number.

"Yes, it's your—" he hesitated "—your son. How do
you feel about giving away the bride at a Mexican wedding? Oh, in about thirty minutes."

There was a burst of Spanish from the other end of
the line. Rick replied in the same language, protesting
that he wasn't up to anything immoral, he was trying to
make sure everything was done properly and that meant
a proper wedding. The general seemed to calm down.
Another hesitation. Rick grinned.

"Thanks," he said, and hung up. He turned to Gwen
and pursed his lips. "Do you have a white dress?"

"Do I have a white dress!" she exclaimed, and ran
into the next room to put it on.

She left her hair long. The dress was close-fitting,
with puffy sleeves and a draped beaded shawl. She
looked young and very innocent. And most incredibly
sexy.

Rick's body reacted to her visibly. He cleared his
throat. "Don't notice that," he said curtly.

"Oh. Okay." She giggled as she joined him and looked
up into his dark eyes. "Are you sure?" she asked hesitantly.

He framed her face in his hands and kissed her with
breathless tenderness. "I don't know why, but I've never
been so sure of anything. No cold feet?"

She shook her head. Her eyes were full of dreams. "Oh, no. Not at all."

He smiled. "Same here. We can share ammunition, too, so it will be cost effective to get married."

She burst out laughing. "I'll be sure to tell my father that when I explain why I didn't invite him to the ceremony."

He grimaced. "I'll have to do the same for my mother. But we don't have time to get them all together. We're eloping."

"Your father will have to be the audience," she said.

"My father." He smiled. "Let's go."

The general was waiting for them at the border. They followed him down a long dusty road to a small village and stopped in front of a mission church with a shiny new bell.

"I donated the bell," the general informed them proudly. "They are good people here, and the priest is a nice young man, from the United States." He hesitated, glancing from one to the other. "I did not think to ask which religious denomination...?"

"Catholic." They both spoke at once, stared at each other, and then burst out laughing.

"We hadn't discussed it before," Rick said.

"Well, it will be good," the general said with a big smile. "Come, the priest is waiting. You two, you're sure about this?"

Gwen looked at Rick with her heart in her eyes. "Very."

"Very, very," Rick added, his dark eyes shining.

"Then we shall proceed."

The general took Gwen down the aisle of the church

on his arm. The whole village came to watch, including a number of small children who seemed to find the blonde lady's hair fascinating.

The priest smiled benevolently, read the marriage service. Then they came to the part about a ring.

Rick turned white. "Oh, no."

The general punched him. "Here. I remember everything." He handed him a small circle of gold that looked just right for Gwen's hand. "Something old. It belonged to my *abuela,*" he added, "my grandmother." He smiled. "She would want it to stay in the family."

"It's beautiful," Gwen whispered. "Thank you."

The general nodded. Rick took the small circle of gold and slid it gently onto Gwen's finger, where it was a perfect fit. The priest pronounced them man and wife, and Rick bent to kiss her. And they were married.

Neither of them remembered much about the rest of the evening. Back at Gwen's apartment, there was a feverish removal of cotton and lace, followed by an incredibly long session in bed that left them both covered in sweat, boneless with pleasure and totally exhausted.

Not that exhaustion stopped them. As soon as they were breathing normally again, they reached for each other, and started all over.

"You know, it never occurred to me that marriage would be so much fun," Rick commented when they were finally sleepy.

Gwen, curled up against him, warm and satisfied, laughed softly. "Me, either. I always thought of it as something a little more dignified. You know, for children and..." She stopped.

He turned and looked down at her guilty face. "Hey. You want kids. I want kids. What's the problem?"

She relaxed. "You make it seem so simple."

"It is simple. Two people fall in love, get married and have a family." His eyes were on fire with his feelings. "We'll grow old together. But not right away. Maybe not at all," he added worriedly, "when my mother realizes that I got married without even telling her."

"My dad is going to go ballistic, too," she replied. "But he couldn't have come even if I'd had time to ask him. He's tied up with military stuff right now."

"Is he on active duty?"

"Oh, yes," she said, and there was another worry. She still had to tell Rick who her dad was, and all about the family he'd married into. That might be a source of discord. So she wasn't about to face it tonight.

She curled up close and wound her arms around him. "For a guy who never indulged, you're very good."

He laughed. "Compliment returned." He hugged her close. "They said it comes naturally. I guess it does. Of course, there were all these books I read. For educational purposes only."

She grinned. "I read a few of those, too."

He bent and brushed his mouth gently over hers. "I'm glad we waited," he said seriously, searching her eyes. "I know we're out of step with the world. But I don't care. This was right for us."

"Yes, it was. Thank you for having enough restraint," she added. "We couldn't have counted on me for it. I was on fire!"

"So was I. But I was thinking about later, generations later, when we tell our grandchildren and great-grandchildren about how it was when we fell in love and got married." He closed his eyes. "It's a golden memory. Not a legalization of something that had gone on before."

She pressed her mouth into his warm, muscular shoulder with a smile. "And the nicest thing is that you're already my best friend."

"You're mine, too." He kissed her hair. "Go to sleep. We'll get up tomorrow and face the music."

"What?"

"I was just thinking," he mused, "that the lieutenant is going to foam at the mouth when we tell him."

"What?" she exclaimed.

"Just a hunch." He thought the lieutenant had a case on Gwen. Maybe, maybe not. But he was expecting fireworks the next day.

Chapter 9

"Fireworks" was, if anything, an understatement.

"You're married?" Lieutenant Hollister exclaimed.

Gwen moved a little closer to Rick. "Yes. Sorry, we would have invited you, but we didn't want the expense of a big wedding, so we eloped," she told him, stretching the truth.

"Eloped." Hollister leaned back in his chair with a grumpy sigh. He glared at Marquez. "Well, it was certainly quick."

"We knew how we felt at once," Rick replied with a smile at his wife. "No sense having a long engagement."

She smiled back. "Absolutely."

"Well, congratulations," Hollister said after a minute. He got up, smiled and shook hands with both of them. "How did your mother take it?" he asked Rick.

Rick grimaced. "Haven't told her."

"Why don't you two take the day off and call it a honeymoon," Hollister suggested. "Gail Rogers can sub for you," he told Rick. "I don't want Barbara coming after me with a bazooka because she heard the news from somebody else."

"Good idea," Rick said. "Thanks!"

"My pleasure. A wedding present. A short one," he added. "You have to be back on the job tomorrow. And when are we losing you?" he asked Gwen.

She wasn't sure what he meant, and then she realized that she belonged to a federal agency. "I'm not sure. I'll have to talk to my boss and he'll have to discuss it with the captain here."

Hollister nodded. "You've done very well. I'll be sorry to lose you."

She smiled. "I'll be sorry to go. I may have to make some minor adjustments in my career path, as well," she added with a worried glance at Rick. "I don't really want to keep a job that sends me around the world every other week. Not now."

Hollister pursed his lips. "We can always use another detective," he pointed out. "You'd pick it back up in no time, and we have all sorts of workshops and training courses."

She beamed. "You mean it?"

"Of course," he assured her.

"Wait a minute, you'd give up working for the feds, for me?" Rick asked, as if he couldn't quite believe it.

"I would," she said solemnly. "I'm tired of living out of a suitcase. And I really like San Antonio." She didn't add that she was also very tired of the D.C. social scene and being required to hostess parties for her dad. It was never enjoyable. She didn't like crowds or parties. To give him his due, neither did her father. But he was certainly going to be in the center of the Washington social whirl very soon. She dreaded having to tell Rick about it.

"Well," Rick said, and couldn't resist a charming smile.

She laughed. "And now for the really hard part. We have to break the news to your mother."

"She'll kill me," he groaned.

"No. We'll take her a pot of flowers," Gwen said firmly. "She's a gardener. I know she wouldn't mind a bribe that she could plant."

They all laughed.

And actually, Barbara wasn't mad. She burst into tears, hugged them both and rambled on for several minutes about how depressed she'd been that women never seemed to see Rick as a potential mate as much as a shoulder to cry on.

"I'm just so happy!"

"I'm so glad," Gwen enthused. "But we still brought you a bribe."

"A bribe?" Barbara asked, wiping away tears.

Gwen went onto the porch and came back inside carrying a huge potted plant.

"It's an umbrella plant!" Barbara exclaimed. "I've wanted one for years, but I could never find one the right size. It's perfect!"

"I thought you could plant it," Gwen said.

"Oh, no, I'll let it live inside. I'll put grow lights around it and fertilize it and…" She hesitated. "You two didn't have to get married?"

They howled.

"She's as Victorian as we are," Rick told his mother with a warm smile.

"That's wonderful! Welcome to the stone age, my dear!" she told Gwen and hugged her, hard.

"Where are you going to live? In San Antonio?" Barbara asked, resigned.

Gwen and Rick had discussed this. "The old Andrews place is up for sale, right in downtown Jacobsville," Rick said, "next door to the Griers. In fact, I put in an offer for it this morning."

"Oh!" Barbara started crying again. "I thought you'd want to live where your jobs are."

Explanation about Gwen's job could come later, Rick decided. "We want to live near you," Rick replied.

"Because when the kids come along," Gwen added with a grin, "you'll want to be able to see them."

Barbara felt her forehead. "Maybe I'm feverish. You want to have kids?"

"Oh, yes," Gwen replied, smiling.

"Lots of kids," Rick added.

"I can buy a toy store," Barbara murmured to herself. "But first I need to stock up on organic seeds, so that I can make healthy stuff for the baby."

"We just got married yesterday," Rick pointed out.

"That's right, and this is November." She went looking for a calendar. "And nine months from now is harvest season!" she called back.

Rick and Gwen shook their heads.

They stayed for supper, a delicious affair, and then settled down to watch the news. Gwen, sitting contentedly beside her husband, had no warning of what was about to happen.

A newscaster smiled as a picture of a four-star general, very well-known to the public, was splashed across the screen. "And this just in. Amid rumors that he was retiring or resigning from the service, we have just learned that General David Cassaway, former U.S. Commander in Iraq, has been named director of the Central Intelligence Agency. General Cassaway, a former covert ops commander, has commanded American troops in Iraq for the past two years. He was rumored to be retiring from the military, but it seems that he was only considering a new job."

Barbara glanced at Gwen. "Why, what a coincidence. That's your last name."

The newscaster was adding, "General Cassaway's only son, Larry, died in a classified operation in the Middle East just a few months ago. We wish General Cassaway the best of luck in his new position. Now for other news…"

Rick was staring at Gwen as if she'd grown horns. "Your brother's name was Larry, wasn't it?" he asked. "The one who was killed in action?"

Barbara was staring. So was Rick.

Gwen took a deep breath. "He's my father," she confessed.

Rick wasn't handling this well. "Your father is the new head of the CIA?"

"Well, sort of," she said, nodding worriedly.

Rick knew about Washington society from people in his department who had to deal with the socialites in D.C. He was certain that there were no poor generals in the military, and the head of the CIA would certainly not be in line for food stamps.

"What sort of place do you live in, when you go home?" Rick asked very quietly.

Gwen sighed. "We have a big house in Maryland, on

several acres of land. My dad likes horses. He raises, well, thoroughbreds." She was almost cringing by now.

"And drives a...?"

She swallowed. "Jaguar."

Rick got up and turned away with an exasperated sigh. "Why didn't you tell me?"

"Because I was afraid you'd do just what you're doing now," Gwen moaned. "Judging me by the company I keep. I hate parties. I hate receptions. I hate hostessing! I'm perfectly happy working a federal job, or a police job, any sort of job that doesn't require me to put on an evening gown and look rich!"

"Rich." Rick ran his fingers through his hair.

"I'm not rich," she pointed out.

"But your father is."

She grimaced. "He was born into one of the founding families. He went to Harvard, and then to West Point," she said. "But he's just a regular person. He doesn't put on airs."

"Sure."

"Rick—" she got up and went to him "—I'm not my family. I don't have money. I work for my living. For heaven's sake, this suit is a year old!"

He turned around. His face was hard. "My suit is three years old," he said stiffly. "I drive a pickup truck. I can barely afford tickets to the theater."

She gave him a strained look. "You'll get used to this," she promised him. "It will just take a little time. You've had one too many upsets in the past few weeks."

He sighed heavily. "We should have waited to get married," he ground out.

"No," she returned. "If we'd waited and you'd found out, you'd never have married me at all."

Before Rick could open his mouth and destroy his future, Barbara got up and stood between them. "She's right," she told her son. "You need to stop before you say something you'll regret. Let Gwen go home for tonight, and you sleep on it. Things will look better in the morning." She went to get her cell phone and dialed a number. She waited until the call was answered. "Cash? Gwen Cassaway's going back to San Antonio for the night and I don't want her driving up there alone, do you have someone who can take her?"

"No…!" Gwen protested.

Barbara held up a hand. She grinned. "I thought you might. Thanks! I owe you a nice apple pie." She hung up. "One of Cash's men lives in San Antonio and he's on his way home. He'll swing by and give you a lift. He won't mind, and he's very nice. His name is Carlton Ames. He'll take good care of you."

Rick was cursing himself for not letting Gwen drive her car down instead of insisting that she come with him. He didn't like the idea of her riding with another man. They were married. At least, temporarily.

"Go home and don't worry," Barbara said, hugging her. "It will be all right."

Gwen managed a smile. She looked at Rick, but he wouldn't meet her eyes. She drew in a long breath and put on her coat and picked up her purse. She walked out to the front porch with Barbara, who closed the door behind them.

"He's still upset about meeting his father," Barbara said gently. "He'll get over this. You just get a good night's sleep and don't worry. It will work out. I'm so happy he married you!" She hugged the younger woman again. "You're going to be very happy together once he gets over the shock."

"I hope you're right. I should have told him. I was afraid to."

"Have you talked to your father?"

She shook her head. "I have to do that tonight." She grimaced. "He's not going to be happy, either."

"Does he have prejudices...?" Barbara worried at once.

Gwen laughed. "Heavens, no! Dad doesn't see color or race or religion. He's very liberal. No, he'll be hurt that I didn't tell him first."

"That's all right then. You'll make it up with him. And with Rick. Oh, there's Carlton!"

She waved as an off-duty police car pulled up at the porch. A nice young man got out and smiled. "I'm going to have company for the ride, I hear?" he asked.

"Yes, this is my new daughter-in-law, Gwen." Barbara introduced them. "That's Carlton," she added with a grin. "She didn't drive her own car and she has to get back to San Antonio to pick it up. Thanks for giving her a ride."

"Should I follow you back down here, then?" he offered.

Gwen shook her head. "I have things to get together in my apartment. But thanks."

"No problem. Shall we go?"

Gwen looked toward the porch, but the door was still closed. She saw Barbara wince. She managed a smile. "I'll see you later, then," she said. "Have a good night."

"You, too, dear," Barbara said. She forced a smile. "Good night."

She watched them leave. Then she went back in the house and closed the door. "Rick?"

He was on the phone. She wondered who he could be calling at this hour of the night. Perhaps it was work.

He hung up and came into the living room, looking more unapproachable than she'd ever seen him. "I'm going for a drive. I won't be long."

"She was very upset," she said gently. "She can't help who her father is, any more than you can."

He looked torn. "I know that. But she should have told me."

"I think she was afraid to. She's very much in love, you know."

He flushed and looked away. "I won't be long."

She watched him go, feeling a new and bitter distance between them, something she'd never felt before. She hoped they could work things out. She liked Gwen a lot.

Rick pulled up to the country bar, locked the truck and walked inside. It was late and there were only a couple of cowboys sitting in booths. A man in the back motioned to Rick, who walked down the aisle to sit across from him.

The older man gave him an amused smile. "Should I be flattered that you called me when you needed sympathy? Why not talk to your mother?"

Rick sighed. "It's not really something a woman would understand," he muttered.

General Machado pursed his lips. "No? Perhaps not." He motioned to the waiter, who came over at once, grinning. "Coffee for my young friend, please."

"At once!"

Rick's eyebrows arched at the man's quick manner.

"He wants to go and help liberate my country," Machado told Rick with a grin. "I have the ability to inspire revolutions."

"I noticed," Rick said dryly.

General Emilio Machado leaned back against the booth, studying the young man who looked so much like himself. "You know, we do favor each other."

"A bit."

The waiter came back with the coffee, placing a mug in front of Rick, along with small containers of cream and sugar, and a spoon. "Anything else for you, sir?" he asked the general with respect.

"No, that will do for now, thank you."

"A pleasure! If you need anything, just call."

"I will."

The waiter scampered away. Machado watched Rick sip hot coffee. "Just married, and already you quarrel?"

"She lied to me. Well, she lied by omission," he corrected coolly.

"About what?"

"It turns out that her father is the new head of the CIA."

"Ah, yes, General Cassaway. He and Grange are friends."

Rick recalled an odd conversation that Gwen and Grange had shared at the first meeting with Machado at the border. It had puzzled him at the time. Now he knew that she had been cautioning Grange not to give away her identity. It made him even sadder.

"He's rich," Rick said curtly.

"And you are not." Machado understood the problem. "Does it matter so much, if you care for the woman?

What if it was your mother who was wealthy, and her father who was poor?"

He shifted restlessly. "I don't know."

"But of course you do. You would not care."

Rick sipped more coffee. He was losing the argument.

Machado toyed with his own cup. "I was a millionaire, in my country," he confided. "I had everything a man could possibly want, right down to a Rolls-Royce and a private helicopter. Perhaps I had too much, and God resented the fact that I spent more money on me than I did on the poor villagers who were being displaced and murdered by my underling's minions as he worked to bring in foreign oil corporations. The oil and natural gas are quite valuable, and the villagers considered them a nuisance that interfered with the fishing." He smiled. "They have no interest in great wealth. They live from day to day, quietly, with no clocks, no supermarkets, no strip malls. Perhaps they have the right idea, and the rest of the world has gone insane from this disease called civilization."

Rick smiled back. "It would be a less hectic life."

"Yes, indeed." His dark eyes were thoughtful. "I was careless. I will never be careless again. And the man who usurped my place and made my people suffer will pay a very high price for his arrogance and greed, I promise you." The look on his face gave Rick cold chills.

"We've heard what he did to private citizens," Rick agreed.

"That is my fault. I should have listened. A…friend of mine, an archaeologist, tried to warn me about what his people were doing to the native tribes. I thought she was overstating, trying to get me to clamp down on foreign interests in the name of preserving archaeological treasures."

"A female archaeologist?"

He chuckled. "There are many these days. Yes, she taught at a small college in the United States. She was visiting my country when she stumbled onto a find so amazing that she hesitated to even announce it before she had time to substantiate her claim with evidence." His face hardened. "There was gossip that they put her in prison. I shudder to think what might have been done to her. That will be on my soul forever, if she was harmed."

"Maybe she escaped," Rick said, trying to find something comforting to say. "Rumors and gossip are usually pretty far off the mark."

"You think so?" Machado's dark eyes were sad but hopeful.

"Anything is possible."

Machado sighed. "I suppose."

The waiter came scurrying up looking worried. "El General, there is a police car coming this way," he said excitedly.

Machado looked at Rick.

"I'm not involved in any attempts to kidnap or arrest you," he said dryly.

"Is the car local?" Machado asked.

"Yes. It is a Jacobsville police car."

Machado weighed his options. While he was trying to decide whether to make a break out the back door, a tall, imposing man in a police uniform with large dark eyes and his long hair in a ponytail came in the door, looked around and spotted Rick with the general.

Rick relaxed. "It's all right," he said. "That's Cash Grier."

"You know him?"

"Yes. He's our police chief. He's a good man. Used to be a government assassin, or that's the rumor," Rick mused.

Machado laughed under his breath.

Cash walked over to their table. He wasn't smiling. "I'm afraid I have some bad news."

"You're here to arrest me?" Machado asked dryly.

Cash glanced at him. "Have you broken the law?" he asked curiously. It was obvious that he didn't recognize the bar's famous patron.

"Not lately," Machado lied.

Cash looked back at Rick, who was going tense.

"Gwen," he burst out.

Cash grimaced. "I'm afraid so. There's been a wreck…"

Rick was out of the booth in a flash. "How badly is she hurt?" he asked at once, white-faced. "Is she all right?"

"They've transported her and Ames to Jacobsville General," he said quietly. "Ames is pretty bad. Ms. Cassaway has at the very least a broken rib…!" Rick was already out of the bar, running for his truck.

"Wait! I'm coming with you!" Machado called after him, and stopped just long enough to pay the waiter, who bowed respectfully.

Cash, confused by the two men, got back in his patrol car and followed the pickup truck down the long road to the hospital. To his credit, he didn't pull out his ticket book when he pulled in behind Rick at the emergency entrance.

"My wife, Gwen Cassaway," Rick told the clerk at the desk. "They just brought her in."

The clerk studied him. "Oh, that's you, Detective Marquez," she said, smiling. "Yes, and she's your wife? Congratulations! Yes, she's in X-ray right now. Dr. Coltrain is treating her…"

"Copper or Lou?" Rick asked, because the married Coltrains were both doctors.

"Lou," came the reply.

"Thanks."

"You can have a seat right over there," the clerk said gently, "and I'll have someone ask Dr. Coltrain to come see you, okay?"

Rick wanted to rush behind the counter, but he knew better. He ground his teeth together. "Okay."

"Be just a sec." The clerk picked up the phone.

"She will be all right," Machado told his son with a warm smile. "She has great courage for one so young."

Rick felt rocked to the soles of his feet. He never should have reacted as he had. He'd upset her. But… she hadn't been driving, and Ames was one of Cash's better drivers…

He turned to the police chief. "Ames wrecked the car? How?"

"That's what I'd like to know," Cash said curtly. "There was another set of tracks in the dirt nearby, as if a car had sideswiped them. I've got men tracking right now."

"If you need help, I can provide a tracker who might even excel your own," Machado offered quietly.

Cash had been sizing the other man up. He pursed his lips. "You look familiar."

"There are very few photographs of me," Machado replied.

"Yes, but we've met. I can't remember where. Maybe it will come back to me."

Machado raised an eyebrow. "It would be just as well if your memory lapses for the next few hours. My son can use the company."

"Your son?" Cash's dark eyes narrowed on the older man. "Machado."

The older man nodded and smiled.

"Gwen had a photo of you. I had to break the news to Rick's mother, about your connection to him."

"Ah, yes, that was how he was told. Ingenious." The general's expression sombered. "I hope she and the officer will be all right."

"So do I," Cash said. "I can't help being concerned about that other car."

Machado came a step closer. "The Fuentes bunch have much reason to interfere with my plans. They are being paid by my successor to spy on me. There is also a very high level mole in the DEA. I do not know who it is," he added. "But even I am aware of him."

"Damn," Cash muttered.

"Yes, things are quite complicated. I did not mean to involve the children in my war," he added, with a rueful glance at Rick, who was pacing the floor.

"No parent would. Sometimes fate intervenes. Her father should be told."

"Yes," Machado replied. "He should." He excused himself and spoke to Rick.

"Her father." Rick groaned. "How am I going to find him?"

Machado grinned. "I think I can solve that problem." He pulled out his disposable cell phone, one of many, and dialed a number. "Grange? Yes. Gwen has been injured in an automobile accident. I need you to call her father and tell him. We don't know details yet. She has at least a broken rib. The rest we don't know...but he should come."

There was a pause. "Yes. Thank you. She is at the Jacobsville hospital. Yes. All right." He hung up. "Grange and her father are friends. He will make the call."

Rick averted his eyes. "Hell of a way to meet in-laws," he muttered.

"I do agree," Machado said. He put an affectionate arm around his son's neck. "But you will get through it. Come. Sit down and stop pacing, before you wear a hole in the floor."

Rick allowed himself to be led to a chair. It was kind of nice, having a father.

Dr. Louise Coltrain came into the room in her white lab coat, smiling. She was introduced to Gwen's husband and father-in-law with some surprise, because no one locally knew about the wedding.

"Congratulations," she told Rick. "She'll be all right," she added quickly. "She does have a broken rib, but the other injuries are mostly bruises. Patrolman Ames has a head injury," she told Cash. "His prognosis is going to be trickier. I'm having him airlifted to San Antonio, to the Marshall Center. He's holding his own so far, though. Do you have a way to notify his family?"

Cash shook his head. "He doesn't have any family that I'm aware of. Just me," he added with a grim smile. "So I'm the one to notify."

She nodded. "I'll keep you in the loop. Detective Marquez, you can see your wife now. I'll take you back..."

"Where the hell is my daughter?"

Rick felt a shiver go down his spine. That voice, deep and cold with authority, froze everyone in the waiting room. Rick turned to find the face that went with it, and understood at once how this man had risen to become a four-star general. He was in full uniform, every button polished, his hat at the perfect angle, his hard face almost bristling with antagonism, his black eyes glittering with it.

"And who's responsible for putting her in the hospital?" he added in a tone that was only a little less intimidating.

While Rick was working on an answer, Barbara came in the door, worried and unsettled by his call. She paused beside the military man who was raising Cain in the waiting room.

"My goodness, someone had his razor blade soup this morning, I see!" she exclaimed with pure hostility. "Now you calm down and stop shouting at people. This is a hospital, not a military installation!"

Chapter 10

General Cassaway turned and looked down at the willowy blonde woman who was glaring up at him.

"Who the hell are you?" he demanded.

"The woman who's going to have you arrested if you don't calm down," she replied. "Rick, how is she?" she asked, holding out her arms.

Rick came and held her close. "Broken rib," he said. "And some bruising. She'll be all right."

"Who are you?" General Cassaway demanded.

Rick turned. "I'm Gwen's husband. Detective Sergeant Rick Marquez," he said coldly, not backing down an inch.

"Her husband?"

"Yes. And he's my son," Barbara added.

"And also my son," General Machado said, joining them. He smiled at Barbara, who smiled back.

"You two are married?" Cassaway asked.

Barbara laughed. "No. He's much too young for me," she said.

Machado gave her an amused look. "I do like older women," he admitted.

She just shook her head.

"I want to see my daughter," Cassaway told Lou Coltrain.

"Of course. Come this way. You, too, Rick."

Cassaway was surprised at the first name basis.

"We all know each other here," Lou told him. "I'm a newcomer, so to speak, but my husband is from here. He's known Rick since Barbara adopted him."

"I see."

Gwen was heavily sedated, but her eyes opened and she brightened when she saw her husband and her father walk into the recovery room.

"Dad! Rick!"

Rick went on one side to take a hand, her father on the other.

"I'm so sorry," she began.

"Don't be absurd." Rick kissed her forehead. "I was an idiot. I'm sorry! I never should have let you go with Ames."

"Ames! How is he?" she asked. "The other car came out of nowhere! We didn't even see it until it hit us. There were three men in it..."

"Did you recognize any of them?"

"No," she replied. "But it could have been Fuentes. The last of the living brothers, the drug lords."

"By God, I'll have them hunted down like rats," Cassaway said icily.

"My father will beat you to it," Rick replied coolly.

"Just who is your father?" Cassaway asked suddenly. "He looks very familiar."

"General Emilio Machado," Rick said, and with a hint of pride that reflected in the tilt of his chin.

Cassaway pursed his lips. "Grange's boss. Yes, we know about that upcoming operation. We can't be involved, of course."

"Of course," Rick replied with twinkling eyes.

"But we are rooting for the good guys," came the amused comment.

Rick chuckled.

"So you're married," Cassaway said. He shook his head. "Your mother would have loved seeing you married." He winced. "I would have, too."

"I'm so sorry," she said. "But I hadn't told Rick who you were." She bit her lip.

"What did that have to do with anything?" the older man asked, puzzled.

"I'm a city detective," Rick said sardonically. "I wear three-year-old suits and I drive a pickup truck."

"Hell, I drive a pickup truck, too," the general said, shrugging. "So what?"

Rick liked the man already. He grinned.

"See?" Gwen asked her husband. "I told you he wasn't what you thought."

"Snob," the general said, glaring at Rick. "I don't pick my friends for their bank accounts."

"Sorry," Rick said. "I didn't know you."

"You'll get there, son."

"Congratulations on the appointment," Rick said.

The general shrugged. "I don't know how long I'll last. I don't kiss butt, if you know what I mean, and I say what I think. Not very popular to speak your mind sometimes."

"I think honesty never goes out of style, and has value," Rick replied.

The general's eyes twinkled. "You did good," he told his daughter.

She just smiled.

Out in the waiting room, Cash Grier was talking on the phone to someone in San Antonio while the general thumbed through a magazine. Barbara paced, worried. Gwen's father was a hard case. She hoped he and Rick would learn to get along.

Cash closed his flip phone grimly. "They found a car, abandoned, a few miles outside of Comanche Wells," he said. "We can't say for sure that it's the one that hit Ames, but it has black paint on the fender, and Ames's car is black. We ran wants and warrants on it—it was stolen."

"Fuentes," Machado said quietly. His dark eyes narrowed. "I have had just about enough of him. I think he will have to meet with a similar accident soon."

"I didn't hear you say that," Cash told him.

"Did I say something?" Machado asked. "Why, I was simply voicing a prediction."

"Terroristic threats and acts," he said, waving a finger at Machado. "And I'm conveniently forgetting your connection with the Pendleton kidnapping for the next hour or so. After that," he added with pursed lips, "things could get interesting here."

Machado grinned. "I will be long gone by then. My son needed me."

Cash smiled. "I have a daughter," he said. "She's

going on three years old. Red hair and green eyes and a temper worse than mine."

"I would like to have known my son when he was small," Machado said sadly. "I did not know about him. Dolores kept her secret all the way to the grave. A pity."

"It was nice for me, that you didn't know," Barbara said gently. "When I adopted him, he gave me a reason to live." She stood up. "Do you think things happen for a reason?" she asked philosophically.

"Yes, I do," Machado replied with a smile. "Perhaps fate had a hand in all this."

"Well, I suppose…" she began.

"I have to get back home," General Cassaway was saying as he walked out with Rick. "But it's been a pleasure meeting you, son." He shook hands with Rick.

"Same here," Rick told him. "I'll take better care of your daughter from now on. And I won't be so inflexible next time she springs a surprise on me," he added with a laugh.

"See that you aren't. Remember what I do for a living now," he told the younger man with a grin. "I can find you anywhere, anytime."

"Yes, sir," Rick replied.

The general turned to Machado. "And you'd better hightail it out of Mexico pretty soon," he said in a confidential tone. "Things are going to heat up in Sonora. A storm's coming. You don't want to be in its way."

Machado nodded. "Thank you."

"Oh, I have ulterior motives," Cassaway assured him. "I want that rat out of Barrera before he turns your country into the world's largest cocaine distribution center."

"So do I," Machado replied quietly. "I promise you, his days of power will soon come to an end."

"Wish I could help," Cassaway told him. "But I think you have enough intel and mercs to do the job."

"Including a friend of yours," Machado replied, smiling.

"A very good one. He'll get the job done." He shook hands with Machado. Then he turned to Barbara. "You've got a smart mouth on you."

She glared at him. "And you've got a sharp tongue on you."

He smiled. "I like pepper."

She shifted. "Me, too."

"She's a great cook," Rick said, sliding his arm around her shoulders. "She owns the local café here, and does most of the cooking for it."

"Really! I'm something of a chef myself," Cassaway replied. "I grow my own vegetables and I get a local grandmother to come over and help me can every summer."

Barbara moved closer. "I can, too. I like to dry herbs as well."

"Now I've got a herb garden of my own," the general said. "But it isn't doing as well as I'd like."

"Do you have a composter?" Barbara asked.

His eyebrows lifted. "A what?"

"A composter, for organic waste from the kitchen." She went on to explain to him how it worked and what you did with it.

"A fellow gardener," Cassaway said with a beaming smile. "What a surprise! So few women garden these days."

"Oh, we have plenty around Jacobsville who plant gardens," Barbara said. "You'll have to come and visit us next summer. I can show you how to grow corn ten feet high, even in a drought," she added.

Cassaway moved a step closer. He was huge, Barbara thought, tall and good-looking and built like a tank. He had thick black hair and black eyes and a tan complexion. Nice mouth.

Cassaway was thinking the same thing about Barbara. She was tall and willowy and very pretty.

"I might visit sooner than that," he said in a low, deep tone. "Is there a hotel?"

"Yes, but I have a big Victorian house. Rick and Gwen can stay there, too. We'll have a family reunion." She flushed a little, and laughed, and then looked at Machado. "That invitation includes you, also," she added. "If you're through with your revolution by then," she said ruefully.

"I think that is a good possibility, and I will accept the invitation," Machado said. He kissed her hand and bowed. "Thank you for taking such good care of my son."

She smiled. "He's been the joy of my life. I had no-body until Rick needed a home."

"I only have a daughter," General Cassaway said sadly. "I lost my son earlier this year to an IED, and my wife died some years ago."

"I'm so sorry," Barbara said with genuine sympathy. "I miscarried the only child I ever had. It must be terrible to lose one who's grown."

"Worse than death," Cassaway agreed. He cleared his throat and looked away. He drew in a long breath. "Well, my adjutant is doing the ants' dance, so I guess we'd better go," he said, nodding toward a young officer standing in the doorway.

"The ants' dance?" Barbara asked.

"He moves around like that when he's in a hurry to do something, like he's got ants climbing his legs. Good man, but a little testy." He shrugged. "Like me. He suits me." He shook hands with Rick. "I've heard good things about you from Grange. Your police chief over there—" he nodded toward Cash, who was talking on the phone again "—speaks highly of you."

Rick smiled. "Nice to know. I love my job. I like to think I'm good at it."

"Take care of my little girl."

"You know I will."

He paused at Barbara and looked down at her with quiet admiration. "And I'll see you later."

She grinned. "Okay!"

He nodded at the others, and walked toward the young man, who was now motioning frantically.

Cash joined them a minute later. "Sorry, I wasn't trying to be rude. I've got a man working on the hit-and-run, and I've been checking in. There was an incident at the border crossing over near Del Rio," he added. "Three men jumped a border agent, knocked him out and took off over the crossing into Mexico. We think it was the same men who ran Ames off the road."

"Great," Rick muttered. "Just great. Now we work on trying to get them extradited back to the States. That will be good for a year, even if we can get a positive identification of who they are."

Machado pursed his lips. "I would not worry about that. Such men are easy to find, for a good tracker, and equally easy to deal with."

"I didn't hear that," Cash said.

Machado chuckled. "Of course not. I was, again, making a prediction."

"Thanks for coming with me," Rick told Machado. "And for the shoulder earlier."

Machado embraced his son in a bear hug. "I will always be around, whenever you need me." He searched the younger man's face. "I am very proud to have such a man for my son."

Rick swallowed hard. "I'm proud to have such a man for my father."

Machado's eyes were suspiciously bright. He laughed suddenly. "We will both be wailing in another minute. I must go. Grange is waiting for me in the parking lot."

"I can't say anything officially," Cash told the general. "But privately, I wish you good luck."

Machado shook his hand. "Thank you, my friend. I hope your patrolman will be all right."

"So do I," Cash said.

Rick walked Machado to the door. Outside, Winslow Grange was sitting behind the wheel of Machado's pickup truck, waiting.

Machado turned to his son. "When the time comes, I will be happy to let you become my liaison with the American authorities. And it will come," he added solemnly. "My country has many resources that will appeal to outside interests. I would prefer to deal with republics or democracies rather than totalitarian states."

"A wise decision," Rick said. "And when the time comes, I'll be here."

Machado smiled. *"Que vayas con Dios, mi hijo,"* he said, using the familiar tense that was only applied to family and close friends.

It made Rick feel warm inside, that his father already

felt affection for him. He waved as the two men in the truck departed. He hoped his father wouldn't get killed in the attempt to retake Barrera. But, then, Machado was a general, and he'd won the title fairly, in many battles. He would be all right. Rick was certain of it.

Gwen came home two days later. She wore a rib belt and winced every time she moved. The lieutenant had granted her sick leave, but she was impatient to get back on the job. Rick had to make threats to keep her in bed at all, at Barbara's house.

"And I'm a burden on your poor mother," Gwen protested. "She has a business to run, and here she is bringing me food on trays…!"

"She doesn't mind," Rick assured her.

"Of course she doesn't mind," Barbara said as she brought in soup and crackers. "She's working on planning a fantastic Thanksgiving dinner in a couple of weeks. I'm going to invite your father," she told Gwen and then flushed a little. "I guess that would be all right. I don't know," she hesitated, looking around her. "He's head of the CIA and used to crystal and fine china…"

"He doesn't use the good place settings at home," Gwen said dryly. "He likes plain white ceramic plates and thick Starbucks coffee mugs and just plain fare to eat. He isn't a fancy mannered person, although he can blend into high society when he has to. He'll think of it as a welcome relief from the D.C. whirl. Which I'm happy to be out of," she added heavily. "I never liked having to hostess parties. I like working in law enforcement."

"Me, too," Rick said, smiling warmly at his wife. "I'm just sorry about what happened to you and Ames."

"Yes. Have we heard anything about Ames?"

"Cash Grier said that he regained consciousness this morning," Barbara said with a smile. "It's all coming back to him. He remembered what the men looked like. He got a better view of them than you did," she told the younger woman. "He recognized Fuentes."

"Fuentes himself?" Gwen was shocked. "Why would he do his own dirty work?"

"Fuentes knows that you're married to me, and that I'm General Machado's son," Rick said somberly. "I think he was trying to get back at the general, in a round-about way. He may have thought it was me driving. He wouldn't have known that you were with Ames."

"Yes," Barbara said worriedly. "And he may try again. You can't go anywhere alone from now on, at least until Fuentes is arrested."

"He won't be," Rick said coldly. "Dozens of policemen have tried to pin him down, nobody has succeeded. He has a hideout in the mountains and guards at every checkpoint. An undercover agent died trying to infiltrate his camp a few weeks ago. I'd love to see him behind bars. It's trying to get him there that's the problem."

"Well, your father's not too happy with him right now," Barbara remarked.

"And the general has ways and means that we don't have access to," Gwen agreed.

"True," Rick said.

"I think we may hear some good news soon about Fuentes and his bunch," Barbara said. "But for now, my main focus is getting your wife back on her feet," she told her son. "Good food and a little spoiling always does the trick."

"You're a nice mother," Rick said.

"A very nice mother and I'm so happy that you're going to be mine, too," Gwen told her with a warm smile. She shifted in the bed and groaned.

"Time for meds," Barbara said, and went out to get them.

Rick bent and kissed Gwen gently between her eyes. "You get better," he whispered. "I have erotic plans for you at some future time very soon."

She laughed, wincing, and lifted her mouth to touch his. "You aren't the only one with plans. Darn this rib!"

"Bad timing, and Fuentes's fault," Rick murmured as he brushed her mouth tenderly with his. "But we have forever."

"Yes," she whispered, beaming. "Forever."

Thanksgiving came suddenly and with, of all things, snow! Rick and Gwen walked out into the yard at Barbara's house and laughed as it piled down on the bare limbs of the trees around the fence line.

"Snow!" she exclaimed. "I didn't know it snowed in Texas!"

"Hey, it snowed in South Africa twice in August," he pointed out. "The weather is loopy."

She smiled and hugged him, still wincing a little, because her rib was tender. She was healing quickly, though. Soon, she would be whole again and ready for more amorous adventures with her new husband.

"Is your father coming down?" he asked Gwen.

"Oh, yes. He said he wouldn't miss a homemade Thanksgiving dinner for the world. He can cook, but he hates doing it on holidays, and he mostly eats out. He's very excited. And not only about the meal," she added with an impish grin. "I think he likes your mother."

"Wouldn't that be a match?" he mused.

"Yes, it would. They're both alone and about the same age. Dad's quite a guy."

"But he's head of a federal agency. He lives in D.C. and she owns a restaurant here," Rick pointed out.

"If they really want to, they'll find a way."

"I guess so." He turned to her, in the white flaky curtain, and drew her gently to his chest. "The best thing I ever did in life was marry you," he said somberly. "I may not say it a lot but I love you very much."

She caught her breath at the tenderness in his deep voice. "I love you, too," she whispered back.

He bent and drew her mouth under his, teasing the upper lip with his tongue, parting her lips so that his could cover them hungrily. He forgot everything in the flashpoint heat of desire. His arms closed around her, enveloping her so tightly that she moaned.

He heard that, and drew back at once. "Sorry," he said quickly. "I forgot!"

She laughed breathily. "It's okay. I forgot, too. Just another week or two, and I'll be in fine shape."

He lifted an eyebrow and looked down at her trim, curvy body in jeans and a tight sweater. "I'll say you're in fine shape," he murmured dryly.

"Oh, you!" She punched him lightly in the chest.

"Shapely, sexy and sweet. I'm a lucky man."

She reached up and kissed him back. "We're both lucky."

He sighed. "I suppose we should go back inside and offer to peel potatoes."

"I suppose so."

He kissed her again, smiling. "In a minute."

She sighed. "Yes. In a minute…or two…or three…"

Ten minutes later, they went back inside. Barbara gave them an amused look and handed Rick a huge pan full of potatoes and a paring knife. He sighed and got to work.

The general came with an entourage, but they were housed in the local hotel in Jacobsville. General Cassaway did allow his adjutant and a clerk to move into Barbara's house with him, with her permission of course, and he had a case full of electronic equipment that had to find living space as well.

"I have to keep in touch with everyone in my department, monitor the web, answer queries, inform the proper people at Homeland Security about my activities," the general said, rattling off his duties. "It's a great job, but it takes most of my time. That's why I've been remiss in the email department," he added with a smile at Gwen.

"I think you do very well, considering how little free time you have, Dad," she told him.

"Thanks." He dug into the dressing, closing his eyes as he savored it and the giblet gravy. "This is wonderful, Barbara."

"Thank you," she replied, with a big smile. "I love to cook."

"Me, too," Gwen added. "Barbara's teaching me how to do things properly."

"She's a quick study, too," Barbara replied, smiling at her daughter-in-law. "Her corn bread is wonderful, and I didn't teach her that…it's her own recipe. She's very talented."

"Thanks."

"What about this Fuentes character who sideswiped that car you were in?" he asked Gwen suddenly.

"Strange thing," she replied, tongue-in-cheek. "Fuentes seems to have gone missing. Nobody's seen him since the wreck."

"How very odd," the general remarked.

"Isn't it?"

"How about the young man who was driving you?" he added as he dipped his fork into potato salad.

"He's out of the hospital and back at work," Gwen said warmly. "He's going to be fine, thank goodness."

"I'm glad about that." He glanced across the table at Rick. "I understand that your father has left Mexico."

Rick smiled. "Yes, I did hear about that."

"So things are going to heat up in Barrera very soon, I would expect," the general added.

Rick nodded. "Very soon."

"No more talk of revolution," Barbara said firmly. She got to her feet with a big grin. "I have a surprise."

She went into the kitchen and came back in with a huge coconut cream pie. She put it on the table.

"Is that...?"

"Coconut cream." Barbara nodded. "I heard that it's someone's favorite."

"Mine!" General Cassaway said. "Thanks!"

"My pleasure." She cut it into slices and put one on a saucer for him. "If you still have room after all that turkey and dressing..."

"I'll make room," he said with such fervor that everyone laughed.

The general stayed for two days. Rick and Gwen and Barbara drove him around Jacobsville and introduced him to people. He fit in as if he'd been born there. He was coming back for Christmas, he assured them. He had to do a vanishing act to get out of all those holiday parties in Washington, D.C.

Rick heard from his father, too. The mercenaries had landed in a country friendly to Machado, near the border of Barrera, and they were massing for an attack. Machado told Rick not to worry, he was certain of victory. But just in case, he wanted Rick to know that the high point of his life so far had been meeting his own son. Rick had been overwhelmed with that statement. He told Gwen later that it had meant more to him than anything. Well, anything except marrying her, of course.

They moved back into her apartment, because it was closer to their jobs, leaving Rick's vacant for the moment.

She went home early one Friday night and when Rick walked in the door, he found her standing by the sofa wearing a negligee set that sent his heart racing like a bass drum.

"Here I was trying on my new outfit and there you are, home early. What perfect timing!" she purred, and moved toward him with her hair long and soft around her shoulders, her arms lifting to envelope him hungrily.

He barely got the door closed in time, before they wound up in a feverish tangle on the carpet....

Chapter 11

"Your ribs," Rick gasped.

"Are fine," Gwen whispered, lifting to the slow, hard rhythm. Her eyes rolled back in her head at the overwhelming wave of pleasure that accompanied the movements. "Oh, my gosh!" she groaned, shivering.

"It just gets better…and better," he bit off.

"Yes…!" A high-pitched little cry escaped her tight throat. She opened her eyes wide as he began to shudder and she watched him. His body rippled in the throes of ecstasy. He closed his eyes and groaned helplessly as he arched up and gave himself to the pleasure.

Watching him set her own body on fire. She moved involuntarily, lifting, lifting, tightening as she felt the pleasure grow and grow and grow, like a volcano throwing out rocks and flame before it suddenly exploded and sent fiery rain into the sky. She was like the volcano, echoing its explosions, feeling her body burn and flame and consume itself in the endless fires of passion.

She couldn't stop moving, even when the pinnacle was reached and she was falling from the hot peak, down into the warm ashes.

"No," she choked. "No…it's too soon…!"

"Shhhhh," he whispered at her ear. "I won't stop until you ask me to." He brushed her mouth with his and moved back into a slow, deep rhythm that very quickly brought her from one peak to an even higher one.

He lifted his head and looked down at her pretty pink breasts, hard-tipped and thrusting as she lifted to him, her flat belly reaching up to tempt his to lie on it, press it into the soft carpet as the rhythm grew suddenly quick and hard and urgent.

"Now, now, now," she moaned helplessly, shivering as the pleasure began to grow beyond anything she'd experienced before in his arms. "Oh, please, now!"

He pushed down, hard, and felt her ripple around him, a flutter of motion that sent him careening off the edge into space. He cried out, his body contracting as he tried to get even closer.

They shuddered and shuddered together, until the pleasure finally began to seep into manageable levels. He collapsed on her, his body heavy and hard and hot, and she held him while they started to breathe normally again.

"That was incredible," she whispered into his throat.

"I thought we'd already found the limit," he whispered back. "But apparently, we hadn't." He laughed weakly. He lifted his head. "Your rib," he said suddenly.

"It's fine," she assured him. "I wouldn't have felt it

if it wasn't fine," she added with a becoming flush. She searched his dark eyes. "You're just awesome."

He grinned. "So are you." He lifted an eyebrow. "I hope you plan to make a habit of meeting me at the door in a see-through pink negligee. Because I have to tell you, I really like it."

She laughed softly. "It was impromptu. I was trying it on and I heard your key in the door. The rest is history."

He kissed her softly. "History indeed."

He started to lift away and she grimaced.

"Sorry," he said, and moved more gently. "We went at it a little too hard."

"No, we didn't," she denied, smiling even through the discomfort.

He led her into the bedroom and tucked them both into bed, leaving the clothes where they'd been strewn.

"We haven't had supper," she protested.

"We had dessert. Supper can wait." He pulled her into his arms and turned out the light. And they slept until morning.

Christmas Day brought a huge meal, the whole family except for General Machado, and holiday music around the Christmas tree in the living room of Barbara's house. Rick and Gwen had bid on the nearby house and the family selling it accepted. They were signing the papers the following month. It was an exciting time.

Barbara and General Gene Cassaway were getting along from time to time, but with minor and unexpected explosions every few hours. The general was very opinionated, it seemed, and he had very definite ideas on certain methods of cooking. Considering that he'd only started being a chef five years before, and Barbara had been doing it for years, they were bound to clash. And they did. The more they discussed recipes, the louder the arguments became.

Gwen had resigned her federal job, with her father's blessing, and was now working full-time as a detective on Rick's squad at San Antonio P.D.

Her fledgling efforts had resulted in murder charges against Mickey Dunagan, the man arrested but not convicted on assault charges concerning a college coed. He was also the subject of another investigation on a similar cold case, in which charges were pending. He'd been seen at the most recent victim's apartment before her death in San Antonio.

Faced with ironclad evidence of his guilt, a partial fingerprint and conclusive DNA matching fluids found on the victim's body, he'd confessed. A public defender had tried to argue that the Miranda rights hadn't been read, but the prisoner himself had assured his legal counsel that he'd been read them, and that he stood on his confession. He'd started crying. He hadn't meant to hurt any of them, but they were so pretty and he could never even get a girl to go out with him. He'd killed that other girl, too, because she'd made fun of him and laughed.

This girl he'd just killed, she'd been kind. He didn't care if he went to prison, he told Gwen. He didn't want to hurt anybody else.

She'd handed him over to the prosecutor's office with a sad smile. A murderer with a conscience. How unusual. But it didn't bring the dead women back. On the other hand, the cold case squad was feeling a sense of satisfaction. They owed Gwen a nice dinner, they told her, and would deliver any time she asked. She also spoke with the parents of the dead women, and gave them some consolation, in the fact that the killer would be brought to justice and, most likely, without a long and painful trial that would only bring back horrible memories of the tragedies.

The San Antonio patrolman, Sims, who'd gone on stakeout with Rick and Gwen, had been resigned from the force suddenly, with no reason given. Nobody in the department knew what had happened.

Patrolman Ames in Jacobsville was happily back on the job and with no apparent ill effects.

Down in Barrera, there were rumors of an invasion. It was all over the news. General Cassaway, when asked about the truth of those rumors, just smiled.

Gwen handed Rick a wrapped gift and waited patiently for him to open it.

He looked inside and then back at her with wonder. "How did you know...?"

She grinned and nodded toward Barbara, who laughed.

"Thanks!" he said, pulling out a DVD of an important United States vs. Mexico soccer match that he'd had to miss because of work. "I'll really enjoy it."

"I know you saw the results, but it was a great game," Gwen said.

"Here. Open yours," he said, and handed her a small present.

She pulled it open. It was a jeweler's box. She pulled the lid up and there was a small, beautiful diamond ring.

He pulled it out and slid it onto her finger. "I thought you should have one. It isn't the biggest around, but it's given with my whole heart."

He kissed it. She burst into tears and hugged him close. "I wouldn't care if it was a cigar band," she said.

"I know. That's why I wanted you to have it."

"Sweet man," she murmured.

He sighed. "Happy man," he added, kissing her hair.

She looked up at him with eyes full of love. "You know," she said, glancing toward her mother and General Cassaway, who were looking at recipe books they'd given each other, "I think this is the best Christmas of my life."

"I know it's the best of mine," he replied. "And only the first of many."

"Yes," she said, smiling from ear to ear as she touched his cheek with her fingertips. "The first of many. Merry Christmas."

He kissed her. "Merry Christmas."

The sudden buzz of his cell phone interrupted them. He reached into his pocket with a grimace. It was probably a case and he'd have to go to San Antonio on Christmas Day....

He looked at the number. It was an odd sort of number....

"Hello?" he said.

"Feliz Navidad," a deep voice sang, "Feliz Navidad, Feliz Navidad, something-somethingy felicidad!"

"You forgot the words?" Rick laughed, delighted. "Shame! It's '*Feliz Navidad, próspero año y felicidad,*'" he added smugly.

"Yes, shame, but I am very busy and my mind is on other things. Happy Christmas, my son."

"Happy Christmas to you, Dad," he said, glowing because his father had taken time out of a revolution to wish him well.

"Things are going fine here. Perhaps soon you and

your lovely wife will come to visit me, and I will send a plane for you."

"That would be nice," Rick said. He mouthed "Dad" to Gwen, who grinned.

"Meanwhile, be a good boy and Santa Claus will send you something very nice in the near future."

"I didn't get you anything," Rick said with sadness.

There was a deep chuckle. "You did. The hope of grandchildren. That is a gift beyond measure."

"I'll do my best," Rick replied, tongue in cheek.

There was an interruption. "Yes, I will be right there. Sorry. I have to go. Wish me luck."

"You know I do."

"And Happy Christmas, my son."

"Happy Christmas."

He hung up.

"That was a very nice surprise," Rick said.

She smiled. "Yes."

"It's not a simple recipe," the general was growling. "Nobody can make that right! It's a stupid recipe, it curdles every time!"

"It's not stupid, and yes, you can," Barbara growled back.

"I'm telling you, it's impossible! I know, I've tried!"

"Oh, for heaven's sake! Come on in here and I'll show you. It's not hard!"

"That's what you think!"

"Stop growling. It's Christmas."

The general made a face. "All right, damn it."

"Gene!"

He sighed. "Darn it."

"Much better," she said with a grin.

"I won't be reformed by a cook," he informed her. "And just in case you didn't notice, I'm head of the CIA!"

"In this house, you're an apprentice chef. Now stop muttering and come on. This is one of the easiest sauces in the world, and you won't curdle it if you'll just pay attention."

The general was still muttering as he followed Barbara into the kitchen. There was a loud rattle of pots and pans and the opening of the fridge. Voices murmured.

Rick pulled Gwen into his arms and kissed her hungrily. "I love you."

"I love you, too."

"See? I told you! That's curdling!"

"It's not curdling, it's reducing!"

"Damn it, you put the butter in too soon!" the general was raging.

"I did not!"

Rick rolled his eyes. "Do you think you could do something about your father?"

"If you'll do something about your mother," she returned with a grin.

"I'm not raising the heat. That book is wrong!" the general snapped.

Rick looked at Gwen. Gwen looked at Rick. In the kitchen, the voices were growing louder. Without a word, they went to the front door, opened it and ran for their car.

Rick was laughing. "They won't even miss us," he said as he started the vehicle. "And maybe if they're left alone, they'll make peace."

"You think?" she teased.

He drove off to the house they were buying, cut off the engine and stared at it.

"We're going to be very happy here," Gwen said, sighing. "I'll make a garden and your mother can teach me how to can."

"Yes." He pulled her close. "If she and your father don't kill each other," he added.

"They'll have to learn to get along."

"Ha!"

The phone rang. Rick opened it. "Hello?"

"Could you come home for a minute?" Barbara asked.

"Sure. If it's safe," he teased. "What do you need?"

"Well, we could use a little help in the kitchen."

"Making the sauce?"

"Getting hollandaise sauce out of hair. And curtains. And cabinets. And on walls…"

"Mom!" he exclaimed. "What happened?"

"He thought I was making it wrong and I thought he was making it wrong, and, well, we sort of, uh, tossed the pan up."

"Are you okay?"

"Actually, you know, I think he was right. It tastes pretty good with less salt."

"I see."

"He's looking for another frying pan, so could you hurry?" she whispered, and then hung up.

"What's going on?" Gwen asked.

He grinned as he started the car. "War of the Worlds Part I. We get to help clean up the carnage in the kitchen."

"Excuse me?"

"They trashed the hollandaise sauce all over the kitchen."

"At least they're speaking," she pointed out.

He just shook his head. The general and his mother

might eventually agree to a truce, but Rick had a feeling that it was going to be a long winter.

He pulled Gwen close and kissed the top of her head. He could manage anything, he thought, as long as he had her.

She sighed and closed her eyes. "Too many cooks spoil the broth?" she wondered aloud.

"I was thinking the same thing," he agreed. "Let's go referee."

"Done!"

They drove home through the colorful streets, with strings of red and blue and yellow and green lights and garlands of holly and fir. In the middle of the town square was a huge Christmas tree full of decorations, under which were wooden painted presents.

"One day," Rick said, "we'll bring our kids here when they light the tree."

She beamed. "Yes," she said, and it was a promise. "One day."

The tree grew smaller and smaller in the rearview mirror as they turned down the long road that led to Barbara's house. It was, Rick thought, truly the best Christmas of his life. He looked down at Gwen, and he saw in her eyes that she was thinking the very same thing.

Two lonely people, who found in each other the answer to a dream.

* * * * *

CARRERA'S BRIDE

Chapter 1

It was a hectic evening at the Bow Tie casino on Paradise Island. Marcus Carrera was standing on the balcony smoking a cigar. He had a lot on his mind. A few years ago, he'd been a shady businessman with some unsavory contacts and a reputation that could send even tough guys running. He was still tough, of course. But his reputation as a gangster was something he'd hoped to leave behind him.

He owned hotels and casinos both in the States and in the Bahamas, although he was a silent partner in most of them. The Bow Tie was a combination hotel and casino, and his favorite of all his holdings. Here, he catered to an exclusive clientele, which included movie stars, rock stars, millionaires and even a couple of scalawags. He was a millionaire several times over. But even though his operations had all become legitimate, he had to hold

on to his vicious reputation for just a while longer. The
worst of it was that he couldn't tell anyone.

Well, that wasn't entirely true. He could tell Smith.
The bodyguard was a really tough customer, an ex-
everything military, who kept a six-foot iguana named
Tiny for a pet. The two of them were becoming a land-
mark on Paradise Island. Marcus sometimes thought his
guests were showing up as much to see the mysterious
Mr. Smith as to gamble and lounge on the sugar-sand
beach behind the hotel.

He stretched hugely. He was tired. His life, never calm
even at the best of times, was more stressful lately than it
had ever been. He felt like a split personality. But when
he remembered the reason for the stress, he couldn't regret his decision. His only brother was lying in a lonely,
ornate grave back in Chicago, the victim of a merciless
drug lord who was using a dummy corporation in the
Bahamas to launder his illegal fortune. Carlo was only
twenty-eight. He had a wife and two little kids. Marcus
was providing for them, but that didn't bring back their
husband and father. It was a damned shame to die over
money, he thought furiously. Worst of all, the money-
laundering banker who had set Carlo up for the hit was
still running around loose and trying to help a renegade
Miami gangster buy up casinos on Paradise Island. They
wouldn't be run cleanly, as Marcus's were.

He took a draw from the cigar. It was a Havana cigar,
one of the very best available. Smith had friends in the
CIA who traveled to Cuba on assignment. They could
buy the cigars legally and give them as gifts to whom-
ever they pleased. Smith passed them on to his boss.
Smith didn't smoke or drink, and he rarely swore. Mar-

cus shook his head, chuckling to himself. What a conundrum the man was. Sort of like himself, he had to admit.

He lifted his leonine head to the breeze that blew eternally off the ocean. It ruffled his thick, wavy black hair. There were threads of silver in it now. He was in his late thirties, and he looked it. But he was an elegant man, despite his enormous height and build. He was well over six feet tall, as graceful as a panther, and just as quick when he needed to be. He had huge hands, devoid of jewelry except for a Rolex on his left wrist and a ruby ring on his left pinky finger. His skin was olive tan. It was set off stunningly by the spotless crisp white shirt he wore with his black dinner jacket and bow tie. The crease in his black slacks was knife-straight. His wing-tipped black leather shoes were so shiny that they reflected the palm trees on the balcony where he was standing, and the pale moon overhead. His fingernails were flat, immaculately clean. He was close-shaven and polished, never with a hair out of place. He was obsessive about grooming.

Perhaps, he thought, it was because he was so damned poor as a child. One of two sons of immigrant parents, he and Carlo had gone to work at an early age helping their father in the small automotive repair shop he owned with two other partners. The work ethic had been drilled into them, so that they knew that work was the only way out of poverty.

Their father had run afoul of a small-time local hood. He was beaten almost to death in his garage after he'd refused to let the hood use it for a chop shop, to process parts from stolen cars.

Marcus had been twelve at the time, not even old enough to hold a legitimate job. His mother worked as

a cleaning lady for a local business in their neighborhood. Carlo was still in grammar school, four years behind Marcus. With their father unable to work, only what
their mother brought home kept food on the table. But
soon they couldn't pay rent anymore. They ended up in
the street. Both of the elder Carrera's partners claimed
that they had no obligation to him, since their agreement
was only verbal. There was no money to hire attorneys.

It had been a bleak existence. Forced to ask for wel-
fare, Marcus had seen his mother humbled and broken,
while his father lay mindless in a bed from the massive concussion, unable to recognize his family, even
to speak. A blood clot finished him a few months after
the beating, leaving Marcus and Carlo and their mother
alone.

When her health began to fail, Marcus was faced with
seeing his brother and himself end up in foster care,
wards of the court. He couldn't allow them to be separated. There was no family in the States to appeal to,
not even any friends who had the means to help them.

With dogged determination, Marcus got a name from
one of his tough friends and he went to see the local
crime boss. His grit convinced the man that he was
worth taking a chance on. Marcus became a courier for
the mob, making huge amounts of money almost overnight. He had enough to get a good apartment for his
mother and brother, and even managed health insurance for them.

His mother knew what he was doing and tried to dis-
courage him, but he was mature for his age, and he convinced her that what he was doing wasn't really illegal.
Besides, he asked her, did she want to see the family
broken up and her kids made wards of the court?

The prospect horrified her. But she started going to mass every morning, to pray for her wayward son.

By the time Marcus was in his early twenties, he was firmly on the wrong side of the law and getting richer by the day. Along the way, he caught up with the drug boss who'd had his father beaten, and he settled the score. Later, he bought the garage out from under his father's two former partners and kicked them out into the street. Revenge, he found, was sweet.

His mother never approved of what he was doing. She died before he made his first million, still praying for him every day. He had a twinge of regret for disappointing her, but time took care of that. He put Carlo in a private school and made sure that he had the education Marcus lacked. He never looked back.

Women came and went in his life infrequently. His lifestyle precluded a family. He was happy for Carlo when the young man graduated from college with a law degree and married his childhood sweetheart, Cecelia. Marcus was delighted to have a nephew and then a niece to spoil.

Once, he let himself fall in love. She was a beautiful socialite from a powerful Eastern family with money to burn. She liked his reputation, the aura of danger that swirled around his tall head. She liked showing him off to her bored friends.

But she didn't like Carlo or the friends Marcus kept around, mostly people from his old Chicago neighborhood, who had as many rough edges as he did. He didn't like opera, he couldn't discuss literature, and he didn't gossip. When he mentioned having a family, Erin only laughed. She didn't want children for years and years, she wanted to party and travel and see the world. But when she did want them, it wasn't going to be with a man who couldn't even pretend to be civilized, she'd added haughtily. And that was when he realized that his only worth to her was as a novelty. It had crushed him.

By that time, Marcus had already seen most of the world, and he wasn't enchanted by it. The end came unexpectedly when he threw a birthday party for Erin at one of his biggest hotels in Miami. He missed Erin and went looking for her. He spotted her, disheveled and drunk, sneaking out of a hotel room with not one, but two rock stars he'd invited. It was the end of the dream. Erin only laughed and said she liked variety. Marcus said she was welcome to it. He walked away and never looked back.

These days, he'd lost much of his interest in women. It had been replaced by an interest in textiles and needlework. Nobody laughed at him since he'd started winning international competitions. He met a lot of women who were good with their hands, and he enjoyed their company. But most of them were married or elderly. The single ones looked at him oddly when they heard his name and the gossip. Nobody wanted to get mixed up with a hood. That was what had led to the decision he'd made recently. It was a life-changing event. But one he couldn't talk about.

He was sick of being a bad guy. He was more than ready to change his image. He sighed. Well, that wasn't going to be possible for a few months. He had to play the game to the end. His most immediate problem was finding a conduit to a necessary contact who was staying at a hotel in Nassau. He couldn't be seen talking to the man and, despite Smith's tight security, it was risky to use the telephone or even a cell phone. It was a knotty problem. There was another one. The man he was supposed to help in some illegal activities was due to talk to him tonight. So far, he hadn't shown up.

He put out the cigar reluctantly, but there was no smoking in the hotel or the casino. He couldn't really complain. He'd set the rules himself, after his young nephew and niece had come for a week with their mother, Cecelia. Smoking in the dining room had caused his nephew Julio to go into spasms of coughing. The boy was taken to a doctor and diagnosed with asthma. Since he had to protect Julio, and little Cosima, he decided to ban smoking in the resort. It hadn't been a popular decision. But, hell, who cared about popularity? He only smoked the rare cigar, though, he consoled himself. He didn't even really like the things anymore. They were a habit.

He stalked back into his luxurious carpeted office. Smith was scowling, peering at a bank of closed-circuit television screens.

"Boss, you'd better look at this," he said, standing straight. He was a mountain of a man, middle-aged but imposing and dangerous-looking, with a head shaved bald and green eyes that could be suddenly sparkling with amusement at the most unexpected times.

Marcus joined him, peering down. He didn't have to ask which monitor he should look at. A slight blonde woman was being manhandled by a man twice her size. She was fighting, but to no effect. The man moved and Marcus saw who he was. His blood boiled.

"Want me to handle it?" Smith asked.

Marcus squared his shoulders. "I need the exercise more than you do." He moved gracefully into the private elevator and pushed the down button.

* * *

Delia Mason was fighting with all her strength, but she couldn't make her drunk companion let go of her. It was demeaning to have to admit that, because she'd studied karate for a year. But even that didn't help her much. She couldn't get away. Her green eyes were blazing, and she tried biting, but the stupid man didn't seem to feel the teeth making patterns in his hand. She hadn't wanted to come on this date in the first place. She was in the Bahamas with her sister and brother-in-law, getting over the lingering death of her mother. She was supposed to be enjoying herself. So far, the trip was a dead bust. Especially, right now.

"I do like…a girl with spirit," he panted, fumbling with the short skirt of her black dress.

"I hate a man who…won't take no for an answer!" she raged, trying to bring her knee up.

The man only laughed and forced her back against the wall of the building.

She started to scream just as his wet, horrible mouth crushed down onto hers. He was making obscene movements against her and groaning. She'd never been more powerless, more afraid, in her life. She hadn't even wanted to go out with this repulsive banker, but her rich brother-in-law had insisted that she needed a companion to accompany her out on the town. Her sister Barb hadn't liked the look of the man, either, but Barney had been so insistent that Fred Warner was a true knight. Fred was a banker. He had business at the casino anyway, he told Delia, so why not combine business and pleasure by taking Delia along? Fred had agreed a little reluctantly. He was already nervous and then he'd had one drink after another in the bar downstairs waiting for

Delia, trying to bolster his courage. He mumbled something about getting into bed with a rattlesnake to keep his business going. It made no sense to Delia, who almost backed out of the date at the last minute. But Barney had been so insistent…

Delia sank her teeth into the fat lower lip of the man and enjoyed his sharp yelp of pain for a few seconds. But the pain made him angry and his hand suddenly ripped down the neckline of her dress and he slapped her.

The shock of the attack froze her. But just as she was trying to cope with the certainty of what was about to happen, a shadow moved and Fred was spun around like a top and knocked down with a satisfying thud.

A huge man, immaculately dressed and menacing, moved forward with pantherlike grace.

"You son of a…!" the drunken man shouted, scrambling to his feet. "I'll kill you!"

"Go for it," a deep, darkly amused voice invited.

Delia moved forward before her rescuer could, and swung her purse at Fred, landing a solid blow on his jaw.

"Ouch!" Fred groaned in protest, grabbing his cheek.

"I wish it was a baseball bat, you second cousin to a skunk!" Delia spat, red-faced and furious.

"I'll loan you one," Marcus promised, admiring her ferocity.

Fred gaped at the man and his eyes flashed. "Who the hell do you think you are…!" Fred demanded drunkenly, moving forward.

Marcus planted a huge fist in his gut and sent him groaning to his knees.

"What a kind thing to do," Delia exclaimed in her broad Texas accent. She smiled at the stranger. "Thanks!"

Marcus was noticing her torn dress. His face hardened. "What are you doing here with this bargain basement Casanova?" he asked.

"My brother-in-law offered him to me as a companion," she said disgustedly. "When I tell Barb what he tried to do to me, she'll knock her husband out a window for suggesting this date!"

"Barb?"

"My big sister, Barbara Cortero. She's married to Barney Cortero. He owns hotels," she confided.

Marcus's eyebrows lifted suddenly, and he smiled. His luck had just changed.

She looked up at the big man with fascination. "I really appreciate what you did. I know a little self-defense, but I couldn't stop him. I bit a hole in his lip, but it didn't slow him down, it just made him mad, and he hit me." She rubbed her cheek and winced.

"He hit you?" Marcus asked angrily. "I didn't see that!"

"He's a real charmer," she muttered, glancing down at the drunk, who was still holding his stomach and groaning.

Marcus pulled out his cell phone and pressed in a single number. "Smith?" he said. "Come down here and take this guy back to his hotel. In one piece," he added. "We don't need any more trouble."

There was a reply. Marcus chuckled and flipped the phone shut. He looked at Delia curiously. "You're going to need to stitch that dress up," he remarked. He slid out of his dinner jacket and slid it over her shoulders. It was warm from the heat of his big body and it smelled of expensive cologne and cigar smoke.

She looked up at him with utter fascination. He was a

handsome man, even with those two jagged white scars on his cheek, cutting through his olive complexion like roadmaps. He had big, deep-set brown eyes under thick eyebrows. He was built like a wrestler and he looked dangerous. Very dangerous.

"Stitches," she murmured, spellbound.

He was watching her, too, with amused curiosity. She was small, but she had the heart of a lioness. He was impressed.

The elevator opened and Smith walked out of it, powerful muscles rippling under his dark suit as he approached the small group.

"Where shall I deliver him?" he asked in his gravelly voice.

Marcus looked at Delia and lifted an eyebrow.

"We're all staying at the Colonial Bay hotel in Nassau," she stammered.

He nodded toward Smith, who put out one huge hand and brought Fred abruptly to his feet.

"Let go of me or I'll sue!" Fred threatened.

"Attempted sexual assault is a felony," Marcus said coldly.

"You can't prove that!" Fred replied haughtily.

"I've got cameras everywhere. You're on tape. The whole thing," Marcus added.

Fred blinked. He scowled and peered at the older man. Through the fog of alcohol, recognition stiffened his face. "Carrera!" he choked.

Marcus smiled. It wasn't a nice smile. "So you remember me. Imagine that. Small world, isn't it?"

Fred swallowed hard. "Yeah. Small." He straightened. "I actually came here to talk to you," he began, swaying unsteadily.

"Yeah? Well, come back when you're sober," Marcus said firmly, giving the man a look that he hoped Fred would manage to understand.

Fred seemed to sober up at once. "Uh, yeah, sure. I'll do that. Listen, this thing with the girl, it's all a...a misunderstanding," he added quickly. "I had a little too much to drink. And she just kept asking for it..."

"You liar!" she exclaimed.

"We've got tape," Marcus said again.

Fred gave up. He gave Marcus an uneasy look. "Don't hold this against me, okay? I mean, we're like family, right?"

Marcus had to bite his tongue to keep from spilling everything. "One more stunt like this, and you'll need a family—for the wake. Got me?"

Fred lost a shade of color. "Yeah. Sure. Right." He pulled away from Smith and tried to sober up. "I was just having a little fun. I was drunk or I'd never have touched her! Sorry. I'm really sorry!"

"Get him out of here," Marcus told Smith, and he turned away while the drunken man was still trying to proffer apologies and excuses. He gave Fred a long look.

"I'll...call you," Fred choked.

Marcus nodded without Delia seeing him.

He took Delia by the arm. "Come on, we'll get a needle and thread and fix your dress. You can't go home looking like that."

She was still trying to figure out what was going on. Fred seemed to know this man, even to be afraid of him. And strange messages were passing between them without words. Who was this big, dark man?

"I don't know you," she said hesitantly.

He lifted an eyebrow. "Repairs first, introductions later. You're perfectly safe."

"That's what my sister said I'd be with Fred," she pointed out, tugging his jacket closer. "Safe."

"Yeah, but I don't need to attack women in dark alleys," he stated. "It's sort of the other way around."

He was smiling. She liked his smile. She shrugged and her perfect lips tugged up. "Okay." She managed a smile of her own. "Thanks."

"Oh, I was just there to back you up," he said lazily, letting her go into the elevator in front of him. "You'd have done okay if you'd had a shotgun."

"I'm not so sure," she said. "He was inhumanly strong."

"Men on drugs or alcohol usually are."

"Really?" she asked in a faint stammer.

He gave her a worldly appraisal as the elevator carried them up to his office. "First experience with a drunk?" he asked bluntly.

"Well, not exactly," she confessed on a long sigh. "I've never had an experience like that, at least. I seem to draw drunks the way honey draws flies. I went to a party with Barb and Barney last month. A drunk man insisted on dancing with me, and then he passed out on the floor in front of God and everybody. At Barb's birthday party, a man who had too much to drink followed me around all night trying to buy me a pack of cigarettes." She looked up at him with a rueful smile. "I don't smoke."

He chuckled deeply. "It's your face. You have a sympathetic look. Men can't resist sympathy."

Her green eyes twinkled. "Is that a fact? You don't look like a man who ever needs any."

He shrugged. "I don't, usually. Here we are."

He stood aside to let her exit the elevator.

She stopped just inside the office and looked around, fascinated. The carpet was shag, champagne colored. The furniture was mahogany. The drapes matched the carpet and the furniture. There were banks of screens showing every room in the casino. There was a bar with padded stools curled around it. There were computers and phones and fax machines. It looked like a spy setup to Delia, who never missed a James Bond film.

"Wow," she said softly. "Are you a spy?"

He chuckled and shook his head. "I'd never make the grade. I don't like martinis."

"Me, either," she murmured, smiling at him.

He motioned her toward the huge bathroom. "There's a robe behind the door. Take off the dress and put on the robe. I'll get some thread and a needle."

She hesitated, her eyes wide and uncertain.

He pointed to the corner of the room. "There are cameras all over the place. I'd never get away with anything. The boss has eyes in the back of his head."

"The boss?" she queried. "Oh. You mean the man who owns the casino, right?"

He nodded, trying not to smile.

"You're a…" She almost said "bouncer," but this man was far too elegant to be a thug. "You're a security person?" she amended.

"Something like that," he agreed. "Go on. You've had all the hard knocks you're going to get for one night. I'm the last person who'd hurt you."

That made her feel guilty. Usually she was a trusting soul—too trusting. But it had been a hard night. "Thanks," she said.

She closed the door and slid out of the dress, leaving her in a black slip and hose with her strappy high heels. She put on the robe quickly and wondered at her complete trust in this total stranger. If he was a security guy, he must be the head guy, since he'd told the other guy, Smith, what to do. She felt oddly safe with him, for all his size and rough edges. To work in a casino, a man must have to be tough, though, she reminded herself.

She went out of the bathroom curled up in the robe that had to be five sizes too big for her. It dragged behind her like the train of a wedding gown.

Her rescuer was seated on the desk, wearing a pair of gold-rimmed reading glasses. Beside him was a sewing kit, and a spool of black thread. He was already threading a needle.

She wondered if he'd been in the military. She knew men back home who were, and most of them were handy around the house, with cooking and mending as well. She moved forward and smiled, reaching for the needle at the same time he reached for the dress.

"You sew?" she asked.

He nodded. "My brother and I both had to learn. We lost our parents early in life."

"I'm sorry." She was. Her father had died before she was born. She'd just lost her mother to stomach cancer. She knew how it felt.

"Yeah."

"I could do that," she said. "I don't mind."

"Let me. It relaxes me."

She gave in with good grace and sat down in a chair while he bent his dark head to the task. His fingers, despite being so big, were amazingly expert with the needle. And his stitches were short, even, and almost invisible. She was impressed.

She looked around the huge office curiously, and on an impulse, she got to her feet when she spotted a wall hanging.

She moved toward it curiously. It wasn't a wall hanging after all, she noted when she reached it. The pattern was familiar. The fabric was some of the newest available, and she had some of it in her cloth stash back home. Her eyes were admiring the huge beautiful quilt against one wall, hung on a rod. It was a symphony of black and white blocks. How incredible to find such a thing in the security office of a casino!

"Bow tie," she murmured softly.

His head jerked up. "What's that?" he asked.

She glanced at him with a sheepish smile. "It's a bow tie pattern, this quilt," she replied. "A very unique one. I could swear I've seen it somewhere before," she added thoughtfully. "I love the variations, and the stark contrast of the black and white blocks. The stitches are what make it so unique. There are stem stitches and chain stitches…"

"You quilt." It was a statement and not a question.

"Well, yes. I teach quilting classes, back home in Jacobsville, Texas, at the county recreation center during the summer."

He hadn't moved. "What pattern do you like best?"

"The Dresden Plate," she said, curious at his interest in what was primarily a feminine pursuit.

He put her dress down, opened a drawer in the big desk, pulled out a photo album and handed it to her, indicating that she should open it.

The photographs weren't of people. They were of

quilts, scores of quilts, in everything from a four-patch
to the famous Dresden Plate, with variations that were
pure genius.

She sank back down in the chair with the book in her
lap. "These are glorious," she exclaimed.

He chuckled. "Thanks."

Her eyes almost came out of their sockets as she
gaped at him. "You made these yourself? You quilt?"

"I don't just quilt. I win competitions. National and
even international competitions." He indicated the bow
tie pattern on the wall. "That one won first prize last year
in a national competition in this country." He named a
famous quilting show on one of the home and garden
channels. "I was her guest in February, and that quilt
was the one I demonstrated."

She laughed, letting out a heavy breath. "This is incredible. I couldn't go to the competition, but I did see
the winning quilts on the internet. That's where I remember it from! And no wonder you looked so familiar, too. I watch that quilting show all the time. I saw
you on that show!"

He cocked a thick eyebrow. "Small world," he commented.

"Isn't it just? I'm sorry, I don't remember your name.
But I do remember your face. I watched you put together
a block from the bow tie quilt on that television show.
Well, I'm impressed. Not that many men participate,
even today."

He laughed. "We're gaining on you women," he said
with a twinkle in his dark eyes. "There's a Texas Ranger and a police officer who enter competitions with me
these days. We travel together sometimes to the events."

"You're good," she said, her eyes going back to the book of photos.

"I'd like to see some of your work," he remarked.

She laughed. "I'm not quite in your league," she said. "I teach, but I've never won prizes."

"What do you do when you're not teaching?"

"I run an alterations shop and work with a local dry cleaner," she said. "I do original fashions for a little boutique as well. I don't make a lot of money at it, but I love my work."

"That's more important than the amount of money you make," he said.

"That's what I always thought. One of my girlfriends married and had a child, and then discovered that she could make a lot of money with a law degree in a big city. She took the child and went to New York City, where she got rich. But she was miserable away from her husband, a rancher back home, and she had no time at all for the child. Then they filed for divorce." She shook her head. "Sometimes we're lucky, and we don't get what we think will make us happy. Anyway, I learned from watching her that I didn't want that sort of pressure, no matter how much money I could make."

"You're mature for your age. You can't be more than twenty…?" he probed.

Her eyebrows arched and she grinned. "Can't I?"

Chapter 2

"I'll bite, then," he murmured, going back to pick up her dress and finish his neat stitches. "How old are you?"

"Gentlemen are not supposed to ask ladies questions like that," she pointed out.

He chuckled, deep in his throat, his eyes on his fingers. "I've never been called a gentleman in my life. So you might as well tell me. I'm persistent."

She sighed. "I'm twenty-three."

He glanced at her with an indulgent smile. "You're still a baby."

"Really?" she asked, slightly irritated.

"I'll be thirty-eight my next birthday," he said. "And I'm older than that in a lot of ways."

She felt an odd pang of regret. He was handsome and very attractive. Her whole young body throbbed just being near him. It was a new and unexpected reaction. Delia had never felt those wild stirrings her friends talked about. She'd been a remarkably late bloomer.

"No comment?" he queried, lifting his eyes.

"You never told me your name," she countered.

"Carrera," he said, watching her face. "Marcus Carrera." He noted her lack of recognition. "You haven't heard of me, have you?"

She hadn't, which he seemed to find amusing.

"Are you famous?" she ventured.

"Infamous," he replied. He finished the neat stitches, nipped the thread with strong white teeth and handed the dress back to her.

She took it from him, feeling suddenly cold. The minute she put the dress back on, their unexpected tête-à-tête was over. She'd probably never see him again.

"There's something about ships that pass in the night…" she murmured absently.

His jaw tautened as he looked at her, his reading glasses tossed lightly onto the top of the desk. He summed her up with his dark eyes, seeing innocence and attraction mingled with fear and nerves.

His eyes narrowed. He'd rarely been drawn to a woman so quickly, especially one like this, who was clearly from another world. Her connections were going to make her very valuable to him, but he didn't want to feel any sparks. He couldn't afford them right now.

"What's your name?" he asked quietly.

"Delia Mason," she replied.

"You're Southern," he guessed.

She smiled. "I'm from Texas, a little town called Jacobsville, between San Antonio and Victoria."

"Lived there all your life?" he probed.

She gave him a wicked grin. "Not yet."

He chuckled.

"Where are you from, originally?" she asked, clutching her dress to the front of his robe. "Not the Bahamas?"

He shook his head. "Chicago," he replied.

She sighed. "I've never been there. Actually, this is the first time I've ever been out of Texas."

He found that fascinating. "I've been everywhere."

She smiled. "It's a big world."

"Very." He studied her oval face with its big green eyes and soft, creamy complexion. Her mouth was full and sweet-looking. His eyes narrowed on it and he felt a sudden, unexpected surge of hunger.

She moved uncomfortably. "I guess I'd better get dressed." She hesitated. "Do the cabs run this late?" she added.

"They run all night, but you won't need one," he said as he closed up his sewing kit and put it away. He thought of driving her back himself. But it was unwise to start things he couldn't finish. This little violet would never fit into his thorny life. She couldn't cope, even if she'd been older and more sophisticated. The thought irritated him and his voice was harsher than he meant it to be when he added, "I'll have Smith run you back to your hotel."

The thought of a journey in company with the mysterious and dangerous Mr. Smith made her uncomfortable, but she wasn't going to argue. She was grateful to have a ride. It was a long walk over the bridge to Nassau.

"Thanks," she mumbled with suppressed disappointment, and went into the bathroom to put her dress back on.

She hung the robe up neatly and then checked her face in the mirror. Her breath sucked in as she saw the terrible bruise coming out on her cheek. She put a lot of face powder over it, but it didn't do a lot to disguise the fact that she'd been slapped.

She did the best she could and went back out into the security office. He was standing out on the balcony with his hand in his pockets, looking out to sea. He was a sophisticated man. He had a powerful figure, and she wasn't surprised that he was in security work. He was big enough to intimidate most troublemakers, even without those threatening dark eyes that could threaten more than words.

The wind caught strands of his wavy black hair and blew it around his ears. He looked alone. She felt sorry for him, although it was probably unnecessary and would be unwelcome if she confessed it. He wasn't a man to need pity, she could see that right away.

She thought of not seeing him again, and an emptiness opened up inside her. She'd just lost her mother. It was probably a bad time to get involved with a man. But there was something about this one that drew her, that made her hungry for new experiences, new feelings. She sighed heavily. She must be out of her mind. A man she'd only just met shouldn't have such an effect on her.

But, then, her recent past had been traumatic. The loss of her mother, invalid though she'd been, had been painful. It was worse because Delia's mother had never loved her. At least, not as she loved Barb; dear Barb who was beautiful and talented, and who had made an excellent marriage. Delia was only a seamstress, unattractive to men and without the live-wire personality of her much-older sister. It had been hard to live in the shadow of Barb. Delia felt like a bad copy, rather than a whole person. Her mother had been full of suggestions to improve her dull daughter. None of them had been accepted. Delia was satisfied with herself, loneliness and all. If only her mother had loved her, praised her even just once in a while. But there had been only criticism. A lifetime of it. She often wondered what she'd done to make her mother dislike her so. It really felt as if she were being punished for something. Nobody knew, least of all Barb, how difficult it had been for Delia at home. She'd done what was expected of her, always.

But when she looked at this man, this stranger, she wanted to do crazy things. She wanted to break all the rules, run away, fall off the edge of the world. She didn't understand why he should make her so reckless, when she'd always been such a conventional person. Apparently there was something to that old saying, that different people brought out different qualities in you, when you let them into your life. He must be a bad influence, because she'd never wanted to break rules before.

As if he sensed her presence—because he couldn't have heard her quiet steps above the wind as she joined him on the balcony—he turned suddenly and looked right at her.

She didn't say a word. She moved beside him and stared out over the ocean, enjoying the sound of the wind, and farther away, the subdued roar of the surf.

"You're very quiet," he remarked.

She laughed nervously. "That's me. I've spent my life fading into the background of the world."

He gave her an assessing gaze. "Maybe it's time that changed."

Her heart skipped a beat as she looked up at him in the dim light from the office. His dark eyes met hers and held them while the wind blew around them in a strange, warm embrace.

He made her think of ruins, of mysterious places in shadow and darkness, of storms and torrents of rain.

"You're staring," he pointed out huskily.

"I've never met anyone like you," she said unsteadily. "I'm just a small-town country girl. I've never been anywhere, done anything really reckless or exciting. I've never even been in a casino before in my life. But… but…" She couldn't find the right words to express what she was feeling.

His chin lifted and he moved a step closer, so that she could feel the strength and heat of his body close to her. "But you feel as if you've known me all your life," he said huskily.

Her eyelids flickered. "Well…yes…"

He reached out with one big, powerful hand and lightly brushed her cheek with his fingertips. She trembled at that whisper of sensation and shock waves ran down her slender body into her sensible stacked high heels.

"Oh, boy," he ground out.

"What's wrong?" she asked in confusion.

"And I'm old enough to know better, too," he said, obviously thinking out loud. He looked confounded, even irritated, so she wasn't really prepared when he suddenly reached for her.

His big arms lifted her up against him as his head bent. His dark eyes riveted on her soft, parted lips. "What the hell. It's midnight and you're about to lose a slipper…"

While she was trying to puzzle out the odd remark,

his head bent, and his hard, warm mouth moved into total possession of her lips.

Instinctively she started to struggle, but his mouth opened and she gasped at the unexpected flood of sensation that left her trembling. But not with fear. She melted into the powerful muscles of his chest and stomach, and drowned in the clean, spicy scent of his skin. She felt the sigh of his breath against her cheek while the kiss went deeper and slower and hungrier...

In a daze of longing, she felt his arms crushing her against him while his face slid into her warm throat and he stood there in the wind, just holding her. His arms were warm against the chill of the wind coming off the ocean. She should have protested. She shouldn't be behaving this way with a total stranger, she shouldn't even be here with a man she didn't know.

But all the arguments meant nothing. She felt as if she'd just come home after a long and sad journey. She closed her eyes and let him rock her in his big arms. It was an intimacy she'd never felt in her life. Her mother had never been affectionate with her, even if Barb had. But that was in the past. Now, just the act of being held was a new experience.

Marcus was dumbfounded by what he'd done; by what she'd let him do. He knew by her response to him that she knew next to nothing about men. She didn't even know how to kiss. But she trusted him. She didn't protest, didn't fight, didn't resist. She was like a warm, cuddly kitten in his arms, and he felt sensations that he'd never experienced before.

"This was stupid," he said after a minute, the strain audible in his deep, raspy voice.

"You don't look like a stupid man to me," she said dreamily, smiling against his shoulder.

He drew in a long breath and slowly put her away. His eyes were as turbulent as hers.

"Listen," he began, his big hands resting involuntarily on her shoulders, "we come from different worlds. I don't start things I can't finish."

"Well, don't blame me," she said with dancing eyes. "I almost never seduce men on dark balconies."

He scowled. She had a quick mind and a quirky sense of humor. It didn't make things easier. She appealed to him powerfully. But he was at a point in his life when he couldn't afford attachments of any sort, especially her sort. She was more vulnerable than she might think. What he had to do might put her in the path of danger, if he kept her around. And he was in a bad place to start looking for romance.

"Ordinarily I wouldn't mind being seduced," he said. "But I'm not available."

She felt embarrassed. She stepped back, flushing. "Sorry," she stammered. "I didn't think…!"

"Don't look like that," he said harshly. He turned away from the embarrassment. "Come on. I'll have Smith drive you back."

"I could get a cab," she said, wrapping the tatters of her pride around her like an invisible cloak.

"Don't be absurd," he said, his voice curt.

Delia couldn't hide her discomfort at the thought of enduring the drive back to Nassau in the company of Mr. Smith.

"Surely you aren't afraid of him?" Marcus drawled

softly. "You aren't afraid of me, and I'm worse than Smith in a lot of ways."

Her eyebrows arched. "Are you, really?" she asked in all honesty.

He chuckled in spite of himself. "You don't know anything about me," he murmured as he studied her with indulgent amusement. "That's kind of nice," he added thoughtfully. "It's been a long time since anybody was as comfortable with me as you seem to be."

"Now you're making me nervous," she told him.

He smiled. It was a rare, genuine smile. "Not very, apparently."

She moved a little closer, tingling all over as she approached him. He made her hungry. She gazed up at him. "I think I've got it figured out, anyway."

"Have you now?"

"You're Mr. Smith's boss," she said.

He pursed his lips and started to speak.

"You're a bouncer," she concluded before he could get the words out.

He was actually dumbfounded. He just stared at her with growing amazement.

"It's nothing to be ashamed of," she said firmly. "Somebody has to keep the peace in a place like this. Actually, my father was a deputy sheriff. I wasn't even born until after he died, so I don't remember him. But we still have his gun and gunbelt, and the deputy sheriff's badge he wore."

"How did he die?" he asked abstractly.

"He made a routine traffic stop," she said quietly. "The man was an escaped murderer."

"Tough."

She nodded. "Mom was left with me and Barb, although Barb was sixteen at the time, almost seventeen." She sighed. "Barb is beautiful and brainy. She married Barney, who's worth millions, and she's been deliriously happy ever since."

"So it's just you and your mother at home," he guessed.

She grimaced. "My mother died last month of stomach cancer," she said. "It's why I'm here. Barb thought I needed a break, so she and Barney squared it with my boss at the dry cleaner—I do alterations for them—and then they dragged me on a plane. I hope I still have a job when I go home. Nobody seems to understand how hard it is to get work in a small town. I have monthly bills to pay and hardly any savings, so my job is very important." She smiled ruefully. "Barb doesn't understand jobs. She married Barney just out of high school, when I was two years old, so she's never worked."

"Lucky Barb." He watched the expressions play on her delicate features. "I guess Barb helped when your mother was so sick?"

She nodded. "She paid all Mama's medical and drug bills, and even for a nurse to stay with her in the daytime while I worked. We'd never have made it without her."

"Did she do any of the nursing?"

"She came and stayed with us for the last few months of mother's life," she said quietly. "She and Barney decided that it was going to be too much for me, so they even got nurses to do the night shift. But mostly it was Barb who nursed her, until she died. Mother didn't want me with her. Barb and Mom were very close—it wasn't like that with Mother and me. She didn't like me very much," she added bluntly.

He revised his opinion of the older sister. She'd done her part.

"Are you close, you and your sister?"

She laughed. "We're closer than mother and daughter, really. Barb is terrific. It's just that she thinks I can't walk unless she's telling me how to do it. She's sixteen years older than me."

"That's a hell of an age difference," he pointed out.

"Tell me about it. Barb's so much older that I must seem more like a child than an adult to her."

He scowled. "How old was your mother when you were born?"

"Forty-eight," she laughed. "She said I was a miracle baby."

"Mmmm," he said absently.

"How old was your mother when you were born?" she asked curiously.

He chuckled. "Sixteen. In the old days, and in the old country," he drawled, bending closer, "women married young. She and my father were betrothed by their families. They only saw each other in company of a *dueña,* and they were married in the church. The first time they kissed each other was on their wedding day, or so my father always said."

She looked puzzled at the Spanish word he'd used for chaperone. "I thought you were Italian," she blurted out.

He shook his head. "My parents were from the south of Spain. I'm a first-generation American."

"Do you speak Spanish?"

He nodded. "But I read it better than I speak it. My parents wanted me and my brother to speak English well, so that we'd fit in better than they did."

She smiled, understanding. She moved slowly back

into the office and he followed, closing the sliding door onto the balcony.

"I'll ride with you to your hotel," he said after a minute. He picked up the phone and told someone to take over for him while he drove into Nassau and back.

She took one last look at the beautiful black and white quilt in its frame on the wall. "That really is majestic," she remarked.

"Thanks. I'd love to see some of your work."

She grimaced. "I don't even have photos of it, like you do," she said. "Sorry."

"I may get down to Texas one of these days," he said offhandedly.

She smiled. "That would be nice."

He glanced back at her. "It might not be, when you know more about me," he said, and he was suddenly very solemn.

"That isn't likely."

"You're an optimist. I'm not."

"Yes, I noticed," she teased.

He chuckled as he opened the door to let her out into the hall.

Mr. Smith was waiting beside a huge black super stretch limousine in front of the hotel and nightclub.

Delia actually gasped. "You can't mean to drive me back in that!" she exclaimed. "Your boss will fire you!"

"Unlikely," Marcus said, with a speaking glance at Smith, who was trying not to laugh out loud. "Get in."

She whistled softly as she slid onto the leather seat and moved to the center, to give him room to get in.

Smith closed the back door and went to the driver's seat.

Delia was stagestruck. She looked around wide-eyed, fascinated by the luxurious interior. "You could go bowling in here!"

"It's nice when you're ferrying around a crowd of tourists," he stated. "Want something to drink?"

He indicated the bar, where a bottle of champagne and several bottles of beer and soft drinks were chilling in ice.

She shook her head. "No, thanks. Is that television?" she added, indicating a flat screen just in front of her near the ceiling.

"Satellite television, satellite radio, CD player, phone…"

"It's incredible," she said softly. "Just incredible!"

"Your sister's married to a millionaire," he pointed out. "Don't you get to ride in limos?"

She shook her head. "There wouldn't be any need for her to drive down to Jacobsville in one. They fly to San Antonio and rent a car. At home, they've got a Jaguar sports car."

"I thought you might visit her and ride in limos," he teased.

"In New York?" she asked. She shook her head. "We'd usually go down to Galveston together for vacation on the beach. I've never been to New York, and since Barney travels so much and Barb goes with him, they're rarely home. I don't even go up to San Antonio unless I have to, when I buy supplies. I'm very much at home in the little house I shared with Mama. We have a handful of chickens and a dog named Sam."

"Who's looking after them?"

"A neighbor," she said. "Although, Sam's being

boarded. He's bad to get in the road. You have to watch him constantly."

"What breed is he?"

She smiled. "He's a German shepherd—black with brown markings. I've had him for eight years. He's a sweetie."

"Any cats?"

She shook her head. "Mama was allergic. We couldn't even have Sam in the house."

Smith was pulling out into the main road that led over the bridge to Nassau. Marcus leaned back against the soft leather of the seat. "I've never seen a chicken close up, except on television," he remarked.

She grinned. "Come to Texas and I'll let you pet one."

"You can pet a chicken?"

"Of course you can," she said, laughing.

He liked the sound of her laughter. It had been a long time since he'd done much of that. His life was lonely and dangerous, and he had a natural suspicion of people. He'd seen women who looked like virginal innocents roll a man and take everything he had.

"Why were you at the club in the first place?" he asked unexpectedly.

She sighed. "Because Fred said he wanted to talk some business with the manager of the casino and we might as well go there as anyplace else on the island. But he got cold feet and started drinking." She was oblivious to the look on Marcus's leonine face. "He's mixed up in something illegal, I think, and there are some people he's dealing with who want to hurt him." She bit her lip as she looked up at Marcus. "I probably shouldn't have mentioned that. The owner of the casino's your boss, right?"

"Sort of," he confessed.

"Well, Fred kept throwing back hard liquor until he could hardly stand up. I wanted to go back to my hotel by then, because he was getting really out of hand. I had to fend him off in the taxi, and when we got to the club, I was going to go inside and call a taxi to take me back. But Fred got angry when I said that, and reminded me that he'd bought me an expensive dinner. He said I owed him a little fun," she added coldly. She grasped her purse tight in her hands and glanced at Marcus. "I guess I've led a pretty sheltered life until now. Do men really expect a woman to have sex with them just because they buy her a meal? Because if that's the way of it, I'm buying my own dinners from now on!"

Her expression amused him. He laughed softly. "Well, I can only speak for myself, but I've never considered a steak currency for sex."

She smiled in spite of her irritation. "It shows that I don't date much, huh?" she said matter-of-factly. "Even after I was in high school, I had to fight Barb and mother to get to go out with a man. Mother would call Barb if anyone asked me on a date. They said men were devious and they'd say all sorts of things to get you into bed with them, and then they'd leave you pregnant and desert you." She shook her head. "God knows where they got those ideas. Barb married Barney just after high school graduation, and Mother didn't go out with anybody at all after Daddy died."

"She didn't?" he asked abruptly, surprised.

"She was sort of old-fashioned, I guess. She said she and Daddy were so happy together that any other man she dated would fall short of that perfection. So she spent her time doing charity work and raising me."

"I didn't think there were any women like that left in the world," he said honestly.

"What was your mother like?"

He smiled slowly. "She was the kind of woman who kissed cuts and bruises and made homemade cookies for her kids. She worked herself half to death to give us the things we had to have for school," he added, his face taut.

"Was she pretty?"

"What a question. Why?"

"Well, you're very good-looking," she said, and then flushed as she realized she might be overstepping boundaries.

He chuckled. "Thanks. I think you look pretty good, too."

"Oh, I'm plain," she replied. "I don't have any illusions about being beautiful. But I can cook, and I'm a fair seamstress."

He reached out and touched a loose strand of her blond hair, contemplating the high coiffure she wore it in. "How long is your hair?" he asked suddenly.

"It's to my waist in back," she said self-consciously. "My boss at the dry cleaner where I do alterations says I look like Alice in Wonderland with it down, so I keep it in a bun or a ponytail most of the time."

"You don't cut it, then?"

She shook her head. "I look terrible with short hair," she said. "Like a boy."

Both thick eyebrows went up. "Excuse me?"

She shifted on the seat. "I'm rather bosom-challenged."

He burst out laughing.

She was really blushing, now. "I can't think of a better way to put it," she confessed. "But it's the truth."

His dark eyes were kind and indulgent. "Men have individual tastes in women," he said. "I come from a background where women have ample curves. They say it's what we're not used to that attracts us, and that's how it is with me."

She stared at him, uncomprehending.

"I don't like women with ample...bosoms," he explained.

She just looked at him, her eyes wide and hopeful. "You...don't?"

He shook his head. "And I've never met a woman who kept chickens until now, much less one who knew a Bow Tie pattern from a Dresden Plate."

She smiled. "I've never met a bouncer who could quilt before," she replied.

He chuckled. Let her keep her illusions. He'd never said what he did for a living on that quilt show he was on, or even in the competitions. He just said he was a Chicago businessman. He was enjoying this anonymity. It was rare for anyone not to recognize at least his name, if not his face.

"Would you like to see Blackbeard's Tower?"

Her lips parted. "Blackbeard, the pirate?" she asked.

"The very one." He leaned toward her conspiratorially. "He's not there."

She laughed. "That's all right, I'd rather see it without his ghost," She twisted her purse in her hands. "When?" she asked, without looking at him.

He hesitated. He had a meeting that he didn't really want to attend. Of course, he'd have to go. "I've got a lunch appointment. How about somewhere between one and two o'clock tomorrow?"

Her wide eyes lifted to his, radiant and happy. "I'd like that," she said huskily.

"I'll call for you in the lobby."

She smiled. "Okay!"

He hesitated. "You may hear some things about me when Fred tells your sister what happened," he told her. "Try not to believe them. Or at least, wait and make up your own mind when you get to know me a little better. Okay?"

She was curious, but she smiled. "Okay."

"One more thing," he added, when Smith was pulling up into the circular driveway that led to the hotel entrance. "If Fred calls you a liar and says it didn't happen—and he might—you tell your sister and brother-in-law that I've got a tape of it and they're welcome to look at it any time they like. It would stand in any court of law."

"You think I should have Fred arrested?" she exclaimed.

He was torn between what was right and what he was bound to do. He couldn't afford to have Fred in jail right now. "No," he lied. "But you shouldn't go out alone with him again."

"I don't plan to," she assured him.

Smith was opening the door. Tourists standing inside the glass doors were gaping at the huge black limousine.

"They probably think we're rock stars," she said with twinkling light eyes.

"Let them think what they like. You're sure you're okay?" he added.

She nodded. Her eyes caressed his broad face. "Thanks. For everything."

He shrugged. "You're welcome. I'll see you tomorrow."

"Between one and two, in the lobby," she agreed.

Smith held out a hand and helped her out on the passenger side of the huge vehicle. He grinned at her.

She flushed, because she was still nervous of him, and it showed.

"Well, good night," she said to Marcus.

He smiled. "Good night, angel."

She walked on clouds all the way into the hotel, past staring tourists, and straight into the elevator.

Barb was beside herself when Delia used the key to let herself into the suite.

Her blond hair was mussed from her busy, beautifully manicured fingers. "Baby, where have you been?" she exclaimed, rushing forward to hug Delia half to death. "Oh, I've been so worried! Fred came back with this wild tale about your being kidnapped by some gangster…!"

"Fred tried to assault me outside the casino in a dark corner," Delia said angrily, and she pointed to her cheek. "When I wouldn't cooperate, he slapped me!"

Barb gasped.

Barney, her husband, came into the room in an evening jacket. His balding head shone in the overhead light and his dark eyes narrowed. "So you're finally back! Fred was worried sick…"

"Fred assaulted me," Delia began again.

"Now, baby, you know that's not true," Barney said, his voice softening. "Fred told me you got a little upset because he was just slightly tipsy…"

"Look at my cheek!" she raged. "I wouldn't let him have sex with me, so he slapped me, as hard as he could!"

Barney hesitated, and his dark eyes began to glitter. "Fred said the owner of the casino gave you that bruise," Barney said, but with less confidence and growing anger.

"There's a videotape of the entire incident," she said curtly. "And the head of security for the hotel says you're welcome to see it. Both of you. Anytime you like!"

Chapter 3

There was a stunned silence. Barb's breathing was audible as she looked from her husband to her sister.

"I think Fred's lying," Barb said finally.

Barney stared at her. "Fred said she didn't do a thing for him, and he's used to real lookers. I'm sorry, baby," he told Delia, "but that's the truth. It doesn't make sense that Fred would be that out of line with a woman who didn't appeal to him."

"A bowl of gelatin would have appealed to him at the time, Barney," Delia said in her own defense. "He was stewed to the gills."

"I'll talk to Marcus Carrera," Barney said curtly. "He'll tell the truth. He may be a pirate, but he's an honest pirate."

"You know the head of security at the casino?" Delia asked.

"Honey, I don't know what *you've* been drinking," Barney said drily, "but Carrera is the owner of the Bow Tie. The closest he comes to security is when he turns Smith loose on somebody who's tried to cheat him. They say he used to do his own dirty work in the old days in Chicago. Maybe he still does."

"Mr....Carrera owns the casino," Delia parroted.

"He owns lots of stuff," Barney replied casually. "Hotels and casinos, mostly, in the Caribbean and one off the coast of New Jersey. The Bow Tie's his newest one. He's been down here for a while. Since the oil-drum incident, anyway."

Delia sat down, hard. She was feeling sick. "What oil-drum incident?"

Barney chuckled. "This really bad character did something nearly fatal to one of Carrera's friends. They found him floating down the Chicago River in an oil drum. Well, most of him," he amended. "There are still a few parts missing."

"Parts?" Delia exclaimed.

"Now, now, baby, nobody said Carrera did it by himself. He's always had people around him who would do what they wanted him to," he continued. "But he's got a reputation that scares even bad people. Nobody ever crosses him unless they've got a death wish."

"That isn't what that Dunagan man said," Barb reminded her husband.

He frowned at her. "Dunagan was just passing on gossip," he said with deliberate firmness.

"Well, there is some gossip about that Miami gangster—what's his name, Deluca?—who's trying to set up his own operation down here on Paradise Island. They say he's got his hand into all sorts of illegal gambling in

Florida and now he wants to take over a casino or two in the Bahamas."

"He got caught for running an illegal betting operation," Barney replied. "He opened a couple of shops so people could bet on greyhound and horse racing. But he reneged on the payoffs or lied about the bets that were placed. He did three years. Had a really good lawyer," he added with a grin.

Barb gave him a cold look. "He's a crook."

"Sure he is," Barney agreed. "But he's got a lot of muscle, and that beautiful daughter who travels around with him. They say he uses her to set up men. But she's got the personality of a spitting cobra."

"How exactly did you get home, baby?" Barb asked suddenly.

"The head of security drove me over in a big black stretch limousine," Delia said with a big smile. "It was incredible!"

"I forgot you'd never been in one," Barney said, sighing. "I wanted to bring you up to stay with us in New York and show you the town. But your…mother wouldn't hear of it," he added curtly. "She hated my guts. She said she didn't want you around me."

"But, why?" Delia asked, appalled. Nobody had ever told her that.

Barb gave Barney a warning glance. "Mother was jealous of Barney because he took me away from her," she said. "They never got along. You know that."

"Yes," Delia admitted, "but that doesn't explain why she didn't want me to go to New York."

Barney turned away, looking uncomfortable. "She thought you might like it there and want to stay."

"She didn't want to lose you, baby," Barb said, but she didn't sound very comfortable herself.

"But she never liked me," Delia exclaimed.

"What?" Barb asked sharply.

Delia had never admitted that to them. She hated doing it now, but perhaps it was time to get it out in the open.

"She didn't like me," she confided miserably. "Nothing I did was ever right. She didn't like my hair long, but she liked it less if I had it cut. She didn't like the clothes I wore—they were too dowdy. She ridiculed the ones I designed and made myself. She said I was lazy and shiftless and that I'd never amount to anything…"

"Baby, you can't be serious!" Barb exclaimed, horrified.

"I never understood why," Delia said heavily, sitting down. "It was almost as if she hated me, but when I asked her if she did, she got all flustered and said of course she didn't, that it wasn't my fault that I was the way I was."

Barb and Barney exchanged curious glances. They not only looked shocked, they looked guilty. Delia wondered why.

"Baby, why didn't you ever tell me this?" Barb asked gently, her green eyes soft and loving.

Delia grimaced. "It wouldn't have been right, for me to talk like that about my own mother. And what could you have done, anyway? You and Barney had your own lives."

"She never said why she made it so hard on you?" Barney asked.

Delia glanced at him and thought, not for the first time, how strange it was that his face and hers were remarkably similar, from the small ears to the rounded chin and the very shape of his eyes. She'd even asked Barb once if he was kin to them, because of the resemblance. But Barb had laughed and said of course not.

Not that she didn't look like Barb, too, with the same green eyes and blond hair. Their mother had dark hair and blue eyes. But, then, Delia knew that she and Barb were throwbacks to their paternal grandmother, because Delia's mother had said so.

"I'm sorry," Barb said, moving to hug her sister close. She'd always been affectionate like that, since Delia's earliest memories. Barb hugged her coming and going, praised her, teased her, sent her presents on every holiday and birthday and all the time in between. Delia had never wanted for anything, especially not love. In fact, until three years ago, Barney and Barb had lived in San Antonio. They were always around. But when they were, Delia's mother was on her best behavior. She loved Barb best, and it showed. She was sharp with Delia, though, and Barb had occasionally remarked on it. She didn't realize how harsh their mother could be, when she wasn't there.

"Maybe I could come to New York and visit one day," Delia mentioned.

Barb's face lit up. "That would be great! We could take you to all the touristy places and you and I could go shopping together!"

Delia smiled. "I'd like that."

"We still haven't finished talking about Fred," Barney interrupted.

"She's not going out with him again," Barb said firmly, with an arm around her sister.

"I wasn't going to suggest that," Barney said gently.

"But I need to have a talk with him about his behavior tonight," he added, dark eyes flashing. "He had no right to manhandle her!"

"I agree wholeheartedly," Barb said. "At least you got home safely."

"Yeah, and Carrera didn't send Fred home in a shoe box, either, apparently," Barney murmured.

"You said Mr. Carrera doesn't kill people," Delia reminded him. She couldn't believe that he did. She didn't want to believe it.

"He's calmed down a bit," Barney replied. He poured himself a drink. "He hasn't bumped anybody off recently, at least. He's keeping a low profile. I expect that's why he's down here in the Bahamas. Lying low."

"You look sick, baby," Barb said worriedly. She sat down beside Delia and patted her knee. "You've had a bad night. Why don't you go to bed and get some sleep?"

"I think I'll do that," Delia said.

"Did you actually talk to Carrera?" Barney asked curiously.

Delia nodded, her throat too tight for speech.

Barney chuckled. "That's one for the books. He never mingles with the customers. I guess he was afraid you might sue him, if Fred's lying. He wouldn't like the publicity."

"I thought you believed Fred," Barb said curtly.

He shrugged. "If Carrera got involved, it's no wonder Fred's trying to smooth things over. Nobody wants to cross him. Least of all Fred. He's been working out a business proposition he wants to involve Carrera in. I don't know what sort, but Fred does have a genius for making money." He sipped his drink, frowning. "I might try to get in on it myself," he added with a glance at Barb.

"You stay out of business with Carrera," Barb said flatly. "I like you alive, warts and all."

"Did Smith bring you back to the hotel?" Barney asked Delia.

"He and Mr. Carrera did."

There were shocked stares.

"Fred tore my dress and Mr. Carrera sewed it up for me." She faltered.

Barney finished the drink in one swallow.

"That's right, he quilts," Barb said, brightening. "Delia teaches quilting. You told him, right?"

Delia nodded.

"No wonder he was nice to you," Barney agreed. "He's a sucker for a fellow quilter. We heard he gave a guy a week's paid vacation in one of his hotels for two yards of old cloth."

"Antique fabric is very valuable," Delia said softly, "and extremely hard to get."

"They say he keeps an album of his quilts." Barney chuckled.

"He does. I saw it. He's won international competitions," Delia replied. "His needlework is marvelous." She showed the mend to Barb, who couldn't find the stitches.

"That's really something," Barb had to admit.

"If he ever shoots me, I'll ask him to sew me a quilted shroud," Barney quipped.

Barb stared at him. "Why would he want to shoot you?"

Barney looked uncomfortable. Then he shrugged. "No reason right now. I had thought about suggesting we all take in a show at the casino. We might get special treatment now, what with him sewing up Delia."

Barb glowered at her husband. "We're not putting her in his path again. I do not want my baby sister running around with a criminal!"

"He's not a criminal. Not exactly," Barney said. "He's a nice guy as long as you don't try to steal from him or threaten anybody close to him."

"I don't want to find out," Barb said firmly. She turned to Delia. "You stay away from that man. I don't care how nicely he sews, either."

Delia wanted to tell them that Marcus had asked her out the next day, but she didn't quite have the courage. It was hard to stand up to Barb, who was mature and brimming with authority. Delia had never refused to do anything Barb asked.

But she remembered the hungry kiss she'd shared with Marcus on the windswept balcony, the feel of his arms around her, the warm strength of him in the cool evening. She tingled all over with memory. She wanted to be with him.

The only thing that bothered her was his reputation. What if he really did kill people...?

Barb was studying her expression. "Dee, did you hear me?" she asked. "I said, I don't want you going around with a gangster."

"I heard, Barb," Delia replied.

"He's loaded, you know," Barney interrupted. "They say he's worth millions."

"It's how he got it that bothers me," Barb replied.

"There are worse crooks heading up corporations all over the world," Barney said carelessly. "He's certainly got the Midas touch when it comes to business. At least he's honest, and he never makes idle threats. He loves senior citizens."

"So does the Japanese mafia, the Yakuza," Barb shot back.

Barney threw up his hands. "Everything's black-and-white with you."

"I'll go to bed and let you two finish your argument in private," Delia offered.

"You do that, baby," Barb said gently. "I'm glad you're okay. Imagine, riding around Nassau in the company of a killer!"

"They never proved that he killed anybody," Barney argued.

"They never proved he didn't!"

Delia slipped out of the sitting room and closed the door on the loud voices. She got ready for bed in a daze. She couldn't believe what Barney said about Marcus. Surely she'd have sensed evil if it was in him. He'd been kind, and comforting. He'd even been affectionate. He was attracted to her, as she was to him. Was it so wrong to spend time with him?

She worried about what Barb would say. And then she thought, *I'm a grown woman. I have to make my own decisions about people.*

She remembered suddenly what Marcus had said to her, about not believing what she might hear about him; about waiting until she knew him better to make that sort of judgment.

It was going to be too much temptation anyway, to turn away from him now. She was already hooked. She couldn't stop thinking about him. She was going to go to Blackbeard's Tower with him, even if she had to do it covertly.

She remembered that he'd said he'd meet her in the lobby, and she began to worry. It was a long shot, but what if Barb and Barney happened to be in the lobby at the same time?

The thought kept her awake late into the night.

She dreamed about the hot kiss they'd shared on his balcony, as well. She'd always been a sensible, practical sort of person. But when Marcus Carrera touched her, she lost her head completely and became someone else. She'd never understood why women gave up their principles and slept with men before they were married. But it was becoming clear that sometimes physical attraction overran caution. Her body throbbing, she felt stirrings that she'd never experienced in her life. She could barely stand to have the sheet touch her body, she was so feverish with just the memories. Marcus's body close to hers, his big hands flat on her back, his mouth biting into hers hungrily. She actually moaned. It was dangerous for her to see him again, because she wanted him with a blind, mindless passion. She knew already that she couldn't resist him if he put on the heat. And he might be as helpless to stop it as she already was.

She was very curious about sex. Her mother had been reticent and reluctant to even talk about it, just like Barb. But Delia had friends who indulged, and they told her the most shocking things about men and women in bed together. She thought of Marcus that way and her body ached for him.

She knew that if he asked her out, she'd go with him as often as he liked. She'd lived in a cocoon all her life, without refusing to do whatever she was told. But she was twenty-three now, and already falling in love with that big, dark man from the casino. For once, she was going to do what pleased her, and she'd live with whatever consequences there were. She wasn't going to spend the rest of her life alone without even one sweet memory to cherish in her old age. And if she had to go against Barb to do that, she was willing. It was, after all, her life.

When Delia woke, she felt as if she hadn't slept at all. She couldn't believe that Marcus was a killer, no matter what anyone said. He had been tender with her, generous, kind. Surely a gangster wouldn't have been so accommodating to a perfect stranger.

But what did she know about gangsters? She was a small-town girl with no knowledge of people with mob connections, except by gossip. There had been some excitement in Jacobsville, Texas, over the past few years. A drug lord had decided to build a distribution center there, and a group of local mercenaries had stopped him. A local girl had been kidnapped in revenge and taken to the drug lord's home in Mexico, and her stepbrother had rescued her. There had even been a shooting when Christabel Gaines and her guardian Judd Dunn had run afoul of a murderer; Christabel had been shot by one of the notorious Clark brothers, who had killed a young woman up around Victoria. Clark was now serving a life sentence without hope of parole.

But other than those episodes, Jacobsville was mostly a quiet place to live. Delia lived in a cocoon of kind people and rustic charm. She was unsophisticated, not really pretty, and rather shy.

So, why, she wondered, would a rich, worldly man like Marcus Carrera even want to take her sightseeing? If he was as rich as Barney said he was, surely he could get any sort of women he liked—beautiful women, talented women, famous women. Why would he want to take Delia out? Maybe he was desperate for company? She laughed at that thought. But then she remembered the torrid kiss they'd shared, and her heart raced. Perhaps he felt the same way she did. It didn't have a lot to do with looks, social position or wealth. Nobody could explain physical attraction, after all.

That fiery passion was unsettling to a woman who'd never felt it in her life. She couldn't even consider an affair, she told herself. And he didn't seem to be a marrying man. Surely if he'd wanted to marry, he'd have done it, at his age.

There was another consideration—if she was going to go against her own best instincts and go out with him, she'd have to lie to Barb. She'd never done that in her life. Barb had loved her, sacrificed for her, taken care of her even more than her own mother had. In all honesty, she loved Barb more than she'd loved her poor mother. But the alternative was to forget Marcus and stand him up. Her heart ached at just the thought of not seeing him again. This sudden hunger to be with him, to hold him, to kiss him was overpowering. She couldn't bear to stand him up. Even after only a brief meeting, her eyes ached for the sight of him.

She told herself that she was an idiot. But she was going to meet him, no matter what the consequences. She couldn't help herself.

In the end, her fears of Barb seeing her with him in the lobby evaporated when Barney had an emergency call about his business back home. His headquarters was in New York, but he was opening a new hotel in Miami, and there were major problems with the contractor who was building it. The man had walked off the job, with his entire crew, after an argument with one of Barney's vice presidents. Barney was going to have to fly there and solve the problem. Barb, who was in charge of the interior design for the building, would necessarily have to go as well, since the contractor had been authorized to supply the materials she required.

"I hate leaving you here alone, baby," Barb said worriedly. "Would you like to fly down to Miami with us while we sort this out?"

Delia thought fast. "I think I'd rather stay here, if you don't mind," she said. "I really wanted to get in some sunbathing on the beach."

"Are you sure you'll be okay?" Barb persisted.

"She's a grown woman, for God's sake. You're only her sister, not her mama," Barney said furiously.

Barb flushed. "Well, I worry!" she defended. "What about Fred?" she added.

"Fred's gone to Miami, too, for the week," Barney muttered, searching for his wallet. "I didn't know he had business interests there," he said with an odd smile.

"There!" Delia said, relieved. "That solves the problem."

Barb was frowning. "You aren't going off with Carrera anywhere, are you?" she asked suspiciously.

Delia managed to look dumbfounded. "Chance would be a fine thing!" she exclaimed. "I mean, look at me," she added, spreading her arms wide. "Tell me why a man that rich would look twice at a plain nobody of a seamstress from a little town in Texas."

"You are not plain!" Barb argued. "The right clothes and makeup and you'd be a knockout. In fact, we just outfitted you, didn't we, and you have yet to wear a single thing I bought you!"

"I will. I promise," Delia said in a conciliatory tone.

Barb sighed. "No, you won't. You spend your life in sweats and old shirts. In fact, you didn't even have any shirts without pictures or writing on them until I brought you down here and took you shopping."

"I'll wear the new clothes," Delia promised, and she meant it. Marcus might like her in something pretty.

"We need to talk about this," Barb continued.

"But not right now," Barney said impatiently, looking at his Rolex. "We have to go right now or we'll miss our flight."

"All right," Barb said reluctantly. She hugged Delia. "You keep this door locked while we're gone," she began. Barney was opening the door and motioning to her. "Don't open it unless you know who's outside!"

"Yes, Barb," Delia said automatically.

"And do not go out at night alone…" Barb continued.

Barney had her by the arm and was dragging her toward the door. She laughed. "Don't take candy from strangers!" she called merrily. "Don't go too near the ocean, and don't pet stray dogs!"

"I won't, I promise." Delia chuckled.

"I love you!"

The door closed on the last word.

"I love you, too!" Delia called after her.

There was a skirl of laughter and then silence.

Delia tried on three of the new outfits Barb had bought for her before she settled on a simple white peasant blouse with a lace-edged white cotton skirt and a wide magenta cotton wrap belt. She'd found the outfit in one of the local stores, and the saleslady, an elegant, tall woman, had showed her how to wrap the belt around her waist several times and tuck it in. The result was very chic, especially with Delia's small waist.

She was vibrating with nervous energy and indecision about her choice when the phone rang and made her jump. She ran to answer it.

"Yes?" she said at once.

There was a deep chuckle, as if he knew she'd been sitting on hot coals waiting for him and was pleased by it. "I'm in the lobby," he said.

"I'll be right down."

She hung up and darted to the door, only then realizing that she was barefoot and had forgotten both her purse and the room key. With a rueful laugh at her own forgetfulness, she ran back to get her shoes and purse and key.

Eight breathless minutes later, she arrived in the luxurious lobby, having spent five minutes waiting for the elevator.

She stepped out into the lobby and looked around worriedly for Marcus. And there he was, lounging against the wall opposite the bank of elevators, lazily elegant and smiling.

He was wearing a green knit shirt with brown slacks. He looked big and expensive and sexy.

He was looking, too, his dark eyes intent on her trim figure and especially her wealth of long, wavy blond hair that she'd left cascading down to her waist in back.

He smiled then, warmly, and she went straight to him, almost colliding with another hotel guest she didn't even see, causing amused glances from passersby.

"Hi," she said huskily.

"Hi," he returned, his voice deep and soft. "Ready to go?"

She thought about the risks she was taking, the danger she could be in, the anger and betrayal that Barb was going to feel. But nothing mattered except that look in his dark eyes. She threw caution and reason to the winds.

"I'm ready," she said.

Chapter 4

Marcus could hardly believe this was the same shy, conservative woman he'd met only the night before. She looked exciting in that lacy white thing, with her long hair down. He'd had second thoughts about involving her in his life when it was in flux, but in the end, he hadn't had a choice. It had been pure luck that Fred had chosen to bring her along to the meeting they didn't get to have. She was Barney's sister-in-law and that gave him a connection to a badly needed contact. He could pass a message along in a very innocent way, through a woman he could pretend to be interested in. The fly in the ointment was Barbara, Delia's sister, who was not going to approve of her baby sister dating a gangster.

It was amazing, that of all the women he'd known— and there had been some beautiful ones—he honestly was interested in her. It wasn't like him to be attracted to a small-town girl like Delia. She wasn't his style at all. Then, too, there was the question of his past. She thought he was a security guard. She had no idea who, or what, he really was. It wasn't fair to her to let her believe a lie. But he didn't dare tell her the truth. She didn't seem the sort of woman to be comfortable spending time with a gangster, even if he was reformed. And he needed her to spend time with him. For a few weeks, at least.

He reached out slowly and caught her cold, nervous fingers in his, linking them together. It was like touching a live wire. Her hand jerked in his, as if she, too, felt the electricity. Her breath caught audibly. She winced when she realized that he knew exactly what she was feeling.

"Don't look like that," he said in a deep, velvet tone, moving closer. "I feel it, too."

"I haven't slept," she choked out, lost in his eyes.

"Neither have I," he replied curtly. He studied her perfect complexion, the faint flush on her cheeks a dead giveaway of her turmoil. "Where's your sister?"

"On her way to Miami with Barney. Some sort of crisis. And Fred's gone there, too," she added breathlessly.

"To Miami?" He looked thoughtful.

"So Barney said. God knows why. Barney says he's got no business interests there."

"None that Barney knows about, maybe," Marcus mused. He seemed distant for a moment. Then he blinked and smiled down at Delia. "I've got a big day planned for us. Let's go."

"Okay," she said softly.

He didn't ask any questions and she didn't tell him about Barb's warning about him. She was going to pretend that there were no complications. She was going to pretend she didn't know who he was, too. This was one day she was simply going to enjoy. It might be the only one she had with him. She wasn't going to waste it in worry.

They walked out the front door holding hands, but Mr. Smith and the limo were nowhere in sight. A cab was waiting at the entrance instead.

"I didn't want to raise eyebrows, in case your sister had told you something about me," he murmured.

"What would she have told me about you?" she wondered, pretending innocence.

His expression was priceless. He looked relieved. "What did you tell her?"

"That Fred assaulted me and the head of security at the hotel brought me home," she said simply.

"Not my name?" he persisted.

She grimaced. "I didn't think of it until it was too late…"

"Don't think of it," he said tersely. "I'll explain later."

He put her into the back of the cab and climbed in beside her. "Take us back to the Bow Tie, John," he told the driver.

"Yes, sir," the man said with a big grin. "You going around in disguise, huh, Mr. Carrera?"

"Big disguise, and you get a bonus for forgetting it."

"I'm your man."

"You can take her home tonight, as well," he told Harry. "For another bonus."

"I don't know who you are, Mr. Carrera," he said blithely. "Never met you in my life."

Carrera chuckled. "That's the spirit."

"What sort of disguise does he mean?" Delia asked wryly.

"Never mind," he replied. "I thought we'd have lunch before we go out."

"Lovely!" she said.

He felt guilty for a minute about the game he was playing. He didn't want to hurt her, but she gave him a connection he needed very badly. Apart from that, she appealed to him physically in a forbidden way. She was a sweet kid and he was going to spoil her a little, so she wouldn't lose by the association with him. She didn't ever need to know who he really was, and he didn't plan to tell her. Not until he had to, anyway.

They passed over the bridge to Paradise Island, and in daylight she was able to see the incredible assortment of boats moored at the big marina. There were sailboats and motorboats and ferryboats, carrying people from Nassau to Paradise Island on the water instead of the road.

"Just look at all the boats!" she exclaimed, looking out the cab's window. "There's one with black sails!"

"He must be a pirate, then, huh?" he teased, following her gaze.

She turned her head and looked straight into his eyes. She felt him, strong and warm at her back, and her whole body tensed with hunger.

He saw that, enjoyed it, savored it. She couldn't hide anything from him. That was pleasurable, like the touch of her shoulder against his chest. His eyes darkened and he moved back abruptly. This wasn't the place, he told himself, even if he was crazy enough to make a move on her. He had to try to remember what was at stake right now. He had to keep his mind on business, not on Delia.

The casino looked different in daylight, she thought as they got out of the cab. While Marcus was paying the fare, Delia walked over to a bank of hibiscus and touched the red blossoms with a delicate hand. She loved flowers. She had a huge garden at home, full of every sort of blooming plant. But she didn't have hibiscus. They weren't comfortable in her part of Texas through the winter.

"Do you like them?" Marcus asked.

She nodded. "I can't grow them at home. The winters are too cold."

"I thought Texas was hot."

She chuckled. "It is, in the summer. But we actually have snow sometimes in Jacobsville in the winter, and it gets down to freezing. Tropical plants can only be grown in a greenhouse, and I can't afford one."

He reached down and picked one of the flowers, tucking it behind her ear. He smiled. "It suits you."

She laughed self-consciously. "I'm not pretty, but you make me feel like I am. That sounds silly, I guess."

He shook his head. He was searching her green eyes quietly, intently. She blushed, and he smiled. It amused him that she found him attractive, that she reacted to him so hungrily.

She was twenty-three. He was certain that she had some experience, at that age. He was curious to see how much. But he couldn't rush his fences. She was going to fit nicely into the scheme of things. He had to keep her around.

He took her hand in his again. "Let's go. I want to show you around my house."

"You don't live in the hotel?" she asked.

"The boss keeps a penthouse apartment there," he said evasively. "But I like my own space."

He led her around the grounds of the hotel to a

wrought-iron gate in a white stucco fence. He unlocked it and ushered her in.

There was a huge expanse of grass and flowering shrubs and trees. Beyond it, just on the spotless beach, was a sprawling white adobe house with graceful arches and a red tiled roof.

"Wow," she said as they approached it. The porch had white wicker furniture, and there were pots of flowers everywhere, hanging from the eaves of the house, sitting on the ceramic tile of the wide, long porch.

"Do you like it?" he asked, smiling. "I thought you might. I love flowers, too. I planted most of these as seed. A couple of the shrubs were imported. The hibiscus and oleander were already here, but I planted a few more. There's a greenhouse, too, where I raise orchids. You can't see the driveway from here, but it's lined with royal palms."

"Those are the ones with the white trunks, aren't they?"

"Yes."

"Are those casuarina pines?" she added, nodding toward the trees lining the yard, near the beach. They looked like white pines, but with long fronds that waved gracefully in the breeze.

"They are," he said, surprised. "Don't tell me you have those in Texas," he teased.

She shook her head. "I bought a book on native plants and trees the day I got here," she told him. "Everything is so different down here!"

"I like the scenery, too," he said. "But there's something more. It's the sort of place that relaxes you, slows you down."

"In your line of work, I guess it's a relief to get away from brawls," she said.

"Huh?"

"Security work," she prompted.

He smiled ruefully. He'd actually forgotten the role he was playing. "That's right," he said. "I need a place that takes my mind off work."

He led her inside the beautiful house, through open rooms with stone floors that were cool and eye-catching. She thought about how wonderful that stone would feel under bare feet and had to resist taking off her shoes.

"I don't see a television," she remarked when they were in the living room.

"I've got one in the den," he said lazily, "along with all the electronic equipment I have to keep for the sake of security around here. Smith has some of it in his suite. I have the rest."

"Mr. Smith lives with you?" she asked, surprised.

"Well, not in the same room," he said at once.

She laughed at his indignation. "Sorry."

"Damn, woman," he cursed, and then laughed. "Smith takes care of the house for, uh, the boss," he added. "So do I, when I'm off duty."

She knew it was his house, but she didn't let on. She looked around with warm, approving eyes. "It must be great, living here, with the ocean so close."

"It gets a little hectic during hurricane season," he said.

"Which is when?"

He pursed his lips. "From May until late September or early October."

She gasped. "It's late August!"

He chuckled at her expression. "Don't worry. We don't get that many."

"Does the house flood?"

"It has, in the past," he said. "I…the boss, I mean… has rebuilt it once. Otherwise, we just drain it out and have a crew come in and clean out the water damage."

She nodded, as if she understood.

He knew she didn't. He turned and looked down at her. "Cleaning up water damage is a specialized job," he said. "The same people come in after a fire when the hoses have been used on furniture and drapes."

"Oh!"

He grinned at her. "Don't ever be ashamed to admit you don't know something, Delia," he said gently. "It's not a crime."

She smiled ruefully. "Sorry. I just don't want you to think I'm an utter idiot. I don't know a lot about the world."

"Stick with me, kid," he said in a teasing tone. "I'll clue you in."

She laughed with delight. "How exciting."

He pursed his lips and gave her slender body a mock leer. "You're the exciting one. Come on. We'll finish the tour and then we'll drive over to Blackbeard's Tower."

"I can hardly wait!"

He showed her the lavish master bedroom, with heavy Mediterranean furniture and carpet and drapes in earth tones. There was a huge bathroom with a hot tub, and a vanity. The other two bedrooms were similar, if smaller. There was a laundry room, too.

"I don't use it," he told her with a grin. "We have a lady, Lucy, who comes in to cook every day, and two days a week she does laundry for me and Smith. And the boss, of course."

"I have a laundry room, too, but no Lucy."

He smiled. "And this is the garage," he added, opening a door.

She gasped. Inside were five cars. One was the stretch limousine that had taken her back to her hotel the night before. There were four others, none of which she recognized. Well, except for the silver Jaguar. The Ballenger brothers mostly drove Jaguars, so she knew what they looked like. The others were unusual, and she hadn't seen anything like them.

"We'll take this one," he said, guiding her to a small red sports car.

"Wow," she said as he seated her. "This is cute."

He could tell that she didn't know what an Alfa Romeo was, so he didn't expound on how much it cost. "Yes," he agreed, starting the engine. "It's cute."

"Are we going to see Blackbeard's place now?" she asked.

He chuckled. "That's right. Hang on to your seat, honey. This is a car you *drive*."

He shifted gears, whipped it out of the garage, and sent it racing down the driveway. All she saw was a blur of green and white on the way to the road.

Once they were across the Paradise Island bridge again and on the paved road that led around the island, she began to relax. The wind in her hair was delightful. She didn't reach for a scarf or hairpins. She closed her eyes and enjoyed the feel of the wind.

"You're an elemental, aren't you?" he called above the roar of the engine.

"Excuse me?"

"You like wind and storms."

"Yes," she called back, smiling.

"Me, too," he murmured.

They passed small houses and public beaches, where local people were playing in the surf. There were houses recessed down past wrought-iron gates and roadside stands where tourists could buy drinks and food. Everything was colorful. A lot of the small houses were painted in pastel colors, pinks and blues and greens. They looked homey and welcoming, and the people seemed always to be smiling.

Marcus drew up at a deserted beach and pulled off into the small dirt track that led toward a grown-up ruin of a building.

"This is it," he said, helping her out after he'd parked.

"The tower?" she parroted.

"The very same." He led her around the growth of vegetation to a stone ruin, a circular building that had relatively new wooden steps. "Most tourists don't know about this place," he told her. "They can't prove that Blackbeard watched out for treasure ships here, but they think he did. Local legends say so, anyway."

"A real pirate," she enthused. "That's exciting."

"Pirates were all over the Bahamas and the Caribbean," he remarked, nudging her toward the staircase. "Woodes Rogers, who became governor of the Bahamas, was a pirate himself, like Henry Morgan, who later became governor of Jamaica."

"Renegades," she mused under her breath.

"Sometimes a reformed bad man makes a good man," he said quietly.

She laughed. "So they say."

She got to the top and looked out over the remaining gray stone blocks to the ocean. "It's beautiful," she said to herself, noting the incredible color of the ocean, the blistering sugar whiteness of the beach. Between the tower and the beach were sea grape bushes. One of the cabdrivers had pointed them out and told her that they were once used as plates in the early days of settlement.

"Do you like pirates?" she asked, glancing up at him with a wicked smile.

He shrugged. "They're my sort of people," he commented, looking down at her quietly. "I'm an outsider."

Her fingers itched to touch him, but she was nervous about it. He looked formidable.

"You'd be surprised at the number of tough guys who live in my town. We've got everything from ex–black ops to ex-mercenaries. I hear there's even a reformed gun runner in town somewhere. Our police chief, Cash Grier, was in black ops, we heard."

His eyebrows arched. "You don't say?" he mused. He didn't tell her that he knew Cash Grier quite well, or that he'd heard of Jacobsville. He'd helped Grier keep his wife, Tippy, from being victimized after her kidnapping back in the winter.

"I need to visit this town," he said, studying her.

"You'd be welcome," she replied, lowering her eyes shyly. "I could take you around our local points of interest. Not that we've got such exciting ones as this, but Jacobsville was once the center of Comanche country, and there was a famous gunfighter who had property there."

"You like outlaws, don't you?"

She grinned. "Well, they're interesting," she pointed out.

"And dangerous."

She stared at his chin. It had just a faint cleft and looked stubborn. "Life is boring without a little spice."

He moved a step closer and touched her hair. He'd been itching to, ever since he picked her up at her hotel. "Your hair fascinates me. I love long hair."

"I figured that out," she confessed breathlessly.

He chuckled. "Is that why you wore it down? For me?"

"Yes."

He lifted an eyebrow. "Don't you know how to lie?"

"It's a waste of time," she said simply. "And it complicates things."

He couldn't quite meet her eyes. "Yes. It complicates things." He dropped his hand.

She was going to ask him why he'd become so remote suddenly, but a tour bus drove up next to the Alfa Romeo and parked.

"It seems we've been discovered," he said, smiling at her, but not with the same sensuousness as before. "We'd better go."

She followed him down the staircase. They got to the bottom just as six tourists followed a heavyset, laughing tour arrived to the tower. One of the women was young, blonde, sophisticated and dripping expensive jewelry. She gave Marcus a sultry look from her heavily shadowed blue eyes. He ignored her completely, locking Delia's fingers into his as he nodded politely at the tour guide and kept walking.

The blonde shrugged and turned away.

Delia was curious about his lack of interest.

He gave her a keen glance and laughed hollowly. "I may not be Mr. America, but the car attracts women," he hedged. "Even though it's not mine," he added quickly. "I don't like women who find my possessions attractive."

"I guess it would be demeaning," she agreed, because she knew what he was saying. A lot of women over the years must have liked him for his money, his power, his position alone.

"Demeaning." He savored the word. "Yes. That's a good way to express it."

He opened the passenger door of the car and helped her in. "You're perceptive," he mused.

She leaned her head back against the seat. "Everybody says that, but I'm not, really. I just know how to listen."

He got in beside her and laid his arm over the back of her seat. He stared at her until her eyes opened and her head turned toward him.

"Listening is a rare gift," he said. "Most people only want to talk about themselves."

She smiled warmly. "I'm not that interesting, and I haven't done anything that would be worth talking about to people. I do alterations and make quilts. What's exciting about that?"

"As a fellow quilt-maker," he pointed out drily, "I find it very exciting."

She leaned forward and whispered, "I know where to find some floral fabric that dates to 1948, and the lady's willing to sell it for the right price!"

"Darling!" he exclaimed.

She laughed with pure delight at the twinkle in his dark eyes. "You're not anything like I used to picture security people," she told him. "The only bouncer I know is Tiny, who works at Shea's Roadhouse and Bar, and he's, well, he's not much to look at."

"Neither is Mr. Smith's pet iguana—who is also named Tiny," he chuckled ironically. "We should introduce them one day!"

"Funny coincidence." She lifted her hand daringly and traced his big nose, to the crook in the middle. "Has your nose been broken?" she asked.

He caught her hand and pressed the palm to his mouth. "Only once," he said. "But it's so big that I hardly felt it," he teased.

She smiled, looking hungrily at him.

He felt a sudden painful urge to bend and kiss the breath out of her. But it was a public place and this wasn't the time. He kissed her palm again and gave it back to her.

"We'd better go before the tourists get back," he said drily. "Could you eat?"

"I could."

"Great. I had Lucy make us a seafood salad and slice some mangos last night. It'll be cold and sweet."

"I'll enjoy that," she murmured.

Marcus smiled at her radiant delight as the wind tore through her hair once more in the little convertible on the way back to his house. He noted that she didn't protest that it was messing up her hair, or complain about the wind. She seemed to love it.

It had been years since he'd driven a woman on a date. He usually took the limo and had Smith drive him. When he wanted to impress a woman, which was rarely these days, the limo always did the job.

But he'd suspected that Delia wouldn't know an expensive sports car from a domestic model, and he was right. She was so honest, so natural, that she made him feel like a total fraud.

He pulled into a paved driveway that led up to white wrought-iron gates. He pressed a button in the car and the gates swung open.

Delia laughed with surprise. "How did you do that?"

"Magic," he teased. He drove through the gate and it closed automatically behind them.

"It looks different than it did when we left," she mused as she noted royal palm trees on both sides of the driveway, along with masses of hibiscus and bougain-villea and jasmine, all in glorious bloom. Farther along, tall casaurina pines swayed gracefully beyond the grace-ful white adobe house, its eaves dripping with flowers of every color and variety.

He laughed amusedly. "I get the message. I'll slow down so that you can see it this time."

"Your boss must think a lot of you, to give you such a spectacular place to live."

"You really like it?" he asked, pleased by her enthu-siasm.

"Oh, I like it," she said in almost a whisper as he stopped and cut off the engine. Her eyes were every-where, softening as they rested on the flowers. "It's so beautiful."

Other women he'd invited here had used different adjectives: dull, boring, rustic. It was too small, or too primitive, or too remote from the city. The bottom line was that they hated it. He was crazy about the place. He spent hours working in the flowers, fertilizing and pruning and landscaping.

"You must be a terrific gardener," she murmured as they got out and walked across a stone patio to the wide steps and spacious front porch. "I've never seen so many flowers! And that tree looks like a... No, it couldn't be." She hesitated.

"It's exactly what it looks like, an umbrella plant," he confirmed. "And that one over there is a Norfolk Island pine."

"But they're monstrous!"

"Compared to the potted plants back in the States, they certainly are. But here they're in their natural element, and they grow like crazy."

"They're beautiful," she said solemnly.

He smiled. "I think so, too."

He parked the car and led the way into the kitchen, sliding his car keys back into his pocket.

He opened the refrigerator and produced a huge covered bowl full of seafood salad and a covered plate with sliced mango. "There's a lemon meringue pie as well, if you like lemon."

"Oh, it's my favorite," she enthused.

He chuckled. "We'll have it for dessert. It's my favorite, too." He took down plates and glasses and she set the table, arranging the silver he gave her and the napkins, as well.

"What do you want to drink?" he asked.

"I like iced tea, but milk is okay."

He gave her a curious glance. "I usually have coffee..."

"That would be even better, but I didn't want to impose," she added. "You went to a lot of trouble for this."

She was constantly surprising him. Nobody wanted to "rough it" by eating leftovers here, when there were five-star restaurants all over Nassau. Here she was worried about making more work for him. He was impressed by Delia's companionable spirit.

He had the light meal together in no time, and they lingered over a second cup of coffee on the veranda, overlooking the casuarinas and, beyond them, the blinding white sand and turquoise waters of the Atlantic Ocean.

Heavy, low clouds were building around them, blackened and towering into the heavens. The sun had been out earlier, but a storm was clearly on its way into the bay.

"Do you like storms?" she asked absently as she leaned back against a palm tree trunk, watching the churning of the waves on the beach.

"Yes. I'd already figured that you did," he replied.

She smiled. "I should be afraid of them, I expect, because lightning terrifies me. But I love a storm. I love the fury of the wind, and the sound of rain coming down. We have a tin roof on our house. When it rains, it's like a metallic lullaby, especially at night. I don't know why, but rain makes me feel safe."

He was studying her face with intent interest. His dark eyes slid down her trim figure in the gossamer-thin garments she was wearing, and he wondered hungrily what she looked like under her clothes.

As if in response to his mental images, the skies suddenly burst open and rain came down immediately, in torrents.

Delia gasped as the rain soaked her blouse and skirt and drenched her hair.

Laughing, Marcus caught her hand and ran with her to the protection of the roofed patio, where she stood dripping near a wall, trying to shake the water from her skirt.

Marcus's eyes were suddenly narrow and glittery, and he was looking at her with an expression she couldn't fathom.

When she looked down at herself, she understood. The fabric was transparent. He could see right through her clothes, right down to her flimsy bra and panties. It was like being naked.

She started to raise her hands. Seconds later, Marcus backed her against the wall and pinned her wrists to the smooth surface with his big hands, while his knee coaxed her legs apart and his eyes went to her breasts.

Instinctively she began to struggle, remembering Fred.

"I won't hurt you," he whispered softly, holding her gaze. "I won't force you. Trust me."

Her face flushed as he looked down at her again, slowly levering his hips into slow contact with hers while the wind blew wildly around them.

"Your breasts are incredible," he said huskily. "I ache just looking at them. And your mouth has the most seductive curve in your lower lip…"

As he spoke, he bent. He found her mouth and caressed it slowly, tenderly with his lips, while his tongue ran along the inside of her upper lip and drove her heartbeat over the edge. His mind was telling him it was too soon for this. His body wasn't listening.

Neither was Delia's. Throwing caution to the wind, she reached up around his neck, opened her mouth under his and held on for dear life.

Chapter 5

The reaction Delia got with her unexpected response was ardent and a little frightening for a woman who'd never indulged in heavy petting with a man she wanted. It was immediately obvious that Marcus was a man of experience, and that he knew exactly how to get past a woman's reserve.

His big body levered slowly down against hers in a sensuous, lazy movement that made her tremble with new sensations. His knee edged her legs apart so that he could fit himself between them.

She gasped and stiffened at the explosive pleasure.

He lifted his lips a scant inch from hers. His breathing was heavy, his eyes full of dark fire. "What's wrong?" he asked roughly.

She was out of her depth, but she didn't know how

to tell him. He seemed to think she was much more experienced than she was.

"Too fast?" he whispered, biting softly at her mouth. "I'll slow down. Is this better?"

Better? It was torture! His hand slid down her throat, around to her shoulder, and then with anguished slowness to the soft curve of her breast through the wet fabric.

Her legs were trembling. Her hands were gripping his broad shoulders for support. She was dizzy with sensation as his strong fingers worked magic on her soft skin. He teased up and down between her breasts with little brushes of pleasure that only built the hunger without satisfying it.

She arched her back gently and coaxed his fingers lower, but he lifted his head and looked at her curiously.

"You're shy," he mused, laughing tenderly. "I can't believe it."

"I've always been shy," she whispered, shivering as his fingers finally edged out toward the taut, sensitive tip of her breast.

"But there's nothing cold about you, is there?" he breathed at her lips. He nibbled the top one tenderly, tasting it with his tongue before his strong white teeth closed gently on the lower one.

At the same time, his hand shifted, and covered her breast under the dress. Her eyes rolled back in her head with the force of the pleasure. Her soft cry of pleasure was captured by the slow, hard assault of his mouth as it opened hers and his tongue began to penetrate it with long, deep thrusts.

Her body was no longer her own. She felt his hips sink against hers, so that they were intimately pressed together between her long legs. The close contact was agonizing. His hands were under the blouse now, under the bra, against bare, eager skin. She lifted toward them, shivering rhythmically with the gentle thrust of his hips against hers.

"It's no good," he groaned. "I can't stop."

She couldn't even pretend to protest when he suddenly picked her up and strode into the house with her, his head pounding with a desire so sharp and profound that he couldn't even think.

She lay against his chest, feeling his heart beat, feeling his incredible warm strength, her breath catching in her throat with each step. She was trembling with wild little pulses of desire, so aroused that she couldn't bear even the thought that he might stop.

He carried her into the master bedroom, kicking the door shut behind him. He barely took time to lock it before he fell onto the patterned brown coverlet with her body under his.

He ripped at his shirt and hers until they were breast to breast while he kissed her with anguished, ardent passion.

His hands were relentless on her wet clothing, stripping it off expertly and tossing it onto the carpet. She lay nude under him, and her only thought was that his hands were heaven on her cool, bare skin. She moved helplessly as he touched her in ways and places that no man had ever touched her.

When his mouth drew down her throat and onto her breasts she actually gasped at the explosion of delight. When it fixed on to her nipple and slid down over it, she shuddered. There was a wave of heat swelling in her lower body. She was blind, deaf, dumb to anything except raw sensation.

"Are you taking anything?" he rasped at her lips.

"You mean...like the Pill or the shot?"

"Yes."

"No," she whispered miserably.

"It's all right," he said huskily. "You don't have to worry. I'm healthy as a horse. I've got something to use, and I'll be careful with you."

It would have taken more willpower than she had to question what was happening. She was twenty-three years old, and no man had really wanted her. Certainly she'd never wanted anyone so much. A little voice at the back of her head started screaming warnings, but she couldn't hear it.

He stood up and stripped, letting her watch. When he tore off the black silk boxer shorts and she saw him aroused, she gasped. She'd seen one or two pictures of men like that. None of them compared to him.

He liked her rapt stare, but it aroused him even more. He fumbled something out of his wallet and pulled her up into a sitting position.

"Put it on for me," he said gruffly.

She flushed rose red. "I'm sorry," she stammered. "I don't...well, I don't know how."

He grimaced, but the odd statement didn't register through the desire. His hands were unsteady. He couldn't remember being in such a state with a woman until now. Perhaps it was the long abstinence.

He managed to get the prophylactic into place in record time. He laid her back on the coverlet, his eyes intent, his body corded with desire.

"Don't...don't hurt me," she managed weakly.

He felt a hesitation in her that puzzled him, in addition to the quick little frightened plea. But he was much too far gone to ask questions.

"I'd cut off my arm before I'd hurt you, sweetheart," he whispered. "In fact, this is going to be the sweetest hour of your life. I promise."

As he spoke, he bent to her body and his mouth opened on soft, warm skin.

In all her reading—and there had been a lot—nothing prepared her for the minutes that followed. She was shocked, overwhelmed, delighted and drowning in sensations. She should have protested, at least once, but she couldn't manage a single word. Instead she opened her legs for him, lifted her hips for him, writhed in unholy torment as he kissed her slowly, expertly, and kindled such a flame of desire in her that she begged for relief.

He lifted his head and watched her face while his hand caressed her with deadly mastery, making her sob with building pleasure.

He bent to her mouth, brushing it with his lips. "You're ready for me," he whispered huskily. "Do you want to feel me inside you?"

She cried out in torment. "Yes!"

One long, powerful leg inserted itself between hers while his hand slid under her hips and lifted her into sudden, starkly intimate contact.

Her eyes snapped open as he began to move. He watched her wide-eyed shock with throbbing curiosity.

When she stiffened and her nails dug into his upper arms, and he felt the reason for her sudden stillness, he began to realize what was happening.

He paused for a second, his breath ragged as he

searched her eyes. "If I'm your first man, you'd better tell me quick," he bit off.

Her eyes were tortured. The answer was in them, stark and vivid.

He drew in a quick, shaky breath. He swallowed, hard. "It's all right," he whispered reassuringly, taking deep breaths to slow down the anguish of need. "I'm not going to move again. You are," he said gently. "Come on. I'll let you control it."

"I don't know how," she whispered brokenly. "I'm so sorry…"

"For God's sake, there's nothing to be sorry about! Here. Push up against me," he said urgently. "Come on, honey, I can't hold it much longer. Push!"

She obeyed him, grimacing when the pain bit deeply into her.

"Easy," he whispered. His hand moved between them and found the tiny bud that controlled her pleasure. He touched her where his caresses had already made her sensitive, brushing her lightly until she gasped and began to lift toward him instead of away from him. "Do it again. And again. Just like that."

She felt the pain slowly lessen, the pleasure grow, with his expert touch.

"Good girl. That's it. I'll bring you to the edge of pleasure and when you fall, I'll go into you," he breathed sensuously against her open mouth. "I'll go into you hard and fast and deep…"

She moaned hoarsely at the impact of the words and his sensuous caresses, and all at once, there was no more time. She cried out sharply as ecstasy rose up like a hot tide in her body and suddenly exploded into a symphony of pleasure.

She shuddered and shuddered, her eyes half-closed, her body moving rhythmically with his as he pushed down hungrily and she felt the power of him over-whelming her. Throbbing waves of hot sensation built to fever pitch as the sound of his harsh breathing echoed like her own. Waves of delight began to buffet her as the terrible tension finally began to shudder away in ecstasy.

She'd thought the pleasure had reached its peak, but with the sudden hard penetration of his body, her climax shot to an even higher level, one which she thought was certain to kill her. It was almost pain. She sobbed and sobbed as she felt him groan harshly and then shiver against her. His movements, like hers, were helpless, involuntary. It was so sweet that she wept.

When the world came back into focus, she was cling-ing to him with all her strength and still sobbing in the hot aftermath.

"Did you feel it?" she whispered brokenly into his hot, damp throat. "Did you feel it, too?"

"Of course I felt it!" He collapsed on her, giving her his weight as he tried to catch his breath. "I've never been so hot in my life! I'm still not spent. Can't you feel me? I'm dying for you!"

"You…are?"

He lifted his head and looked into her wide, curious eyes. Virginal eyes. She didn't have a clue what was hap-pening. And now it was too late to go back. He moved his hips experimentally and she gasped and lifted toward him as what he'd said became starkly understandable.

"Can you go again?" he whispered tenderly.

"Yes," she replied, her body throbbing with every soft brush of his.

He ground his teeth together. "I can't stop," he groaned.

She reached up and touched his cheeks, slid her fingers into his thick black hair, lifting its crisp waves. "I don't mind," she whispered shyly, having never felt so close to another human being. He was part of her now. Completely part of her, in every way.

"Forgive me," he bit off as he kissed her passionately.

She wanted to tell him that there was nothing to forgive, but already the fever was rising in her body. She felt the first returning throbs of pleasure and closed her eyes.

Eons later, she opened her eyes and realized that they'd been asleep. As she looked at the wealth of bare skin on display under the light sheet, his and hers, she felt suddenly embarrassed and ashamed and guilty. She'd been saving her chastity for marriage. It had never occurred to her to give it away to a man she'd only known for one day! She was horrified at what she'd permitted to happen.

But she couldn't blame him. She hadn't made a single protest. It was her fault as much as his. She could still remember the hot urgency of the need, like an unquenchable thirst in both of them. There had been no way to stop it. It had happened too fast.

At least there wouldn't be any consequences, she consoled herself. He'd used protection.

He opened his eyes, stretched, and gave her a long, quiet look before he drew her into a sitting position beside him and cupped her face in his big, warm hands. "I didn't plan this," he said firmly, with dark, steady eyes. "It was never meant to happen. I just lost control completely when I started kissing you."

"I know," she said miserably. "I lost control, too."

He kissed her softly. "At least tell me you enjoyed it, so I won't feel like drowning myself."

He sounded genuinely upset. She lifted her shamed eyes to his. "It was the most incredible experience of my life," she confessed. "I...loved it."

"So did I," he replied roughly. "It was worth anything. Even my life."

She searched his eyes curiously. He didn't seem the kind of man who would think of sex as a solemn act. Quite the opposite. But he looked totally serious.

"Delia, I've never been with a virgin," he said in a deep, soft tone. His voice was husky, sincere. He touched her face tenderly. "I could barely believe it, even while it was happening."

She couldn't answer him. She was dumbfounded.

"I didn't hurt you too much, did I?" he persisted.

She shook her head. "Only a little. Honest."

He pulled her up off the bed with him and nudged her toward the bathroom. "Let's have a bath. Then we'll sit down and talk."

"A bath?"

"In the hot tub," he said.

He started the water and gathered up washcloths and towels. When the tub was full, he turned on the jets and coaxed her into the water. It was heavenly, although the water stung a little in her delicate feminine core.

"I was afraid of that," he murmured apologetically. "Is it bad?"

"Not at all," she said. "I'm fine. Really."

He leaned back against the edge of the bath and scowled.

"Something's wrong," she guessed. "What?"

"You do know that no sort of birth control is fool-proof?" he asked gently.

Her heart jumped. "Yes."

He sighed. "Delia, what I used is for one time. We went two."

"And...?"

"It tore."

She felt uncertain. Her eyes were troubled.

He grimaced. "Listen, I'd take care of you, if something happened," he told her.

"You mean...a clinic...?"

"No!" He looked horrified. He paused. "Would you...?"

She shook her head. "I couldn't."

He relaxed. He stretched, grimacing as muscles protested. He saw her watching him and he chuckled. "I feel my age sometimes. I'm older than you. A lot older." He looked at her worriedly. "Am I too old?"

"Don't be silly," she said, smiling.

He drew in a long breath. "Hell. I don't know where I am. It was going to be lunch and a tour of the pirate tower. Now look at us."

Her eyes dropped to his broad, hair-covered chest and his muscular arms. They were very strong. She remembered the power of his body above her, driving down against her with furious rhythm.

She blushed.

He lifted an eyebrow. "My, my," he murmured. "Pleasant memories?"

She threw her washcloth at him.

He liked that, and it showed. He caught the cloth and moved suddenly, making a huge wave, as he imprisoned her against the wall of the whirlpool bath. "Now, that was reckless," he whispered, crushing her mouth under his while his hands found her soft breasts and explored them hungrily. "You're sore and I'm wasted."

She linked her arms around his neck and kissed him back, hungrily. Her body was singing to her. She throbbed with remembered pleasure. "You're just dynamite," she whispered unsteadily.

"So are you. Explosive. Passionate. Delicious. I could eat you alive!"

"I thought that's what you were doing," she teased, kissing him sensuously, feeling, for the first time, her power as a woman.

"Delia, this is crazy. We're both out of our minds! We can't have this sort of complication," he groaned.

She lifted her breasts against his chest and moved them seductively. "We can't? Are you sure?"

He kissed her again, savoring the feel of her nude body against his. "You don't know what it's going to be like," he said worriedly. "We're going to want each other all the time. It will show. People will see it."

"Does it matter?" she murmured in a dazed cloud of pleasure.

"Yes, honey, it does," he replied solemnly, lifting his head. "You don't know who I am, what I am. You don't know how dangerous it could be."

That was when she remembered what Barney and Barb had said to her. It assaulted her mind with shattering reality. She looked up at him with wild, frightened eyes that betrayed her knowledge.

He frowned. "You know who I am, don't you?" he asked then. "You knew when I picked you up at your hotel."

She bit her lower lip worriedly.

He eased her away from him and got out of the tub, drying himself perfunctorily before wrapping his big body in a white terry-cloth robe that emphasized the soft olive of his complexion.

She scrambled out of the tub and grabbed one of the big bath towels on the warming rod, wrapping herself in it with growing embarrassment.

He turned with a long sigh and looked at the devastation in her face. "I didn't want you to know," he said gruffly. "At least, not yet. Not until you knew me better."

She laughed inanely. As if they could know each other any better physically!

"Did your sister tell you, or did Barney?" he persisted.

She drew in a long breath. "Both of them."

He didn't move any closer to her. He wanted to. He wanted to pick her up in his arms and cradle and comfort her. He actually winced as he realized what must have been said about him, about his past. He wasn't like that now. He was legitimate in every way, but he couldn't tell her that. He couldn't admit that he'd broken the old ties, given up the old life. So much depended on his actions. He couldn't afford to trust anyone, least of all a woman he barely knew—despite the unusual feelings she kindled in him. He'd already been sold out by one woman he trusted, and that incident had nearly cost him his life.

He was watching her, waiting, uneasy.

She felt sick to the soles of her feet. In the heat of the moment she'd forgotten everything she knew about him. Now, when it was too late, her reason came back.

"I'm not quite as bad as they made me out to be," he said after a minute. "I'm not wanted anywhere in the States. In fact, I was only arrested once, when I was about twenty, on conspiracy charges. But they were dropped. That's gospel."

That made a difference. She relaxed a little as she looked at him. "I don't know a lot about the real world," she said after a minute. "I've been sheltered all my life, by my mother and, especially, by Barb. I've only had one or two dates, and they ran for the border after Barb grilled them when we got home again."

He cocked an amused eyebrow. "Your sister intimidates men?"

She nodded. "She's formidable."

"Are you afraid of her?"

"Not afraid, exactly. But I've never disobeyed her much."

He frowned worriedly. "Did you tell her you were going out with me?"

She blushed scarlet.

"Uh-huh," he murmured.

"She'd have told me not to go," she explained.

That made him feel better. If she was willing to risk her sister's wrath for him, she must feel something.

"And you wanted to go," he said softly.

Her eyes searched his with pure anguish. "It was all I thought about," she confessed. "I wanted to see you, so much."

"I wanted to see you, too." He moved closer, his big hands reaching for her shoulders. He pulled her closer. "Take a chance on me," he coaxed. "I can't make any promises right now, but I can't bear the thought of losing you."

She smiled weakly. "Me, neither."

His warm hands reached up to her cheeks. He

searched her eyes hungrily before he bent and kissed her with aching tenderness.

He wrapped her up tight and kissed her until her mouth felt bruised.

"Stay with me tonight," he ground out against her lips.

"All…night?"

"All night, Delia." He lifted his head. "Yeah, I know, we're both too sore to do much except hold each other, but I want that. I want it more than I can tell you."

So did she. "What can I tell the desk clerk at my hotel if Barb calls and asks where I am? She'll be frantic."

"I've got a friend named Karen." He smiled when she looked jealous. "She's sixty and she loves a conspiracy, especially a romantic one. She'll tell your sister that you met her here at the casino and accepted an offer to go sailing early in the morning. She's got a yacht."

"She does?" she exclaimed. "I've never been sailing!"

He chuckled at the excitement in her eyes. "Would you like to spend the day on the ocean? I'll call her right now."

He held Delia's hand as he went back into the bedroom and pulled his cell phone out of his slacks' pocket on the floor. He tossed the slacks into a chair and pushed a button on the phone.

He dropped down into an armchair and pulled Delia onto his lap. "Hi, Karen," he said with a smile in his voice. "How's it going?"

There was a pause. He tucked Delia against his shoulder and kissed her damp hair. "I've got a girl," he said. There was another pause, and he laughed. "No, this one doesn't gamble or drink. She's from Texas and she teaches quilting." Another pause. He laughed again.

"That's exactly what I was thinking. How would you like to meet her? She's never been on a boat."

He turned his head and looked down at Delia with warm, sparkling eyes. "We'll meet you at the marina at 10:00 a.m. Bring a basket. You bet! See you."

He closed the flip phone. "What's wrong?" he asked when she frowned.

"I don't have a change of clothes," she said. "I'll have to go by the hotel…"

"Baloney. What size are you?"

"I'm…I'm a ten," she replied.

He picked up the phone again and spoke, but this time in fluent Spanish. He nodded and spoke again. He hung up. "They're sending over a selection of shorts, skirts, and sundresses. You've already got those cute little zip-up pink sneakers," he teased, indicating them on the floor.

"You can do that?" she stammered. "I mean, just have people send a shop to you?"

"Bibbi's my cousin," he said lazily. "She runs a boutique in the arcade down the street."

"But she doesn't know me."

"I told her to bring pastels, pinks and blues and yellows," he said. "I notice you like those colors."

"You're just…amazing," she managed to say.

He smiled and bent to kiss her softly. "Wait," he whispered. "You haven't seen anything yet. What do you want for supper?"

"It can't be that late," she began.

He pulled a clock around on the table beside the chair. Amazingly they'd been in the room for three hours.

She started to speak and couldn't.

He bent and kissed her eyelids shut. "I know it seemed quick, but it really wasn't," he whispered. "And we slept."

She looked at his face with wide, curious eyes. "I've never done anything like this," she said, trying to make him understand. "I take forever just ordering food at a restaurant. I'm very deliberate."

"But you rushed into this without being able to think and you're upset," he said perceptively. "If it's any consolation, it was just like that for me. I usually think things through myself. I'm not impulsive. But this was beyond my control."

"That's what I was just thinking."

He touched her mouth with his fingertips, noting its slight swell. "You were waiting until you married, weren't you?"

She nodded sadly.

"But you'd want kids, a home, a place you belonged."

"Yes."

His thumb rubbed at her lower lip and he scowled. "Would you want me, like that? Would you want me to belong to you?"

Her lips parted on a surge of feeling. "Oh, yes."

He was still scowling. "Nobody ever wanted me for long," he said absently. "For my money, sure, for a fling, an affair. But not with the works. A home and kids."

"Why not?" she wondered.

"Maybe I've liked the wrong sort of women."

"What sort?" she asked, because she was genuinely curious.

"Beautiful women with long legs and no scruples," he said simply. "Models, showgirls, even an actress. They liked fancy cars and easy money and plenty of plunder."

"Girl pirates," she said, trying not to look jealous.

Her eyes were sizzling. "Why, you're jealous," he mused, surprised.

"Why would I be jealous of beauty and talent?" she asked wistfully. "I mean, I'm so drop-dead gorgeous and talented—"

"You're beautiful all over, especially your heart," he interrupted. "And I consider quilting an art."

"I've never been a man-killer."

"That's what you think," he said with a grin.

Delia's eyes twinkled. "But I'm nothing to look at," she protested.

He wrapped her up tight and smiled down at her. "I've already told you, beauty is in the eye of the beholder. To me, you're a knockout."

She was suspicious. "You aren't just saying that because you feel guilty?"

He shook his head. "I value honesty above everything. Just like you." He did feel guilty at saying that, because he was involved in the biggest lie of his life, and he couldn't tell her.

Chapter 6

The hotel sent their supper order over to his house in a van. They shared shrimp cocktail, steak and salad, and a bottle of champagne. But Marcus had her stay in the bedroom when it arrived, because he didn't want his staff to know that he had a woman in his house.

"It isn't that I'm ashamed of you," he told her when they sat at the table savoring the delicious food. "But I don't want it to get back to your people."

"Especially Barb," she agreed.

"Yeah."

She finished her meal and reached for a piece of lemon cake with a pudding center as Marcus refilled their cups with fresh coffee that he'd brewed.

"This is delicious," she said with real feeling, savoring it. "I can make a lemon cake, but not with this filling!"

"I'll have the chef share his recipe and you can make it for me."

"But you've got a chef," she argued.

He reached across the table for her hand. "Nothing wrong with home-cooked food. The way to a man's heart…?"

She smiled.

"Has Karen lived in the Bahamas a long time?" she asked.

He nodded. "She's British, but she came down here for a holiday and never went home. She used to be an anthropologist," he added. "She went on digs in Egypt in her younger days. Now, she's happy piddling around in her flower garden or knitting."

"Does she quilt?" she asked.

He nodded. "She taught me machine piecing, although I rarely use it. I much prefer hand-quilting."

"Me, too," she agreed.

The cell phone rang suddenly. He picked it up and listened. "No," he said curtly. "No, I can't. Not today." He looked over at Delia thoughtfully. "That was your fault, not mine. How long are you going to be in Miami? The end of the week. Yeah. You can call me when you get back. We'll see. I said, we'll see. Yeah."

He hung up, but immediately dialed again. "Smith? Listen, I don't want any more calls today. I'm forwarding everything over to you." He listened. "Tell them I'm unavailable until tomorrow night. Got that?" He pursed his lips. "None of your business. Do what I told you. If there's an emergency, you handle it. Yes, I'll back you up. Fine. Thanks."

He put the phone away and pulled his own slice of

chocolate cake over to him. "Don't you like chocolate?" he asked.

"I get migraine headaches from it sometimes," she said. "I don't want to ruin tomorrow."

He grinned and dug into the dessert with gusto.

He liked the windows open at night, Delia noticed. She lay in his arms in the king-sized bed and thought how difficult it was going to be to explain this to Barb. Then she felt the warmth of his big body next to her, and the wonder of intimacy she'd had with him, and she didn't care. Whatever the cost, she was truly happy for the first time in memory. She'd take the consequences and deal with them, whatever they were. He felt her move and his arms brought her close, enfolded her in their warm strength.

"Don't leave me," he whispered, half-asleep. "Don't ever leave me."

"I never will," she whispered back. "I promise."

She curled into his body with a sigh and went back to sleep. If Barb called the hotel to make sure she was all right, they'd tell her that Delia was staying at Karen Bainbridge's house, and Karen would tell them the same thing. It was nice to have an alibi. She didn't consider that it would be the first time she'd lied to Barb. A lot of firsts were happening to her. She'd grown up and she was certainly old enough to make her own decisions, her own choices. Maybe this was terribly wrong, but she'd never wanted anything more than these days with Marcus.

A tiny voice in the back of her mind warned her that some things came at an exorbitant price. She refused to listen. All that mattered was this sweet feeling of belonging, of...love. She sighed softly and fell asleep.

The next morning, Delia was dressed and waiting in the living room when the boutique owner, a pert olive-skinned woman with dancing dark eyes, waltzed in behind two men carrying boxes.

"Hi, Bibbi," Marcus greeted.

"Hi, yourself. I brought a selection," she told Marcus, turning a cheek for his kiss. *"¿Esta ella?"* she added in Spanish, nodding at Delia. *"Bonita,"* she added with a grin.

"She's pretty, all right," Marcus agreed with a smile. "Okay, honey, take a look and pick out what you want."

"Do you take credit cards?" she asked Bibbi.

"I'm paying," Marcus began.

"You are not," Delia said firmly, smiling at Bibbi. "I've got my credit card."

Bibbi gave Marcus a speaking glance. "A woman with principles," she said. "That's a novelty in your life, cousin," she added wickedly. "Yes, I take credit cards and you're in luck, because you hit a sale. All these are thirty percent off."

"Wow!" Delia exclaimed, and dug into the boxes.

An hour and six outfits later, Bibbi took down the information, shook hands, packed up her merchandise and followed the two men who carried it out. She waved at Marcus with a wide grin.

"You're going to be a pain in the butt, aren't you?" Marcus asked Delia as she tried to decide which outfit to wear sailing.

She glanced at him. "About letting you buy me

things? Of course. Did you expect to have to pay me off for last night?" she added seriously.

He stuck his hands into his slacks' pockets. "I always expect to pay for whatever I get," he replied, his tone somber and disillusioned.

She could only imagine the sort of women he was used to. She put her new treasures down and went to him.

"I wanted what happened," she said in a gentle tone. "I didn't do it for personal gain. I don't play that sort of game."

He grimaced. "Sorry," he said tersely.

She searched his dark eyes quietly. "It's all right. We don't know a lot about each other. We're bound to make assumptions."

"A few, here and there, maybe," he agreed. He tugged her close. "We'll stop by a restaurant along the way to Karen's boat and get breakfast. I told her we'd be there about ten. That suit you?"

She smiled. "Yes. But I still haven't decided what to wear."

He went to the pile of clothing and tugged out pink Capri pants and a filmy white cotton top and a black-and-pink floral bathing suit. He handed them to her.

"You're going to be bossy," she surmised.

He grinned. "Count on it. I come from a macho culture. You'll have to be pretty tough to stand up to me."

"I think I'll manage," she replied, smiling back. "Okay, I'll go change."

She started toward the bedroom and suddenly stopped. She turned and found him watching her hungrily.

He cursed under his breath, hating his own weakness as he moved into the bedroom behind her.

He tossed her clothes on the bed and bent to her mouth, sweeping her up against him ardently.

"You're all I think about," he muttered against her mouth. "I'm sure it's unhealthy."

She linked her arms around his neck, tingling at the pleasure it gave her. "There's probably a pill for it."

"I don't want to be cured," he whispered, kissing her again.

His hands worked on her clothes, smoothing off everything except her bra and panties. He looked down at her with unbridled desire and his eyes asked a question as he brushed his thumb against her nipple through the lacy fabric.

She grimaced. "I want to," she assured him.

"But you're still sore," he guessed.

She nodded grimly.

He laughed shortly. "It's my own fault. I was greedy."

"So was I."

He kissed her lightly and reached for the Capri pants, holding them for her to step into. He fastened them around her small waist and then stuffed her into the blouse. He reached up and loosened the hair she'd tucked into a bun. "There," he murmured, studying her. "Much better. I think I like having my own dress-up doll."

"We'll run out of clothes eventually," she said.

He shrugged. "I'll learn to make them."

She laughed. "I don't have to learn. I can already make clothes."

"Show off."

"I'll teach you," she promised.

His smile was wicked. "There are several more things

I plan to teach you, too," he added, and he didn't mean sewing.

"Be still my heart," she whispered.

He kissed her slowly, fiercely. "We've barely touched the surface," he said. "Wait and see."

He put her away after a minute and tugged her by the hand. "Breakfast," he said again. "I'm starved, but food will have to do for now."

She laughed as she went with him.

He stopped at the little sports car and looked down at her for a long time.

"What are you looking for?"

"I was wondering what you looked like when you were a little girl," he said. "I was thinking that kids are nice."

Her heart jumped wildly. "We've only known each other for two days," she began.

"Hell. How long does it take to know how you feel?" he demanded. "Two days, two years, I'd feel the same. There's already a connection between us. Tell me you don't feel it. You want my kids. I can see it in your eyes."

She blushed. "I've always wanted children," she said in a husky, aching tone.

"I haven't really thought about having them until now," he told her. "Maybe I had some vague idea of the future, but nothing definite. You'd look right at home with kids around you."

She nibbled her lower lip. "Aren't you just making the best of a mistake, by saying that?"

"When you know me better, you'll see that I never make mistakes," he said blandly. "Being perfect, I'm above that sort of thing."

"Right."

He grinned. "Get in. We're wasting daylight, isn't that what you Texas girls say? I love Western movies."

"Listen, I can't even ride a horse," she protested.

"I'll bet you look smashing in a cowboy hat."

"We'll have to try one on me and see," she said.

"I'll take you up on that."

She wasn't sure if he was serious, but he certainly seemed to find her fascinating, because all the way to the restaurant he asked about her life back home.

The connection between them was staggering to Delia, who'd had very little to do with men all her life. She felt comfortable with Marcus in a way it should have taken years to accomplish. She loved just looking at him. He was big and dark and imposing, but he had a tender heart. She loved the way he spoke to little children they passed in the restaurant, the easy way he had with waitresses, making them feel at ease and not throwing his weight around. For a millionaire, and a gangster, he was remarkably polite.

The gangster part still nagged at her. So did her easy surrender to him. She'd lived by a code, one that didn't allow for such romantic escapades. She'd planned to get married and then sleep with her husband. She'd made no allowances for letting a man seduce her before then.

But she'd had no control whatsoever with Marcus. She still looked at him and ached to lie in his arms again and thrill to his kisses. It was scary.

She tried to hide it from him, though. It wouldn't do to let him see what a marshmallow she was.

There was also the problem of Barb, and that one wasn't going to go away. Barb was going to be disappointed in her, furious with her for cavorting with a known hoodlum.

There was one more complication that might arise—the consequence of a child. Even if Marcus was willing to do the right thing, how was she going to feel about having the child of a gangster?

She remembered reluctantly what Barney had said about Marcus and people who crossed him. He was a frightening figure to many people. If he had enemies, and surely he must, their child would be right on the firing line with Delia. It was a sudden and sobering thought. Marcus had asked her to trust him until she knew him better. She wanted to. For the moment, at least, she was going to make enough memories to last a lifetime. Just in case. And she wasn't going to think about tomorrow.

Karen Bainbridge was sixty, short, blonde, and a live wire. She didn't look her age. She had beautiful skin and saucy blue eyes. And she liked Delia at once.

"She's just the way I pictured her," Karen told Marcus as they climbed aboard her yacht. She paused to talk to her captain and tell him where they were going, while Marcus handed the picnic basket Karen brought to the steward to be put down below in the galley.

"What's in this?" he asked Karen as he gave it to the man.

"Chicken and biscuits, salad, fruit and a lovely cherry pie," Karen told him. "We have champagne, as well. Tell me, dear, where did you meet Marcus?" she added, pinning Delia with those bright blue eyes.

"At the hotel," Delia began.

"She had an abusive date and I rescued her," Marcus said lazily. "What a shock I had when I took her up to my office and discovered that she knew how to quilt!"

"I'll bet." Karen turned to Delia. "You know, dear, he's never been around women who could sew, except me. And as sad as it is to admit it, I'm simply too old for him. You're much more his style," she added wickedly.

"Yes, she is," Marcus agreed, smiling warmly.

"Tell me about yourself," she encouraged.

Delia hadn't planned to talk much about herself, but Karen was easy to open up to; very much like Barb. She related the abbreviated story of her life, ending with her mother's recent death.

Karen was sympathetic without being artificial. She patted Delia's hand gently. "We all have to learn to let go of the people we love most," she said softly. "It's one of life's hardest lessons. But, just think, someday we have to let go of life, all of us."

"I suppose so," Delia replied.

"Not that you'd dwell on it at your age," Karen said with an indulgent smile. "There's one little thought I'd like to share with you. I heard it from my mother when I was small. All the people we loved, who have died, are still alive in the past. The only thing that really separates us is time."

Delia eyed the older woman curiously. The thought really was comforting.

"See?" Karen added. "It's a matter of perspective. In other words, it isn't what happens to us, it's how we react to what happens to us. That's what separates optimism and pessimism."

"You're a deep thinker," Delia mused.

"I'm old, dear," came the laughing reply. "When you've lived as long as I have, you learn a lot, if you're the least bit observant." She glanced toward Marcus, who was talking to the captain in a relaxed, easy manner. "For instance, you're in love with my friend, there," Karen teased.

Delia drew in a long breath. "Hopelessly. I'm not an impulsive person, but I fell and fell." She met Karen's eyes. "It's only been two days," she said worriedly.

Karen didn't blink. "Love doesn't take a lot of time. It just happens."

Delia managed a watery smile. She stared at Marcus's broad back hungrily. "Do you…know about him?"

"That he runs around in, shall we say, shadowy company? Yes. But he's one of the best men I've ever known. He's a soft touch, and he never deserts a friend in trouble. Reputations are usually exaggerated, child," she added gently. "If I were your age, I wouldn't even hesitate. He's very special."

Delia wiped her eyes, smiling. "I thought so, myself. Sometimes, maybe taking a chance is the right thing."

"Count on it," the older woman advised. "And never judge a book by its cover," she added. "Or a quilt by its fabric alone."

"I won't forget."

They sailed out into the bay and then into the Atlantic Ocean. The high-tech fabric of the sails rippled in the wind and made whispery sounds. Seagulls darted to and fro. Delia sat beside Marcus and felt as if she belonged. Karen told her about the history of New Providence while they ate crisp salads and cold cuts.

Later, Karen drowsed while they sailed, and Marcus held Delia in front of him, idly kissing her neck and her ear and teasing her with the wind blowing noisily off the sea.

"This really is the Atlantic Ocean, isn't it?" she murmured, leaning contentedly back against his chest. "I used to think the Bahamas were in the Caribbean."

"A lot of people do. It's the Atlantic." He kissed her neck. "How do you like your vacation so far?"

"It's the best time I've ever had in my whole life," she said simply.

He hugged her closer. "Mine, too," he said huskily. "How much longer are you going to be here?"

"Three more weeks," she said, hating the thought.

"A lot can happen in just three weeks," he reminded her.

She turned in his arms. "A lot already has," she whispered, lifting her face.

He bent and kissed her warmly, hungrily, groaning deep in his throat as the kiss kindled fierce new fires in his big body.

"You're just incredible," she whispered when he lifted his head. Her eyes were misty with pleasure, her mouth swollen.

He enjoyed the way she looked. "So are you," he replied. "We need to make a quilt together," he mused.

She laughed. "I'd really like that."

"We'll talk about it."

"I like your friend Karen."

He glanced toward the elderly woman, still sleeping peacefully. "I like her, too," he said. "She's an odd bird. But then, so am I."

"Not so odd," she replied, touching his face with the tips of her fingers, exploring its broad strength, its nooks and crannies. "I like your face."

"It's a little banged up," he pointed out.

"It doesn't matter," she said. "It just gives you a sort of piratical look. I find it very attractive," she added shyly.

He chuckled, swinging her back and forth in his big arms. "I would have been a pirate in the old days, I guess." His face hardened. "Maybe I still am."

She put her fingers over his wide, sexy mouth. "You're just Marcus, and I'm crazy about you," she said simply. "Although maybe it's too soon to say that."

He shook his head. "I'm crazy about you, too, baby," he said huskily.

She laughed with pure joy, her eyes radiant with it as she looked up at him. "Is there really a future for us?"

He moved restively, thinking of all the complications in his life right now. He grimaced. "Look, we have to take this one day at a time," he said, searching her eyes. "It isn't what I want, but it's how it has to be. There's a lot going on that you don't know about."

"Not something...illegal?" she faltered.

He cocked an eyebrow. "Do you think I'd involve you in something illegal?" he asked openly.

She sighed. "No. Of course not. I'm sorry."

He touched her mouth with his fingertip, tracing its soft outline. "I will never hurt you deliberately. I promise."

She relaxed. "And I won't hurt you deliberately," she vowed.

"I now pronounce us dedicated to truth." He chuckled.

She reached up and kissed him. "Do we get to do what we did again?" she asked.

He drew in a long breath. "I want to get to know you," he replied. "Sex clouds the issues. Even if it is the best I ever had."

She brightened. "I like that idea, too. I'll bet you were a tough little boy."

"Very," he assured her. "I got in fights from kindergarten up. Broke my poor mother's heart."

"I never got in trouble at all," she replied wistfully. "Unless you count pouring salt on another girl's mashed potatoes because she called me a fat frankfurter in second grade."

"Were you? Fat?"

"Roly-poly," she admitted, smiling. "I lost weight."

"Don't ever get skinny," he said gently. "I like you just the way you are."

She beamed at him. It was, in many ways, the most perfect day so far.

They discussed movies and television shows and even politics, and found that they were amazingly compatible.

"Do you have a DVD player?" he asked her.

She grimaced. "I hate to admit it, but I can't figure out how to hook one up. I'm still using VCR tapes."

"Primitive," he remarked. "I'll have to come to Texas, if for no other reason than to show you how to move into the modern age electronically. Do you like music?"

"Yes. Latin music, especially," she confessed. "I have most of Julio Iglesias's albums, some Pedro Fernandez, some Luis Miguel, and half a dozen others. I even have some of Placido Domingo's opera performances."

"I'm impressed," he teased. "That's a fairly mixed bag."

"All terrific, too."

"Truly. How about reggae?"

Her eyebrows lifted. "What's reggae?"

He grinned. "We've got a Jamaican reggae band playing at the casino. I'll take you there one night and let you see if you like it."

"Could we dance?" she asked hopefully.

He laughed. "I may not look it," he said gently, "but I won dance contests when I was younger."

She was delighted. "I'll bet you still could."

"We'll find out," he promised.

They were on the way to landing at a small, deserted island when Marcus's cell phone rang insistently.

He excused himself and Delia frowned at the expression on his face. He seemed first curious, then angry, then furious. He barked something into the phone and hung up, glowering at the ocean.

After a minute he came back. "Some businessmen from Miami have turned up unexpectedly. We'll have to go back. Now," he added when Karen joined them.

"There will be other days for sightseeing," Karen said in a conciliatory tone. "Marcus, go and tell the captain to make for port, will you?"

"Of course," he said, but he was distracted.

At the marina, Delia said her goodbyes to Karen and let Marcus call a cab for her instead of sending her back in the limo.

"There are plenty of reasons that you don't need to be seen with me right now," Marcus said gently. "And the least of them is your sister. I'm really sorry about today. But I'll make it up to you tomorrow. We'll go sightseeing all over the island. How about that?"

"I'd love it," she said radiantly.

He grinned. "Tomorrow it is, then." He opened the door and put her into the cab without touching her. "See you in the morning."

"Yes. Take care," she said.

"You, too."

He closed the door. She looked back as the cab pulled out of the marina. He and Smith were still standing beside the limo, in deep conversation.

Chapter 7

Delia was up at daylight waiting for Marcus to call. Her whole life was suddenly caught up in his. She could hardly bear being away from him at all.

Barb had phoned soon after Delia got in, and Delia was able to tell her about Karen's yacht and the ocean day trip.

Barb relaxed audibly as she listened. There was no mention at all of Marcus, of course.

"You're sure you're not seeing that gangster?" Barb insisted.

"I was out with a nice little old lady seeing the sights," Delia said in a forcibly relaxed voice. "I'd love for you to meet her when you get back. She's British, but she's lived in these islands for a long time. She knows all the best spots."

"I'll take you up on that," Barb said finally, laughing. "Okay, I'm convinced. But you do keep your door locked at night."

"I do. Honest."

"Have you seen Fred? I heard he might be back from Miami already."

"No, I haven't seen him. Why?" Delia asked, curious.

Barb hesitated. "It was something Barney let slip. I think Fred may be a lot more dangerous than we realized, baby. You steer clear of him, just in case, okay?"

"I will. But why is Fred dangerous?"

She hesitated again, lowered her voice. "Well, I heard Barney tell somebody that he was thick with the Miami mob and that he was laundering money for it."

"Fred?"

"Yes, that's what I thought," Barb chuckled. "But you can't ever tell about people, and mostly the bad guys don't wear signs. Just the same, it would explain why he was so eager to take you to that gangster's casino on Paradise Island. There's a connection there, you mark my words."

"I'm not going to the casino, honest."

"I know that. Are you having a bad time without us? I'm just so sorry…"

"I'm having a ball with Karen and the beach," Delia laughed. "Really."

"I'm not surprised that your idea of fun is hanging out with a woman in her sixties," Barb said softly. "Mama and I were too hard on you, weren't we, baby?"

"I turned out just fine, thanks," Delia laughed again.

There was a sigh. "All right, I'll let you go. But be careful sailing around on yachts. There might be pirates out there, for all you know."

"If I meet one, I'll introduce you."

"You do that. Good night, baby. We should be back late next week or the week after. You're sure you don't want to fly over here and stay with us until we go back?"

Delia was thinking about the extra time she'd have to see Marcus while her sister was away. "I'm very sure," she replied. "Take care."

"You, too. Love you."

"Love you, too." Delia hung up, relieved that Barb hadn't noticed anything suspicious. She was learning to lie very well, she thought sadly. Maybe too well.

She didn't sleep worrying about what Barb had told her. If Fred was mixed up in money laundering for the mob, could that be why he'd gone to see Marcus?

She loved him with all her heart. But she had to admit that she didn't really know him very well. And what if he was mixed up in the mob? After the delight they'd shared, after she'd grown to care so much for him, could she really walk away?

It was barely six in the morning when she woke up and couldn't go back to sleep. She made coffee and sat out on the balcony of her room, watching the waves break on the sugar-white beach. Today Marcus was taking her sightseeing. Should she ask him if he and Fred were in business together? Did she dare? And what would she do if he said yes? The thought that he might end up in prison tormented her.

She tried to eat breakfast, but her stomach rebelled at the smell of eggs. That was so odd. She'd never had a lack of appetite in the morning. She touched her belly lightly and wondered. Could she tell, this soon? Or was she just becoming paranoid?

Paranoid, she decided firmly. All the warnings from

Barb were making her second-guess her own judgment.
She had to take it one day at a time and not borrow trouble.

So she was waiting when Marcus sent a cab for her
the next morning. It was John, the same cabdriver who'd
ferried her over to Paradise Island before. He was young
and personable and seemed to love the conspiracy.

"You like the boss, huh?" he asked her cheekily, in a
crisp, very clear British accent.

She laughed. "Yes. I like the boss a lot."

"He is a good man," he told her, the outrageous smile
gone. "My brother drowned last year when his fishing
boat capsized. He left a wife and six children. That Marcus Carrera, he set up a trust fund for them at a local
British bank, so they never have to worry about money
again. Some people say he is a bad man. But I do not
think so."

She smiled warmly. "Neither do I. What's your
name?"

"I am John Harrington."

"I am Delia Mason. And I'm very glad to meet you,"
she said sincerely.

"The same with me. I am sorry you have to hide your
trips to Paradise Island."

"So am I. It isn't the way I'd prefer to do things," she
added quietly. "But for some reason, Marcus thinks it's
better if we aren't seen together at my hotel."

"He has enemies, ma'am," he replied. "He is protecting you."

Her heart warmed at the suggestion. She hadn't considered that. She began to smile and couldn't stop. Protecting her. She liked that.

Marcus was waiting for her at the door of his house

where John dropped her off. He waited just until the cab was paid and waved away before he pulled Delia into his house, closed the door and kissed her half to death.

His hot face slid into her throat and he held her as if he feared she might be torn from his arms. "I can't bear this," he whispered roughly. "It's torture, being away from you even for a few hours."

Which was exactly how she felt. She kissed his warm neck drowsily. Her whole body throbbed. She wanted him. It was mutual, she could feel the instant response of his big body to her closeness.

His big hand slid around to the upper part of her thigh and tugged, pressing her hard against that part of him that was most male. He groaned.

She felt him shudder and her heart soared. He belonged to her. She'd never been more sure of anything.

"If you want to," she whispered, "I will."

He groaned again, sliding his mouth across her cheek to find her hungry lips. He kissed her with aching need, both hands on her hips now, rubbing her body roughly against his until they both shuddered.

But abruptly, he pulled back, let her go, and turned away to the sliding glass doors overlooking the ocean. He opened them and let the eternal breeze off the ocean cool his fever.

Delia joined him, still unsteady from the unexpected burst of passion. She folded her arms across her chest with a long, heavy sigh.

He glanced down at her, his dark eyes stormy. "I want to," he said without preamble. "But we're not going to," he added firmly. "I'm not going to try to turn you into my mistress. I have too much respect for you."

She was surprised by his straightforwardness. "You

aren't anything like your reputation, you know," she said softly.

He laughed harshly and turned his attention back to the white-capped waves breaking on the sugar-sand beach. "You don't know that part of my life at all," he said. "And I don't want you to."

"Everybody makes mistakes," she began.

He turned and took her by the shoulders. "My past is brutal. But I'm trying to start over, despite how it looks." His fingers contracted. "Listen, I want a family, children, a home—a real home—of my own." He looked tortured. "But there are things I have to do first. I have obligations that I can't share with you, people depending on me."

She was curious. "You're mixed up in something, aren't you?"

"Yes," he said bluntly. "Something bad and dangerous, and I can't share it."

"Are you…in danger?"

He drew in a sharp breath and looked out at the ocean over her blond head. "Yes." Her concern made him ache to tell her the truth. But he didn't dare. He looked down into her wide, trusting eyes and he grimaced. He touched her cheek with a tender hand. "You have to trust me, as hard as that may seem. I know it looks bad, but there is one great truth here—my feelings for you. Those are as real as that ocean out there." He bent and kissed her softly. "I adore you!"

She pushed close into his arms and kissed him back. She felt safe, treasured, comforted. She felt as if she were a part of him.

Marcus was feeling something similar. He should send her back to her hotel and have nothing else to do with her until this was all over. He was putting her life at risk. But he needed her, so desperately.

He stood in the wind, just holding her close, for a long time, his turbulent gaze on the ocean, which seemed as restless and tormented as he felt.

"When it's all over," he said huskily, "you and I will make plans for our future. Deal?"

"Deal," she whispered.

He bent and kissed her, one last time. "We'd better get going," he said gruffly. "Before I do what we both want."

She searched his eyes, uncomprehending. "Why don't you want to?"

He framed her oval face in his big, warm hands. "I've already made one almighty mistake, taking you to bed on our first date. I'm not making it again. My mother raised me to respect innocence. It goes against everything I believe in to make a convenience of you."

"But I'm crazy about you," she whispered.

He actually flushed. "Yeah. I'm crazy about you, too. But we're building a relationship that will last a long time. We need to go about it slowly. Agreed?"

"Agreed," she said reluctantly.

"Besides that," he worried quietly, "I'm too careless with you. I want children someday, that's no lie. But I don't want them right now. It's impossible. My life is too complicated."

Her heart skipped. She could be pregnant, and he didn't want children right now. She gave him a pained look.

"Don't look like that," he said softly, smiling at her. "It was just one time. There's no real risk. Right?" he added, a little uneasily.

"Right," she lied, and forced a smile. "No real risk at all."

"So we won't take any more chances. I was careless. I won't be careless again, and neither will you."

"Got it," she agreed.

"Now," he said, releasing her. "I've got a great itinerary. In the next few days, Miss Mason," he added with a grin, "I'm going to educate you in the folklore and history of the most interesting group of islands on earth!"

And he did. They started out early in the morning and came back at sunset. He strolled her down Prince George Wharf, through the gigantic straw market, where he bought her a beautiful purse and hat adorned with purple flowers. He took her on a carriage ride, where the horse pulling it wore a hat, too.

They saw the water tower, the artificial waterfall, Government House, and where a James Bond film was made. They went out into the ocean on a glass-bottomed boat, with a skipper who serenaded the crew in a reggae beat. They toured Fort Fincastle and Fort Charlotte. They walked along Bay Street and had lunch in quaint bistros. They toured the botanical gardens and Delia raved about the koi pond. They toured a hotel complex where an underwater aquarium was the key attraction. They saw a sponge warehouse and ate conch soup in a restaurant on the bay, where passenger ships were berthed at the wharf and tiny tugboats sailed to turn the big ships in the harbor.

Every night they had supper at Marcus's house, with Smith standing guard. And in the evenings, Delia lay in Marcus's arms on the patio near the big swimming pool, and listened to the waves crash on the beach as they talked about a future.

It was an idyllic time; two weeks of unbelievably sweet memories. During that time, Delia missed her period, and she felt nauseated not only in the morning, but at night, as well. She lost her appetite, and grew so tired that she started going back to her hotel no later than nine o'clock, pleading lack of sleep.

Marcus wasn't suspicious. He knew nothing about pregnant women, never having been around one—not even his sister-in-law when she was pregnant with his niece and nephew. He'd mentioned it once when they were talking. Delia was confident that she didn't have anything to worry about in that sense. But what was she going to do?

It was a problem she didn't want to have to face anytime soon, but the odds were against her being able to hide her condition. Especially when Barb came back. Her sister was a vacuum cleaner when it came to information.

Marcus made a lobster bisque while Delia made a fruit salad and poppyseed dressing, plus homemade rolls, to go with it. They'd shared food preparation only once before, but this particular night they didn't want to have someone bring food in.

Delia loved working in the kitchen with Marcus. They talked as they worked, and Delia teased Marcus about the size of his Shark Chef apron, which featured a cartoon shark grilling shrimp on a barbecue grill.

"We could try it on you, honey," he mused, "but I expect it would wrap around three times. You're tiny compared to me."

"I like that," she said with a warm smile.

He put the bisque off the burner to rest before it was served. Then he caught Delia close and kissed her hungrily. "I like it, too," he whispered at her lips. "You were almost too small for me in bed," he added with a dark affection in his eyes when she flushed. "That's why you got so sore." He bent and kissed her again. "But you'll fit me after the first few times," he added outrageously, teasing her lips with the point of his tongue.

She hid her face against his chest and laughed softly at the thrill of remembered pleasure the words provoked. "Are you...big?" she asked.

He roared.

She hit his chest, still without looking at him. "Well, how am I supposed to know about things like that?" she asked reasonably. "I've only ever seen men in magazines, and they sure didn't look like you did that night!"

He laughed deep in his throat. "You couldn't take your eyes off me," he recalled gently. "I loved it. I can't remember feeling like that in my whole life. It was like flying."

"I felt that way, too." She sighed and curled closer. "I love being with you."

"Yeah. Me, too," he said, but he sounded remote, distracted.

She lifted her head at the odd tone and gave him a long, curious appraisal. His face was taut and his eyes were troubled.

"Have I done something wrong?" she asked worriedly.

"As if you could," he chided. He bent and brushed his lips gently over hers. "I've got a problem or two that I can't share with you. Nothing major. Honest."

"It wouldn't be another woman?" she asked uncertainly.

He laughed softly. "No. It wouldn't be. I haven't had feelings for any woman in a long time." His big hand brushed her cheek. "None of them were ever like you," he added. "You're special."

"So are you," she replied.

"Besides," he added, "how far would I have to look to find another woman who knew quilts the way you do?" he teased.

She laughed. "Speaking of quilts," she added, tugging loose to go to her purse. "I found something in my pocketbook last night that I didn't even know I had. I want to give it to you. It's a pattern for a memory quilt that I'm working on."

She brought it to him. It was a small square with graceful curved lines and a tiny embroidered flower in the center.

"This is beautiful," he commented. "I don't embroider well, though."

"I do. It's one of my better skills. That's why I did the center square of the block like this. It's rather a variation on the Dresden Plate."

"Yes, I noticed, but you've pieced every wedge section individually. This is going to be a lot of work if you hand-quilt it."

"I want to do it by hand," she replied. "It's a labor of love. The fabric in that block comes from dresses worn by my grandmother and my mother, Barb and me," she added, pointing out the different fabrics. "I want to make a quilt that I can pass down to my own children one day. If any of them quilt."

He was studying her face, the block held loosely in

his big hand. "Maybe they'll like it as much as we do," he said quietly.

Which could only intimate that he was interested in fathering her children, and she brightened immediately.

"Thanks for letting me keep this," he told her. "I think I might do the same, with fabric from my niece and nephew's clothing and my sister-in-law Cecelia's. Maybe she's got something left from Carlo, as well."

"Carlo?"

"My brother. The one who died of a drug overdose." He didn't add that it was an injected overdose, that Carlo was killed for tipping off the feds about Fred Warner's Colombian money-laundering connection.

"How terrible for you. And for them," she added. "Your sister-in-law, does she come here to see you with the children?"

"From time to time, in the summer," he said. "The kids are five and six, respectively, and in school now. They're called Cosima and Julio." He smiled with re-membrance. "They're really cute. Smart, too. Carlo was brilliant with figures."

"What led him into drug use, can you tell me?"

He shrugged, moving away to put the quilt block on top of the counter. His fingers traced it lightly. "Why does anybody use them?" he asked coldly. "He was never strong enough for life, in the first place. Every time he and Cece had an argument, or he had pressure at work, or one of the kids got sick, he turned to narcotics for re-lief. I tried to stop him, Cece tried to stop him. We even had his parish priest talk to him. But he didn't want to quit. In the end, he took one hit too many and his heart stopped. He ended up in the hospital and we finally got him into rehab. It was a bad time," he added. "A real bad time. He was back on the right track and mad as hell at the people who got him hooked."

He stopped short of telling her that Carlo had gone after Fred Warner for revenge, since it was Fred who got him hooked. Fred wasn't aware that Marcus knew that. He thought Marcus considered him one of Carlo's friends. "Anyway, Carlo died of an overdose and Cece came apart at the seams. I ended up with the kids, down here in the Bahamas, with a nanny until she could cope again."

"Is she nice?" Delia asked, trying not to feel jealous.

"Yes. She's nice," he replied. "Pretty. Talented. She's a commercial artist. She lives in California now."

"Wow."

He gave her a long look. "Are you jealous?" he asked in a deep, husky tone.

She shifted restlessly. "Maybe. A little."

He laughed. "I've never even kissed her. She's definitely not my type."

"That's reassuring."

"How about you?" he wondered. "Do you secretly pine for Barney?"

She laughed, too. "Oh, sure, I hide under his bed at night hoping he'll notice."

"Barb would have you for breakfast," he commented.

"Probably. Barney's definitely her type, but I think of him as a big, cuddly brother. He's sort of like my hero, in a lot of ways. He's looked out for me since I was little, like Barb. Besides," she added with a flirting look, "I like big, dark men with deep voices."

He smiled broadly. "I like slight little Texas girls."

"That bisque is going to get cold," she said after a minute.

"So it is. We'd better eat it quick."

* * *

After they did the dishes, Marcus pulled her down onto a chaise lounge with him and they listened to classical music while the wind danced in the casuarinas pines and the ocean roared softly along the shoreline.

"It's so nice here," she murmured. "I love the Bahamas."

"Me, too. I feel as if I've come home, every time I come back here. The people are wonderful, and the climate is like paradise."

"It has so much history."

"Yes. And so much beauty." His hand contracted in her long hair. "But it can be a dangerous place, too. When Barb comes back, you and I are going to have to be distant acquaintances. You know that, don't you?"

She sighed. "Yes. I guess so."

"It's not what I want, either, Delia," he confessed. "But I can't afford to rock the boat."

"Can I do anything to help?" she asked him.

He moved restlessly. "This is something I have to do alone," he said, almost absently. His hand smoothed her hair. "Some people are coming here tomorrow," he added. "That means you can't phone me or come over here."

Her heart fell. "I can't talk to you?"

"The phones may be bugged," he replied. "I don't want you in any danger."

"Now you're scaring me," she told him.

His broad chest rose and fell heavily. He'd said too much. He had to backtrack to keep her from getting suspicious.

"They're just businessmen, but it's a big deal going

down, and quickly. I can't have any distractions, is what I mean. Nothing dangerous. Okay?"

She let go of the fear. "Okay," she agreed.

His hand filtered through her soft hair. "Worried about me?" he probed.

Her fingers toyed with a button of his silk shirt. "Always," she confessed.

She made his blood sing. He felt her body in the red sundress warm and fluid against his on the chaise lounge. She smelled of flowers. He could feel the quickness of her breath. It was going to be a long dry spell after this.

His big hand moved under hers and flicked open shirt buttons. He guided her fingers under the silk and taught her the motion and pressure he liked.

He felt warm and strong and just faintly furry. She loved the feel of his chest against her. She bent and drew her mouth along his collarbone, noticing with pride the way his big body shivered at the caress.

"Turnabout is fair play," he said in a husky tone. He unbuttoned the sundress and discovered to his delight that there was no bra under it. He pulled her closer, so that her breasts were pressed into the thick hair that covered his chest. "That's nice," he groaned.

"Yes." Delia slid her arms around him under the shirt, reveling in the wonder of being close to him. She ached to merge into his own body, there in the starlight, with the waves crashing on the nearby beach.

He turned her so that she was under him. His long, powerful leg eased between both of hers and insisted on dominion.

She didn't fight him. She loved the warmth of his big hands on her breasts as he kissed her with ferocious hunger. She arched up to his hands, gasping as the pleasure began to grow all over again.

He moved, so that his hips were directly over hers, so that they were as close as possible without the clothes that separated them.

"Oh, baby," he groaned into her mouth. "This is the closest to heaven it gets in the world. Feel how much I want you, Delia."

What he felt was blatant. His skin was damp with the passion that grew in him by the second.

"What if I can't stop?" he ground out against her mouth.

She relaxed into the soft cushions. "I don't mind," she whispered with aching need. She meant it. She sensed that he was distancing himself from her. He did care, she knew he did, but something was terribly wrong. She didn't want to lose him.

"Delia," he groaned, "we can't do this."

"Why can't we?" she asked, opening her legs to admit the weight of his powerful body between them. She lifted into him.

"This isn't the place... God!"

Just as he protested, her hand went shyly between them and she touched him, shocked at his reaction as much as she was surprised at his potency. Her memory of his body in arousal was less intimidating.

He caught her hand and moved it against him with pure sensual fever. "That's it. Here. Here!" He undid fastenings and seconds later, her hand was against hard, velvety soft skin.

She tried to draw back, but it was too late. He had her firmly in his grip and he was insisting. She followed his whispered commands first with shyness, then with pride, then with abandon as he gave in to the aching need for satisfaction and shuddered violently in her hands.

"It's no good, I can't stop," he ground out, and he stripped her out of the sundress and her underwear with confident finesse.

His shirt hit the pavement along with his slacks and boxer shorts, in short order.

"Yes," he groaned as he went into her with feverish passion. He lifted his head and watched her body accept him, even if it protested just slightly at the power of his possession.

"Marcus," she cried out, shocked and delighted all at once.

He moved again, still watching her. "It's going to be magic," he gasped.

She watched him, watching her, as they moved together on the chaise, while the whispery, urgent sounds of skin on fabric grew loud, like their breathing, in the softly lit darkness.

"What if someone…walks in?" she asked in a last bit of sanity.

"Who the hell cares?" he moaned. "Let them watch…!"

His rough, deep motions sent her out of control, throbbing with hot tension that built and built until finally, abruptly, she stiffened and shuddered and cried out in a hoarse, almost inhuman tone that faded like the night around them as she climaxed over and over again.

He let her wring the last bit of silvery pleasure from him before he drove hard and fast for his own fulfillment. He found it so suddenly that his voice rang out in the darkness as he convulsed over her.

She held him afterward, cradling his weight, caressing his dark, damp hair while he shivered in the aftermath.

"It gets better all the time," she whispered brokenly, kissing his throat.

"It gets more dangerous all the time," he replied roughly. "Delia, I didn't use anything. I was too far gone. I don't want to make you pregnant, baby. I don't dare!"

"Would it really be so terrible?" she whispered daringly.

His teeth clenched. "It would be…the end of the world for me, right now," he said bluntly, shattering the last of her dreams. She didn't know the danger he was in, and he was thinking what a stick it would give his enemies to have a pregnant woman for them to threaten. "I've told you that already. I don't want kids, Delia. Not now!"

Chapter 8

Delia clung to him tightly, her eyes closed as she hid her anguish at what he'd just said to her.

"I know you don't want to hear that," he said wearily. "I'm sorry. But there are things going on that you can't know about. We can't take any more chances. We can't be lucky forever."

"I understand."

"You don't, baby," he said heavily. "But that's all right." He eased onto his side, carrying her with him. "I'm crazy about you," he whispered. "That's the truth."

"I'm crazy about you, too, Marcus," she whispered back. "I'll never feel this way about anybody else as long as I live."

"You'd better not," he growled in mock anger. He kissed her gently. "We'd better get dressed. I have to get you home early tonight. I've got company coming."

"Company?" She felt uneasy.

He smiled. "Male company," he whispered, and kissed her again.

Once they were dressed and he'd phoned for a cab, he held her gently in the hall. "Listen," he said quietly, "don't think I'm trying to back out. I have to keep away from you for a while. It's nothing to worry about, and you're not to feel rejected. Okay?"

She felt worried, and it showed. "I can't even talk to you on the phone?"

"Not until I call you, or get in touch with you through Smith. Got that?" He held her by the shoulders, his hands heavy and firm. "You can't be seen associating with me until I tell you it's safe. Promise me!"

"I promise, Marcus," she faltered.

"You look as if I've thrown you out in the street and it's not like that," he said gruffly. "You're the best thing that's ever happened to me. I'm not going to let you go. So when you're picturing me with other women and worrying about whether I've dumped you, remember what I said. I care about you, very much. As soon as I can, I'll be in touch."

She managed a wan smile. "Okay."

"You can't tell your sister or Barney anything about us. Got that?"

"I wouldn't dare," she confessed.

He looked at her with deep concern. "We've got a future together. I promise you, we have. I'll find a way."

She sighed. "All right. I'll live on dreams for a while."

He traced a line down her cheek. "So will I, and they'll be sweet ones." He bent and drew his lips softly over her swollen mouth. "My sweet innocent. There's nobody else like you on earth, and you're all mine."

She smiled under his mouth. "And you're all mine."

He kissed her hungrily until the sound of a horn outside the door distracted him.

"Can I send you a note?" she asked.

He glared at her. "No notes, no phone calls, don't wave if you see me on the street. You don't know me, except for that night I saved you from Fred."

"Fred." She sighed.

"And stay the hell away from him, no matter what else you do," he said firmly. "Fred is big trouble."

"I noticed," she said, not realizing that they were talking at cross-purposes.

His dark eyes were troubled as he walked her to the front door. "Last month I was a happy, carefree bachelor," he murmured. "Now I'm not only losing my right arm, I'm seeing it off at the curb."

She laughed softly at the analogy. "I'm losing mine, too," she reminded him. "Or maybe I should say I'm going to be a needle without thread."

"Or a block without piecing," he countered, smiling.

She held his big hand in hers and looked up at him one last time. "Be safe," she whispered.

"I'll do my part. You do yours." He opened the cab's rear door for her. "John," he told the driver, slipping him a hundred-dollar bill, "you never saw me in your life and you just came from Karen Bainbridge's house with Miss Mason. Got that?"

"You bet, Mr. Carrera," John said with a grin.

Marcus stood and watched the cab pull away with a grim face. All too soon, he was going to be involved in a struggle he didn't anticipate with joy. But compared to losing Delia, even temporarily, it didn't concern him half as much.

* * *

Delia hid her misery until she was back at the hotel and in her room for the night. She took a long, hot bath and cried all through it. She couldn't shake the feeling that Marcus might be trying to set her down gently, despite his affirmations that he cared for her. Hadn't she heard all her life that men would say anything to get a woman into bed with them?

Now that she didn't have him to reassure her, she lost her confidence. It was all she could do to make herself get up and dressed the next morning and go down to the restaurant for breakfast.

It wasn't much of a breakfast at that, she thought as she sat by the clear waters of the swimming pool under some palm trees. She sipped orange juice and nibbled bacon. She couldn't even look at a fried egg.

She was staring uncertainly at the bacon on her plate when a shadow fell over her.

"It's too late," a deep voice commented.

She lifted her head and looked into a pair of black eyes in a rough, tan face surrounded by dark blond hair. He was tall, slender, muscular, and pleasant. He didn't look the least bit threatening, but there was something about him that made Delia tense inside.

"I'm sorry?" she stammered.

"The bacon. You can't set it free."

She got it. Her face brightened as she laughed. "Smart mouth," she commented.

He grinned. "My middle name," he replied.

She frowned. "I've seen you around here."

"Really?" he asked with a straight face. "When?"

She chuckled. At least he'd taken her mind off the bacon. "I'm Delia Mason," she introduced herself.

"Dunagan," he said, extended a hand.

"Just Dunagan?" she queried, wondering why his name sounded familiar. Hadn't Barney mentioned a man named Dunagan? She couldn't remember.

He grinned. "Mind if I join you?"

She hesitated.

"Let me guess. You're involved," he surmised.

She sighed. "Yes."

"No problem. So am I." He had a thoughtful look. "Of course, she doesn't know it, but why should that worry me?"

She blinked. "You're involved with a woman and she doesn't know?"

He shrugged. "I keep secrets. Are you here alone?" he added.

"With my sister and her husband," she said.

"Thought I recognized you. Your brother's Barney Cortero, right?"

"He's my brother-in-law," she corrected

"He's a good egg," he replied, studying her closely. "Why aren't they with you?"

"They had to go to Miami. But they're due back tonight," she volunteered.

He smiled. "I like Miami," he said. "I spend a lot of time there."

"I've never been to Florida," she said, smiling. "In fact, I've never been anywhere until now."

"Where are you from?" he wanted to know.

"Texas," she said. "You?"

His eyebrows arched. "You aren't going to believe this. I'm from Texas, too. Near El Paso."

"I'm from near San Antonio."

"We've got sagebrush and cactus," he bragged.

"We've got pecan trees and palms."

He shrugged. "To each his own. Maybe I'll see you around, again," he added with a congenial smile.

"Yes. Maybe so."

He winked and sauntered off toward the bar.

She smiled to herself. There was nobody who could compete with Marcus, of course, but her new acquaintance was definitely attractive. Back home, she'd had one date in two years. Now in the space of weeks, she was suddenly irresistible. But it didn't help to know that she was separated from Marcus indefinitely, and that she was almost certainly pregnant to boot. Marcus didn't want children now. What was she going to do?

The first thing was to make sure she really was pregnant. So she went to a drugstore and bought a home pregnancy kit. She used it. The result was positive.

She sat on the edge of the bathtub and stared down at the blue tile floor with her mind in limbo. She was going to have a child. She was twenty-three, unmarried and the child was fathered by a man who'd already said he didn't want children until much further down the road.

Now Delia was faced with a dilemma. Barb couldn't know about it; that was the first priority. She'd be inconsolable and furious, and so disappointed in her sister that it was agony to even contemplate her reaction.

The second priority was to make sure that she didn't slip up and show any symptoms that Barb would recognize. She had to make sure she slept late and didn't get exposed to scrambled eggs. She had to say that she exercised so much during the day that she was exhausted at night. Barb would buy that, because she'd never been pregnant. She couldn't have children at all. Delia wondered why. It was a subject that had never been discussed.

But as to what she was going to do about her child there was no question. She was keeping her baby, no matter what she had to do. If it meant moving overseas for nine months and pretending that she'd adopted a child, she'd do that. She'd do anything. She placed her hand protectively over her flat stomach and smiled dreamily. She was going to be a mother!

She tucked the pregnancy-test kit into a plastic bag, shoved it in her purse, and disposed of it in a trash bin in a nearby arcade. There was now no chance that Barb would find it.

She contrived to look rested, alert and happy when the hotel door opened and a weary Barney walked in with Barb.

"We're back, baby!" Barb exclaimed, and rushed forward to hug Delia warmly. "I'm so sorry we had to be away so long! Are you okay? There wasn't any trouble, or anything…?"

"Barb!" Barney inserted abruptly, and gave his wife a threatening look.

"I meant Fred hasn't been around?" Barb backtracked quickly.

"No, I haven't seen him," Delia assured her sister. "Did you have a nice trip?"

"It was business," Barb said evasively. "Have you been hanging out with the yacht lady?"

Delia chuckled. "Quite a lot. You have to meet her, too," she added with perfect composure. "She's a hoot. You'd never guess she was in her sixties. She's so full of life—and she quilts!"

"Aha," Barb said with a grin. "That's the draw, is it?"

"We've been trading patterns," Delia lied. Of course, she and Marcus certainly had traded patterns.

"And you haven't been seeing that gangster?" Barb added suspiciously.

"Barb, she already told you she hasn't," Barney groaned. "Stop grilling the girl."

Barb grimaced. "I'm sorry. It's just that I worry, especially now…"

"Barb, for God's sake!" Barney interrupted.

Barb flushed, holding up both hands, palms out. "Okay, okay!"

"Have you eaten supper?" Barney asked Delia.

"No, and I'm hungry," she said. She wasn't really, but she couldn't admit that.

"Let's all go get something to eat."

"Have you connected with any of the guests here?" Barb asked as they all went out the door together.

"Actually, I have, with one. His name's Dunagan."

Barney turned to her, frowning. "Dunagan?"

"He's from Texas, too," Delia chuckled.

"Yes, we know," Barb said absently.

"He's dishy," Delia said, playing it to the hilt. "Wavy blond hair, black eyes, nice body, weird sense of humor—just my type."

Barb pursed her lips and her eyes twinkled. "Well, well, progress!"

"Will you stop trying to marry her off?" Barney muttered. "She's just a baby."

"I was eighteen when you married me," Barb pointed out.

Barney gave her a grin. "So I robbed the cradle. That doesn't make it all right."

Barb made a face at him. "Spoilsport. I want to see my…sister happy like I am. What's wrong with that?"

Not for the first time, Delia found it curious that Barb always hesitated before she said 'sister,' as if she had a hard time with it. There was a tremendous age difference, of course, and she'd spent much of her life taking care of Delia. Probably she felt more like a mother than a sister, and who could blame her.

"I'll bet I ruined your love life," Delia mused. "Mama said you took me on your first date with Barney."

Barb didn't look at her. "That was Mama's idea. She thought you'd keep us straight."

"Didn't she trust you?" Delia asked innocently.

"Leave it alone, there's a good girl," Barb replied. "Quick, catch the elevator or we'll be stuck here for ten minutes!" She ran for it, with Barney and Delia trailing behind.

Dunagan was at the restaurant when they walked in, sitting all by himself, waiting for his order. He was wearing white slacks with a patterned silk shirt and a stylish jacket. He looked very masculine and expensive.

He spotted Delia and grinned as she and her party came even with him, behind the waiter.

"Great minds do think alike," he told her. "Care to join me? I need protection! I'm sure that at least two women in this restaurant have evil designs on me." He glanced around covertly.

She smiled. "Sorry. I'm with my sister…"

"Barb, you mean?" he persisted. "Hey, Barney, how's it going?" he added, greeting Delia's brother-in-law.

"Slow and tricky," Barney said. "You're still here, then?"

Dunagan shrugged. "Some jobs take a lot of patient work."

Barney and the younger man exchanged a puzzling look. There was something strange about the way they looked at each other. It was almost as if they were putting on an act.

"What do you do, Mr. Dunagan?" Delia asked as Barney seated Barb and then himself.

"I'm in real estate," he replied, smiling. He produced a card and handed it to Barney. "Right now, I'm trying to peddle some acreage on Paradise Island."

Barney lifted both eyebrows. "That's still on?"

"Definitely," Dunagan said easily. "I've got a buyer on the hook."

"Well, well," Barney replied.

The waiter arrived, and the small talk vanished as the menus were produced.

It was the strangest meal Delia could remember, and she was quietly suspicious of the easy rapport between Barney and Dunagan. Barb didn't seem to be aware of it.

Afterward, Dunagan went into the lobby with them and asked Barney if he knew anything about a statue just outside the hotel door.

The men walked away, talking animatedly.

"What's going on?" Delia asked her sister.

Barb looked innocent. "What do you mean, baby?"

"Barney and Mr. Dunagan are talking on two levels," she said. "I don't understand much, but they know each other. I'm sure of it."

Barb laughed. "You've got a very suspicious mind."

"It runs in my family," Delia said mischievously. "Now, give. What's going on?"

Barb was serious all at once. "I wish I could tell you," she replied. "But I can't. It's a very secret sort of project Barney's working on."

"With Dunagan?"

Barb turned and looked down at her sister. "I can't tell you anything."

Delia grimaced. "I get the feeling that nobody trusts me."

"That's silly. Of course I do. But this isn't my project, and I can't discuss it. Not even with my very favorite sister."

"I'm your only sister," Delia pointed out.

Barb hugged her. "My very special only sister."

Delia relaxed. She was very tired. It was her condition, she supposed. At least she hadn't been sick.

"Sleepy?" Barb asked curiously. "You're usually a night owl."

"I don't know what it is about the Bahamas," she said with a straight face, "but I've been sleepy like this for two weeks. Maybe I'm coming down with something."

Barb chuckled. "The paradise syndrome," she teased. "It's making you lazy."

"That'll be the day," she laughed.

"Yes. It truly will. Why don't you go on up to bed?" Barb asked, nodding toward the two men who were talking outside the hotel, with grim faces. "They may be out there all night."

"That looks like a distinct possibility," Delia said. "I think I will go on up. You sleep good, Barb."

"You, too, baby. Tomorrow we might go out in a glass-bottom boat, would you like that?"

"Yes!" Delia said with forced enthusiasm. "I'd really enjoy it."

"Then we'll do some sightseeing," Barb said. "You're not sick, are you?" she added worriedly.

Delia laughed. "Not me. Good night."

"Lock the door behind you. We've got our key," Barb called after her.

Delia did go up, but she didn't sleep. She laid awake worrying if the driver of the glass-bottom boat she and Marcus had gone out on would recognize her and say anything. They'd been careful most of the time, but on occasion, they'd been careless.

She realized that it would be ridiculous to assume that a boatman would recognize one couple out of the thousands that came through the Bahamas during the summer. But she couldn't help herself.

As it happened, she didn't need to worry. She had a phone call early the next morning.

"It's for you," Barb announced, poking her head into Delia's room. "Some lady with a British accent."

"Karen!" Delia exclaimed, grinning as she dug for the phone. "Hello?"

"Good morning, dear," Karen's accented voice replied. "Would you and your sister and her husband like to come sailing today?"

"I would," Delia said at once. "I'll ask my sister. Barb!" she called, with her hand over the mouthpiece.

Barb opened the door again. "What?"

"Would you and Barney like to go sailing?" she asked. "Karen's invited us out on the yacht."

Barb's eyes widened. "Would we!" she exclaimed. "Sure!"

"Barb said yes," Delia told her friend. "And thanks."

"Come over to my slip at the marina about ten, dear, and I'll pack a nice picnic lunch for us. See you then!"

"We'll be there," Delia promised, and hung up.

"A yacht. Wow!" Barb murmured. "Even Barney's friends don't have yachts. Nobody sails!"

"Karen doesn't, not often." Delia smiled. "You'll love her. She's sweet and British and very eccentric."

"My sort of lady," Barb agreed. "When do we leave?"

"About nine-thirty, to get to her slip at the marina by ten. We'll have to take a taxi."

"I'll tell Barney."

The door closed and Delia's heart raced. She couldn't see Marcus, but being with Karen was almost as good. Perhaps Karen had seen him and had a message for her. If not, perhaps she could take one for Delia. She felt as if she'd had her lifeline cut.

They took a cab to the marina, and Karen was waiting on the pier, all smiles, wearing a huge straw hat with roses all over the brim.

Delia introduced them, and Barney and Barb were immediately charmed by the elderly lady.

"I'm so glad you could all come," Karen said, leading the way down the pier to the slip where her yacht was moored. "It's old, but I love it," she added, leading them aboard the grand white floating mansion. "My husband bought it new in the eighties."

"It's glorious," Delia said with a sigh.

"Very nice," Barney agreed, smiling at Karen. "Barb and I went on a cruise once, but we've never been nautical. A ship like this could change my mind."

"I love the ocean," Barb agreed. "Thank you so much for inviting us," she added. "Delia's been singing your praises ever since we got back from Miami."

"She's a dear girl," Karen replied, smiling at Delia. "And so kind, to keep an old lady company. Guests are thin on the ground for me these days," she added with a meaningful look at Delia, who was immediately alert and concerned. Had something happened to Marcus?

Karen read the expression and shook her head quickly as Barb and Barney wandered off to explore the yacht.

Delia nodded and followed after them, with Karen in the rear.

They sailed for the Out Islands, chatting and listening to Karen's outlandish tales of her first days on New Providence.

There was a swimming pool onboard, although Marcus and Delia hadn't used it. But Barb and Barney were like fish in water. Karen offered them suits and as much time in the pool as they liked before lunch. They took her up on it.

Delia didn't because she wanted to talk to Karen, and she couldn't risk having her sister overhear them.

When they heard splashing in the pool, Delia turned quickly to Karen. "How is Marcus?" she asked at once. "Have you heard from him?"

"No, dear," Karen said worriedly. "I was hoping that you might have."

"Not a word," Delia replied. "In fact, he told me not to contact him. Not even to wave at him on the street. Something's going on. Something bad, I'm afraid."

Karen took Delia's cold hands in hers. "My dear, I feel the same apprehension, but I don't know what we can do about it. I tried to phone him, twice, and that nice Mr. Smith said that he wasn't able to take any calls. Something about an ongoing business deal that he had to concentrate on. But I usually see him going in or out near my house, and he hasn't been."

Delia gnawed her lower lip. "You think he's in some sort of trouble?"

"I can't think of any other explanation. But I'm sure he's all right," she added when she saw Delia's expression. "I'm sure he is."

"I wish I could be," Delia replied, worrying about something else that she couldn't share with Karen, about the child she might be carrying.

"You might talk to Mr. Smith," she said.

"If Marcus doesn't want me to call him, I'm sure he doesn't want me talking to Mr. Smith, either. But if you hear anything, anything at all, will you call me at the hotel?"

"Of course," Karen said quietly. "And you must make me the same promise. I've known Marcus for many years. I'd stake my life on his honesty. And I'll never believe some of the outlandish things I've heard about him."

"Neither will I," Delia agreed. "Not ever."

It was an idyllic day, but disappointing, because Delia had hoped against hope that her friend knew something about Marcus. Now she had no way to find out what was happening in his life.

Barb was suspicious. She kept watching Delia as if she knew Delia and Karen were talking about something they didn't want overheard. Once they were back at the hotel and getting ready to go downstairs to the restaurant for supper, Barb let Barney go on ahead to get a table. She urged Delia out into the room and closed the door.

"You and that sweet little old lady were trading more

than quilt patterns, or I'm a drunken sailor," Barb said gently. "Now what's going on?"

Delia forced herself to look innocent. "Of all the suspicious people," she exclaimed, laughing. "Karen and I were talking about potted plants!"

Barb studied her worriedly. "No. I'm sure it's more than that. It has something to do with Marcus Carrera or I'm a turkey."

"Gobble, gobble?" Delia teased.

"This is serious," came the quiet reply. "Listen, Marcus Carrera is mixed up in a really bad plot, baby. He's working with a gang in Miami to take over gambling on Paradise Island. I overheard Barney talking about it on the phone with someone. But he's been sold out by one of the mob. Federal agents are on his tail. They're going to arrest him."

Delia's face went pale. She couldn't even manage a reply.

Barb grimaced. "So you do know him, don't you? And it's more than just having him rescue you at the casino. I thought so. Baby, you can't go near him again. He's going to go to prison. You don't want to throw your life away on a man like that!"

Delia swallowed hard. "He's not like that."

Barb's eyes widened. "In only three weeks, you know him better than the federal government does. I see."

"No. It's…hard to explain." Delia took a calming breath. "He won't let me near him. He said it was dangerous, that I could get hurt. He said he wouldn't risk me, in any way, and that I wasn't to speak to him on the street."

Barb groaned. "Oh, baby," she said miserably, and

hugged her sister hard. "I'd have cut off my arm to spare you this."

"He's not a criminal."

"They don't arrest people for being nice."

"He hasn't done anything illegal, I know it. And he couldn't have killed people," Delia said fervently. "He's kind, he has a wonderful heart! He makes the most beautiful quilts…!"

"There's a mass murderer who was kind to animals," Barb replied.

"Marcus is not a mass murderer!"

"But he is a criminal, baby," Barb said heavily. "And nothing you can say about him, nothing you can do, is going to keep him out of prison."

Delia swallowed. "I have to warn him," she whispered. "I can't let him be killed!"

"Baby…"

"I love him," Delia choked.

Barb ground her teeth together. "There's something else. I was afraid that you were involved with him, and I wanted to try and spare your feelings. But there's no need now. Listen, he's involved with a woman," she added. "She's been seen at the casino and the hotel with him, at all hours of the day and night. She's young and beautiful and the daughter of one of the gangsters in Miami that he's connected with."

Chapter 9

Delia felt her world crumbling. Marcus had told her to stay away from him, for her own protection. But he was going around with a beautiful woman and connected with the mob in Miami. What if he'd just wanted her out of the way so that he wouldn't make his girlfriend jealous? What if he'd been involved with the other woman all along?

But if he was, why had he slept with Delia?

"He said he was crazy about me," she mumbled miserably.

Barb was looking at her as if she'd lost her mind entirely. "And you believed him?" she exclaimed. "Do you think a man like that cares about the truth?"

"He's not a mobster, he's a good man," Delia protested. "I can't let him go to prison, Barb. I have to go and see him. I have to warn him!"

"You can't go near that casino!" Barb said firmly. "I'm not going to let you get killed! Besides, if you go, Barney will know that I told you about Carrera."

"It will be our secret," she promised. "Barb, I have to know!"

Barb was hesitant. Her face was contorted with worry. "Baby, I don't want you to take the chance. Maybe I can get Barney to go," she added with uncharacteristic flexibility.

"Get me to do what?" Barney asked from behind them.

Barb jumped. "Don't sneak up on me!" she exclaimed huskily.

Barney was looking from one to the other with quiet curiosity. "What have you been talking about?" he asked.

"Marcus Carrera," Delia said bluntly. "I know he's in some sort of trouble with the government. I want to go to Paradise Island and…talk to him."

Barney didn't seem at all surprised by this statement. He cocked an eyebrow. "That might be possible, if you go with a friend of mine. And if you carry a note to Carrera for me."

Barb's jaw dropped. Delia sat down.

"You two must think I'm an idiot," he said easily, perching himself on the arm of the sofa. "I know more about what's going on than I'll ever tell you. But all you need to know is that there's a deep project going on, and I'm involved. Sort of. Anyway, I need to send a note to Carrera and Delia's the only hope I've got of getting it to him. I can't phone him or send a courier over without arousing suspicion."

"You're involved?" Delia asked.

He nodded. "And that's all I'm going to say."

"Is Marcus in danger?" she persisted.

His face was somber. "More than he even realizes right now. I can't afford to let him die. He's essential to what's going on. Are you game? It will be dangerous."

"She's not going!" Barb came out of her trance to protest. "I won't let her get in the line of fire."

"I won't let Marcus die," Delia replied. "I care too much about him."

"He's running around with another woman, and you want to save him?" Barb asked bitterly.

"Even if that's true, I don't want him dead," Delia said with quiet pride, oblivious to Barney's intent stare.

"I'll call my friend. You be ready to go in an hour," Barney told her.

"Barney!" Barb exclaimed, and she took off after him. "I am not letting you get involved with gangsters!"

All Barb's arguments didn't sway either Delia or Barney. She threw her hands up with a harsh groan.

"Don't I have the right to say anything at all?" she exclaimed.

"Sure. Say 'good luck.'" Barney told her.

"We're talking about my...my sister!" she persisted, almost in tears. "She could be killed!"

"Carrera most certainly will be, if I don't get this note to him," Barney replied, handing it to Delia. "Don't open that," he added firmly. "It could cost you your life, and I'm not joking."

"I won't," Delia replied. "Thanks, Barney," she added, grateful to her brother-in-law for almost the first time in their long acquaintance.

"You do know that most of the things they say about him are true?" he asked, but in a kind tone.

She nodded. "It doesn't matter."

He grimaced. "That's what I thought you'd say. Good luck, kid."

There was a quick knock at the door. Barney went to answer it.

"You be careful," Barb said in a choked tone. "If anything happened to you…"

"I'm going to be all right," Delia said confidently.

Before Barb could say anything else, Dunagan walked in, wearing dress slacks with an expensive white shirt and a dinner jacket and black tie. He wasn't smiling. He gave Delia a cursory glance and nodded.

"You look good," he said.

"So do you, but why are you here?" Delia prompted.

"He's your date," Barney said. He held up a hand. "The less you know, the better this is going to go down. Just pretend you're out for a night on the town. Nothing more. And try not to be too obvious when you talk to Carrera. Talk about him rescuing you, and nothing else. Got that?"

"Got it," she agreed. Her knees were beginning to feel like jelly. She was a quilting teacher. How in the world had she gotten herself involved in mob warfare? And what involvement did the mysterious Dunagan have in all this? Was he working with Barney, and were they for the mob or against it?

"Pity people don't wear placards," she murmured, getting her purse and velvet wrap. She was wearing a black velvet dress, strapless, with red roses embroidered on the skirt. The wrap also had embroidered roses. Her blond hair was up in a complicated hairdo. She looked elegant and dignified.

"You can tell the players if you know what to look

for," Dunagan said. He took her arm. "I'll take care of her," he told Barb, who was fighting tears. "I give you my word."

Barb managed to nod. "I love you, baby," she whispered to Delia.

"I love you, too, Barb."

She went out the door with Dunagan.

Just as they got to the hall, she heard Barb's furious voice yelling, "You never told me you were collaborating with gangsters! And just how much trouble are you in?"

A cab was waiting at the curb. To Delia's surprise, it was John.

"How are you this evening, Miss Mason? To the Bow Tie, Mr. Dunagan?" he added.

"Yes," he said. "And hurry, John."

"Yes, sir!"

Delia kept glancing at Dunagan. She couldn't help it. The smiling, carefree tourist she'd become accustomed to was suddenly someone else. He was somber, watchful, and there was a noticeable bulge under his jacket.

He noted her concern and forced a smile. "Don't look so worried," he teased. "Everything will work out."

"Think so?" she asked. She sighed and looked out the window as they approached the high arch of the bridge that led past the marina and over to Paradise Island. "I really hope it will."

She was thinking of all sorts of terrible possible futures. She was pregnant, and nobody knew, not even Marcus. Life was very complicated.

The Bow Tie was crowded. Tourists milled around between the hotel and the casino with its gaming tables, slot machines, and entertainment complexes with live shows.

Delia kept looking around for Marcus. She'd felt over-dressed when she walked in, but she saw everything from people in torn jeans to women in evening gowns and men in tuxedos. Apparently the dress code was very flexible.

Dunagan took her arm and guided her through the carpeted expanse toward the floor of the casino near the cash booths. It was like a scene from a James Bond movie, she thought, fascinated by the roulette wheels and blackjack tables.

"It's like a movie," she murmured.

He chuckled. "More than you realize," he replied.

They approached the entrance to the elevators when Delia spotted Marcus. He was wearing a tuxedo. He looked elegant and wealthy. Next to him was an olive-skinned woman, very beautiful, with long black hair. She was wearing a white silk dress, and she looked as expensive as Marcus. She had him by the arm, and he was smiling down at her.

Delia felt more insecure by the minute. It had seemed so easy when she was planning it. She even had Barney's note in her evening bag as an excuse to speak to Marcus. But when it came right down to it, she got cold feet. She remembered unpleasantly that he'd told her not to contact him. He'd been explicit. Certainly he had a reason, if he was really mixed up with the Miami mob. But where did that gorgeous brunette come in? And was she part of the deal Barney talked about, the secret project that nobody wanted her to know about?

Dunagan urged her forward. She hesitated.

Just as her feet froze, Marcus turned his head, laughing at something the brunette had said. He spotted Delia and the smile wiped clean off his face in an instant. He scowled furiously.

Delia felt unwell. Her stomach was queasy. She wanted to turn around and run. But it was already too late. Marcus and the brunette were moving right toward her.

"Hello, Miss Mason," Marcus said in a deliberately casual tone.

"Mr. Carrera," she replied, nodding at him. It was hard to pretend not to care, when the very sight of him was like water in the desert.

"You know each other?" the brunette asked, her dark eyes snapping.

"Mr. Carrera saved me from a drunken guest here at the casino last month," Delia volunteered.

"A real rat," Marcus drawled. "Doing okay, Miss Mason?" he added.

She forced a careless smile. "Doing fine, thanks."

"Nice place," Dunagan murmured, smiling. "Is there a bar?"

"There are three," the brunette said, running her eyes over him like seeking hands.

"You don't say? I'm Dunagan," he said, moving closer. "Do you mind pointing the way to me?"

"No problem," the young woman replied. "I'll just be a minute, Marcus."

"Delia, wait here, okay?" Dunagan told her. "When she shows me the bar, I'll get some chips on the way back."

"Okay," Delia replied, smiling sweetly.

They were no sooner out of earshot when Marcus exploded. "What the hell is your problem?" he demanded with blazing dark eyes. "I told you…!"

She slid her hand into his, pressing the note into it. "Don't fuss," she said under her breath.

He felt the note and scowled.

"Barney," she said without moving her lips, looking around as if she were searching for Dunagan.

"What has he told you?" he demanded.

"Nothing."

He didn't believe her. The situation was dangerous. Terribly dangerous. He turned and unobtrusively tore open the small envelope, running his eyes over the block printing. His whole face tautened. He slid the note into his pocket and looked down at Delia with an expression that would have stopped a bank robber cold.

"Get out of here," he said coldly. "Don't come back. Ever."

The heartless words made her heart stop. What had been in that note? "Is it that woman?" Delia asked, feeling her heart turning to ice.

"It always was," he said without meeting her eyes. "We had a fight. She was in Miami and I got lonely."

She was pregnant. He'd said he adored her. And all of it, everything, was because he'd been missing his girlfriend?

He looked down at her, and his expression was cruel. "You heard me. Running after me isn't going to win you any points. Don't you have any pride at all? She's wearing my ring!"

Delia knew she was going to die later. He couldn't have made his feelings plainer.

"I'm here with another man, didn't you notice?" she said, gathering the tattered remains of her pride. Her heart was shaking her with its racing beat, and she felt sick all over. "I should think that speaks for itself. I'm a messenger. Nothing more."

"Good," he returned. He jammed his hand into his pocket. "Get out and go back to Texas. You're out of your league here."

"I noticed."

She turned her head and saw Dunagan returning with the brunette, who was glaring daggers at Delia.

"Do you love her?" she asked Marcus in the last second they were alone.

"With all my heart," he said flatly.

She looked up into his hard eyes. "And you cheated on her?" she asked on a hollow laugh.

"We had a fight," he said simply. He smiled cynically. "Did you think you had a chance? You're sweet, honey, but you're plain as old shoes and about as sophisticated as a sand crab. You believe everything a man tells you."

"Not ever again," she replied with a tight smile. She searched his eyes. "They were right about you all the time," she said unsteadily. "You're just a gangster."

"Count on it," he agreed with cold eyes.

She turned away on shaky legs and smiled warmly at Dunagan. "Did you get the chips?"

"Sure did," he told her with a grin. "She showed me where to go. Thanks," he added to the gorgeous brunette.

"No problem," she said carelessly, moving right up next to Marcus with a possessive glance and a speaking glare toward Delia. "Have a good time."

"Oh, we will," Dunagan assured them, steering Delia toward the tables. "Good evening."

Dunagan stopped to speak to a man he knew. While he was distracted, Delia took a minute to catch her breath and try to pull herself together. She'd never dreamed that Marcus would treat her so cruelly. And the way he'd looked at her, as if she were an insect, beneath his notice. Her heart felt as if it had been shattered.

She put a tissue unobtrusively to her wet eyes, but as she put it away in her purse, she noticed a small, dark man with big ears that had curly lobes. His earlobes were so odd-looking that she almost missed seeing the pistol that he was pulling out of his jacket. He was looking straight at Marcus.

Without even thinking of the danger, she turned and walked into him, knocking him off balance.

The small man cursed, gave her a seething glare, quickly stuck the pistol back into his belt and blended immediately into the crowd. He was out of sight seconds later. Marcus hadn't seen anything. Neither had Dunagan.

Delia's heart raced madly as she rejoined Dunagan. "Did you see that?" she asked quickly, without raising her voice.

"See what?"

"There was a small man with a gun. He pulled it out of his belt and was about to shoot Marcus with it. I knocked him off balance and he took off," she said, her eyes worried. "What is going on here?"

Dunagan ground his teeth together. "Where is he?"

"I don't know. He's very ordinary looking except for his earlobes. He just blended into the crowd. I don't know where he went."

"Did he realize that you saw the gun?"

"I don't think so," she replied curtly. "Why is someone trying to kill Marcus?"

He hesitated, just as Mr. Smith came striding into

the room, alerted, no doubt, by his closed circuit camera. People moved out of his way as he joined Dunagan and Delia. Marcus, curious and solemn, glanced toward Smith, with his arm tightly around the brunette as if he wondered why Smith had approached Delia.

"Did you see him?" Smith asked Dunagan.

"I didn't," he replied tersely, "but Delia did. Were you watching?"

"Yes, on my monitors, for all the good it did me. I don't think Marcus noticed anything." He turned to Delia with an urgent expression. "What did you see?" he asked her gently.

"Surely you saw him, too?" she asked softly, careful not to let anyone overhear. "Wasn't he on your monitor?"

He grimaced. "I got a nice shot of his back and the back of his head on tape, along with just a flash of the gun when he pulled it out and put it back up. The other monitors had a sudden, very convenient glitch, which means that he either has an accomplice or he knows his way around surveillance equipment."

"Suspicious," Dunagan murmured.

"Step outside with me, would you?" Smith asked quietly.

They went with him to the entrance. Delia managed not to look back at Marcus, who was still staring toward them, even though her heart was breaking at what he'd said to her.

"Was he aiming at Marcus?" Smith asked Delia the minute they were alone.

"I'm sure of it," she replied. "I walked into him deliberately, but I'm sure he didn't connect me with Marcus."

"What did he look like?"

"He was dark, small, ordinary, but he had unusual earlobes."

"Would you recognize him if you saw him again?" Smith persisted.

"Yes," she said with confidence.

Smith sighed roughly and ran a hand over his smooth head. "I didn't see it coming. That's a first."

Delia's blood was running cold. Someone wanted Marcus dead. Was it the government? Surely they'd go after him with a subpoena, not a hit man?

"Will he try again?" she wondered.

"Of course," Smith replied angrily. "And we won't see him coming next time."

"Maybe we could get a sketch artist," Dunagan ventured.

"No time," Smith replied. "He'll try again tonight. He can't afford to wait now." He looked at Delia. "I need you to stick around. Will you wear a wire, so that you can alert me the instant you see him, if you do?"

"Y-yes, of course," she said, although she wanted desperately to run to Marcus and protect him with her very life.

Smith looked at Dunagan.

"I won't leave her for a minute," he promised Smith.

"Are you packing?" Smith asked surprisingly.

To Delia's surprise, Dunagan nodded, opening his dinner jacket to expose a shoulder holster with an automatic pistol.

"Okay. We'll go to my office and do what's necessary."

"Why is Marcus in danger?" Delia wanted to know.

"I can't say," Smith said tersely. "Let's go."

Delia had a small battery-pack appliance attached to

her dress under the belt at her waist, and the wire ran up just under the shoulder strap of her dress where it was clipped in place by Smith's efficient hands. It was black, and it didn't show. He inserted an earpiece in her ear, as well. She felt the danger like a living thing, more for Marcus than for herself. If he were killed, despite her misery tonight, she didn't know how she'd go on living.

"All you have to do is sing out," Smith assured her, indicating the receiver in his ear. "I'll hear you. I'm going to have the casino ringed around with volunteer staff. He won't get through us."

Delia managed a weak smile. "Gosh, I hope not."

"Keep your eyes open. And be careful," he added. "If this guy is a contract killer, he won't hesitate to shoot anybody who gets in his way, including you."

"They didn't waste any time, did they?" Dunagan said bitterly.

"Not a second," Smith agreed.

Delia glanced from one to the other, totally in the dark. Everyone seemed to know what was going on, except for her. But the thought that some stranger was trying to kill Marcus made her sick at heart. She was carrying his child, and he didn't know. How could she bear it if something happened to him?

"I'll be right beside her," Dunagan added.

It was only then that Delia realized he was wired already. He had an earpiece in his ear, too.

"Gosh, this is cloak-and-daggerish," she murmured.

Smith cocked an eyebrow. "You have no idea," he mused, green eyes sparkling. "All right. Are we ready? Showtime."

"What about Marcus?" Delia asked. "Does he know that somebody's trying to kill him?"

"If you gave him Barney's note, he does," Dunagan replied.

Her breath caught. That explained his expression, his determination to get her out of the casino. He didn't want her out of his life at all. He was protecting her! She felt her heart lift like a balloon.

"But he didn't see the assassin, did he?" Smith persisted.

"I can't be sure, but he didn't even look our way until the man blended into the crowd."

"Come on," Dunagan coaxed. "Let's get back downstairs. I'll be right with you every step of the way."

She gave him a curious smile. "You're not a tourist, are you?" she asked.

He chuckled. "Sort of."

"Don't ask him any questions," Smith told her firmly. "What you don't know keeps you safer. And you watch yourself," he added. "We don't want to lose you."

"I'm going to be fine," she assured him. "The thing is to save Marcus."

"Amen," Smith said.

"Let's go," Dunagan said.

"I'm right behind you," she replied, glancing one last time at Mr. Smith.

Her spirits dwindled a little when they were back on the casino floor and she saw the brunette curled into Marcus's big body while they stood on the staircase overlooking a bank of slot machines, talking to a customer. He was holding her with one arm, still smiling down at her with possession. It broke Delia's heart to see it. Had he really been trying to protect her, or was he genuinely involved with that dynamite brunette? From where she stood, it didn't really look as if he were pretending to be interested. Especially when his big hand strayed down to the brunette's hip and caressed it. She thought of the child she was carrying and fear rippled across her body. She was taking a chance not only for herself, but for the baby, as well, and nobody knew. But she couldn't back out. Nobody else would recognize the man who was trying to kill Marcus. Only her.

She didn't look directly at Marcus, but her eyes were everywhere else, darting to and fro while she tried to locate any sign of the odd man who'd aimed the gun at Marcus earlier. What a lucky break for her that he hadn't realized the bump she gave him was deliberate. It had saved Marcus's life.

Dunagan steered her to a slot machine just below Marcus and gave her a handful of quarters. "Go for it," he coaxed. "Just keep your eyes open at the same time."

She noted that he'd placed her so that she had a clear view of Marcus, who was standing just above her on the staircase between the first and second floors of the casino. He didn't move from the spot. Obviously, Smith hadn't yet spoken to him. Out in the open like that he made a good target, but it was also easy to see anyone approaching him. That had to be deliberate, to keep the hit man from thinking Marcus was aware of his presence, but it was dangerous. Smith was taking a terrible chance on Delia's ability to recognize the assassin.

The only bad spot came when Delia had to make a quick trip to the rest room, but she'd given Dunagan the best description she could and she hoped he could recognize the man if he reappeared.

As she walked out of the cubicle to wash her hands, the gorgeous brunette was waiting for her at the elegant, gilded bank of sinks.

She was primping, pushing at her perfectly coiffed long black hair. She gave Delia a cold going-over.

"I saw you talking to Marcus, while your boyfriend lured me away," she said icily. "Just don't get your hopes up. He belongs to me."

"Does he?" Delia asked.

"And nobody poaches on my territory," she said in a thick northern accent. She even smiled. "Not if they want to stay healthy."

Delia wanted to hit the woman. She was elegant, beautiful, rich, everything Delia wasn't. And Marcus had said he loved her.

"Have you known him long?" she asked.

"Long enough to know that I love him," the woman said smugly. "And I can afford him. You can't. A woman like you would be useless to a man like Marcus. You don't even know how to dress!" she said rudely. "A country rube at a place like this. What a joke! He'd have to hide you in a closet to keep his friends from laughing if they got a good look at you!"

Delia's eyes sparked, but she pretended surprise. "You're kidding, of course," she retorted. "As if I'd want to be seen going around with a gangster!"

The woman's eyes opened wide. She hadn't expected that response.

"I come from respectable, decent people," she added haughtily, "who wouldn't be seen dead in company like this! I have too much pride to lower myself to that level!"

"How dare you!" the woman snapped. "Do you have any idea who I am? My father is filthy rich and so am I!"

Delia washed her hands and dried them nonchalantly. "Filthy is a good word for the sort of rich you are," she said. "Do have a nice evening." She smiled coolly and walked out.

"You...!"

The vulgar word floated on the air so loudly that a couple of heads turned when Delia walked out into the casino, but she paid no attention to her sudden notoriety. Her blood was boiling. She'd have liked nothing better than to knock the woman down. But she had other concerns.

"Wow," came a soft, deep chuckle in her ear. "Remind me never to make you mad."

It was Smith. He'd heard every word. Delia grimaced. She glanced behind her, watching the brunette storm up the staircase toward Marcus. "I'm a bad girl," she whispered.

"She's worse," Smith replied, and walked off toward the roulette wheel, his eyes still on the crowd.

Delia moved back to her slot machine, aware that Dunagan was trying to get her attention from halfway across the room. Her earpiece wasn't working! Dunagan indicated a solitary figure heading for the staircase.

"Oh, my God! That's him!" Delia exclaimed.

Smith and Dunagan came from different directions, trying to converge in time. Delia was closer, and faster.

She went up the staircase like a whirlwind just as the little man aimed the gun a second time at an oblivious Marcus.

Delia ran at him, pushing him just as he fired. He backhanded her with the strength of his whole body and she felt herself go backward, over the railing, down onto the casino floor. She landed with a horrible crash, and she felt as if her body were broken in two. The pain was so terrible that she blacked out.

Meanwhile, Marcus had struggled with the little man when they both wrestled over the railing and they, too, fell onto the carpeted casino floor.

The little man rolled and got to his feet, but by then, Smith had him in an inescapable hold and had handcuffed him seconds later.

Marcus, like Delia, was unconscious from the fall.

"Call an ambulance!" Dunagan growled into his microphone.

There were screams and muffled speculation as people gathered around Delia and Marcus with fascinated horror. The brunette was lying over Marcus's chest, crying hysterically when the ambulance sirens began to sound.

Chapter 10

Delia came slowly back to consciousness. She moaned. Her stomach felt as if it had been ripped open. Her head was splitting.

"Baby?"

She opened her eyes and looked up at Barb with blank, curious eyes. "Barb?"

Barb was crying. "Oh, baby, thank God you're alive," she whispered hoarsely. "We were scared to death when Dunagan called us! I thought you were dead when we first got here!"

"I fell." Delia's mind was swimming. "There was a man with a gun... Marcus?"

"He was still unconscious when we got here," Barb said coldly. "And good enough for him!"

"Is he going to live?" Delia asked worriedly. "Please!"

Barb hated Carrera. She didn't want to answer the

question, but Delia did look so miserable. She couldn't refuse her. "I haven't seen him, but Barney said they think he'll live," she said reluctantly. "It was a concussion, just a little worse than yours. That brunette is all over him like measles," she added disgustedly.

Delia closed her eyes. She was sick with grief, anguish, bitterness. At least Marcus was alive, even if the venomous brunette was in possession. Then like lightning striking, she thought about the baby she was carrying and the terrible pain in her stomach. She gasped.

Her hands went to her stomach. She looked up at Barb with icy fear, wanting to ask but afraid, too.

Barb's face was eloquent. "You lost the baby, Delia. I'm sorry."

Delia's eyes clouded. Tears rolled helplessly down her cheeks. It had been Marcus's child. He wouldn't know. He was still unconscious. If he had concussion that severe, he could die, too, despite what the doctors were telling people.

Barb moved as close as she dared and held the younger woman gently. "Damn him!" she choked. "Damn him!"

"I loved him," Delia whispered brokenly. "I wanted our baby."

Barb ground her teeth together. "Why didn't you tell me?"

"Because I knew what you'd think," Delia said miserably. "You're so upright, Barb. You'd never have made a mistake like that."

Barb's face was contorted with pain, although Delia couldn't see it. "I would have done anything I could for you," she replied. "Anything, baby!"

Delia held her closer, her face awash with tears. "I'm

so sorry I didn't trust you!" she said, knowing how much it had hurt her sister to be kept in the dark.

"There, there," Barb whispered, stroking her hair. "It's going to be all right, you'll see. You're safe now."

"Dunagan?" Delia asked.

"He and Barney have gone off with some men in suits," Barb muttered. "Good grief, I feel like a mushroom lately! Nobody tells me anything!" She lifted her head. "Just what were you doing when you fell, Delia? How did you fall?"

Delia didn't want to involve Barb. If Dunagan and Barney had kept quiet, she had to do the same.

"The railing at the casino gave way," she lied.

Barb sat up and stared down at her curiously, and not with an expression of trust. "Barney said you got knocked off the staircase by a man who stole from the casino and was trying to get away from security."

"Did I say the railing gave way?" Delia touched her temple. "I must still be in shock."

"I must be wearing a sign that says, Lie To Me," Barb corrected darkly.

"It's for your own good," Delia replied. Her hands went back to her flat stomach. She was in shock right now, but it was going to be bad when it wore off. She didn't even want to have to face it yet.

Barb got up from the bed and sat down in a chair, grateful that the nurses hadn't seen her. Sitting on beds was strictly forbidden.

"Did they arrest a man in the casino, or did Barney say?" Delia asked hesitantly.

"The Bahamian police arrested a man for attempted murder, in fact," Barb told her. "Dunagan had put handcuffs on him and Carrera's head security man was sitting on him when the police arrived, according to Dunagan."

"Ouch," Delia murmured. "Mr. Smith is huge and the would-be killer was only a little guy—" She stopped abruptly.

"I am *so* ready to thump you when you're better!" Barb said through her teeth. "You saved that gangster's life, didn't you? And risked your own to do it!"

Delia closed her eyes. "I'm really tired, Barb," she whispered, becoming conveniently drowsy. "I just want to sleep for a while."

Barb relented, but her eyes were worried. "Okay, baby. We'll talk when you feel better. I'm just happy that you're going to be all right. Delia," she added slowly, "I'm sorry about the baby. But you don't have a clue what it would have been like to have it and keep it and be unmarried. You just don't."

"Like *you* know!" Delia said with loving sarcasm, her eyes still closed.

Barb's eyes were haunted. "I'm going to go and see where Barney got to. I'll be back soon, I promise."

Delia was getting drowsy for real. "Okay." She sighed.

Barb went out of the room and down the hall to intensive care. She paused at the desk.

"Marcus Carrera," she said slowly. "Can you tell me how he is?"

"Are you a member of the family?" the nurse asked.

"No," Barb replied, glancing through the window where the slinky brunette was leaning over Marcus in his bed. "But my sister saved his life."

"Then she must have been the young woman who knocked down the man with the gun," the nurse said at once, smiling. "My brother is a policeman, he told me.

What a brave young lady!" She didn't notice that Barb paled and gasped. The nurse was looking through the glass into the intensive care room where the brunette and Marcus were. "He's just recovered consciousness. He's going to be fine. Well, in time," she added, leaning closer. "He doesn't know who he is, though," she whispered. "He's lost his memory completely."

Barb was secretly relieved. That might spare Delia a lot of pain down the road. At least it would make the last week of Delia's vacation a peaceful one, once she knew how things stood. Barb was going to make sure that she had a good time.

"Thanks," Barb told the nurse. "I won't say anything about it, except to my sister."

The nurse just smiled.

Barney was coming down the hall when Barb approached Delia's room. He was alone, and he looked worried.

"How is she?" he asked.

"Sleeping, when I left," Barb replied. She folded her arms tight across her chest. "Am I ever going to find out what's going on?" she asked him. "According to a nurse, my sister foiled an assassination attempt on the gangster down the hall!"

He pulled her down the hall to the waiting room and sat down with her in a corner, away from other visitors.

"I'm sorry I couldn't tell you sooner, but it was impossible. They've got a contract killer in stir over in Nassau," he told her. "He was sent here from Miami with explicit instructions to take out Carrera."

"Who sent him, the government?" she asked, still shocked from what the nurse had told her.

"No," he replied tersely. "It was a renegade gangster who's trying to set up a money laundering operation down here with the first of many casinos he hopes to buy. He's living in Miami and bucking the northern mob, and they don't like it. But so far he hasn't ticked any of them off. This will change things. Carrera has friends. Lots of them." He took a breath. "That hood in Miami made a big mistake using a killer with a rap sheet the size of this guy's. He's still wanted for two murders in New Jersey, and federal marshals are already on the way to pick him up after his extradition hearing."

"We're going to be in the middle of a turf war," Barb groaned.

"No," her husband replied. "You don't understand. Carrera's little brother was knocked off by a money launderer right here in the Bahamas, a banker with mob connections and ties to the Colombian drug cartel. Carrera's been after him for weeks. He's working with the feds."

Barb's jaw fell.

"I thought you'd take it like that," Barney murmured. "You can't tell Delia," he added firmly. "She's already done more than I'm comfortable with. She saved Carrera's life last night, twice. The first time she bumped into the assassin and put him on the run, before he knew who she was. The second time, she stopped him just as he fired. She and Carrera went over the banister in the struggle." He shook his head. "Smith and Dunagan were just a few feet away, but they'd never have been in time. They had a communications breakdown. When Carrera's back on his feet, Smith's going to be in serious trouble, I'm afraid."

"Barney, Carrera won't know him," she said slowly. "He won't know anybody, including Delia. I just came from intensive care. Carrera's regained consciousness, but he's got amnesia. He doesn't remember a thing."

"Amnesia? Oh, that's just great!" Barney growled. "Just great! We're in the middle of a sting, and he's the pivot. Without his cooperation, the little Miami rat we're trying to trap may just get his foot in the door down here!"

"That's not our problem," Barb told him. "I just want to get my sister out of the hospital and back home."

"I know that. But we can't leave just yet," he said apologetically. "I'm working with Dunagan because I'm thick with the money laundering banker," he added. "I have to finish what I started."

"Why are you mixed up in this?" Barb demanded. "And who is Dunagan?"

He grimaced. "I did a little artful doctoring of my taxes last year. If I do the feds this little favor, I get to pay the penalty and not lose half my livelihood."

"Barney!" she exclaimed. "How could you!"

He patted her hand. "No need to sound so self-righteous, doll, we both know you're not."

"Delia doesn't know, and she's never going to!" Barb shot back.

He was hesitant. "There's something I have to tell you. You aren't going to like it," he added. "The money laundering banker's name is Fred Warner."

She stiffened. "Fred, who tried to assault Delia?"

"It gets worse. Fred got mad at Carrera for punching him over Delia that night, and he reneged on the deal he'd made with Carrera. He ratted him out to the Miami guy. That's why the assassin came after him. They know Carrera's working with the feds, and they're planning to take him out. Right now, he's the only one who knows what they're up to—except for me and Dunagan—and with his memory gone, we're in the hot seat together."

Barb felt sick. "There's more, right?"

"Fred's not through getting back at people," he told her. "He's been talking to a private detective. I don't know what he's after, but he's looking for revenge on me, too. It's just as well they detected my little income tax artwork, because Fred would have turned me over to the government in a heartbeat."

"He couldn't find out about my past, could he?" she asked worriedly. "Mama's dead. Nobody else alive knows…"

"We know, though, don't we?" Barney said quietly. "There may be records somewhere that he can get into. I don't know. I just thought you should be prepared."

"I should have told her years ago, after we got married," Barb said miserably. "She'll never forgive me."

Barney pulled her close and held her. "Cross bridges as you get to them, honey. Don't anticipate them. We've been through more than this together. We'll manage."

"If we could just rewrite the past," she said sadly, resting her cheek on Barney's shoulder.

"Nobody gets to do that." He kissed her forehead. "Did you tell her about the baby?" he added sadly.

"Yes, but I'm sure she guessed," Barb said. Tears stung her eyes. "My poor Delia. She loved the fourteen-karat heel. She wanted that baby so much."

"We know how that feels," he replied, smoothing her hair. "A baby in the family would have been nice. I don't guess she told Carrera?"

"Of course not," she replied. "And he's practically sewn to that hard-wired brunette who's staying with him at the hospital, so it's just as well."

"I suppose. Amnesia. Imagine that." He sighed. "Dunagan and I are going to have our work cut out for us now."

"Well, you just keep my baby out of any future plans, you hear me, Barney?" she added firmly. "We're not going to risk losing her, too. No matter what."

"You know I'd never let Delia get hurt," he said with a sad smile. "Has it occurred to you that we've made a tragic error of judgment? Your mother helped it along, but we could have overridden her."

"It was too late by then."

He grimaced. "Most of it was my fault."

"I helped," she reminded him gently. She reached up and kissed him. "I do love you, so much," she whispered. "It was worth everything!"

"For me, too, honey," he replied, and kissed her back.

"We can't let Delia be hurt anymore," she said.

"I'll do my best to prevent it. You don't think it might be wiser to just tell her the truth about her past now?"

She shook her head. "Not until I have to."

"Then we'll try to head off Fred. Come on. Let's get a bite to eat while Delia's sleeping. I'm starved and they must serve breakfast around her somewhere!"

She went along with him, only later remembering that he never had told her who, or what, Dunagan was.

Marcus had a hell of a headache, and it didn't help that Roxanne Deluca wouldn't stop fussing over him. He hadn't recognized her, but she'd introduced herself and told him they were engaged. He noted the ring on her left hand and took it for gospel.

"What do I do for a living?" he asked her, sounding dazed.

"You own hotels and casinos all over the world," she told him easily. "And you and my father are in business together."

"We are? What sort?"

She gave him a calculating look. "I'll tell you all about it later."

He put a hand to his head. He felt sick and his temples were throbbing. "How did I end up in here?"

"You accidentally fell in the casino and hit your head," she lied glibly.

"Am I clumsy?" he mused.

"Not usually."

He closed his eyes. "I'm sleepy."

"Go to sleep, then, darling," she told him sweetly. "I'll be right here when you wake up."

"Okay," he mumbled.

She stayed until she was certain he was asleep, then she went out into the hall next door to the restroom and used her cell phone. "Daddy?" she said after a minute. "He's in the hospital. He doesn't remember anything. No, he's not faking, I'm positive, I asked a doctor. You can say anything you want to and he won't be able to contradict it. Pity, he's quite attractive. I know, Daddy, I'm not going soft. We can take him down at our leisure. Let me know where and when, and I'll get him there when you've got somebody to do the job. And please get somebody efficient! I'll be in touch. *Ciao.*"

She closed up the cell phone and walked back to Marcus's room. Barb opened the rest room door cautiously and made sure the brunette was out of sight before she walked back down the hall toward Delia's room. She had something very interesting to tell her husband.

* * *

The second day that Delia was in the hospital, she had an unexpected visitor—Karen Bainbridge, who walked in the door with an enormous bouquet of tropical flowers tied with a ribbon.

"I'm so glad that you're both going to be all right," Karen said. "But for Marcus to have lost his memory— I'm so sorry."

Delia forced a smile. "I'm sorry, too, but at least he's still alive. Do sit down! I'm so glad you came."

"Your sister isn't here with you?" Karen asked curiously.

"She and Barney went back to the hotel to get me some more nightwear," Delia said. "We thought I'd be released today, but they want to keep me until tomorrow."

"You're all right?" Karen asked, concerned.

"Yes. I…just had some minor complications," she replied, not wanting to tell the sweet elderly lady about the miscarriage.

Karen gave her a slow, penetrating look. "I told Marcus what you did, you know," she said gently. "That you saved his life. He doesn't remember who you are at the moment, but he was surprised and very grateful that you took such a risk on his behalf. I wanted to stay longer, but that woman with him seems very possessive. It wasn't until Mr. Smith walked in that she backed off and stopped interfering."

"Mr. Smith?"

She nodded. "He's been running the enterprise while Marcus is here. He's quite intelligent."

"Yes," Delia agreed.

"That woman almost didn't let me into Marcus's room. Mr. Smith moved her aside and invited me in.

Marcus had no idea what was going on, but I imagine Mr. Smith will tell him sometime."

Delia was miserable at how possessive that other young woman was, and she couldn't hide it.

"There, there, dear," Karen said softly, reaching out to touch Delia's hand. "You mustn't give up. I'll never forget the way Marcus looked at you, the day we went out on the yacht together."

"She's wearing an engagement ring, and she says he gave it to her," Delia replied solemnly. "At the casino, before we fell, Marcus told me they'd had a fight and that was the only reason he had anything to do with me. He said I had no place in his life."

Karen was shocked. "He can't have meant it."

"He won't remember it now," Delia continued. "He won't remember me, either. But he made it very obvious that he didn't want anything more to do with me. At first," she added hesitantly, "I thought he was in danger and he was protecting me by telling me not to come near him. That was before she told me about the engagement. He told me, too, at the casino."

Karen's face fell. "I'm sorry. You seemed like such a perfect couple—and so much in love with each other."

"It did feel like that, for a while." She leaned back against her pillows with a deep breath. "You know, I felt as if I'd known him forever. Now I feel like a fool." She looked at Karen. "Life teaches painful lessons."

"Indeed it does, my dear. My fiancé was killed in Vietnam. I was never able to love anyone else," the older woman replied gently.

"Karen, I'm so sorry."

She smiled wistfully. "We might have been divorced a week after the wedding, who knows? But the memories are very sweet. He was an American, from Oklahoma. His parents had a ranch that had been in his family for a hundred years." She stared down into her lap. "He was riding in a helicopter, airlifting wounded men, when the helicopter was shot down."

"It must have been devastating," Delia ventured.

"It took years to get over it," Karen agreed. She looked at the younger woman sympathetically. "Death or rejection, it's all loss, and it hurts. But you can get over this, too, my dear. I'll help. Any time you want to go sailing, all you have to do is call me."

"I'm very grateful," she replied. "Thank you."

"And now, let's talk about something cheerful! What do you think of my new crop of orchids?" she asked, indicating the bouquet she'd brought with her. She refrained from mentioning that Marcus had given them to her over the years and that her orchids were descended from his. Poor Delia. Her heart ached for the girl. She'd heard about the baby Delia lost, and she knew without asking that it was Marcus's. She'd told Smith that Delia had lost the child she was carrying. Smith had been shocked. She'd asked him not to share that with Marcus, because of the brunette. Smith had been utterly furious, and hurt. Karen sensed that he felt a responsibility for that loss. But he'd promised he wouldn't tell Marcus that in addition to losing his memory, he'd lost a child, as well.

Roxanne was raising so much havoc in Marcus's room that the nursing staff finally ordered her out. She vowed to return with an attorney, but she left.

Smith stood beside Marcus's bed like a stone statue.

"Have you remembered anything, Mr. Carrera?" he asked his boss.

Marcus still felt as if his head was coming off. The nausea was easing a little, thanks to his medication. He stared up at the big, bald man with wide, blank dark eyes. "I don't know you," he said. "I don't know that woman who keeps coming in here, either, but I'll never believe I was stupid enough to get engaged to her. She's a lunatic!"

Smith grimaced. He didn't dare tell Marcus the truth. It would put the boss in more danger than he was already in.

Marcus was glaring at him. "You know all about me, don't you?"

"I've worked for you for a year, now," Smith said.

Marcus grimaced. "There was an old woman who came to see me. She said a young woman down the hall threw herself at a man who was trying to shoot me. She saved my life. I don't remember her. And why was someone trying to kill me?"

Smith ground his teeth. "Your doctor says we can't tell you anything yet. He says your memory will come back all on its own, but you have to give it time."

"I could be dead before then."

"I'm not letting anybody kill you," Smith promised him. "You may have lost your memory, but I've still got mine. I know all I need to know, in order to protect you. I'm afraid you'll just have to trust me."

"Why is that young woman in the hospital?" Marcus persisted.

Smith drew in a calming breath. If he didn't say, Marcus would ask a nurse, and that might provoke gossip. "She was pregnant," Smith said flatly. "The father of the child didn't know, if that was your next question. She's not married."

Marcus thought about that for a minute: His face was taut with strain, as if he were trying to remember anything about his past. He sat up in the bed and swayed a little. "Will they let you walk me down the hall?"

Smith hesitated. "I'll go ask."

He knew where Marcus wanted to go. It was possible that seeing Delia would trigger his memory. But if he meant to do it, it needed to be before Roxanne came back and took over again.

He asked the nurse, who agreed that Marcus could go down the hall if Smith was careful to support him.

"Your nurse says you can go walking," Smith said, helping Marcus into a burgundy bathrobe.

"Good. I want to see that young woman before my so-called fiancée gets back here. Let's go."

Delia saw her door open with a feeling of apprehension, especially when she realized that Marcus had come to see her.

He looked dazed, and he was moving very slowly. Smith gave her a quick warning glance, which she interpreted to mean that she wasn't to tell Marcus anything. She nodded back.

Marcus stopped at the foot of her bed and stared at her. He saw a plain, green-eyed young woman with tangled blond hair and a slender body. She wasn't pretty or exciting. She didn't seem his sort of woman at all.

He frowned. "Smith said you saved my life," he said without preamble.

"So they tell me," she replied in a heavily Texas-accented voice.

His eyebrows arched. "My God, what an accent!" he laughed. "Where are you from?"

She glowered at him. "A little town in south Texas that nobody from Chicago probably ever heard of."

He glanced at Smith curiously. "Am I from Chicago?"

Smith nodded.

Marcus looked back at the young woman in the bed. "How do you know where I'm from? Are we acquainted?"

She looked at Smith worriedly.

"Don't look at him, look at me," Marcus grumbled. "Do I know you?"

Delia took a breath. "You saved me from an assault at your casino," she said, compromising with the truth. "I saved you from an assault. We're even."

"Not quite." Marcus stared at her while odd flashes of sensation wound through his big body. "You were pregnant, they said. You lost your child."

Delia fought to keep her feelings from showing. "God's will," she said in a tight tone.

His eyebrows arched. "You're religious?"

She avoided his eyes. "Yes."

He was scowling again. "I think I was, too... Did you want your baby?" he asked bluntly.

She ground her teeth together. It hurt to answer that question. It hurt to look at him and have him know about their baby, and not be able to tell him that it was his, as well.

"Yes," she bit off. "I wanted it."

"The father, did he want it, too?"

She glared at him, fighting tears. "He didn't know. But if he had, it wouldn't have made any difference. He didn't want me. He certainly wouldn't have wanted a child of mine."

He couldn't let it go. He felt something when he looked at her. He didn't understand why he should feel sad. "Did you love him?"

She couldn't force herself to meet his searching gaze. "Yes. I loved him."

He didn't say anything. He just looked at her. "I'm sorry," he said finally, "about your child."

She didn't look up. "Thank you."

"Thank you for what you did," he replied.

"As I said," she choked, "I was repaying a favor."

He winced. He didn't know why it hurt him to hear her say that. His mind was spinning. He moved and almost lost his balance. Smith caught him, but he noted an instinctive surge forward from that young woman in the bed. She was concerned for him, even in the midst of her grief. Why should that make him feel guilty?

"We should go," Smith said deliberately, "before your fiancée comes back and misses you. There'll be a scene."

"God knows, we've had enough of those," Marcus muttered. He was still watching Delia. "They say I'm rich. If you need anything, all you have to do is ask."

"I don't need a thing, but thanks," she replied, forcing a smile. Her eyes wouldn't go up far enough to meet his.

"Get better," Marcus said as he turned away.

"You, too."

"I'll be fine. My condition's not a patch on yours," she said without thinking.

A patch. A patch. A four-patch, a nine-patch, those were quilting terms. He turned so quickly that he almost fell again. "You make quilts!" he said abruptly.

Chapter 11

Delia felt her heart rise into her throat. He'd remembered! Would that trigger other memories?

But his lack of recognition was evident as he looked at her. "I don't know where that came from," he said, looking blank. He smiled politely. "*Do* you quilt?"

"I teach quilting back home," she replied. "We... spoke about it after you saved me from the man I was with."

He put a hand over his eyes as if he wanted to wipe away the fog that concealed his past. "Someone mentioned that I quilt, too, as a hobby."

"You've won competitions with your designs," she agreed.

He nodded, but he wasn't thinking so much about quilts as he was wondering why he'd had such an extensive conversation with a woman who didn't appeal to his senses at all. She seemed like a kind woman, but she didn't stimulate him or make him wish for a closer acquaintance. There couldn't have been anything between them, he decided.

He smiled politely. "Thanks again. I'd better be going."

"I hope you regain your memory," Delia said, with equal politeness.

He shrugged. "If I don't, it's probably no great loss," he said, chuckling. "It might be nice to start fresh."

"It might, indeed," Delia agreed, although he was twisting a knife through her heart.

He nodded to Smith, who got under his arm and steadied him down the hall to his own room. Smith felt sick to his soul about Delia. He gave her a last look, grimacing at the moisture growing in her eyes. Poor little thing, he thought miserably.

The next day, they released Delia and let her go back to the hotel, with instructions to rest for a day or two before doing anything strenuous. Since her plans had to do with sunbathing and sightseeing, she didn't think of that as a problem.

Marcus was also released. Roxanne followed behind the limousine as Smith drove him to his beach house. She carried in her suitcase and looked as if she had plans to take over.

"You'd better stay at the hotel," Marcus told her.

"We're engaged," she retorted.

He stared at her for a long time. "I want my memory back. That's more likely to happen if I'm here on my own with no distractions."

"He's here," Roxanne fumed, glancing at Smith ruefully.

"He cooks," came the reply. "Besides, he'll be running the casino and the hotel in my absence, so he's unlikely to be around much anyway."

Roxanne paid close attention to that statement. She looked thoughtful.

Smith noticed and decided to make a couple of phone calls. He was going to add some extra gardeners to the house as well—men he'd worked with before who were handy with sidearms. He didn't trust Roxanne or her father one bit, and he was suspicious of her concern for Marcus, as well as the mysterious engagement that nobody knew anything about. It could be real, he decided, but only Marcus would know. And Marcus had no memory.

"Smith, take her over to the hotel and book her into a suite," Marcus said.

"Yes, sir."

Roxanne glared at him but she backed down. "All right, darling, if that's the way you want it. But all you have to do is phone me if you get lonely."

"Thanks," he replied.

She pulled her suitcase on wheels back out the door as Smith led the way. Marcus watched her go with mixed feelings, the most prominent of which was suspicion.

Later, when Smith returned, Marcus was dressed in lightweight white slacks with a red-and-white patterned shirt. He was standing out on his balcony with the wind ruffling his hair. He'd been drawn to the balcony, as if something important had happened to him there. He wished he knew what it was. The harder he tried to remember, the worse his head throbbed.

He turned at Smith's approach. "Who is that woman?" he asked.

"She's Deluca's daughter. He's a Miami hood who wants to own crooked casinos down here and launder money through a local banker," Smith said honestly. "Her father doesn't like you, so don't believe it when she tells you he's your biggest fan. You didn't have any plans to marry her, either."

Marcus put a big hand to his forehead and groaned.

"Sorry, boss," Smith said at once. "I shouldn't have said that."

"I wanted to know." The pain was terrible. He lifted his head, trying to focus. He looked right at Smith. "Who tried to kill me?"

"An insignificant little contract killer with a four-page rap sheet," Smith said. "Listen, boss, I'm not sure I should be telling you this stuff."

"There's nobody else who can." Marcus moved to the balcony overlooking the ocean. "Who sent him after me?"

Smith hesitated.

Marcus pinned him with threatening dark eyes. "Spill it!"

"Deluca," he said.

Marcus raised both eyebrows. "Why?"

Smith ground his teeth together. Well, it might save the boss's life if he knew. He had to tell him. "You're trying to shut Deluca down," he said tautly.

"That doesn't make sense!"

"Yes, it does." Smith moved closer. "You had a brother, Carlo. He married Cecelia Hayes, his childhood sweetheart. They had two beautiful little kids, Cosima and Julio. Carlo finally got off drugs and straightened out, but before he could get his life back together, he was killed by the banker Deluca's working with, because he informed about some Colombian cocaine shipments to the feds. He died and you swore to get even. You've been working with the feds to shut down the banker and keep Deluca from coming in here and starting up crooked gaming." Smith cleared his throat. "The banker doesn't know you found out about him being involved in Carlo's death, but he did find out you were working for the government, and he was angry that you hit him to save Delia Mason from him that night at the casino. So he sold you out to Deluca and Deluca sent a cleaner after you. That's it in a nutshell."

Marcus felt ill. He leaned hard against the balcony. He had a brother, a niece and nephew, and he didn't remember any of it. A man was trying to kill him.

"Where does Roxanne come in?" he asked.

"She was hanging around you with a peace offer from her father that you were considering. She was supposed to keep you unsuspecting while the killer did his work. But Delia Mason got in the way. When you got amnesia Roxanne moved in and pretended you were engaged. She was overheard talking to her father on a cell phone to tell him you were vulnerable and they could take you on at their leisure."

"In other words, he'll send someone else to tie up the loose ends," Marcus guessed.

"Exactly. But you have amnesia and you trust Roxanne, so they won't play such a close hand this time. They'll feel safe."

Marcus smiled. "Good. Can you get me in touch with the feds I'm working with, unobtrusively?"

"That's going to be tricky. One of them cuffed the

perp in plain view of Roxanne. He was playing the part of a tourist, but he's blown his cover. He was seen in the company of Delia's brother-in-law, who's also helping the government with this sting operation. That means I can't get you close to the feds. And if I'm seen with them, the jig's up, too."

"What about the woman, Delia?" he asked.

Smith grimaced. "Good God, boss, she's been through enough!"

Marcus glared at him. "Do you think she's safe? She foiled the hit, didn't she? Do you think Deluca will let that slide?"

"I hear from my sources that he's got something on her sister that he's planning to use, by way of revenge. He can't kill her, everybody would know who did it."

"Everybody will know who did it if he hits me, too," Marcus reminded him.

"Maybe. But Deluca's daughter is supposedly engaged to you, which means he's not got a visible motive for killing you."

Marcus sighed angrily, and glared out over the ocean. "I can't remember a damned thing. I still don't understand why the Mason woman risked her life and her child's life to save mine. She isn't my type. I don't even find her interesting. Surely I didn't encourage her?"

Smith didn't dare answer that question. "You saved her from the money-laundering banker," Smith said, trying to sound nonchalant. "It's hero worship."

Could it be that simple? He turned back to Smith and saw nothing in that calm countenance. He shrugged. "I guess that could explain it."

Great, Smith thought, relieved.

"Who was the old woman who came to see me?" Marcus persisted.

"Karen Bainbridge. You're friends. You got her interested in orchids. She grows them for nurseries now."

"Orchids. Karen." He frowned. "I grow orchids?"

"Yes. You've got a greenhouse full of them."

"And I make quilts." He shook his head. "I can't believe I do that."

"Why not? I knit."

Marcus's eyes were shocked. Smith was over six feet, solid muscle, with a military special ops background. He was a dead shot as well. "You knit?"

Smith shrugged. "I quit smoking because it bothered Tiny." He saw the blank look he was getting. "Tiny is my iguana. She lives in my room, in a giant cage."

"A giant iguana." Marcus frowned. "Do I like her?"

"Yes. But the point is, since I quit smoking, I've got to have something to do with my hands. You used to smoke cigars. You said that's why you started quilting."

"Orchids. Cigars. An old woman for a friend and a plain, uninteresting girl from Texas saved me from a hit man. It wouldn't pass as fiction, much less fact!"

Smith pursed his lips. "It would make a great novel."

Marcus glared at him. "I pay your salary, right?"

"Right."

"Get out there and find the feds. Tell them I'm game to help them nab this Deluca guy, but I'll need direction. I don't remember anything, and I won't know the players. They'll have to work out the logistics."

"I'll get right on it."

"That girl," Marcus said hesitantly. "Maybe I should send her some flowers or something."

Smith hesitated. It would give Delia false hope, and

make her recovery even more difficult. "Not a good idea," he replied finally. "Roxanne might get upset and do something unexpected."

He sighed. "Good point. Okay. I'm going to stick around here. Get busy."

"Yes, sir."

Delia laid on the beach, soaking up the sun and trying not to go crazy thinking about the child she'd lost. It was every bit as bad to remember the look on Marcus's face when he'd stared at her in the hospital. She could tell that he found nothing remotely attractive about her, that he was supremely disinterested in her. It broke her heart because it made her question if he'd really felt anything more than desire for her when they were together. Perhaps it was exactly as he'd said; the brunette and he had argued, and he'd gone out with Delia for revenge. It made sense. A man like that wouldn't be attracted to a plain woman. It went against the grain.

She watched the water lap up on the shore with sad eyes, one hand lying quietly on the flat stomach that no longer contained her child. It was going to be hard to get over that. She probably never would.

A shadow fell over her. She looked up and Barney was standing there, wearing a neat suit. Amazing how familiar he looked sometimes, she thought. She'd always been fond of Barney, and he'd spoiled her rotten as a child. It was one of her greatest blessings that her sister's husband was honestly fond of her.

"Hi, Barney," she said, and smiled.

He pulled up a chair and sat down, facing her. "Hi, baby," he said, addressing her exactly as Barb always had. "I need to talk to you."

"It's about that Miami guy that Marcus is mixed up with, isn't it?" she asked. "Marcus is still in the line of fire. Is the government after him?"

He nodded. "No. Marcus is working for the government," he told her bluntly, "but you can't say that to anybody, you hear me?"

"I do." She looked at him, wounded now that her faith in Marcus had paid off just as he'd pushed her out of his life. He'd been a good guy all along. "Then who's after him?" she asked.

"Deluca is, and he isn't going to quit. Marcus doesn't remember anything, but he wants to go ahead with the sting."

"But Deluca's hit man missed!"

"Deluca won't mess up if he sends another one. We have to get him off the street as soon as possible. We found a way to communicate with him through a cab-driver, but we're going to bait a trap for Deluca and it's dangerous. All of us think it would be a good idea if you went back to Jacobsville before it goes down."

Delia looked at him with pained eyes. "Why do I have to go? Nobody knows I was going out with Marcus, we kept it very low-key. Besides, he's engaged. That brunette stingray's living with him, isn't she?" she added coldly. "I'm no threat to anybody."

"She isn't living with him. She's staying in the hotel." He studied his clasped hands, trying to find a way around what he knew he should be telling her. "Delia, it's best if you go home. I can't tell you why."

"Is it because Marcus's enemies might target me?"

He hesitated. "You're not in any physical danger," he said.

"Barney, you're hiding something from me," she said with certainty. "This isn't like you."

He grimaced. "There are things you don't know," he began. "Like who your father is."

"Who my father is?" she ventured, shocked. "But my father died before I was born. I was premature...!"

He cleared his throat and there was a dull flush across his cheeks. "Well, that isn't exactly how it was. But what you have to know is that Fred's mad at us. He told Deluca that Marcus was going to sell him out, and that's why a hit man got sent in Marcus's direction."

That explained a lot. "But Marcus doesn't remember that!"

"If he does, he's dead. The Deluca woman told her father that Marcus doesn't remember anything about him, so he thinks he's safe. Deluca will be working on a replacement for the hit man. We're watching Marcus like a hawk. They won't catch us off guard again. But you're another matter. Fred's got some...well, some information he shouldn't have, about you."

She sat up, concerned. "What could he do with it?"

Barney looked pained. "Damn it, I told Barb she should have talked to you about this. She won't. She's scared to death to tell you."

"Barney, you're scaring me."

He took a deep breath and looked into her eyes. "I don't mean to. It's just, you need to know what's going on. I guess I'll have to tell you..."

"Barney!"

Barb's taut voice carried down the beach as she walked toward them in platform sandals, sinking to her ankle in the deep sand with each step. She grumbled all the way.

"What are you two talking about?" she asked suspiciously.

Barney sighed. "I was about to tell Delia..."

"...About our plans for dinner?" she finished for him. "We're taking you to this exclusive seafood place. There's a movie star in town and he eats there every night." She mentioned the name of a Texas movie star who'd been in a recent Western. He was Delia's favorite.

"That would be nice, Barb," Delia said, but she knew Barb had interrupted them deliberately. Whatever Barney knew, Barb didn't want Delia to know.

"I was telling her that we want her to go back to Texas, as soon as possible," Barney added coolly.

Barb didn't say anything for a minute. "At the end of the week," she said then. "Let her have a little vacation first."

"The longer she stays, the worse the risk," Barney reminded his wife.

"What risk?" Delia asked. "You just said I wasn't in any danger."

"Not that kind of danger," Barney said.

Barb and her husband exchanged an odd look.

"The end of the week, then," Barney said, rising. He kissed Barb's cheek. "You should tell her," he added softly.

"Tell me what?" Delia exclaimed, exasperated.

"Barney was only teasing," Barb said when he left. "Now, suppose we wander down Bay Street to the straw market? I feel like a new hat!"

Delia was still weak, but she knew the exercise was good for her. She bought a small wooden elephant and a new straw bag to take home with her. Barb was unusually animated, but not very forthcoming. Something was definitely going on.

That evening at the restaurant, Marcus came in with Roxanne on his arm. Delia tried not to look at him. It hurt so much to see him with the other woman.

He paused at their table to speak to them. He looked at Delia carelessly, summing her up as part of the furniture. He smiled at Barb and invited them over to see his orchid collection the next day.

"We'd love to, thanks," Barney said at once, taking advantage of the public invitation to do some private business with Marcus.

Roxanne grumbled, "But we were going out tomorrow!"

"You may be. I'm not," Marcus told her. "I'll see you about eleven, then?" he asked Barney and Barb. He didn't look at Delia at all as he and Roxanne passed on to their table. Delia felt like sinking under the carpet.

Marcus had orchids everywhere, but especially in the enormous, expensive greenhouse with its own climate control.

He acquainted them with the various species of orchid, and showed them how the beautiful flower grew only in bark, not in soil. The colors ranged from pink and white, to spotted yellow and deep orange. There were huge bracts of flowers, and tiny ones. The containers that held them were as unique as the orchids themselves.

While Barney and Barb were enthusing over one particular species, Delia found herself briefly alone with Marcus. He was wearing light Bermuda shorts and a patterned green-and-white shirt that made his eyes look even darker. She had on a blue-and-white sundress with white sandals, her long hair hanging around her shoulders. She was still pale from her ordeal.

"You seem to be doing well," he remarked, feeling uncomfortable with her.

"So do you, Mr. Carrera," she replied politely. "Your orchids are…"

"Who are you?" he asked huskily, his gaze as intent as his tone. "I don't know you, but it upsets me just to look at you. Why?"

She sketched him with her eyes, her heart breaking as she realized that he might never remember anything that had happened between them. Amnesia was unpredictable. "We were only acquaintances," she lied. "Nothing more."

"I know that," he said irritably. "You're not my type of woman at all. You're not glamorous or particularly pretty, you obviously buy your clothes off the rack, your body is too thin, you don't even wear clothes well. I could never have been involved with you," he agreed angrily. "But it was more than a nodding acquaintance. Were you connected with the casino somehow?"

Her heart felt as if he'd stepped on it. He couldn't make it plainer that he had no romantic interest in her. He was certain he couldn't have cared for her.

She lowered her eyes to the orchids nearby. "No," she said. "I don't gamble."

He sighed angrily. "Why do you do that?"

"Do what?" she exclaimed, looking up.

"You look at me as if I'm killing you," he bit off.

She forced a laugh. "How silly. I'm having a nice time looking at the orchids. What sort is this?" she added, pointing to an ordinary purple-and-white phalaenopsis.

He hesitated, as if he wanted to press it, but he gave

in and answered her question. Then he stepped close to show her the way the bracket of flowers grew and the tension exploded between them. He turned to her, a breath away, and saw every quick beat of her heart moving the fabric at her breasts. He felt an electricity that grew quickly explosive as he felt the heat from her body.

His jaw tautened almost to pain as his dark eyes met her green ones at point-blank range. His lips parted on a rush of breath. His big hand went to her cheek and his fingers drew down it involuntarily. Heat exploded in him.

Delia felt it, too, but she'd had enough. She moved away from him and back to the safety of Barney and Barb without a word.

Marcus stared after her, scowling, feeling as if he were on the brink of some incredible revelation. But it hung there, just out of reach, taunting him, tormenting him. She'd meant something to him in the past, he could taste it. What had she been, a minor amusement? Why was he attracted to such an ordinary, dull woman? It must be the concussion, he decided finally, still knocking him off balance.

For the rest of the visit, he ignored Delia, hating the sensations he'd felt with her. He showed his guests the new koi pond he was building of sandstone, a mammoth undertaking with plumbing for all the necessary filters and an expensive liner to boot. He wondered if he'd liked the colorful Japanese fish before? Until he lost his memory he'd apparently not had a yen for koi. The pond had a waterfall, also of sandstone. It was going to be beautiful, when it was finished.

He found time to get Barney alone, and they spoke

about Deluca. Then, all too soon, they were ready to leave.

While Barney was getting Barb into the back of the cab, Marcus hesitated beside Delia. "You lost your child saving my life," he said sadly. "I'm sorry."

Tears stung her eyes. "Tragedies happen to most people at one time or another," she said, trying not to let it show that it was killing her to stand beside him like this and pretend they weren't involved. She loved him!

He felt empty somehow, especially when he saw the tears she was trying valiantly to stem. "You really loved that baby, didn't you?"

She nodded jerkily. She couldn't speak.

"Why?" he ground out. "Why did you take the risk, to save me, a man you didn't even know except as a chance acquaintance?"

She couldn't look at him. "It was an impulse. I saw the gun in the man's hand and I just reacted."

"At what cost!" he said heavily.

She forced her eyes to lift. He looked tormented. She adored him. It was so strong a feeling that she couldn't hide it, and he saw it in her face.

It was like peering into a dark room and seeing just a sliver of light. He wanted to force the memory, but he couldn't. "Tell me," he said under his breath.

She managed a sad smile. "Dragging up the past benefits no one. I'm glad you're still alive, Mr. Carrera. The other…" She took a deep breath. "I believe in acts of God. It wasn't meant to be, for whatever reason. I have to accept that and live with it."

He searched her soft eyes and felt again that jolt of sensation. He frowned. "I don't understand why it hurts me to look at you," he said under his breath.

She averted her eyes and moved away. She couldn't bear to talk about the past anymore. He'd made it clear that she didn't appeal to him in the least. He didn't want her except physically; he probably never had. He was engaged, after all, to the sort of woman he'd told her he liked—beautiful, sophisticated and rich. "You've already made your feelings clear. After all, what would a rich, powerful man like you want with a dull, plain nobody of a woman like me? Goodbye, Mr. Carrera," she said, and felt as if her heart was breaking right in two. "I hope life treats you better than it's treated me."

As she went to get into the cab, Delia met Marcus's eyes across the car and she winced at his closed, angry expression. She didn't look at him again.

He stood and watched the car drive away. Her sarcasm had made him angry. But he felt as if he'd just cut off an arm, and he didn't know why.

That night, while Barney and Barb went to a show downstairs in the lounge, Delia answered the phone and found herself talking to Fred Warner.

"Think you scored real good against me, didn't you, honey, but the joke's going to be on you. Why do you think a millionaire like Barney married a little schoolgirl from Texas when he could have had a debutante, ever think about that?"

"What?" she exclaimed, too shocked to fight.

"You idiot, he looks just like you, and you never noticed? Barney married Barb because she had his baby! He was married when she got pregnant, so your grandmother went away with Barb and told everybody it was her kid. Barb's not your sister, you dope. She's your mother!"

He hung up.

Delia was sitting on the sofa with her head spinning. She couldn't move. She couldn't breathe. Barb was her mother. It had to be a lie. Surely it did!

But things kept going through her mind. Barney did look like her. They favored more than Delia and her late mother had. Barney had been affectionate toward her all her life. He loved her. Barb loved her. It was more than sibling love.

Why hadn't Barb told her? Why had she let her grow into a woman believing that her grandmother was her mother? Why?

She sat and worried and seethed for the next hour and a half until Barney and Barb came back.

They came in the door laughing, having been dancing most of the time after the floor show ended. They were happy, upbeat, cheerful. Until they saw Delia's rigid features.

"I had a phone call from Fred Warner," Delia said coldly, staring at them.

Barb let out an unsteady breath. She put down her evening bag with careful deliberation.

"And…?" she said, trying to sound casual.

"He said that Barney was my father and you were my mother." Her eyes pleaded with them to deny it.

Barney seemed to slump. He sat down on the sofa, leaning forward. "It was only a matter of time, I told you," he said to Barb in a subdued tone. "I told you to tell her the truth!"

"Then…it's true," Delia choked.

Barb burst into tears and ran for the bedroom. She closed the door behind her.

Barney was left, staring at Delia, who looked as if the whole world had fallen on her.

"Why?" she asked harshly.

He spread his hands expressively. "I was married, baby," he said heavily, "to a woman who would have done anything to hold on to all that nice money I had. She never loved me. She only wanted what I could give her. I met Barb while I was in San Antonio on a business deal." He smiled reminiscently. "She was staying overnight with a girlfriend and she went to the same bar where I was. She was dressed real sexy and she was wearing some sophisticated makeup. I thought she was in her twenties." He sighed. "One thing led to another. When I realized what a kid she was, and how innocent, it was already too late. She went home and never mentioned me to your mother, not even when she got pregnant. It was two years before I found out. By then I was divorced, and your grandmother had told everyone that you were her baby, to save Barb's reputation. You were born seven months after your grandfather died, so they said you were premature."

"All these years," Delia said on a sob.

"I wanted to tell you a million times," Barney said, in anguish. "But Barb couldn't bear to have you know. You were brought up so carefully, sheltered so much, so that you wouldn't make the same mistake Barb did."

"But I did anyway," she said flatly.

"Yeah." He grimaced. "If we'd made you go home, maybe you'd never have had to find out. Damn Fred!"

She looked up at him. "It would have come out one day, Barney," she said, feeling oddly sorry for him. He did look so devastated. Not unlike Barb...

"What will you say to Barb?" he asked gently.

Her face closed up. "I don't want to see Barb again right now. I want to go home, Barney. In the past week, my whole life has fallen apart. I'm leaving tomorrow. First thing."

"Okay," he said after a minute. "If that's what you want."

"That's what I want," she said flatly. Then she hesitated. "What about Marcus?" she asked reluctantly. "Will they try again to kill him?"

Barney sighed. "I don't know, baby, but I imagine they will. He's got friends," he reassured her. "Good friends. We'll do everything we can to keep him safe. I promise."

She swallowed hard. "Thanks."

"Barb and I ruined your life," he said. "You don't owe me a thing."

She looked up, her eyes wet with tears. He was her father, and she'd never known. She wished she'd never had to find it out like this. Life, she thought miserably as she went back to her own room, could be cruel.

Chapter 12

The next morning, Delia was up just after daylight and packed when Barb knocked and immediately came into the room.

Delia stared at her as if she were seeing a stranger. Barb's eyes were red and swollen and she looked as devastated as Delia felt.

"I know you don't want to talk to me," she said quickly. "But just give me one minute, please!"

Delia didn't speak. She was still devastated by what she'd learned.

"I was sixteen. Mama was very strict and I thought she was an old fogy," Barb said huskily. "So I snuck off one weekend and went to San Antonio with a friend of mine. We bought some cheap dresses and smeared on lots of makeup and went to a bar. Barney was there alone. We started talking and when he left, I went with him. I didn't know he was married," she added miserably, wiping at her eyes with a tissue. "But I knew I loved him, and he loved me. I had to go home, and I was afraid to tell him how old I really was, so I just left without a word."

Delia sat down and folded her hands, waiting for the rest.

Barb sat down, too. At least Delia was listening, she thought. "When I knew I was pregnant, it was devastating, not only because I didn't know what to do, but because I was going to have to tell Mama what I'd done. I knew she'd be ashamed of me, but I couldn't hide it. Daddy had just died and she was miserable. But the thought of a new baby sort of snapped her out of the depression," she added with a faint smile. "I disguised my condition with big clothes and tent dresses until I was almost due, and then we went away for a couple of months and stayed with a cousin of Mama's. We said the baby was Mama's when we came back home."

"Why?" Delia demanded.

"Because even today in small towns it's hard for a child to grow up illegitimate," Barb said, her tone sad and resigned. "I didn't want your childhood to be any harder than it had to be. I figured Barney would hate me if he ever found out how young I'd been, and that I'd probably never see him again. So we let you think that my mother was your mother, too. But when you were two years old, Barney finally tracked me down. By then he was divorced, and he was still crazy about me. When he saw you, he just fell in love. So he married me. We wanted to take you with us," she added, "but Mama went crazy. She said she'd do anything to keep you, right up to running away with you to another country and hiding out like a fugitive." She grimaced. "Barney and I were afraid she might do it, so we got a house in San Antonio and I was at the house almost every day until you graduated from high school and got a job. We didn't move to New York until you were self-supporting."

"I remember," Delia said heavily.

"We loved you so much, both of us," Barb said, studying her closely. "We still do. We've been bad parents, and we've made a lot of mistakes. I know you need time to come to grips with it all. I won't push and neither will Barney." She stood up. "But I hope someday you can forgive us."

Delia was too confused and still too grief-stricken over Marcus and her baby to manage forgiveness for that big a deception. She didn't look at Barb. After a minute, the other woman's hopeful expression drifted into one of despair and she turned away.

Barb lowered her head and moved to the door. She hesitated, but she didn't look back. "We'll always be there if you need us, baby," she said gently. "And we'll always love you. Even if you…can't love us back, because of what we did."

Her voice broke with tears. She went out the door and closed it firmly behind her. Delia stared at it with dead eyes. It was just too much at one time. She had to go home, she had to get away from here! Maybe when she was back in a normal place, she could get her life back together again. Maybe she could accept that Barb had done the only thing she could have done, in the circumstances.

The plane ride home seemed terribly long, because Delia dreaded arriving back in Jacobsville. So much pain

overwhelmed her. She'd lost Marcus, her baby and now
her own identity, all in less than a week.

Her heart was broken. She cried until her eyes were
swollen. She didn't know how she was going to cope
with it all. She loved Marcus. That was never going to
change. But he didn't remember her, and he might never.
She couldn't get their last meeting out of her mind. He
knew there was something between them, but he had no
memory of it. The sight of his tormented face, his sad
eyes, would haunt her always. But what they'd had for
those few weeks would last her all her life.

She needed time to mourn her child, get over Marcus, and come to grips with what she'd just learned about
Barney and Barb. They were her parents. She'd always
believed that her father had died before she was born,
and that Barb's mother was also her mother.

Now she began to see the past for what it was. Barb
had always been more protective of her than her grandmother had, and she'd been sheltered by both of them.
But her grandmother had always blamed her for Barb's
lapse of judgment. Her grandmother had taken out all her
resentments and anger on Delia, without Barb knowing.
Looking into Barney's face was like looking in a mirror, not to mention that she shared Barb's coloring, but
Delia hadn't wanted to see those things. She'd accepted
a lie. Now she knew everything.

She had to find a way to cope. It would take time to
get used to the idea of her changed identity. She knew
that, in the end, she couldn't hate Barb. She'd done what
she thought was best for Delia, without realizing that
Barb's mother was going to make Delia pay for Barb's
mistake by persecuting her child. She was only disappointed that Barb and Barney had lied to her for so many

years. Maybe they did have a legitimate reason. And they certainly didn't know how hard her grandmother had been on her all those years.

Marcus had been brooding ever since Delia's visit with her sister and brother-in-law. The feelings he had were unexpected and inexplicable. She wasn't his type of woman, so why did he feel such turmoil when he was with her? Why did she look at him as if he meant something to her? Why did she look as if he was hurting her every time they were together?

He couldn't find any answers, and nobody would talk to him about Delia, not even Karen Bainbridge. His memory wasn't any closer than it had been, either. All of it combined to make him irritable and frustrated.

Roxanne Deluca was still around, and she was behaving very suspiciously. She was trying to coax him into taking her to one of the deserted islands in the Bahamas chain. She'd even chartered a boat without telling him.

"You need to get completely away from here for a day, and I'm taking you to a deserted island with me, tomorrow morning." she said, cuddling close to him. "We'll be like Adam and Eve, darling," she teased breathily.

He knew she was up to something, and it probably had to do with a new contract on his life. He was grateful that Smith had been so forthcoming about the situation, or he might have been killed without ever knowing the reason.

"Okay, then," he said. "Come on over about nine in the morning, and we'll go from here. That suit you?"

She smiled broadly. "Yes, it will. I'm so glad you're better, darling."

"When were we getting married?" he asked her.

She hesitated. "Oh, in December," she said, thinking fast.

"December." He nodded, pretending to go along with it.

"We're going to be so happy," she exclaimed.

Later, when she'd gone back to the hotel, he called the cab company and asked for John to come to his house. He paid the cabbie, John, for a double trip that he wasn't going to take, to allay suspicion, and gave him a note for Dunagan.

"Give it to Barney Cortero," he told John quietly. "He'll get it to Dunagan. Don't do it yourself. Got that? And make sure he gets it today. Or you can come to my funeral."

John grimaced. "Yes, sir, Mr. Carrera. You can count on me."

Unfortunately John went across the bridge too fast and T-boned a passing jitney. The wreck gave him a light concussion and a broken rib and sent him directly to the hospital for treatment. It wasn't until the next morning that he was conscious enough to remember the note. He asked the nurse for the shirt he'd been wearing. She handed it to him. He extracted the note and grimaced as he read it. Carrera and Roxanne were going to the marina at nine for a trip to one of the Out Islands. It was now ten o'clock.

"I must have a telephone, at once," John croaked to the nurse. "It's a matter of life or death!"

Barney was just about to leave the room to join Barb downstairs for brunch. They'd overslept and he was still a little groggy. But as he reached the door the phone rang. He ignored it and went out into the hall.

But something nagged at him. He hadn't heard from Carrera, and he'd expected to. What if it was Marcus?

He unlocked the door and went back inside, lifting the phone just as it stopped ringing.

"Hello? Hello?" he repeated.

A thin, weak voice came on the line. "Mr. Cortero?" a husky voice queried. "This is John. I drive a cab. Mr. Carrera sent me with you last evening with a note, but I was in an automobile crash. I'm in the hospital."

"I'm sorry. What's in the note?" Barney asked.

John read the note to him. "You know which island this is?" he added and gave directions.

"Thanks, John. There isn't a minute to lose!" Barney hung up and dialed Dunagan on his cell phone. "It's me," he said when Dunagan picked up. "We've got an emergency."

Marcus had packed a gun, just in case, and he wore it in an ankle holster under the flaring denim of his jeans. If they took him out, he was going to go down fighting.

Roxanne was dressed in a flirty white sundress, her long dark hair sleek and expertly cut. She smelled of expensive perfume, and she was beautiful, but she had the eyes of a cobra.

"You love to go exploring undeveloped islands," she said in a chatty tone as they sailed out of port. "We've done this several times, but not lately."

He didn't believe her. She didn't look like the sort of woman who liked exploring primitive places. He was betting that she planned to lead him right into a trap. He was going along with it. By now, Barney and Dunagan would be waiting for the gangsters when they made their play. He smiled to himself, thinking how surprised

Roxanne was going to be when her father found himself in federal custody.

The crew of the sailboat seemed oddly familiar, but Marcus couldn't place them. He was getting bits and pieces of his life back, in odd dreams that woke him in the middle of the night. A shadowy woman had been the main attraction in them, a woman with a loving, sweet personality who made him whole. It hadn't been Roxanne, he was certain. He'd thought that perhaps he'd run into the unknown woman at the casino. It was a magnet for beautiful, rich women. He was sure that she was extraordinary. He sensed that he hadn't been involved with anyone for a long time, until just recently. But so far, he hadn't run across the mystery woman. Sometimes he could almost feel her in his arms, the sensations were so real. Then he woke up, and he had no memory of what she looked like. It was, he thought absently, like the powerful, odd sensations he felt with Barney's sister-in-law Delia. His attraction to her was as inexplicable as it was shocking. But, then, Delia was a plain, sweet down-home sort of girl, not the type to appeal to his sophisticated tastes. It couldn't have been her.

Well, he had plenty of time, once he got rid of Deluca, to search for his mystery woman. He'd have the leisure, then, to wait for his memory to come back.

"You're very quiet," Roxanne commented as they approached the deserted island she'd described to him.

"I was just trying to remember my recent past," he said easily. "I remember my childhood, my parents, the place I went to school." He shrugged and slid his hands into the pockets of his jeans. "But I can't remember what I did a week ago."

Roxanne seemed to relax. "Don't force it," she said. "It will come back."

He glanced toward her. "Think so? I wonder."

"We're here," she said, pausing to give the crew the order to drop anchor so that she and Marcus could go ashore in the small rowboat.

"You can still row, can't you?" she teased.

"I suppose I'll remember how when I start," he agreed. He gave the crew a searching look, because they still looked familiar to him.

One of them, a tall Berber with the traditional mustache and beard, raised an eyebrow and gave an imperceptible jerk of his head to indicate that Marcus shouldn't look at him too hard.

That was when he knew that the crew of the sailboat wasn't working for Roxanne. He actually grinned before he climbed down the ladder into the dingy.

"You're very cheerful all of a sudden," Roxanne remarked.

He chuckled. "I have a feeling that I'm going to get my memory back very soon. I don't know why, but I do."

"You may be right," she said, without looking at him.

He rowed the boat into the shallows and they jumped out. He tugged it up on the beach so that it wouldn't wash out to sea.

"Now what?" he asked Roxanne.

"Now, let's go exploring!" she said enthusiastically, catching his big hand in hers. "If I remember right, there's a little shack just through there…"

All his instincts for self-preservation were standing up and shouting at him. He moved along with her, but vigilantly, his eyes ever searching for the glint of the sun on a gun barrel, or a shadowy figure nearby.

"I'll bet we'll find a nice cozy little nook in here," she told Marcus, and went up onto the porch of the run-down shack. "Why don't you go on in, and I'll look around for some driftwood so that we can build a fire in the fireplace, like we did before," she added deliberately, smiling. "I'm sorry you can't remember it. We had a really good time here!"

She turned to go down the beach.

He stepped up onto the porch. But instead of going inside, he bent, as if to retie the rawhide lace on his deck shoes. As he squatted down, he palmed the ankle gun.

His heart raced madly. He wondered what the sailboat crew had in mind. If a contract killer was hiding here waiting for him, he'd have to manage alone.

Roxanne, sensing something, turned around and frowned. "What's wrong?" she asked, trying to sound nonchalant.

"Nothing, I just had to tie my shoelace," he called, rising.

"Go on in and wait for me, darling," she cooed.

Wait, the devil, he thought, gritting his teeth. He opened the door and threw himself to one side just as a shot rang out.

He fired without even thinking, reacting to the shot as he had in the old days. The old days…

Everything became crystal clear in seconds. The man in front of him clutched his chest with an expression of disbelief and slumped to the floor, a red stain spreading over the back of his shirt as he landed facedown on the wooden floor of the shack.

"Did you get him?" Roxanne yelled.

"No such luck, baby," Marcus returned. He kicked the killer's gun aside and stepped onto the porch, his dark eyes blazing as he looked over the rail at her. "And that's the second time you and your father have struck out."

Roxanne's mouth fell open. Before she could do anything, say anything, three men came out from the back of the shack with leveled guns.

"Put your hands up, Miss Deluca," the Berber said pleasantly, "unless you want to join your father's hired man in hell."

Roxanne put her hands up at once. She could hardly believe what she was hearing. "He's…dead?"

"Looks that way," Marcus said, his voice even and cold. He came down the steps with the pistol still in his hand. "Was he the only one?" he asked the Berber.

"Yes. We searched thoroughly. Are you all right?"

Marcus laughed hollowly. "Apparently." He gave the taller man a curious appraisal. "Who the hell are you guys?"

"Friends of Mr. Smith," the Berber told him with a grin. "And that's all you need to know. We were barely in time to bluff the crew Miss Deluca had hired and tell her they had a prior engagement and sent us to replace them. Luckily she swallowed it. Dunagan said to tell you that he's found an 'associate' of Mr. Deluca's who's willing to spill his guts in exchange for immunity. His name's Fred Warner."

"Fred!" Roxanne exclaimed. "The weasley little coward…!"

"Sticks and stones, Miss Deluca," the Berber said. "Let's go."

"What about him?" Marcus asked, nodding toward the shack.

"Bahamian police are already on the way. They were looking for the guy in Nassau, but we figured Miss Deluca here had him waiting for you in a secluded place. So we came along for the ride."

"Thanks for the backup," Marcus told them.

"Our pleasure. Now, we'd better get going."

Barney, Barb and Dunagan had supper together that night, after statements had been given to the police and the body of the contract killer had been tucked away in the local morgue. The man, like Deluca's other hired gun, had a rap sheet as long as a towel. Deluca had been picked up in Miami on federal racketeering charges stemming from statements made by his banker, Fred Warner. Roxanne Deluca was arrested for conspiracy to commit murder. Once jurisdiction was established, the two of them could expect a lengthy stay in jail.

They'd invited Marcus to eat with them, so they could fill him in on everything that had happened about Deluca. Even Barb hadn't protested. She was so lonely for Delia that she'd given up her vendetta against the man who'd wronged her. Marcus hadn't completely regained his memory, but he felt more optimistic that he would, despite all the unsettling business of the day. Bits and pieces of the past were fitting themselves into place with each passing hour. He noticed that Barney and Barb were positively morose. Dunagan was manfully trying to keep the conversation going all by himself.

"You two look like the world just ended," Marcus commented.

"Personal problems," Barney replied.

"We all have them," Marcus said heavily.

"It's a good thing you're a dead shot," Dunagan said. "Because John was in a wreck and we didn't even know what was going down until you were halfway to the island with Roxanne."

Marcus smiled, having heard that from the Berber. "Your guys showed up, at least, but they couldn't go ashore with us without arousing Roxanne's suspicions. But I always carry a hidden gun. Old habits die hard." He scowled. "How did I know that?"

"Looks like your memory's trying to reboot," Dunagan said, grinning.

"I wouldn't mind. It's like living in the dark." He stared at Barney curiously. "It's odd how much your sister-in-law looks like you," he said out of the blue.

"That's because she's actually my daughter," Barney said miserably.

Barb took a big swallow of her drink. "And my daughter, too," she added. She gave Marcus a wry glance. "It's almost funny. I was so determined to keep her away from you, because I thought you'd wreck her life. And Barney and I did it all by ourselves."

Marcus frowned. "What do you mean, keep her away from me?"

Barney was trying to give Barb hand signals but she was already three sheets to the wind and she wasn't looking at him.

"She was going around with you while Barney and I were in Miami," she said heavily. "She thought the sun rose and set on you. I didn't know how far things had gone until…ouch!"

She rubbed her shin, where Barney had kicked it. He gave her a hard look, which she finally interpreted. Marcus had lost his memory and they'd said not to tell him a lot about the past. It could be dangerous.

"Don't mind me," Barb said, trying to backtrack. She

laughed inanely. "I'm drunk. I think we'd better go, Barney. I need some sleep."

"Me, too," Barney agreed. "Good to see you all in one piece, Marcus," he said.

"And thanks for the help," Dunagan added, rising. "We won't forget."

Marcus shrugged. "It's been my year to play Good Samaritan. Back in the spring, I helped bag a guy who kidnapped Tippy Moore. Remember her, the supermodel who became a movie star?" he recalled with a smile. "She married an old friend of mine, Cash Grier. He's a police chief in a small town in Texas." He paused, shocked. Those memories had come back without any work at all.

"Jacobsville," Barb informed him. "That's where Delia and I are from."

Marcus was very still. Jacobsville. Small town. Texas. Cash Grier. Tippy's kidnapping. He remembered! He'd visited Tippy in the hospital in New York. He'd been in the hospital in Nassau with a concussion. Delia had been down the hall. He'd gone in to see her without knowing why. She'd looked so familiar to him. She'd been pregnant...

"Good night," Barney called as he and Dunagan shepherded a weaving Barb out the door.

Marcus waved, but he barely heard them. His mind was going full tilt. Delia had been pregnant. She'd saved his life. She'd lost her baby. Her baby.

He signed the tab—no big deal, because he owned the hotel—and went up to his office. Smith glanced at him with subdued concern.

"I heard what happened," he said. "I'm sorry I wasn't there. It was all I could do to get the guys together and send them after you. They were working on a job for a friend of mine, in the area. It was a lucky break for me, because I couldn't find Dunagan or Barney and I had no idea what was going on."

Marcus waved away the apology. "Tell me about Delia," he said curtly.

Smith hesitated.

"Barney's wife said I was going around with her."

Smith grimaced. "Well, yes."

Marcus stilled. "Smith—she was pregnant. Was it… mine?"

Smith's eyes closed and opened. "Yes," he said huskily.

Marcus sat down behind his desk. The baby was the key that opened the lock. He had sudden, sharp flashes of memory. Delia, laughing up at him with the wind blowing through her blond hair as he drove her in the convertible. Delia, in his arms, loving him with unbridled passion despite her utter innocence. Delia, looking at him as if he were some sort of hero when he saved her from Fred. Delia, with tears in her eyes, understanding that he didn't remember her or know about the baby. Delia, walking away from him with her heart breaking…

"Dear God, I let her go!" he burst out. "She was pregnant. She lost the baby, lost me, lost everything. I told her she wasn't my kind of woman, that she could never appeal to me. I actually said that to her. And then, I just let her walk away, without a word! She must have been devastated!"

"Boss, you didn't know who she was," Smith said gently. "She understood."

He put his face in his hands and groaned in utter

anguish. "She lost our baby, saving my life," he whispered. "She fell!"

Smith didn't know what to say. He said nothing.

Marcus continued, "She ran right into that little weasel and knocked the gun out of his hand. He was going to kill me. She saved my life and what did I do? I acted as if I couldn't have cared less about her! I was convinced that I'd never have gotten mixed up with some plain little small-town woman from Texas. I was looking for the mystery woman in my past, for someone beautiful and rich and sophisticated. Delia was standing right in front of me, and I treated her like a stranger. What an idiot I was!" He moved to the balcony and opened the sliding glass doors to let the wind in. He stood there, shattered, vulnerable, hating himself.

"She went home, didn't she?" he asked belatedly.

"Yes," Smith replied.

"And why not? I suppose she thought I'd never get my memory back. I know I looked at her as if she couldn't have interested me any less. She'd been hurt, she'd lost the baby, she'd lost me…" Marcus's eyes were tormented. "No wonder she looked at me as if I were killing her, when I walked into her hospital room." His eyes closed and he fought tears. "After all she'd been through, I turned my back on her, too."

"You didn't know," Smith said again.

"I should have known," Marcus said heavily. He pushed back his unruly hair with a big hand. "I lit up like a rocket whenever she came near me. I ached to hold her when she was close to me. Even that didn't register."

"You were hurt, too."

"Not enough," he said icily. "Everything I got, I damned well deserved. There was going to be a baby," he added, and the pain almost doubled him over. "A baby, Smith. My baby. She…lost it."

Smith closed his eyes. He couldn't bear to see the torment in that dark face. Marcus Carrera was one tough customer, but he was melting in front of Smith's eyes.

"I'm sorry about that," Smith said.

"She just found out that her sister was really her mother, and her brother-in-law was really her father," Marcus added dully. "That, the baby, me…I guess she figured she didn't have any reason to stay here. She probably felt as if we all sold her out."

"She needs time," Smith said wisely. "It's a lot to have to adjust to."

"Yeah." Marcus moved back into the office, his manner distracted. "I'd like to just rush down to Texas and scoop her up and bring her right back here. But you're right. She's going to need time. So I'm going to give her a few months, to get over the worst of it. Meanwhile, I've just thought of a project that may help my case when I go after her."

"Go…after her?"

Marcus smiled faintly. "Half a man can't live, Smith," he said simply. "Not for long, anyway. I'm going to marry her."

Smith's green eyes sparkled at the idea of his boss, a loner by nature, being so smitten with a woman.

Marcus gave his bodyguard a speaking glance. "You've never married, I guess?"

Smith shook his head, smiling. "I'm too picky."

"There were rumors that you were crazy for Kip Tennison," Marcus added.

"I was responsible for Kip and her son for several years, you know," Smith told him. "I'm terribly fond of them both, but her heart always belonged to Cy Harden and I always knew it."

"You didn't stay with them."

Smith chuckled. "Harden and I didn't quite come to blows, but we're too much alike to get along. Besides, since they had their second child, Kip's given up most of her work for the Tennison corporation and she's working as a vice president for Harden's companies. It's her former brother-in-law who's in the line of fire now. I wasn't needed." He cleared his throat. "Harden never did take to Tiny. I think he had a secret lizard phobia."

"Maybe it was an excuse to get rid of the competition." Marcus chuckled.

Smith shrugged. "A man as good-looking and talented as I am would inspire jealousy in most men," he said with a straight face.

Marcus grinned. "Just as well I got landed with you. When Delia comes back, you're going to be needed more than ever. I expect to found a small dynasty down here," he added, the smile fading to sadness as he thought of the child he'd lost before he even knew it existed. "Babies are nice. In fact," he mused, breaking out of his somber mood as he turned, "I've got some nice blue and pink batik prints and a few fat quarters of whimsical fabric that would make the sweetest little quilt…"

He was gone before Smith had to hide his amused smile.

Chapter 13

Delia had always loved Christmas. It was her favorite
season. Jacobsville pulled out all the stops for the holiday season, beginning just at Thanksgiving, decorating
everything in sight. There were garlands of pine and colored lights strung across the street that went around the
town square, and every door had a wreath and a red bow.
There were Christmas trees in almost every window, including one right next to the statue of Big John Jacobs.
There were lighted reindeer, Santa Clauses and snowmen, and wreaths on the lawns of businesses and homes.
In holiday dress, Jacobsville was absolutely without peer.

It was getting easier to look back, Delia thought, although she still grieved for Marcus and her baby. But she
felt the pain grow dimmer as time passed. She missed
Barb and Barney, as well. She hadn't spoken to them,
but she had sent Barb a card just a few days ago for

Thanksgiving, and had one sent right back in return. By Christmas, she hoped, they might be speaking again and visiting. She'd never spent a Christmas without Barb and Barney that she could remember.

She was sorry she'd been so hard on them. It must have been difficult for them to have to give her up to Barb's mother, and more difficult to keep the secret all the long years in between. They loved her. Of course they did, and she loved them. But they should have told her the truth years ago.

She wondered if Marcus had gotten his memory back. She supposed not, because he hadn't been in touch with her all these months. But, then, would he contact her? He'd looked at her without any spark of interest most of the time. He'd even told her that she could never appeal to him as that Deluca woman did. Anyway, it was probably just revenge and desire and nothing more on his part. It even made sense. He'd gotten mad at his fiancée, picked up Delia, seduced her and then felt guilty. It would explain why he hadn't wanted her to contact him after their night together. Whatever had gone before, or whatever might have been, he was engaged. He might even be married by now. Certainly he might even welcome his loss of memory, because it would keep him from having to explain his lapse of fidelity with Delia to Roxanne Deluca.

She did write to Mr. Smith, however, in care of the Bow Tie, without putting her name or return address on the envelope. To her surprise, he wrote back immediately. She learned that there had been another attempt on Marcus's life, but that some mercenaries who were friends of Smith had saved him. The perpetrators were now in custody, including a Miami mobster who'd planned it all—and Fred Warner was right in custody along with him. He cautioned her not to mention it to anyone. As if she knew anyone who'd even be interested, she mused. She was so grateful that Marcus was still alive and out of danger, even if he did marry that Deluca woman. Amazing, she thought, that he'd been targeted by the Miami mobster yet he was engaged to the same mobster's daughter. It didn't make sense.

Nevertheless, it had been a joy to know that Marcus wasn't doing anything illegal, that he'd worked with the government to shut down the illegal operations. Sadly, it wouldn't have mattered if he hadn't been. She'd loved him so.

She hadn't heard from Mr. Smith after that. It was as if there was a conspiracy to keep her in the dark. Perhaps he'd mentioned that he'd written her to Marcus, and Marcus hadn't approved.

All her rationalizing didn't keep Marcus out of her thoughts. She dreamed about him every night. When she put a quilt block together, she thought about him. When she taught a quilting class, she thought about him. Her life was empty in a way it never had been before. She felt as if she'd been cut in two. Even worse was the loss of her child. She'd loved babies all her life. She'd dreamed of having one of her own. Now she could hardly bear to look at baby clothing, or furniture, or even photos of her customers' children and grandchildren. It was like a knife through her heart.

But she was adjusting. She felt far more mature than she had been. She was less unsure of herself, less nervous around people. She'd grown emotionally. She was certainly stronger than she'd ever been. But she missed Marcus. Oh, how she missed Marcus!

412					*Carrera's Bride*

She was putting the final touches on the second short-ened sleeve of a garment she was altering when she heard the bell go out front, where she had her small of-fice open to the public. Leaving the shirt on her sewing machine table, she walked to answer the door, smiling automatically as she opened it. It didn't occur to her to wonder why the customer didn't just walk in. Every-body else did.

But when she saw who her caller was, she was dumb-founded. She couldn't even manage a single word of greeting.

Marcus was doing some hard looking of his own. She'd grown thin in the three months they'd been apart, he thought. She was finer-drawn, from the grief. But her green eyes were wide and surprised and brimming over with delight that she couldn't hide. He relaxed, just a little.

"Mr. Carrera," she greeted hesitantly.

"I know who you are, Delia," he said quietly. "I know what happened. My memory came back. Fortunately it came back before Deluca's second hit man took his best shot at me."

She stared at him hungrily. "I'm so glad he missed," she said softly.

He shrugged. "I guess you didn't know exactly what was going on, did you?" He grimaced. "Can I come in?" he asked, glancing behind him uneasily. "I've never had so many people stare at me before. I feel like a lobster at a seafood restaurant."

"Certainly," she said belatedly, stepping aside to let him in. She paid great attention to closing the door be-hind him while she tried to get her wits back about her.

"I was just at the police department to see Cash Grier," he explained.

"You know our police chief?" she asked, surprised.

"Yeah. One of the guys who kidnapped his wife, Tippy, back in the winter worked for me at one time. I helped the feds put him away," he added.

She didn't know what to say. She didn't know why he was here. "Are you married now?" she asked, trying to sound nonchalant.

"Married?" he asked blankly.

"Roxanne Deluca said you were engaged to her."

"She told me that when I lost my memory. Roxanne's dad was setting me up for another hit," he replied blandly. "I knew Roxanne, but we were never engaged. She wanted me to believe we were, so that she could lead me into a trap."

"But…why?" she asked. "I don't understand."

He perched himself on the edge of her desk and studied her intently. She'd cut her beautiful long hair. He grimaced, because he'd loved the length. She was wearing a dress that was obviously homemade, and not sexy at all. She dressed, and looked, like a woman who didn't care how she appeared to men ever again. He was responsible for that. It hurt him.

"The trap?" she prompted, because it made her uncomfortable to have him look at her that way.

"I've been working with the feds to shut down Fred Warner."

"Yes, I know."

"Do you?" he asked quizzically. "Well, Fred was laundering money for Deluca, who wanted to move in on Paradise Island and set up his own casino. You can probably imagine what sort. Crooked. Anyway, Fred was already doing dirty banking for one of the bigger drug cartels in Colombia."

"Your brother was killed by them," she recalled.

He looked at her, surprised. "I guess I did tell you that." He smiled apologetically. "Some things are still a little blurry. Yes, Carlo was killed by the cartel when he tipped off the feds about a shipment. They injected him with an overdose of cocaine to make it look like an overdose, but the medical examiner wasn't fooled."

"Was he working for the government, too?" she wondered.

His face was taut. "No. He wanted to get back at the guy who got him hooked. Your old pal Fred Warner," he added.

Her lips parted on a soft rush of breath. So that was the connection.

"But the Colombian cartel Fred was laundering money for wanted revenge for that lost shipment, so they went after my brother and killed him," he said sadly, his face hardening. "I swore I'd get Fred for doing that, so I cultivated him with a phony offer of working with me and Deluca. Deluca had contacted me, that's true, and I drew the feds in before I approached Fred."

"But it didn't bring back your brother," she murmured sympathetically.

"No," he agreed, his tone sad. "If he'd just left that damned Fred Warner alone, and not tipped off the law about the cocaine shipment, he might still be alive," he added coldly.

She felt his sadness. "He did the right thing, though. You know he did."

"Yes. The right thing. But he died for it." He grimaced. "I never could understand why he couldn't stop using. I smoke cigars occasionally, but I can quit any time. I don't like addictions, so I don't have any. Carlo was different."

"I've known people who drank and couldn't stop," she replied gently. "I've always connected alcoholism and drug addiction with chemical imbalance. It seems to me that addictive personalities are basically depressed people who are trying desperately to find substances that will lift their moods. In fact, it does the opposite, and just makes it worse."

He searched her face quietly. "That's one of the first things I liked about you," he said. "You're not judgmental. You always look for reasons why people do the things they do. Me, I just shoot from the hip."

She lowered her eyes. "I thought you didn't like anything about me."

He ground his teeth together. He hated the memory of that last conversation they'd had before she left the Bahamas.

She turned. "I'm glad you came by," she said. "But I really have to go back to work now."

"Delia."

She didn't want to look at him again. It hurt too much. But she forced herself to face him.

He was holding something in a bag. She hadn't noticed until now. He held it out to her, almost hesitantly.

She took the carrier, set it on the desk and opened it. Tears blinded her to its beauty for a few seconds. She lifted it out, blinking away moisture, and spread it slowly on the surface of the desk.

It was a baby quilt. It had a block with a Texas landscape and one with Navy Pier in Chicago. Another one was of Blackbeard's Tower in Nassau, and a house with casuarina trees on the ocean. It had a block of a man and a woman at a table on the beach. It had one of a yacht, another of a woman making a quilt, and a man cutting a pattern. In one, there was a couple holding hands silhouetted against the ocean and the moon. In the center, there was a baby dressed in a lacy white gown and a white cap, with a halo over its head.

"It's our baby," she whispered brokenly, without choosing her words.

"Yes," he bit off.

She looked up. His face was tragic, as she imagined her own might be. There was a suspicious moisture in his own eyes.

It was too much. She ran to him, one arm holding the quilt, the other open to embrace him.

He swept her up without a word and stood just holding her, rocking her, while she cried and cried. Tears ran down her cheeks and into the corners of her mouth. She cried until the pain became almost bearable, and still he held her close.

"The past three months have been pure hell," he whispered roughly at her ear. "A hundred times I've picked up the phone to call you and put it down, or started to write a card, or thought about buying an airplane ticket. But I didn't think you'd even speak to me, and I didn't want to upset you any more. Barb and Barney said you weren't having anything to do with them. Well, until three days ago, they got a card from you." He chuckled, although his voice sounded oddly hoarse. "Then I figured, hey, if she can forgive them, maybe she can forgive me. So I got on a plane and flew to San Antonio. It's taken me two days just to get up the nerve to come down here."

She rubbed her wet eyes against his throat. "Did you rent a car?"

"Hell, I rented a limo. I'm not driving you around in some budget sedan and having your friends say I was too cheap to do the thing right."

She pulled back and looked up at him with her whole heart in her eyes, smiling through the tears. He looked older, too, and almost as worn as she did. She reached up, hesitantly, to touch the dark circles under his eyes. There was moisture there.

He caught her hand and pulled it to his mouth, as if he didn't want her to know how it had affected him, when she saw the quilt.

"I was so glad that Dunagan and Mr. Smith's friends kept you safe," she confessed, smiling through her tears.

His eyebrows lifted. "How did you find that out? You haven't been talking to Barb or Barney. They'd have told me."

She looked sheepish. "Mr. Smith wrote to me," she admitted, "and I wrote back, to a post office box he's got in Nassau."

He caught his breath. "So that's how you knew what was going on! If I'd known that, I wouldn't have been so miserable. I'll shoot Smith for not telling me!"

"No, you can't do that," she said with a smile. "I made him promise not to tell you. I was worried, and since I wasn't speaking to my...parents," she said the word for the first time, "there was no other way I could know how you were."

"You cared how I was, after the way I treated you?" he asked with humility.

She touched his wide mouth with her fingertips. "You

didn't remember me," she said softly. "You couldn't help it."

"You gave up on me," he accused. "You went away and left me with that poisonous brunette."

"I thought you might really be engaged to her," she pointed out. "She said you were, and you'd already told me not to contact you, after we went out with Karen on the yacht. I knew about her father, but it wouldn't be the first time a woman got involved with a man against her father's wishes. For all I knew, I could have been a fling."

"Some fling," he murmured, his eyes eating her. "I breathed you from the minute we met. I've been half a man for months."

She managed a weak smile. "Me, too."

He lifted an eyebrow.

"Figuratively speaking," she corrected.

He bent and touched his mouth to her soft lips, tenderly. "I want to take you out to supper tonight. I've got something for you. There's a hotel in San Antonio, the Bartholomew," he added. "I booked a table for seven o'clock. Okay?"

"Why do you have to go to San Antonio to give it to me?" she wondered. "It will be expensive, to have the limousine go there and back again…"

"I'm rich. Didn't you notice?"

She sighed. "I was too busy noticing how sexy you were," she confessed.

He grinned.

She lifted the quilt in her hands and looked at it again, this time with pleasure as well as pain. "This is beautiful."

"We'll keep it in a special place. But I'm working on another one," he added. "One with blocks with numbers and letters in them, and little animals in separate blocks. I'm going to do a blue and pink and yellow one, so it will work for a boy or a girl."

She was confused. "Why?"

He looked down at her with poignant feeling. "I thought, if I asked nicely, you might give me another baby."

Her heart felt near to bursting. That didn't sound like he wanted an affair.

"We'll talk more about it tonight."

"It isn't very fancy, is it?" she worried. "I don't have a lot of nice clothes, Marcus."

"Anything you wear will be fine," he promised, but in the back of his mind, a plot was already forming. "What time do you close up?"

"At five."

"I'll be here about five-thirty. That okay?"

She nodded.

He reached down to kiss her, softly. "Don't forget."

"How could I?" she wondered in a breathless tone.

He turned to go, pausing with his hand on the door handle. "I'm glad you're better," he said. "I had hell living with the things I said to you. It was worse, knowing you lost the baby saving me."

"You think I could have stood by and let him shoot you?" she asked sadly.

"No more than I could have let him shoot you, honey," he replied huskily.

She fed her eyes on him. He was beautiful to her. She never got tired of looking at him. And a man like that had come all this way to take her out to eat. She was amazed.

"I'll see you later," he promised, and winked as he left the shop.

He walked right into an elderly lady who'd been standing outside the door. He apologized and backed into a young couple. As he turned to apologize again, three people he hadn't seen excused themselves for being in the way. A few yards away, a woman was taking pictures of the black super stretch limousine sitting outside Delia Mason's combination house and shop.

"Nice day, isn't it?" the elderly woman asked, grinning from ear to ear.

"Yeah. Real nice."

Marcus dived into the limousine with a total lack of grace and slammed the door. "Get me the hell out of here!" he told the driver.

At precisely five o'clock, Marcus knocked on Delia's front door, peering warily around him while the limousine sat at the curb with its motor running.

Delia opened the door, still in the dress she'd been wearing earlier, shocked. "You said five-thirty!" she exclaimed. "I haven't even started to dress…!"

"I know." He took a long box from under his arm and handed it to her. He put another box on top of that one. He pulled a jewelry case out of his pocket and added that to the stack. "Five-thirty," he said.

She knew the labels on the boxes. One was that of a couture fashion house, the other a leading shoe manufacturer. He hadn't got these things off any rack. "But you don't know my size!"

"I called Barb," he replied.

He climbed back into the limousine and it took off. Delia closed the door. It felt like Christmas.

* * *

Inside the big box was a black silk dress, just her size, and cut to emphasize her slender figure. It fell to her ankles in soft ruffled folds. In the shoe box was a pair of high heels to match. In the jewelry case lay a thick gold necklace encrusted with emeralds and diamonds, and two matching earrings lay in the center of it. She knew before she looked that the gold was 18 karat and the stones were genuine and of the highest quality. Barb had taught her about fine jewelry.

She got out her best underwear, which was still a poor match for the finery Marcus had brought, and started dressing. Fortunately her blond hair had some natural wave, and it didn't look bad at all to her. She used more makeup than normal and pulled out a fancy black velvet coat that Barb had given her to wear with the dress.

When Marcus knocked at the door, she was ready.

"I forgot about the coat," he remarked. "We can get you a fur if you want one. I'll phone and have one sent down right now—"

"I can't wear fur, Marcus," she interrupted softly. "I'm allergic. Sorry."

"Are you allergic to cats and dogs?"

"No. I've got a dog, remember? Sam has a fenced yard out back and a doghouse. My pet chicken, Henrietta, has her own little fenced corner and a henhouse. I'll introduce you to them another time. I'm only allergic to fur coats."

"Thank God." He noted her curious stare. "While I had amnesia, I adopted two big Persian cats."

"Why?" she asked.

He shrugged. "Search me. That was just after I put in a koi pond."

"I remember you showing it off before I left the Bahamas. I still can't believe you have a pond full of those beautiful, colorful Japanese fish like the ones we saw in that botanical garden we visited."

He was surprised she knew about koi. He hadn't remembered. Or had he?

She was fascinated. "When we walked around the garden, I told you that I loved them. You said you weren't that interested in fish!"

He laughed. He had remembered. "I've thought about doing some koi quilts."

Her eyes brightened. "Oh, I'd love to do some of those, too."

"Then we'll have to talk about having you come live on Paradise Island," he murmured drily. "Because I don't think my nerves will let me live here."

"Why?" she asked blankly.

He turned and pointed to the limousine. On the sidewalk near it, the same woman was taking photographs of it again. A new couple was standing near a tree, apparently talking, but they were both staring at Marcus and Delia. An elderly woman down one end of the street was pruning roses. Two girls in the upstairs window of the house next door were giving Marcus thumbs-up signals. And a police car was going slowly down the street while the officer driving it looked at the floor show. Out back, the dog was raising the devil. He was going to upset her hen, Henrietta, in her nice little caged lot, and there would be no eggs for days.

"I forgot that Callie Kirby and her stepfather lived here before she married Micah Steele," Delia said on a sigh. "They still tell stories about their courting days."

"The crowds, you mean?" he asked, glowering at the crowd nearby.

"It's a very small town," she pointed out. "The only real crime we've had in years was when our local mercenaries shut down a notorious drug dealer. Oh, and Tippy Moore batting a would-be assassin on the head with an iron skillet. They say when Cash Grier got there, the man ran out to the police cars pleading for the officers to save him from Tippy."

He chuckled. "I've met the lady, and I don't doubt the story."

She smiled up at him. She touched the emeralds gingerly. "You shouldn't have done this," she said.

"You needed a dress and some accessories," he said simply, catching her by the hand. "Lock the door and we'll take a bow before we leave."

She fiddled with the lock, only half hearing him. "A bow?"

He pulled her into his arms, bent her back against one of them, bent and kissed the breath out of her.

When he let her go, the elderly woman had her hand on her heart and looked as if she might faint. The couple nearby was watching, openmouthed. The girls at the window were cheering. The woman taking the photo of the limousine was now snapping pictures of Marcus and Delia. And the police car was stopped in the road, blocking traffic, while the man inside leaned out the window to shout at them.

"I'd give that a Nine-Plus on a scale of Ten!" Police chief Cash Grier called to Marcus.

"You're blocking traffic, Grier!" Marcus called back.

Grier just chuckled and waved as he drove off.

Marcus escorted Delia to the car with continental

flair, waited while the uniformed driver opened the door, put her inside and dived in after her.

"So much for satisfying our public," he teased, laughing at her still-dazed expression.

The restaurant was crowded, and Delia was still reeling from Marcus's stage kiss. She gave her coat to the clerk at the coat room and took Marcus's hand as they followed the waiter to their table.

Sitting at it were Barney and Barb, dressed to the nines and looking nervous and even a little frightened.

That softened Delia's heart even more. She went straight to Barb with her arms wide open.

Barb ran into them and hugged her close, crying. "Oh, baby, we've missed you so much!"

"Hello, stranger," Barney added, opening his own arms to be hugged.

"I'm sorry," Barb began.

"No, I'm sorry," Delia said at the same time, and laughed because they sounded like echoes. "I just had to get used to it," she added. "But now I'm glad. I'm so glad! I love you both very much."

"We love you, too, baby," Barney said, and turned away before he lost his composure.

"I told you it was going to be a surprise," Marcus told Delia with a grin.

"It really was," Delia said, laughing through her tears. "Oh, I'm so glad to see all of you!" she exclaimed, including Marcus as she swept her eyes over the three most important people in her life. "I'm sorry I've been such a pain," she added softly to her parents. "I'll try to make up for it, honest."

"You had so many hard knocks, baby," Barb told her.

"It's no wonder it hit you so hard. We understood." She glanced at Marcus with a wry smile. "And Marcus has kept our spirits up, too."

"We were all sort of in the same boat," Marcus explained. "None of us wanted to rush you, but it was a lonely game."

He seated Delia while Barney seated Barb, and the waiter brought menus for them.

After they ordered, Delia looked around the table. "I don't understand why we're here tonight, though. Is it some sort of special occasion?"

"You might say that," Marcus mused.

Barb and Barney smiled mysteriously.

"What, then?" Delia persisted.

"You'll just have to wait until after dessert," Marcus teased. "But I promise, it will be worth waiting for."

Dinner was exquisite. Delia had never eaten food so wonderful. And the desserts were rolled from table to table on a trolley, so that the guests could choose their own. Marcus liked a deep chocolate cake. Delia picked a crème brûlée and savored every single bite.

With the dinner came wines, a delicious white with the fish and a dry red with the beef, and champagne with dessert.

The bubbles tickled Delia's nose. She laughed. "I don't think I've had champagne more than once in my life. Mother didn't approve of spirits," she added. Then she stopped, and looked at Barb. "I mean, Grandmother didn't approve of spirits," she corrected, and her eyes were full of love.

Barb bit her lower lip. "Thank you, baby," she said softly. "But I know it's going to be hard for you to get used to calling me Mother. You just go right on calling me Barb. It doesn't matter, honest."

But it did, and Delia knew it. She reached over and touched Barb's hand gently. "You've been like a mama wolf all my life, protecting me and sheltering me and taking care of me. I've always thought of you as more mother than sister, and especially now. I'm glad you're my mother. And I'm glad Barney's my dad," she added, smiling at him, too. "It was a surprise, but it's not a bad one. It was just that so much was going on at the time. I think I went a little crazy."

"No wonder," Marcus replied. "You lost everything, didn't you?"

"Yes. But what doesn't kill you makes you stronger, don't they say?" she replied. "I've matured."

"You have," Barb said.

"But you're still my baby," Barney told her with a loving smile.

"Thanks."

He shrugged. "What are dads for?"

"That's something I can't wait to find out for myself," Marcus murmured, giving Delia's shocked face a speaking glance. "And that reminds me..."

He reached into his jacket pocket and pulled out a small, square jeweler's box, one that matched the box Delia's necklace and earrings had been in. He opened it and sat it just in front of Delia's dessert plate. Then he waited, watched, his breathing all but suspended.

She stared at the rings openmouthed. There was an emerald solitaire in an exquisite heavy gold setting, surrounded by small diamonds, next to what was obviously a matching wedding band.

"It looks like…" she began.

"It is," Marcus said quietly. "I'm asking you to marry me, Delia."

Chapter 14

Delia stared at the rings with her heart in her throat. He was telling her that he wanted to marry her. She shouldn't have been surprised, not after he brought her the baby's memory quilt. But she was.

She looked up at him with tears in her eyes.

He grimaced. "I know. You're remembering what I said to you, that you weren't my type, that I didn't believe I could ever have been interested in you. But the doctors explained it to me. Even when I had amnesia, I was still trying to protect you. Deluca was after me and you were in danger if you were near me." He smiled gently. "You see, it wasn't that I didn't care. I cared so much that even amnesia didn't affect it."

She curled her small hand into his big one and looked at him with her heart in her eyes. "Yes, I'll marry you, Marcus."

"They weren't kidding, you know, when they said I had a reputation," he added, his expression solemn. "I have got a past, and I was a bad man."

"No bad man could make a quilt like the one you brought me today," she said simply, and swallowed hard to keep the lump in her throat from choking her.

His fingers tightened on hers.

Barb and Barney exchanged puzzled looks, but Marcus and Delia weren't sharing that memory. It was too personal.

"Yes, Marcus," Delia repeated. "I'll marry you."

He grinned from ear to ear.

"We're going to need a lot more champagne," Barney said on a chuckle, and signaled to a waiter while Barb mopped up her tears.

"Would you like to be married in Jacobsville?" Marcus asked when they were briefly alone in his hotel room while he planned to phone for the limo driver to pick them up.

"I would," she agreed.

"We can get a license and a blood test and a minister in three days," he said. "Or would you like to wait until Christmas?"

She searched his eyes hungrily. "I'd rather starve to death than wait."

His eyes flashed. "So would I."

In a matter of seconds, the phone call to the limo driver was forgotten, her dress was on the floor, followed by his jacket, and a trail of hastily removed clothing made a trail all the way to the king-size bed.

They barely made it under the covers before his big body was crushing her down into the crisp, cold sheets.

"I'm sorry, I really am starving," he groaned as he nudged her long legs apart and lowered himself between them. He looked into her wide, misty eyes. "Is it all right?"

"What do you mean, is it all right?" she gasped.

"Are you taking anything?" he emphasized.

She shook her head.

He hesitated.

She looked straight into his eyes and deliberately lifted her hips and brushed them against his in a long, slow, sensuous plea.

He shivered.

He bent and brushed his mouth softly over hers. The urgent ferocity was suddenly gone. He hesitated, shifted, took a deep, long breath and kissed her with aching tenderness. The sudden shift from raging passion to exquisite tender patience caught Delia by surprise. She met his eyes with patent curiosity.

"I'll explain. Here," he whispered, tugging her legs up beside his so that they were lying curled together like an intimate puzzle. "If we're going to make a baby, we have to do it with love, not lust," he added, and his voice actually trembled.

She caught her breath and tears misted her eyes. "A baby?" she whispered brokenly. "Do you mean it? It's not too soon for that?"

"No. It's definitely not too soon," he whispered, closing her wet eyes with kisses. "A baby will only make everything more perfect than it already is."

"Yes," she sobbed at his ear, clinging closer as she felt him pressing intimately into her body.

He shifted against her, smiling as his hands began to caress her slowly, with aching tenderness. He kissed her

Diana Palmer 431

face, brief little teasing kisses that matched the infinitely slow, sweet movements of his big body. The only sound in the room was the soft whisper of flesh against flesh, the tiny sounds that pulsed out of her throat as the pleasure began to build.

His big hands cradled the back of her head. "I'm sorry you cut your hair," he said. "I loved it long."

"I was grieving," she replied. "I'll let it grow…" She cried out as his hands found her more intimately than they ever had before.

"Do you like that?" he murmured. "Let's try this."

"Marcus…!"

His mouth explored her as if she were a flower, touching and tasting, and arousing sensations that lifted her completely off the bed.

By the time he reached her breasts, she was shivering. One big hand was between them, coaxing her body to accept him.

Her short nails bit into his big arms as he began to possess her with slow, deep, intimate strokes.

"It wasn't…like this," she tried to tell him.

"No, it wasn't," he whispered. His eyes were somber as they held hers while his body moved into stark, total possession. "We've never made love like this, before, not even when it was the very best pleasure we shared. But this is different, my darling. This is…creation itself."

She throbbed. Her body pulsed with every brush of his powerful body. She made a sound she'd never heard, deep in her throat, as the pleasure began to climb like a fever.

"Hold on, tight," he whispered. "We're going to fall right…over…the edge…of the world…!"

He pushed down, hard, and she lifted up to meet

him. The motion was frantic, potent, fierce. All that tenderness that had led up to it made the culmination even more shattering. They clung to each other, shuddering, pulsating, as the pleasure burst into a thousand fiery explosions and lifted them into near unconsciousness.

She heard his harsh voice throbbing in her ear as he convulsed over her shivering body. She wept, because it was unbearable. She didn't think she could live through it.

"I'm...dying," she sobbed.

"So am I," he ground out unsteadily, his body moving helplessly against hers in the pinnacle of ecstasy.

She couldn't let go, not even when their hearts stopped racing out of control. She clung to his damp back, holding on as he rolled sideways, with her still pressed to him.

He shivered one last time. "I never had it like that in my life with anyone, not even with you," he whispered, awed.

"Me, neither."

He laughed wickedly, deep in his throat. "Yeah, but I wasn't a virgin," he whispered outrageously.

She laughed, too, amazed that intimacy could be so sweet and so much fun at the same time.

He curled her against him and rolled onto his back with a rough sigh. "Now we have to get married quick, so that we don't have to let out the wedding gown I packed for you."

"Wedding...gown?" she stammered.

"It's gorgeous," he said wearily, tugging her into a more comfortable position. "Acres of lace, a keyhole neckline, an embroidered hem of white roses to match the embroidered veil, and a white rose garter."

"You bought me a wedding gown?" she exclaimed. "When?"

"A few days after my memory came back," he murmured drowsily. "I was going crazy, I missed you so much. I knew you had to have a little time, but I had to do something to keep myself sane. So I flew to Paris and went through all the couture houses looking for just the right gown. It's in a hanging bag in my closet. Want to see?"

"Do I!" she replied, touched.

He dragged himself out of bed, opened the closet, and drew out a couture bag. He hooked it over the closet door and unzipped it. Lace flowed out onto the floor. Delia jumped out of bed and went to look at it, fascinated by the almost ethereal beauty of it.

"Marcus, this must have cost a fortune!" she exclaimed.

"It did," he mused. "But I'd have mortgaged the hotel to get it. I think you'll be the most beautiful bride this town ever saw."

She looked up at him with eyes that adored him. "You'll certainly be the most handsome groom," she told him.

She moved against him and reached up to lock her arms around his neck and coax his mouth down to hers. Neither of them was wearing clothing, and it had been a long time that they'd been apart. He felt her bare breasts and long legs against his and his body hardened at once.

She lifted her eyes to his and pursed her lips. "Well?" she asked. "Are you up to it?"

He bent and swung her up into his arms with a bear-ish grin. "Honey, suppose you tell me if I am?"

He tossed her into the middle of the bed and followed her down.

It was morning before they woke. He rolled over and looked at the clock and sighed. "I guess the limo driver gave up on us and went to bed, too," he told her with a wry grin. "I booked him into the hotel, just in case."

"You wicked man," she teased.

"Hey, it's been a long dry spell," he defended himself. "I haven't touched another woman in all this time, you know."

She beamed. "I hoped you hadn't, but it's nice to know for sure."

"Trust me, do you?" he asked.

She nodded. She nuzzled her face against his. "I love you, Marcus," she whispered. "I love you so much, it hurts."

He buried his face in her throat. "I love you just as much," he groaned. "I never knew it could hurt so much to be separated from someone!"

"Hurt...?"

"You lost our baby, and you were gone before I even knew it. I couldn't even comfort you. Worse, I had to live with the knowledge that I'd caused it."

"But, you didn't," she said at once. "Marcus, you didn't! I couldn't have let that man kill you! What sort of life would I have had, without you?"

"Maybe a better one than you will have," he said worriedly. "I've still got enemies. We might have some bad times yet."

"I don't care. I'll stand with you with our backs to the wall and fight right alongside you, if I have to!" She lifted her head and stared at him with a ferocious, loving expression. "Texas women have always been fierce when their families were threatened. You're my family, now, too," she whispered. "And I'll love you all my life."

He bent and put his mouth softly over her parted lips. "I would die for you, baby," he whispered in a choked tone. "I'll give you anything you want!"

She snuggled close, feeling safe and loved and cherished. "I only want a baby, Marcus," she said softly.

His arms tightened. "So do I!"

She closed her eyes. "I have a feeling that we won't have a long time to wait," she murmured with a smile.

When they got back to town, Marcus checked into the Jacobsville hotel to allay any gossip about him and his Delia, and he invited his friends Cash and Tippy Grier to have dinner with them, along with Barb and Barney.

But what started out as a simple social evening mushroomed.

Cash had arranged for his friends Judd Dunn and Marc Brannon, as well as Jacobsville police officers Palmer and Barrett, and Sheriff Hayes Carson, to meet him in the lobby of Marcus's hotel just after supper. And he didn't mention it to Delia.

He left her talking with Barb, Barney and Tippy while he tugged Marcus out to the lobby on the pretext of discussing something personal with him.

"Oh, no," Marcus said when he saw the lawmen, most of whom were wearing their uniforms. "No, you're not to arrest me on some old, forgotten charge like jaywalking and lock me up before my own wedding…?"

"Nothing of the sort," Cash replied immediately, grinning. "No, we have another objective in mind."

Marcus shook hands all around, but he was puzzled at why these guys were gathered around him.

"We asked the Hart brothers how to go about this," Cash said merrily. "They arranged each others' marriages even when their brothers didn't want them to. And they gave us a rundown of the entire process. So here's how it goes. I'll take you over to get the license first thing in the morning. Judd's arranged for Dr. Lou Coltrain to do the blood tests tomorrow at eleven. Marc's arranged for the county ordinary to perform the ceremony two weeks from Friday in her office." He grimaced. "I forgot to ask, did you want a minister, as well…?"

Marcus was reeling. In shock, he nodded and mentioned that he and Delia had barely had time to discuss that, but they were agreed on the denomination and said they'd take care of that, also.

"We'll rent you a tux," Cash added, pursing his lips when Marcus gave him the size.

"I'll phone Neiman-Marcus and have them ship one down for me, with the accessories." Marcus waved that detail away.

"That leaves the invitations," Cash continued.

"All in hand," tall, blond Officer Palmer said with a grin. "My wife works for a big engraving company. They print invitations and business cards and such."

"I've lined up caterers for the reception," Officer Barrett added, smiling. "And I've arranged for the local bank's community room to hold it in."

"I've taken care of the flowers," Marc Brannon chuckled. "Josette's friends with our best local florist."

"Who put the announcement in the local weekly and daily papers and alerted the news media?" Cash asked.

There were shocked gasps.

Cash held up a hand. "Tippy and I will take care of that."

"News media?" Marcus asked darkly.

"Not to worry," Cash said, grinning. "I know exactly the people to call. We won't have any tabloid reporters here. I've already asked Matt Caldwell to run down that local ordinance that he used to keep reporters away from his wife, Leslie, when they were after her a few years back. It works great!"

"I think that's about everything," Hayes Carson mentioned, "except for the escort to the airport, and I'll do that personally. Can't have our newlyweds hassled by traffic on their way out of the country, right?" He chuckled.

Marcus shook his head. "And I was just wondering how to go about getting the details wrapped up." He smiled sheepishly. "Thanks, guys. Thanks a million."

"Don't worry about the dog and the chicken, either," Hayes added with a wicked grin. "I've already got places ready for them out at my ranch until you decide when you want them shipped to the Bahamas."

Delia just beamed. "Thanks, Hayes. You, too, guys!" she added to the others.

They all managed to look humble. They hadn't mentioned the tin cans, the confetti, the soap and ribbons they planned to affix to the rented limousine while the reception was going on. Or that they'd already phoned

Mr. Smith in the Bahamas and given him explicit instructions about Marcus's house for when the newlyweds went home after their week on St. Martin in the Caribbean.

Every detail of the service had been worked out, perfected and carried out without a hitch by Marcus's willing accomplices, to Delia's surprise and secret amusement. It didn't even bother her that preparations for it had been taken out of her hands. She helped address the invitations and they were hand-carried by cowboys that worked for the surrounding ranches—most specifically the Harts, the Ballengers, the Tremaynes and Cy Parks.

The wedding was incredible. News media from two continents showed up with satellite trucks and reporters. Print media sent reporters with cameras and tape recorders. Limousines came to town bearing men in dark suits, two groups of which seemed to line up to glare across the pews at each other. Another pew was populated by rough-looking men who kept watching the men in the dark suits. Lawmen covered one, including police chief Cash Grier and his wife, Tippy, along with assistant chief Judd Dunn and his wife, Christabel, former Texas Ranger Marc Brannon with his wife, Josette Brannon, Jacobsville police officers Palmer and Barrett and their wives, and Sheriff Hayes Carson. Another group of local mercenaries and their wives covered a separate pew—Dr. Micah Steele and his wife, Callie, Eb and Sally Scott, Cy and Lisa Parks—with Harley Fowler who wasn't married. All five Hart brothers, Justin and Calhoun Ballenger, the Tremayne brothers attended, with all their wives, and so did the doctors Coltrain and Dr. Morris and his wife. Tom Walker and his wife showed up with Ted Regan and his wife, the Donavans, the Langleys and even the attorney, Blake Kemp with his secretary Violet. Any of the local gentry who didn't attend simply weren't in town at the time. It was an event, with a capital "E."

There were some unexpected guests, too, including a man named Tate Winthrop from Washington, D.C., with his wife, Cecily. He worked in personal security, or so Marcus told Delia, and Marcus had done him a favor to help keep Cecily out of danger.

Delia also noticed some well-known national politicians, two movie stars, three or four singers and a whole rock band of the notorious type. She couldn't say that Marcus wasn't gregarious, in his way. He certainly had a duke's mixture of friends and acquaintances.

But the one person Delia noticed most was Barb, standing at her side at the altar, having served as her matron of honor. Mr. Smith had flown up just for the day and he was serving as best man for Marcus.

The church leader, an elderly man with a contagious smile, performed the service with dignity and affection, and at the end, where they exchanged rings and kissed each other tenderly, there wasn't a dry eye in the house.

Later, at the reception, Delia's gown was the center of attention.

"You can tell it's from Paris," Barb remarked, hugging Delia warmly. She'd been ecstatic ever since the announcement in the newspapers when she and Barney were listed for the first time as Delia's parents. It had stirred quite a lot of local gossip, but the nicest possible kind.

"It's just beautiful." Violet Hardy sighed, smiling at Delia. "I don't suppose I'll ever get to wear anything like that," she added. Violet was just a little overweight, although she had a beautiful face. She worked for local attorney Blake Kemp, who'd brought her to the wedding, to everyone's surprise. Kemp's aversion to women was well known.

"You never know, Violet," Delia whispered with a speaking glance at Blake Kemp, who was speaking to Cy Parks. Violet actually giggled.

The local people who didn't go to the wedding were waiting outside at the end of the reception, as the couple left in a shower of rice and good wishes.

The limo driver, long-suffering but a good sport, stood dignified and silent beside his elegant vehicle, which was now covered with soaped well wishes, ribbons and bows, with a string of cans, shoes and ribbons dangling from the rear bumper.

"Congratulations, Mr. and Mrs. Carrera," he said with a smile, and opened the door for them with a flourish.

"Thanks," they echoed, diving inside under another barrage of rice.

They waved at the crowd one last time before the door closed.

The next morning, they were cuddled together like spoons, in a king-size bed in a luxurious beach house in St. Martin. It had been a long, passionate wedding night and they'd slept late. Marcus had woken first and called room service to send up breakfast. Then he'd curled Delia into his body and dozed until it arrived.

There was a knock on the door.

Marcus kissed his wife awake warmly and threw on a terry cloth robe so that he could answer the door, while she stayed in bed behind a closed door.

It was room service, with breakfast. Marcus let the waiter in, with his cart, and directed him where to leave it. He gave the smiling waiter a big tip and saw him out. Before he went to get Delia, he lifted the lids from the dishes and took a deep breath of the delicious scrambled eggs, bacon, sausage and toast.

He went back into the bedroom, tugged the cover from Delia's pretty nude body, bent and kissed her breasts with breathless tenderness.

"I don't want to stop, but we need to eat something," he whispered, pulling her gently to her feet. "For my part, I'd keep you like this," he added, smiling.

"We'd never be able to go out and see the sights." She laughed.

He kissed her. "Spoilsport. Who wants to see other sights when these are so perfect?" he asked. "Come on. We've got food. I don't know about you, but I'm starving!"

"Where's my gown?"

He slid it over her head. "Waste of time to put it on, baby," he told her with a grin. "It's coming right back off after breakfast."

She tucked her hand into his and let him lead her to the table. But an unexpected thing happened when she smelled the scrambled eggs.

She barely made it to the bathroom in time. He was right behind her, wetting a cloth to bathe her face when she could get up. He helped her wash out her mouth so tenderly that she could have bawled, then he picked her up, cuddling her like a small, frightened child, and carried her right back to bed.

He put her against the pillows with breathless care.

"Oh, baby," he said softly, "I never dreamed we'd do it this quick!"

She met his eyes and managed a watery laugh. "Me, neither," she replied. "Marcus, I think I'm pregnant!"

"Yeah," he agreed, smiling from ear to ear. "Doesn't it look like it, though?"

She drew him down to her and kissed him until her mouth hurt.

"Now we've got a real dilemma," he whispered.

"Hmm?"

He grinned against her lips. "Who do we call first?"

"My parents!"

"Mr. Smith will be ticked," he said. "And he's the best babysitter we'll ever find. He was with Kip Tennison's little boy from birth."

She beamed. "What a lovely thought!"

"I've got it," he said. "You call Barb and Barney on the room phone." He went to the dresser and picked up his cell phone. "I'll phone Smith with my cell phone!" He stuck it in his robe. "But, first, we have breakfast. I'll bring you a nice glass of milk and some toast. You can have breakfast in bed!"

She sighed and smiled up at him with love glowing from her eyes. "You are going to be the nicest husband and best daddy in the whole world," she said with heartfelt conviction.

And he was.

* * * * *

***

Just for an instant, Gabriel worried about putting Michelle
in the line of fire, considering his line of work. He had
enemies. Dangerous enemies who wouldn't hesitate to
threaten anyone close to him. Of course, there was his
sister, Sara, but she'd lived in Wyoming for the past few
years, away from him, on a ranch they co-owned. Now he
was putting her in jeopardy along with Michelle.

But what could he do? The child had nobody. Now that
her idiot stepmother, Roberta, was dead, Michelle was truly
on her own. It was dangerous for a young woman to live
alone, even in a small community. And there was also the
question of Roberta's boyfriend, Bert.

Gabriel knew things about the man that he wasn't eager to share with Michelle. Bert was part of a criminal organization, and he knew Michelle's habits. He also had a yen for her, if what Michelle had blurted out to Gabriel once was true—and he had no indication that she would lie about it. Bert might decide to come try his luck with her now that her stepmother was out of the picture. That couldn't be allowed.

Gabriel was surprised by his own affection for Michelle. It wasn't paternal. She was, of course, far too young for anything heavy. She was a beauty, kind and generous and sweet. She was the sort of woman he usually ran from. No, strike that, she was no woman. She was still unfledged, a dove without flight feathers. He had to keep his interest hidden. At least, until she was grown up enough that it wouldn't hurt his conscience to pursue her. Afterward...well, who knew the future?

***

Don't miss TEXAS BORN
by New York Times *bestselling author Diana Palmer,*
the latest installment in
THE LONG, TALL TEXANS *miniseries.*

Available October 2014 wherever
Harlequin® Special Edition books and ebooks are sold.